CONSUMMATE BETRAYAL

By

Mary Yungeberg

Mary Y

Enjoy!

CONSUMMATE BETRAYAL

Copyright © 2011, 2014 Mary Yungeberg

ISBN: 978-1500830427

Nicholas Guilak cover photo by Bjoern Kommerell
Cover design by Mirna Gilman, BooksGoSocial
nicholasguilak.com and Booksgosocial.com

ACKNOWLEDGEMENTS

First of all, special thanks to Nicholas Guilak, who agreed to read the manuscript and graciously allowed his image to portray Rowan for the cover. You have my utmost gratitude.

Many people gave generously of their time and expertise in the creation of this story. Among them are airline industry professionals, doctors and nurses, firearms instructors and my buddy, a very special former (never ex!) Marine and Secret Service agent. Your insight helped a great deal and your stories are amazing. To everyone who patiently answered phone calls and emails and listened over endless cups of coffee, thank you very much.

My heartfelt thanks to Laurence O'Bryan and Mirna Gilman at BooksGoSocial.com. The updated covers for each book in the Rowan Milani Chronicles are exceptional.

For the editing expertise, thank you Nancy and Virginia. Any errors are mine alone.

Finally, to my (extended) family – Ernie, Christopher, Heather, Mike, Becky, Loretta, Pat, Bobbie and Helen – your endless encouragement and support has been invaluable. I am humbly grateful for each of you.

Consummate Betrayal

Every man has his secret sorrows which the world knows not;

and often times we call a man cold when he is only sad.

Henry Wadsworth Longfellow

CHAPTER ONE

New Year's Eve
Sa-id Harandi looked around the living room of his Old Town Alexandria, Virginia home and rubbed his hands together, pleased with his preparations. Flames popped and snapped in the fireplace, providing the warm, cozy ambience he hoped his guest would enjoy. On the round walnut table a bottle of single barrel Jack Daniel's whiskey and a squat, crystal tumbler reflected the fire's glow. Glancing at his watch, he headed for the kitchen to retrieve the simple repast he'd created that afternoon.

He chuckled, thinking about the token rebuke he'd no doubt get from Rowan Milani, the son of his oldest friend. *You know I don't like Iranian food, Sa-id. Why do you persist in shoving it down my throat?* "Because it's your heritage and you should be proud," he murmured. He'd known Rowan for more than thirty years and had watched him grow from an insouciant young boy to a driven, dangerous man. He sighed. The transformation had been fraught with grief for everyone involved.

The doorbell chimed, ending his reverie, and he placed the tray of kebabs, baklava and fruit on the table next to the whiskey before walking to the door. Checking the viewer, he saw his guest standing on the front stoop, dressed in a royal blue, cable knit sweater and black jeans with a black leather jacket slung over one shoulder. He smiled and turned the deadbolt, flinging the door wide. "Rowan, come in, please. It's a pleasure to see you."

Rowan stepped through the door, flashing a quick smile in return. "It's always good to see you, Sa-id. Sorry I'm late."

Grateful for an evening devoted to simple friendship, he grasped Rowan's forearm, gazing into the intense, dark eyes. "How are you? And how are your parents and your sister?"

The younger man raised a brow and his smile twisted, almost into a sneer. "I'm fine, and I'm sure my parents and Bettina are as well."

He let go of Rowan's arm and frowned. "Surely you were with them for Christmas."

The sardonic gaze remained. "We've been over this a thousand times, Sa-id. Let's not reprise it tonight, OK?"

Regretting how he must have sounded, he gestured toward the table with both hands. "Forgive me, I'm a rude host. Pour a drink and sit down. I hope you don't mind. I grew nostalgic this afternoon and went to the market for a few old favorites, the kind of things your father and I used to snack on, years ago in Tehran."

Hoping his apology was adequate, he watched Rowan toss the leather jacket on the sofa and wondered for a moment how many pistols and knives his friend had concealed on his person. He shook his head to chase the thoughts away and ignored the edginess threatening to unravel his peace of mind. When he and Rowan met, their agenda didn't revolve around their long friendship, but he hoped – had planned for this evening to be different. Meeting the younger man's gaze, he saw that the whisker-smudged face held only affection. "You never stop trying to shove Iranian food down my throat. Aren't you having your usual wine?"

Relieved that he hadn't offended his friend, Sa-id smiled. "It's in the fridge. Go on now and pour your whiskey while I get it."

When he returned with the crisp 2002 Chateau Montelena chardonnay, he could see only the back of a shaggy, dark head against the top of the sofa facing the fireplace. Rounding the corner, he took a seat in the adjacent recliner. Rowan looked up from where he'd slouched, legs stretched toward the fire with the tumbler of whiskey clasped in both hands, resting on his belly.

"This is nice, Sa-id. Thanks for the invite. I didn't have any plans for New Year's Eve and this beats another airplane seat or cold hotel room."

The unsettling edginess gripped him again as he watched Rowan scratching his jaw through the whiskers. He knew the younger man hated wearing a beard, but his line of work made it necessary from time to time. "You have travel plans I presume?"

Rowan glanced at him and then looked away, taking a long draught of whiskey before replying, "In a week or so, but until then I'm doing some research – and growing a beard, of course."

Realizing he'd been staring unseeing, Sa-id blinked and sipped the fruity wine. "Ah, research? That sounds interesting." He tried to smile but failed, producing a grimace instead. "I'm sorry. For some reason, I can't seem to relax tonight. I truly want to celebrate the end of a productive year and the start of a wonderful new one, for both of us."

After giving him a smirk, Rowan tossed back the rest of the whiskey. "It's all right, Sa-id. My only plan for tonight is to relax and suffer through whatever crap I have to eat for this early celebration of Nowruz that you're foisting on me. I can't believe you haven't pulled out a bowl of cucumber yogurt to go with our drinks." He sniffed. "And the scent of Persian spices is stuffing up my sinuses. Please don't tell me you've got a big pot of Polow somewhere to go with those kebabs."

Shaking his index finger, Sa-id rose from the recliner. "You're incorrigible. Just for that, we're going to dig into that *crap*, right now." He swallowed more wine. "You should embrace your Iranian heritage, Rowan."

He held his breath and waited while Rowan stood up and turned away to refill the tumbler with whiskey before sliding back down on the sofa and scowling up at him. "For God's sake, Sa-id, how many times do we have to rehash this?"

Disturbed by the reservoir of anger he glimpsed in Rowan's eyes and fearful that he'd stirred the rage residing beneath the younger man's veneer of civility, he sank back down on the recliner. "Forgive me for overstepping my bounds, but mark my words – you cannot escape who you are. And regardless of your American birth, your father is Iranian and his blood flows through your veins."

Rowan snorted and shook his head. "And my mother would tell you that hot Italian blood makes me who I am. My father embraced his new country with passion. Bettina and I were raised as American children. You know that Sa-id, you were there." Rowan sounded weary. "I could repeat his stories in my sleep."

Sipping the wine and listening, Sa-id thought about how much he'd like to share the culture he still valued and missed. However, with Rowan, his efforts would be rebuffed. Before he could respond, his friend continued. "Hell, I don't even have an Italian name to honor my mother's side of the family. They went overboard when they chose a Celtic name, don't you agree? *Rowan* is not an appropriate name for a proud son of Iran, Italy or America."

Thinking back to the young couple and the multitude of dreams he'd shared with Khalil and Janice Milani, Sa-id couldn't help smiling. "Yes, of course I remember. And I know the depth of gratitude your father has for the United States. But still – you should understand Iranian culture. It's part of you."

Rowan looked at him and raised a brow. "My understanding of Iranian culture isn't lacking, believe me. I know what my life would be like if I'd been raised as a dutiful Shiite in the Islamic Republic." Rowan shrugged. "Now please – enough of this useless conversation. Let's enjoy the evening. I'm starving. How about we order a pizza?"

Mid-January
Sa-id leaned back in his chair and rubbed his eyes as the documents he wanted printed. While he waited, he gazed at the gently falling snow, illuminated by the street lights outside his

office window at the Council of American-Islamic Relations headquarters in Washington, DC. When the printer stopped, he yawned and glanced at his watch. It was almost seven o'clock in the evening, much later than he'd planned to stay. Careful to erase the tracks of his subterfuge, he switched off the computer monitor and shoved back his chair.

Rowan and the President would appreciate what he'd found. He'd been a liaison and a secret conduit of information to his friend on behalf of the United States for more than eight years. Following the trail of money, funds that CAIR funneled to numerous Islamic organizations abroad on behalf of the Muslim Brotherhood, he enabled Rowan to intervene and stop many terror plots before they could threaten America.

Sa-id shoved the papers, still warm from the printer, into his briefcase. Another clever plan, this one originating in Pakistan, would be stymied. Thinking about how Rowan would handle this particular situation, an involuntary shudder rippled through his body. It was best he didn't know too much about his friend's activities. He just watched, listened, and forwarded information.

It was the least he could do for the country that allowed him to live at peace and in complete freedom, instead of complying with harsh Islamic Sharia. And yet, he'd maintained his identity as an Iranian, possessing dual citizenship. Smiling sadly, he wondered if his homeland would ever escape the debilitating, choking dysfunction of the Islamic Republic.

Poised with one hand on his briefcase and the other on his coat, his eyes widened as the door to his office swung open. Two men entered and he looked from one to the other in confusion. They wore dark blue jackets and lanyards with CIA printed in heavy letters. One was stocky, with black hair and close-set blue eyes that he would call beady. The other was like a massive bull, tall, broad-shouldered and muscular, with blond hair and hard brown eyes.

The stocky man stepped in front of him, and Sa-id caught the aroma of grilled onions. "Mr. Harandi, my name is Seth Hancock." Pointing at his companion, whose body filled the doorway, the agent continued. "This is Lucien Talbot. We're with the CIA and we'd like to talk with you about your activities at CAIR."

Sa-id stared first at the cold eyes and then the thin lips, compressed in a firm line. Doing his best to stop the shaking in his legs, he attempted to sound calm and reasonable. "My activities? I'm a computer security specialist. I'm responsible for many aspects of the network and computer systems here. How does that concern the CIA?"

The bulky man gripped his upper arm with a heavy hand. "We have a car waiting. Come with us now, please."

Apprehension burgeoned to panic as Sa-id realized he was trapped. How could this be happening to him? This was the United States, not Iran, where this kind of abduction was common. For a moment, he thought about Rowan and his concealed weapons. He'd give anything to have his friend's courageous presence with him now. "It's late. Couldn't we meet tomorrow? I could take the day off and come to Langley, or wherever you choose."

The agent jerked his head in an impatient gesture. "Right now, Mr. Harandi. We need to talk with you tonight."

Secured to a wooden chair by yards of duct tape that held his body upright and his arms and feet immobile, Sa-id waited. The bone chilling cold made his teeth chatter, and he squirmed in helpless terror. So far, neither of the men had returned to talk with him. Of course, that must have been a ruse. But he couldn't imagine what they wanted with him or why they would employ such tactics.

After shoving him into the back seat of a black Suburban with darkened windows, the big blond had torn a length of duct tape from a fat roll, bound his wrists behind his back, covered his mouth and then pulled a black hood over his head. They'd driven for what seemed like hours and he had no idea whether they were still in the District, or if they'd taken him into the surrounding area outside the Beltway. They must be somewhere remote, or else how could he have been hustled from the vehicle like a criminal without attracting attention? Despair filled his heart, and beneath the hood, he closed his eyes.

Dozing fitfully, he jerked awake when someone yanked the hood from his head. Fluorescent lights switched on, flooding the room with blinding light. Blinking, eyes watering at the harsh brightness, he strained to see who was standing in front of him. A thickset man with heavy jowls and slicked back onyx hair stared at him.

"Sa-id, you are very cunning. It has taken some time to expose your duplicity, valuable time that has seen the death of many holy warriors."

The calamity he'd feared, that had lurked in the recesses of his mind for years, had overtaken him. He'd been careful, diligent and meticulous about security. Now, though, it had all come to naught. But wouldn't the CIA know he worked on behalf of the United States? Why had the agents handed him to this man? He tried to sort through his jumbled thoughts, but nothing made sense.

The man who'd pulled the hood from his head stood in front of him, breathing hard. Dressed in an elegant black suit with a white shirt and red silk tie, he looked out of place in the dingy room that reeked of diesel fuel. A work bench and shelves, filled with boxes and tools lined the dull gray walls. A pile of greasy looking rags sat in one corner and assorted rakes and shovels were propped against the wall next to the work bench. A closed wooden door appeared to be the only exit, and he wondered if he was in someone's rural workshop.

As he watched, his adversary strode back and forth, black patent leather loafers gritting on the filthy cement floor. "Sa-id, you will tell me the name of your associate, the one who takes the knowledge you give him and uses it to murder the Brotherhood's warriors. This man – he is like a ghost, defying Allah's will in many countries. That will not, *must not*, stand."

Reaching out, the man tugged on the duct tape covering his mouth and ripped it off, making Sa-id's eyes water as he gasped in pain. "Let me speak plainly, Sa-id. You are Iranian and I will honor you by dealing with you justly, as the holy Koran dictates. Tell me the name of your associate now, and I will see that you return to your homeland in safety."

Sa-id didn't know if he could talk. Voice weak, he began, "I don't understand. I have no such associate. And I do not wish to return to Iran. The United States has been my home for many years."

The man patted his cheek. "I have invested many dollars in my quest for the ghost agent who has caused so much destruction. The Brotherhood has lost patience, and so have I. You will tell me his name."

The cruelty in the dark eyes struck terror deep inside Sa-id. But he could never betray Rowan or the United States. "No, I have nothing to tell you. I have no information about an agent who kills holy warriors in defiance of Allah. Please take me home."

The repulsive stranger chuckled. "I am not in the mood for sophistry. It seems that the depraved culture of your precious United States has captured your soul. Allah's refining fire will set you free."

Sa-id waited, fists clenched in helpless consternation while his tormentor pulled a needle and syringe from an inside suit pocket, shoved up Sa-id's shirt sleeve and uncovered his arm. "Your deception and the actions of your associate have cost the

Brotherhood much treasure. Allah's law will be satisfied. The price must be paid, Sa-id, and it starts with you."

The man traced the vein in Sa-id's arm with an index finger and inserted the needle with care. Cold eyes locked with his as the contents of the syringe flowed into his body. "When you awaken, I will have amputated your right hand, in the Iranian tradition of punishment."

Chest constricting in horror, Sa-id could only whisper, "Please, you must believe me. I don't know what you're talking about, and I have no covert associate."

His captor bent in front of him, inches from his face. He could smell sweat and see individual droplets on the thick forehead. The obsidian eyes gleamed. "No more lies, Sa-id."

As Sa-id's head tipped forward, his gaze focused on the patent leather shoes, so out of place on the grimy cement. Then he passed out.

A Week Later

Sa-id lay on his back on the work bench beneath the fluorescent lights, his body wracked with pain. Out of the corner of his eye he saw the pole and a flask of fluid that kept him alive intravenously. His butcher's face appeared above him. Fevered eyes gazed into his and a gentle hand smoothed the hair off his forehead. "Sa-id, why do you choose to suffer? I have told you; it will never end."

The madman had carved gaping wounds on Sa-id's body while he moaned and shook in agony. Now the man grasped the bandaged stump where Sa-id's right hand had been and dragged it up, so he could see it. "To honor your Iranian customs, I took your right hand. Today I will take your left foot and you will not only witness my surgery, you will experience each cut of my knife and saw in excruciating detail. After that, I will wrap your wounds and return you to Iran in shame."

Breathing in labored, heaving gasps, Sa-id twisted his head weakly back and forth. "No, oh no, please don't." Tears he couldn't stop poured from his eyes, running down his cheeks and into his ears. Whimpering, he pleaded with his torturer. "Please, please, I can't tell you." When he closed his eyes, Rowan's smiling face swam before him and he heard the affectionate voice. *This is nice, Sa-id, thanks for the invite. I didn't have any plans.*

Light slaps on both cheeks had his eyelids fluttering open. The mad face turned greedy. "Give me the name of your associate, Sa-id, and I will give you a martyr's death."

How had it come to this? Sobbing, his heart breaking, Sa-id knew it was time, to give the man the name he so desperately desired and then to die. He took a shuddering breath and murmured softly, "Rowan Milani."

Tears spilled down his cheeks again and a keening moan escaped his lips at the horror of what he'd done. "I'm so sorry, Rowan. Forgive me, please." Victory shone in the eyes above him and a smile creased the hellish face. The knife sliced across his throat, brutal yet mercifully quick. Darkness claimed him, and his suffering ended.

First Week in February

The President had been explicit. Eliminate the threat and send a strong message. Rowan slid into his first class seat on the US Air flight from Phoenix to Denver with a sense of weary satisfaction. The President's objectives had been achieved expeditiously, as usual. Settling into the soft leather, he thought about the month he'd invested with the two jihadists in Mexico. Holed up in a grimy, bug and rodent infested hotel on the edge of Puerto Penasco, he'd patiently deceived the two men until they trusted him. Until they were convinced he could take them and their precious cargo: four pounds of anthrax, across the porous southern border of the United States and all the way to the nation's capital.

One of the men who'd bought into his carefully crafted deception was a chubby Columbian named Laszio, a small-time drug lord turned terror thug wannabe. The other, a lanky Arab named Bashir, had come straight from a training camp in Pakistan. Hardcore al Qaeda, the jihadist wore the trademark tennis shoes the operatives prized, and lectured him nonstop about his beloved Koran for the entire month. Remembering the fanaticism in the young terrorist's eyes, Rowan shook his head. Bashir couldn't wait to slice through the belly of the Beast and wreak havoc.

The previous moonless evening, he'd persuaded the two men that the time was right to cross the border with the anthrax. The holy warriors had chuckled in good humor while Rowan screwed the suppressor on his Glock 36. In case a wandering gringo border agent crossed their path, he'd told them with a wink and a smirk. After bouncing along in nearly total blackness on a rutted, sandy road that ran parallel to the border, he'd motioned Bashir to stop. Turning to the back seat, he shot Laszio point blank, grateful as always for the sub-compact forty-five caliber pistol that placed a respectable hole through the man's left eye and plastered most of the rest of his head against the back window.

The obliteration of the tubby Columbian had momentarily stunned Bashir, but by the time he'd pulled his knife, the skinny Arab was scrabbling in the dark for the door handle, like the rat he was. Irritated by the martyr turned coward, Rowan had grabbed the frightened man by the hair, wrenched his head back and yanked the knife across his throat. He could just as easily have shot Bashir, but it was a matter of principle. Since beheading was al Qaeda's preferred method of execution, it was only appropriate. Besides, he'd been asked to deliver a strong message and he thought the knife, more than the pistol, accomplished that.

Leaving the two men slumped over in the blood-splattered rusted Chevy Malibu, Rowan had taken the anthrax loaded suitcase and slid across the border. The other members of the black ops team had relieved him of the lethal package for delivery to Washington, DC. Kuwaiti professor Abdallah Nafisi had suggested during a speech widely publicized on the internet that one person with courage could bring anthrax across the border, "spreading the confetti," as he called it, easily killing upwards of 300,000 Americans. The vaunted professor had encouraged a finale on the lawn of the White House. Rowan would love to be a fly on the wall when the despicable man discovered that his four precious pounds of anthrax had indeed been delivered to Washington, but with different results than he'd intended and financed.

Blinking burning eyes and smothering a yawn with his fist, Rowan sniffed as his nose started to run. The first yawn spawned a second and his eyes watered along with his nose. Wishing they'd close the aircraft door and get underway, he gazed with disinterest at the eclectic collection of people lugging their crap down the narrow aisle toward coach. As the last of the passengers trudged past his seat, he noticed with swiftly lit anger that the man seated across the aisle was watching him, wary suspicion in his eyes. With an aggravated scowl, Rowan turned away and pushed himself deeper into the seat, folded his arms across his chest and glared at the seatback in front of him.

The thing that angered; no the thing that enraged him, was that he served his country, helped keep it safe so people like the pudgy jerk staring at him could sleep at night. Yet he was cast as the suspicious character, and why? Well, he knew why. It was the same every time, but his choices had made it even worse this time. He'd been rushed, pulled on black jeans, a black sweater and unfortunately a black leather jacket. But none of that should matter. It wasn't right that he had to take extra steps, be careful how he dressed and conducted himself because of his Iranian heritage.

No one needed to remind him of September 11, 2001. It held what could be called deep personal meaning. On that day, the monsters had destroyed everything that mattered to him – had annihilated the better part of him. That was why he risked his life on black ops whenever he wasn't on assignment as an FBI special agent attached to an Anti-Terrorism Task Force. He lived to eliminate the Islamic terror masters. They had taken everything from him, extinguished his future, ambushed his dreams, and turned them into nightmares. It was only fair that he return the favor, as often as possible.

Casting a sideways glance at the man across the aisle, he reasoned angrily to himself that it wasn't his fault his father had emigrated from Iran and married an American woman of Italian extraction, the two of them passing along their distinctive features to him, their only son. He was an American, born in the United States, and he used his appearance, along with his ability to speak Farsi and Arabic to serve his country in ways a lot of other people couldn't, or didn't have the balls to. Gazing out the window at the sun-baked concrete, watching a ramp worker dragging a set of chocks, he sighed. He was neither Arab nor a terrorist, but God forbid that the truth come between people and their preconceived judgments against him.

The door closed and the aircraft jerked into motion as the pushback from the gate began. Resolutely shoving the angry, frustrating thoughts aside, he yawned again and closed his eyes. He was anxious to reach Denver and watch for coverage of the early morning covert operation. News of the whole sordid affair should be breaking by the time he arrived.

As the edges of his mind turned foggy with sleep, he remembered an old song that reminded him of his life, something about dirty deeds being done dirt cheap. Well, except for the cheap part. He smiled as his mind began to drift. His expertise came with a hefty price tag, but he'd received no complaints, just regular, discreet deposits in two designated accounts. As he stretched through yet another yawn, he hoped the strong message he'd delivered and the prompt elimination of the threat would meet with the President's approval.

The twin jet engines rumbled as the plane lifted into the sky, minor turbulence making it a bumpy ride. Two sweet hours of sleep were his for the taking. After being awake and adrenaline-wired for the previous thirty-six, he didn't want to waste a minute. Reclining the seat, he folded his hands in his lap and slept.

Looking out the window of Club Gascon, his favored London restaurant, Muusa Shemal sipped his tea and reflected over the meal he'd just enjoyed, bunching fingers to his lips in silent reverence. The foie gras was beyond compare. Rich, buttery and delicate, it was the specialty of the house. And the milk fed lamb with dates and baby carrots was delicious. The whole meal had been exquisite, and he decided to commend the chef before leaving.

A rare sunny afternoon, the day matched his mood for celebration. He'd been elated, expressing endless thanks to Allah since returning from the United States. The ghost agent, the jinn who slid in and out of countries like a wisp of smoke, leaving behind dead bodies and ruined operations, many foiled almost before they'd begun, had been identified. Someday, when he stood over Rowan Milani, teaching him about retribution, he would relate the story of Sa-id Harandi and his remarkable loyalty. The Iranian man had endured his ministrations for a week before betraying his friend. Now, if it pleased Allah, the FBI agent in Denver would agree to detain Rowan Milani, and he could put the next phase of his plan into motion. If not, he would send the CIA operatives in his hire to the elusive man's next destination. A feral smile rippled across his face. Allah decreed that he bring the jinn to Egypt, where the Brotherhood waited to exact revenge. The CIA's adage played over and over in his mind. *If you want someone to disappear – never to see them again, you send them to Egypt.*

Spearing an errant piece of lamb with his fork, he chewed thoughtfully, considering the fools in America's Intelligence organizations, so easily beguiled. They were swine, greedy, and blinded by the dollars he'd waved in their faces. That they accepted his lies about Rowan Milani's allegiance and would secretly deliver one of their own into his hands was testament to the moral rot of the entire kafir nation. They were useful idiots, but they had no honor, and that sickened him.

Rowan woke as the aircraft touched down, grimacing at the scene outside the window. An overcast sky dispensed snow that swept across the tarmac in waves as the jet roared slowly to its designated gate. First stretching then shivering, he realized that his bare feet inside his battered, old slip-on shoes were freezing. Being from California, wearing socks was something he didn't do, unless absolutely necessary.

With any luck his connecting flight to Sioux Falls, South Dakota would be on time. He must be a fool for taking an assignment there in February. It was right up his alley, though. Something was happening, and he feared a new chapter in the war on terror was commencing. Reams of intelligence, along with intensifying internet chatter pointed to a major event somewhere in the vast heartland of the country. Groups of special agents, coordinating with local Law Enforcement and Homeland Security had been assigned in varying locales to address what they all thought was an incipient threat.

He'd been asked to join the operation in Sioux Falls by his boss, Ralph Johnston. A longtime friend and colleague, Ralph treated him more like a son than a subordinate. Special agent Chad Cantor, his only friend in the Bureau besides Ralph, was also assigned to Sioux Falls. Chad was one of precious few people who had never looked at him with suspicion or questioned his allegiance to his country because of his Iranian heritage. They'd become good friends over the years, and he looked forward to working with Chad, who'd grown up in South Dakota and was staying at his father's home in Sioux Falls for the duration of the assignment.

While tasked with his duties in South Dakota, he intended to pursue what he and the President had discussed in general over the last several years and in detail during their last meeting. He'd expressed his disagreement with conventional wisdom, which said that the most devastating attack to the nation would occur in a single, spectacular event. It wasn't that he didn't think an attack like that would happen. But as he'd explained to the President, he thought the more pernicious threat stemmed from the virulent message of domination by the Islamists and submission of the infidels to the ultimate caliphate they wanted to establish in America.

He'd read the fatwas and shared long conversations with terrorists around the globe about the secret jihad Islamists waged in mosques around the United States. Hell, he'd seen the fourteen page plan they called *The Project*, netted in a raid carried out by Swiss authorities on Youssef Nada, a long-time member of the Muslim Brotherhood in Switzerland, after 9/11. *The Project* detailed the Brotherhood's twelve-point strategy, in essence a long-term plan to infiltrate and destroy Western culture.

The FBI's investigation and indictment of the Holy Land Foundation several years later uncovered the Brotherhood memorandum describing a major jihad to destroy Western civilization from within. These people were dead serious about lowering the Stars and Stripes and running the star and crescent of Islam up the pole in its place. And they didn't care how long it took them.

The leader, the man assigned by the Muslim Brotherhood to spearhead the sabotage of the United States had evaded identification, flying below the radar for years, teaching the faithful how to devastate the infidel nation from within. If he could infiltrate a mosque and get close to the principal players, he knew he could identify this particular leader and eliminate him. Dealing a blow like that to the Brotherhood might make them think twice about their beloved *Project.* At the very least, it would slow their progress.

The President had given tacit approval to his plan. *Do whatever's necessary to cut the head off the snake, Rowan,* had been the President's exact words. When he'd said they were dealing with a hydra, the President had smiled. *Then make sure your knife is damn hot when you find this bastard.*

The sound of the aircraft door opening, accompanied by a blast of cold air ended his introspection. Running a weary hand over his face, he caught the gaze of the plump passenger across the aisle. With a jerk of his head, he motioned the man to precede him off the aircraft, which he did like a scared rabbit. Fingers of snow lined the jetway, and an icy breeze hurried him along its sloping walkway. If it was this cold in Denver, he could only imagine the weather in South Dakota.

Breaking news of his nighttime endeavor played on CNN as he arrived in the boarding area for his United Airlines flight to Sioux Falls. Spotting an empty seat practically beneath the flat screen TV, he sat down to enjoy the spin. The Mexican government thought the brutal murder of two innocent Mexican citizens along the US border highly suspicious. He snorted. They were calling those two innocent citizens? Clasping his hands together, he leaned forward to hear more. Mexican authorities could find no witnesses, but suspected illicit American involvement, which they didn't appreciate. Hell, the Mexicans couldn't police their own people, let alone the likes of Bashir and Laszio. They should be grateful for his help.

Walking to the gate podium to present his FBI credentials and the paperwork necessary for carrying his firearm onboard the aircraft, he noticed a few concerned stares. It had been too early, he hadn't thought it through, but as he touched the stubble that darkened his jaws, conscious of the shaggy hair brushing the collar of his jacket, he wished he had. He'd clipped off the beard and hurriedly shaved, but that had been nearly twelve hours ago. A suit and tie would have helped, but it was too late now. The gate agent smiled, which was encouraging. "Special agent, we're almost ready to board. Would you like to come with me and hand off the paperwork to the captain?"

Smiling neutrally, he did his best to affect a tame demeanor. "Yes ma'am, that sounds good." She led him down the jetway to the captain who stood sipping coffee in the galley, looking annoyed at being disturbed. Great. He was one of those, impressed with his position and anxious for everyone to know he was in charge. The captain inspected his ID and detached a copy of the paperwork while he stood quietly next to him, trying not to shiver. "Mind if I take my seat now, sir?"

A good six inches shorter than he was at six feet, carrying excess weight that bulged over his belt and gave his face a round, petulant look, the captain grated on his tired mind. Struggling to control his temper, he clenched his jaws while the man considered, drank more coffee and then gestured with the Styrofoam cup. "Sure, go ahead."

Sneering while he shoved his laptop and briefcase into the overhead bin, thinking *Pillsbury Doughboy,* he scooped up the pillow and blanket set out by the flight attendants and dropped into his first class seat. He tucked the pillow behind his head and huddled under the thin blanket. Almost as an afterthought he buckled the seat belt, then closed his eyes and dozed.

Fred Ralston, Special Agent in Charge of Denver's FBI Field Office stared at his phone. Not sure how to handle the disturbing call he'd received a few hours earlier, he folded his hands on the cluttered desk and pondered his next move. The caller had insisted on anonymity, but claimed to know the identity of an

American operative involved in a terror plot gone bad, resulting in the previous evening's double murder along the US-Mexico border. Anxiety tightened between his shoulders as he replayed the call.

You can retire, Mr. Ralston, if you apprehend this man. His name is Rowan Milani and he murdered two men in Mexico. We believe he is planning a terror incident. He's at your airport, booked on a United Airlines flight to Sioux Falls, South Dakota. Find a way to detain him. Your country will call you a hero and we will reward you generously.

Ralston put his hand on the receiver and stopped. Did he want to start this ball rolling? Did he want to mess around with another man's life, especially a high profile, sometimes controversial agent like Rowan Milani over an anonymous call? Twisting his shoulders to relieve the tension, he weighed his options. Milani gave heartburn to damn near everyone he interacted with at the Bureau. *Arrogant* and *jerk* were common adjectives often used in tandem to describe the special agent.

He sighed and shook his head. Milani got away with things FBI special agents were forbidden to do, such as traveling in first class, albeit at his own expense. *Saving the taxpayers money* was Milani's explanation, always accompanied by a cocky smirk. Occasionally he'd wanted to utilize the special agent's talent in an investigation, but couldn't locate him. He seemed to be nowhere, for weeks at a time. But when anyone tried to delve into Milani's activities, they ran into a brick wall and he knew the reason for that. Milani's boss, Ralph Johnston, safeguarded his special agent's privacy vigorously. He'd heard a few whispers about Johnston, too. Those in the know said that he and the President were long-time friends.

Shit, he'd love to get a warrant and hang onto Milani long enough to get some real answers. But he couldn't justify a warrant and besides that, he owed Rowan Milani the benefit of the doubt. Jerk or not, he was one of them and anyone could make an anonymous phone call. Still, he could ask the special agent to have a talk, especially since Milani wasn't traveling with his extra-vigilant boss. Everyone in the Bureau would support him on that.

Decision made, he picked up the phone and speed dialed the special agent on duty at Denver International Airport. "Banks, this is Fred Ralston. Are you prepared to meet with Rowan Milani? He's booked on a United flight at gate B17. It's imperative that we talk with him, even if it means delaying that flight."

He paused, massaging his forehead while he considered. "Follow procedure Banks, and keep this low-key. Get a cup of coffee and have a chat downstairs in one of the holding rooms. Watch yourself, though. I've dealt with Milani before and believe me – he's not going to be happy about any of this. Reassure him that we just need to find out what's up with that phone call. It's possible he can shed some light on it. I've seen a news report that verifies two people were killed on the border last night, and Milani did fly in from Phoenix. I'll keep investigating and get back to you in a couple hours. Let me know what you find out."

Rowan woke groggily when someone shook his arm. "Special agent Milani, you need to wake up. Hey, Rowan, I need to talk to you." Yanking his arm away, he opened his eyes wide and stared at a tall, balding man standing beside his seat. At the front of the aircraft, the captain and a flight attendant huddled next to the gate agent. They all looked frightened. He rubbed his eyes and frowned at the man, who pulled FBI credentials and flashed them in his face. "I'm special agent Leonard Banks. Something's come up and I need to talk to you, but not here. Would you mind deplaning with me?"

Wanting to make the man wait, he stretched and yawned, then shoved the blanket aside, unbuckled his seat belt and stood up, following the special agent to the front of the plane. Banks shuffled into the cramped space next to the captain, forcing the gate agent and flight attendant into the galley. Rowan looked from the captain to the FBI special agent and back. "One of you wanted to speak to me?"

The tall man addressed him before the captain could reply. "Special agent Milani, like I said, you and I need to have a chat. But first, I'd like you to step off the aircraft with me." Following the man's gesture out the door of the plane, he saw a Law Enforcement Officer standing in the jetway. What the hell was going on? The cowardly anxiety he read in all their faces brought the submerged but always simmering rage he lived with bubbling to the surface. It wouldn't be the first time he'd been pulled from a flight because another passenger was concerned about a Middle Eastern man seated in first class. But it had never required the presence of another FBI special agent to make it happen.

The rage had him breathing hard and he clenched his jaws, told himself he'd better bring it down a notch. But goddamn it, he hadn't done anything except sit in his seat and go to sleep. Glaring at the captain, he planted his hands on his hips. "What exactly is the problem? What are you afraid of, and why do I need to deplane?"

Watching the captain's ample face turn pink, he knew he'd angered the doughboy. "Look special agent Milani, I don't know what's going on. I received a call from the FBI telling me that my aircraft can't leave as long as you're on it and that you might cause a problem. What was I supposed to do? I asked the gate agent to call security. This is my aircraft and whether you stay or leave is my decision, so let me be clear. Gather up your things and deplane right now."

Something was amiss and his sleep deprived brain couldn't put it together. But it wasn't worth pursuing. He'd lost, big-time. Now it would be hours before he arrived in South Dakota and even longer before he'd see a comfortable bed. Fighting to contain the rage, he nodded at the captain. "Of course sir, I'll get my things and deplane immediately. But there is one more thing."

The captain had been turning to reenter the flight deck and swung around abruptly. "What is it?"

He gave the chubby man a shrewd look. "If you consider me a threat to your aircraft, then you need to unload my checked piece of luggage. Otherwise, there is no point in removing me. If I pose a threat, my luggage does as well." He was pushing the envelope with that one, but he didn't care.

The rotund man took two quick steps toward him and poked him in the chest. "You have made a threat against a commercial airliner – *my* airliner, and I can't let that pass."

Speechless, he stared down at the flushed, bloated face, thinking about how easy it would be to choke the life out of the annoying man. A fresh wave of anger rolled over him when he glanced at the insipid FBI special agent. The man stood with his hands outstretched in a supplicating gesture. "Hey, everyone, take it easy. Captain, no one's making any threats, either to the aircraft or your crew. Rowan, let's take a walk, get some coffee."

Drawing a breath, he clenched his fists at his sides and willed his hands to remain there instead of around the captain's neck. That he of all people would threaten a commercial airliner was beyond the pale. Ignoring Banks, he addressed the captain. "I did not threaten your aircraft."

But the doughboy would not be denied his victory. "You can consider yourself persona non grata on any United Airlines flight for at least the rest of the day and most likely longer." The captain motioned to the special agent. "Please escort this man out of here. The flight attendant will bring his things. Good day, special agent Banks. Thank you for your help."

It was over now. He'd be lucky to get a flight anywhere, for the foreseeable future. Still seething, he trudged to the top of the jetway, sandwiched between Banks and the cop. After they stepped from the jetway into the gate area, Banks turned and smiled, first at him and then the police officer. "Sorry to have taken your time. We don't need your services."

The officer nodded and raised an arm in a brief wave. "No problem. You gentlemen have a great day."

Watching the man head down the concourse, the anger receding in the face of monumental exhaustion, he yawned and then glanced at Banks. The special agent still had a smarmy smile on his face. It would be fun to rearrange the smile with his fist, but since that wouldn't be considered civilized, he wiped his nose with the back of his hand instead. "What now, special agent Banks?"

Banks rubbed his hands together and gestured down the concourse. "How about that cup of coffee I mentioned? Then we'll head downstairs to one of our holding rooms so we can have some privacy. It's possible my boss, Fred Ralston will want to talk with you as well."

Twenty minutes later, he found himself sipping a paper cup of Seattle's Best coffee, seated on a bench in a small room, somewhere in the bowels of the airport. A security camera with a glowing red light sat high up in the corner, and offhand, he thought he'd enjoy flipping it off. When Banks closed the door and leaned against it, he stared at the special agent and wondered if he'd get some answers. Banks gulped coffee, placed his cup on the desk and sighed. "Sorry for the rigmarole, Rowan. It's just that the conversation we need to have is sensitive and not appropriate for the front of an airplane or a coffee shop on the concourse."

The bench he was sitting on was damned uncomfortable and all he wanted to do was lay his head on the desk facing it and go to sleep. Yawning again, he sat the cup of tepid coffee on the floor and gazed wearily at Banks. "All right, why don't we start by you telling me what the hell's going on?"

Banks clasped his hands together and frowned at him. "First of all, keep in mind that I'm not the enemy here, OK? You and I, we're on the same team."

The special agent's ass-kissing disposition irritated him and he nodded impatiently. "Yeah, sure, I get it. You and I, teammates. Now, what exactly did you want to talk about?"

The hesitation he saw in the special agent's face had the anger lighting up again. Banks grabbed his cup from the desk and swilled more coffee, then started in. "Fred Ralston got an anonymous call this morning. The caller said you were involved in a double murder in Mexico last night." The special agent shrugged. "We thought you could clear that up for us. I mean, shoot, it was an anonymous call."

Expecting the usual apology about appeasing anxious passengers, the surprise that widened his eyes and dropped his jaw was genuine. He scratched the itchy whiskers on his chin and smirked at Banks. "That's the craziest thing I've heard in a long time, Leonard. You're telling me Ralston thought an anonymous call held enough weight to drag me off a plane and bring me down here to your holding room? What's next? You want to haul me downtown to the Field Office for interrogation?" Fighting rising anger again, he held his breath and glared at Banks.

A red stain crept up the special agent's neck and spread across his face, but he had to give the guy credit. Banks just ran a hand across the top of his gleaming head and chuckled. "I understand how you feel. Let's keep it simple. Tell me where you've been for the past several days. We'll verify the information and you'll be on your way."

Thinking he'd like to say *fuck you*, he stared at the man drumming his fingers on the wall and decided he was in too deep. Something was off kilter, or must have gone terribly wrong with the operation after he'd left. Since he had no clue, he opted for silence, wishing he'd thought of that earlier, on the plane.

Mary Yungeberg

Banks waved an arm. "Rowan, you know the drill. I need answers, to take to my boss." Banks looked at him intently. When he didn't speak, the special agent shoved off the wall and gestured with the coffee cup. "I'm at a loss, Rowan. I wish you'd clear this up for me. Not talking isn't going to inspire confidence. I'm afraid Fred will insist that you come downtown to the Field Office. Why don't you help me out, so we can both put this behind us and get on with our lives?"

Staring at Banks, he felt like a pawn on a chess board, being maneuvered by an unseen hand, unwittingly shifted where he didn't want to go. And now he had to lie. Trying for a defeated look, he shrugged. "Oh hell, all right, Leonard. But I can't say much. We're conducting private training at a ranch not far from Flagstaff. I haven't been near the border. I've been with a bunch of guys, 24/7 for almost a month." He paused and gave the special agent a conspiratorial wink. "But that's not for public consumption, you understand? This training is part of the Anti-Terrorism Task Force I'm attached to and if my boss finds out I said anything, he'll have my ass."

Banks nodded, mouth open, and he thought the guy looked like a big carp, fresh out of water. "Oh, I see, I see. Well, now I can understand your reticence." The special agent tugged on the sleeve of his suit jacket and glanced at his watch. "Tell you what, I need to call Fred and let him know we've gotten to the bottom of this. He may not even want to talk to you further." Banks tilted his head. "He'll probably just touch base with the facility, to verify your presence. In any case, I'll be back shortly. You OK with hanging around here for a while longer?"

The whole proceeding had gone beyond tedious, and he wanted nothing more than to escape the stuffy, grimy room. But he had to keep playing the game for as long as possible. Faking a smile, he told Banks what he wanted to hear. "Sure, Leonard, that's no problem. Do what you need to and I'll hang out here."

After the special agent left, shutting the door firmly behind him, Rowan bent his head, closed his eyes and heaved a gusty sigh. One thing he'd told Banks hadn't been a lie. Ralph would have his ass for the entire debacle, starting with the disagreement between him and the fat captain on an aircraft that was probably being unloaded in order to retrieve his dangerous suitcase. His boss was a former Navy SEAL, if there was such a thing, and a stickler for appearance and decorum. He'd sure as hell shot both out of the water today. Fumbling in his jacket pocket, he pulled out his phone and sighed again. It figured that there'd be no service in the *holding* room.

Rubbing his eyes, he gazed blearily at the door and wondered how the damaging scenario would play itself out. When he didn't arrive in Sioux Falls, Chad would call Ralph. That was a good thing, since Ralph was the only one who could get him out of whatever he'd fallen into. But would Ralph find out in time to make a call and stop the process? Picturing Fred Ralston's disbelieving gray eyes and unsmiling mouth, he grimaced. Ralston didn't like him, never had, and he couldn't imagine the man being satisfied with his story. That meant he was headed downtown to the Field Office, which would not be pleasant.

Once in an interrogation setting with Ralston, he wasn't sure he could keep his temper in check. God only knew what would happen to him then. With the futility of his circumstances setting in, weariness overtook the simmering rage. Sleep in any form was better than sitting hunched over on the hard bench. Gauging the distance to the desk, he thought if he leaned over carefully, it might work.

Laying his head on the cool surface, he contemplated how he'd gone from minding his own business, dozing peacefully in first class to a filthy room somewhere in the depths of the airport. The situation was beyond his purview, too much for his enervated mind. Trying unsuccessfully to pillow his head, he gave up and let his arms droop. Despite the discomfort and the gnawing uneasiness that things were not as they should be, he slipped immediately into exhausted sleep.

CHAPTER TWO

At fifty-five Ralph Johnston had been Special Agent in Charge of a small, elite FBI Anti-Terrorism Task Force, operating out of Bureau headquarters in Quantico, Virginia since shortly after 9/11. He stayed trim and vigorous by maintaining the military discipline that had become second nature through years of practice. Over six feet by several inches, he generally took no shit and didn't suffer fools, at all.

Sliding his large frame down the aisle of the aircraft, he looked for row twelve. It was business class. He'd been bumped up since there were no seats available in coach. Leaving Dulles that morning on a United Airlines flight to Chicago with the intention of connecting to Sioux Falls, South Dakota, he'd been disgusted to find that his flight from O'Hare had canceled. Frustration set in as he realized he'd be flying over Sioux Falls in order to get to Denver, only to board a flight there and fly back to Sioux Falls.

United wouldn't transfer his ticket to Legacy Airlines, so he could connect directly from Chicago to Sioux Falls. Oh no, and the reason United had canceled the flight boggled his mind. Settling into his seat, he motioned to the flight attendant and ordered a Glenlivet on the rocks. Considering the domino effect of the cancelations, he scowled. The aircraft slated to fly his tired butt from Chicago to Sioux Falls had originated in Denver and was still there.

A security breach of some kind had delayed and finally canceled the flight from Denver to Sioux Falls, thus canceling the flight from Sioux Falls to Chicago O'Hare, which would have positioned the aircraft to fly back to Sioux Falls from Chicago with him and seventy or so other crabby passengers. United had canceled that leg as well and that was why he was sitting in business class on a Boeing 777 sipping scotch. A customer service agent, who'd been as disgusted as he was, told him that all the flights from O'Hare to Sioux Falls were full, but Denver still had a few open seats on an Airbus 319 later in the evening. Bully for him. He'd better have one more drink, because this flying back and forth across the country bullshit made absolutely no sense.

Chad Cantor stood near the United Airlines ticket counter in Sioux Falls, apart from the long, restless line of passengers waiting to rebook their canceled flight. He needed to inquire about his missing colleague. His blond hair and blue eyes usually attracted favorable attention from women like the one behind the counter. Hopefully, combining his looks with his FBI credentials would entice the lobby agent to tell him what had happened to Rowan. Smiling affably when the agent looked up from her computer, he hoped for the best.

Eyeing him appreciatively, the young woman inspected his ID. "What can I help you with special agent? Are you checking in for a flight this afternoon?" Her navy blue uniform didn't do her justice, but she filled it in a pleasing way and had aquamarine eyes that looked daring. Her name tag said *Mandy*.

Pulling his gaze away from the uniform, he smiled at her again. "No, I'm not flying today. Actually, I'm concerned about a colleague who was booked on your canceled flight from Denver. I know you aren't supposed to give out personal information, but since he's with the FBI, I thought maybe you could help me. He hasn't called and I'm wondering if he managed to get on another flight."

Mandy looked at him, tapping manicured nails on the countertop. "Since you have proper FBI credentials, I'll take a look for your colleague. What's his name?"

"Rowan Milani is his name, and I'm pretty sure he'd be seated in first class." The look on Mandy's face made him pause. Something must have happened to Rowan.

Embarrassment filled her eyes. "Uh, your colleague, special agent Milani, right?" Without waiting for his reply, she continued. "He caused that flight and two others to cancel and his ticket has been revoked. I'm afraid he won't be allowed to fly on United Airlines for a while." She looked at him unhappily. "Sorry to break the bad news."

Stunned to open-mouthed speechlessness, he wondered what Rowan had gotten into this time. It had to be bad, whatever it was. Rowan was too hotheaded for his own good, and he wondered if his friend had been arrested. "Mandy, do you know what happened, by chance?"

Hesitation written on her face, she frowned and glanced down at her computer, eyes moving as she read something and then looked back up at him. "All I know is that he made a threat against the aircraft, at least that's what they're calling it. Evidently he was asked to deplane and got into an altercation with the captain, and it says the FBI escorted him off the aircraft."

Staring in disbelief, he almost started laughing and then thought about the seriousness of the charges his friend could be facing. He could only imagine how angry Rowan must have been if he were asked to deplane, and there was only one reason they'd make him do that. "Thanks Mandy, I appreciate your help."

With one last smile, her good looks forgotten in his concern for his colleague, he wandered away from the counter, cell phone already at his ear. Finding Ralph was his first priority and then he'd figure out what they'd done with Rowan. Ralph's phone went directly to voice mail and he didn't bother leaving a message. He'd better talk to his boss personally because Ralph would blow a gasket when he heard this news.

Finding the number for the FBI's office at Denver International Airport took a few minutes. "Yeah, Milani was asked to deplane. He couldn't resist baiting the captain and now the flight has canceled, due to a concern about his suitcase. My boss got his ass chewed by someone from United who's pissed off about lost revenue and the FBI's perceived inability to properly screen its own agents for security. Now he wants to talk more to Milani, downtown at the Field Office."

Chad slapped his forehead and rolled his eyes. This guy sounded seriously hacked off. "Special agent Banks, I'd like to speak to Rowan. Can you put him on the phone for me, please?"

Banks chuckled. "That would be a NO. He agreed to wait in our holding room while this crap gets sorted out and I'm not in proximity. Doesn't he have a phone with him? Call him yourself, special agent Cantor."

Folding his six foot five inch frame into a chair in the lower level waiting area, he flipped his phone shut and put his head in his hands, the man's sarcastic words still echoing. *He's not an easy guy to talk with, you know what I mean? His attitude complicates things, makes people mad.* This was unbelievable.

Flipping the phone open, he punched Rowan's number, but the call went to voice mail. Scowling, he tried Ralph again, relief flooding his mind when his boss answered the phone tersely. "Ralph Johnston."

"Ralph. Boss, where are you?" Reaching the one person who could stop what was happening to Rowan before it went too far left him weak-kneed.

"Chad, I'm in Denver. What do you need?" When he finished his story, the phone went silent. Then he heard Ralph cursing quietly. "I'll call you back. I'm going to fix this mess right now." Slumping lower in the chair, he closed his eyes and snapped the phone shut. Thank God Ralph was in Denver. If they hauled Rowan downtown for interrogation, there was no telling what would happen.

* * *

Ralph couldn't wait to get a hold of the man who'd escorted Rowan from the plane. Within minutes of his call, the special agent on duty at the airport met him on Concourse B, led him through a labyrinth of hallways and down a private service elevator into the dreary basement of the airport to the FBI's cramped office. Leonard Banks looked like a weasel to him, the kind who'd kissed butt and slithered into advances rather than earning them. Judging by how the man acted, Rowan would surely have intimidated him by the sheer force of his personality. Not to mention of course that Rowan could be such a jerk when angered.

He glanced around the office, raised his hands and turned back to the special agent. "Where is Rowan? He is here, correct? You haven't moved him downtown?"

Banks looked at him uneasily. "No sir, we haven't moved him anywhere. We've been talking and he's waiting for me in one of our holding rooms. You can take a look right here, we've got video surveillance." Shrugging, giving him an exaggerated smile, the man pointed to a row of monitors.

Sliding around the desk, he squinted at the monitor Banks thumped with an index finger. Was that Rowan? What the hell was he doing? He turned and glared. "Leonard, how long has my subordinate been sitting on a bench in that room?"

Banks stared at him and swallowed. "Well, he and I talked, and then I needed to call my boss and take care of a few other things that happened because of his smart mouth. It's only been a couple hours. He told me he didn't mind waiting."

Concern building over the direction he thought the morass was heading, Ralph frowned. "Do you have written verification of specific charges against special agent Milani? Do you have a warrant for his arrest?"

Banks blinked and took a step back. "No, of course we don't have a warrant for his arrest. Like I said, all we've done is chat.

And like I said, he agreed to wait. We're not actually *holding* him. But I don't mind telling you, he's confrontational, difficult to reason with and borderline belligerent."

He couldn't help a chuckle. "I'm well aware of my subordinate's personality quirks. However, my main concern is that you've kept a colleague in an uncomfortable situation for going on three hours. You know what? Let's go. I've seen enough."

Rowan kept thinking he needed to move, but he was too tired. Thought he heard Ralph's voice and knew he must be dreaming. His arms and back ached, his neck was stiff and pins and needles jabbed his legs. Opening his left eye, he winced at the scratchy dryness. Opening the other eye wasn't possible because his face was plastered flat against something hard, and slimy wetness clung to his chin. As the fog cleared, the ugly events of the past few hours pushed their way back to the forefront of his mind.

While his muscles protested, he struggled to push himself upright. Unable to remember when he'd ever felt worse without the helpful assistance of Jack Daniel's whiskey, he tipped his head back and saw Ralph. He painstakingly twisted first his neck and then his back. It felt good to wipe the spit off his chin, and he needed to find a bathroom, soon. Moving his legs to bring feeling back, he focused on Ralph. "What the hell are you doing in Denver, boss?"

Ralph glowered at him. "It's nice to see you too, and you're welcome. Why I'm here is a long, jacked up tale for another day. Why you're here is my immediate concern. Look Rowan, it's getting to where I can't let you out in public anymore. You want to explain this shit to me?"

Massaging the back of his neck, he glanced at Banks, who was leaning against the door. Rage overflowing at the endless delays and the game playing he'd been forced to endure, he looked at Ralph and angled his head toward Banks. "Ask him." That would be the extent of his input, he wouldn't say more. Even with Ralph's reassuring presence, he wasn't sure that an overarching authority couldn't haul him downtown for further *conversation* anyway. Clenching his jaws, he sat silently and waited for Ralph to speak.

Looking at Rowan's face, Ralph saw the telltale rage and was surprised his subordinate had the smarts to shut up for once. Rowan must be gravely concerned, or he'd have let the lanky man leaning against the door have it with both barrels. Giving Banks a placid smile, Ralph decided it was time for baldy to pay the piper. He'd enjoy making him squirm. "Leonard, this is your opportunity to tell me, or rather us," he gestured at Rowan, "What is going on here? I am most interested to hear your explanation. Enlighten us, please." He crossed his arms and stared.

Banks ran a hand over his head, eyes darting from him to Rowan. "You gentlemen need to understand something. I'm acting on orders from my boss. As I told Rowan, he is concerned about special agent Milani's possible connection to something that happened in Mexico last night."

Ralph shot a quick glance at Rowan, whose face looked purposely blank. When he'd seen the breaking news in O'Hare, it crossed his mind that his subordinate might be involved. But he'd forgotten about it in his never-ending saga of flight across the midsection of the country. "Leonard, refresh my memory. Who is your boss in Denver?"

The man smoothed his wrinkled suit and smiled. "Fred Ralston is my immediate superior and the Special Agent in Charge. As I said, he's got a lead on suspected American covert involvement in this deal that went down in Mexico. We needed Rowan's input to clear things up. I spoke to Fred just before you arrived, and he would still like to chat personally with special agent Milani, to clarify where he's been."

Giving Rowan another surreptitious glance, he noticed his friend had gone still. Banks had definitely struck a nerve. Well, by God, no one was going to question his special agent about complicity in something that had happened in Mexico. But how had Fred Ralston put Rowan together with that operation? He looked at Banks. "What kind of lead are you talking about?"

Banks shrugged. "Fred got an anonymous phone call naming Rowan as the American operative who murdered two people along the border between Mexico and the United States. The caller mentioned a possible terror incident."

Ralph knew it was time to get his friend out of harm's way before someone higher up decided to investigate the merits of that phone call. If they took Rowan downtown, all hell would break loose, in more ways than one. "Leonard, your boss needs to quit smoking peyote." Watching as Banks' entire head turned crimson, he hid a smile behind his fist and cleared his throat.

Enjoying the man's discomfort, he continued. "And you can quote me on that. For crying out loud, he got an anonymous phone call? Give me a break. He's got no proof, no reason to question special agent Milani regarding some bullshit that happened in Mexico. I'm putting an end to this right now."

Bank's mouth opened and closed and his eyes got round. "Before you, I mean, before Rowan can leave, I need to clear it with my boss."

Ralph stepped in front of Banks and tugged gently on the angular man's tie. "Listen closely. Rowan Milani is my subordinate and my responsibility. As you stated, you're not holding him. He agreed to wait while you sorted things out. And now, he is leaving with me and there is not diddly squat either you or your boss can do about it. You may inform Special Agent *in Charge* Ralston that he may forward whatever hard evidence he has, to me. Move away from the door, Leonard. Right now."

Ralph looked at Rowan as they belted themselves into deep, comfortable seats on the Learjet his friend had chartered without batting an eye. Rowan's panache always amazed him. His special agent had plunked down a platinum American Express card and signed the forms with a flourish, as though chartering a private jet was an everyday occurrence. Then Rowan pulled a couple hundred-dollar bills from his wallet that was thick with the green stuff and pushed them over the counter with a rakish wink at the customer service agent. Some things never changed. No matter how much he lectured about discretion, Rowan did whatever the hell he pleased, tossing money to the locals no matter where they were on assignment. He would probably give the pilots even more.

Rowan gave him a fatigued smile and stuffed his cell phone in his jacket pocket. "Chad's picking us up at the airport." Stifling a yawn, his special agent waved vaguely toward the flight deck where the captain and first officer conferred quietly. "We should be getting underway shortly. And I think we arrive around ten o'clock tonight, with the time change. Hell, its fifteen degrees with light snow in Sioux Falls."

He gave Rowan a grim smile. "Don't worry, you'll survive. Hey, I talked to that pinhead Fred Ralston. He isn't planning on pursuing an investigation of you, based on an anonymous call." Kneading the back of his neck, he looked at his friend. "Man, it hacked me off when Banks said you couldn't leave without Ralston's approval. And he gets off with a reprimand for leaving you in that dump for three hours. What a pathetic schmuck."

The cabin lights dimmed, and Ralph craned his neck to look out the window. The engines started their wind-up as they taxied through the darkness past glittering blue and white runway lights. Reclining his seat, he glanced at Rowan, sitting with his hands in his lap, eyes closing as his head dipped. Now probably wasn't the time, but the question had been burning in his mind since that afternoon. "Say, I'm wondering about something."

His special agent opened bloodshot eyes. "What's on your mind, Ralph? Thinking about Mexico?"

How had Rowan read his thoughts? "You might say that. I noticed when Banks started talking about it you got kind of quiet."

The roar of the engines made conversation difficult, and he could see that Rowan was waiting until they were airborne to reply. Watching the younger man as they ascended smoothly and banked toward the east, he decided it wasn't any of his business. As the engine noise leveled off, he spoke. "I'm sorry, I should know better than to ask stupid questions about things that don't concern me. Forget I said anything."

Rowan stared at him. Marveling at the unrepentant face, he searched for a smidgeon of warmth in the dark eyes. What a difference the years had made, he thought sadly. He and Rowan had been friends for a long time, and every once in a while he still missed the man he'd known before September 11, 2001. That singular event had created the rocky, usually smoldering exterior special agent Milani presented to the rest of the world. It was too bad, but that's the way it was. He turned away, slid down in his seat and closed his eyes, feeling the engine vibration throughout his body, lulling him to sleep.

Rowan tapped his forearm. "Hey, Ralph."

Turning his head, he opened his eyes and gazed sleepily at his friend. "What?"

Rowan gave him an indifferent shrug. "I was asked to eliminate a threat and send a strong message. So that's what I did."

Watching from the warmth of the customer lounge provided by the Fixed Base Operator on the private side of the airport, Chad muttered to himself as the Learjet taxied in, guided to a stop by a parka clad agent with glowing orange wands. It was about time. Turning up the collar of his overcoat and pulling on fur lined leather gloves, he stepped into the frigid air to meet his boss and colleague.

He'd done everything he could think of to make sure Rowan would be comfortable once he arrived in Sioux Falls. A *Men's Wearhouse* bag in the trunk of the car contained assorted pairs of socks and boxers. Rowan could easily talk someone at the hotel into getting his clothes washed, but this way he'd be spared the humiliation of handing over his underwear. A bottle of ninety-four proof, single barrel Jack Daniel's whiskey nestled in a paper sack next to the socks and boxers. Smiling to himself he thought about how much Rowan would enjoy that. It was fun to surprise his surly friend once in a while, let him know he cared.

Thanks to Mandy, his new confidant at United Airlines, Rowan's suitcase would arrive by FedEx in the morning. The captain of the flight Rowan had been yanked from made a ramp agent search through ninety-seven bags in the cargo pit twice before a call to US Air confirmed that the suitcase had never made the transfer to United in Denver. Mandy made a few calls and arranged the FedEx transport at the risk of being ostracized by her co-workers and the station manager.

Every airline employee and manager in Sioux Falls wanted Rowan's rear end because of United's three canceled flights. In a small airport, that many cancelations affected all the airlines. United needed seats for almost two hundred people, stretching the goodwill and capacity of both Delta and Legacy.

Mandy had spilled the juicy insider information after a few drinks and some extra attention, first at a bar and then in his bedroom. Humming the old Barry Manilow song that popped unbidden into his mind, *Well you came and you gave without takin', but I sent you away, Oh Mandy.* He snickered. He'd taken one for the team, and Mandy was none the wiser. Oh well. She was cute and kindhearted, but not all that smart. Besides, he'd enjoy telling Rowan how much he'd sacrificed on his behalf.

Teeth chattering, eyes watering from the cold, he waited at the bottom of the aircraft stairs in swirling snow. Breathing in acrid fumes from the jet exhaust as the engines wound down, he squinted up at Ralph, silhouetted by the arc lights overhead as he stepped carefully down the stairs. With a grunt his boss tilted his head back and smiled, breath billowing in a frosty cloud. "Your colleague will be right along. He's enriching the lives of the captain and first officer as we speak."

Chad laughed and wiped his eyes. Looking up, he saw Rowan standing sleepily in the doorway of the jet, scowling and blinking at the snow, then lingering as he zipped up his black leather jacket. He had to chuckle when Ralph cast an irritated glance upward and bellowed. "Rowan, for crying out loud, let's go. We don't have all night. It's plenty cold, in case you hadn't noticed."

Grabbing Ralph by the arm, Chad leaned close. "Boss, I need to talk to you privately tonight, just for a minute." Ralph nodded and didn't say anything as Rowan stepped onto the tarmac, shoulders hunched into his jacket, hands jammed in the pockets. Judging from the look on his friend's face, his first impression of South Dakota wasn't favorable.

With a bad-tempered glare at both him and Ralph, Rowan jerked his head in annoyance. "Well, come on. Let's go before we all freeze to death standing here. Where's the damned Lincoln? You're still driving that piece of junk, right?"

Shaking his head, Chad laughed again and smacked his colleague on the back. "It's great to see you too, Rowan. The Lincoln is in the parking lot. I left it running so it'd be nice and warm for your wimpy California ass. You'll be in your room in the Executive Wing at the Sheraton before you know it. You can even take a hot bath."

Danielle Stratton glanced at the tall, blond-haired man as he pulled on an overcoat and leather gloves and then strode out the door after her friend Ed marshaled the Learjet into its parking spot. For the last hour he'd alternately sat and then paced around the plush customer lounge on the private side of the airport. While she waited in the cushy leather chair, watching advertisements for the company's services on the giant flat screen, he made a few phone calls and grumbled to himself.

Whoever he was meeting had delayed her as well. Tugging on the ponytail restraining her dark red hair, she knew she should never have agreed to give Ed a ride home. As his boss, the part-time job he'd taken, working on the private side of the airport was not her problem and neither was his broken truck. But here she was, because he was also her friend.

Shoving her coat sleeve up, she stared at her watch and yawned. As station manager for Legacy Airlines in Sioux Falls, her day started when the operation opened at five o'clock in the morning and didn't end until the final turn left for Chicago at six o'clock in the evening. Everyone told her she was too dedicated and they were right. At thirty-three, she'd been in the airline industry for thirteen years and didn't like the chaos anymore. Someday, it would be nice to have a life that consisted of more than baggage service problems, on-time departure statistics and ungrateful passengers.

When the tall blond went out the door with a muttered *finally,* she decided to check out the passengers so important that they were arriving by private jet at almost eleven o'clock in the evening. Wandering over to the tables and chairs facing the floor to ceiling windows, she took a seat and waited. First a man who looked like he could be her father's age came down the steps, stopping to talk with the guy she'd been watching. Both men looked up, and she followed their gazes to the door of the aircraft. Oh my. Who was that?

Too *hot* was the only way to describe the man who paused in the doorway of the jet before slouching down the stairs. Once on the ground, he looked cold as he hurried toward the building with the other two men. And God love him, he needed a shave, but the sooty whiskers only added to his decadent good looks. Drawn by instant, overpowering desire, she wanted him, right now. She could feel strong arms wrapping around her, eager lips finding hers and the burn of rough stubble on her cheeks.

Good grief, what was wrong with her? Taking a deep breath, she felt the heat spreading across her face. Shoulders tense, palms damp, she watched him move through the customer service lounge with a lithe swagger, vigorously rubbing his hands and blowing on them. The blond guy smacked him on the back and said something she couldn't hear. Tossing back thick black hair, he laughed out loud, gave his tall friend an insolent grin and answered with a word that made the older guy guffaw.

Watching the three men interact filled her with inordinate, foolish jealousy. They were obviously good friends and she felt cheated out of something special. Who was this man and how long was he going to be in Sioux Falls? Of course, flying in on a private jet put him way, way out of her league.

When he slipped out the door and into the darkness, she felt letdown, as though she'd missed an important opportunity and now it was gone. How could she feel such breathtaking attraction to someone she didn't even know? Telling herself to get over it, she decided that by morning she probably wouldn't even be able to remember what he looked like.

Turning back to the window, she propped her elbows on the table, rested her chin in her hands and watched Ed methodically chock the wheels, close the cargo bin and the aircraft door, buttoning up the jet for the night. Disturbed that a man she'd never seen before and most likely would never see again could leave her feeling so bereft, she sighed disconsolately. In her heart she knew she was a fool to think she'd forget what he looked like anytime soon.

Watching Rowan hustle through the revolving door at the Sheraton, Chad turned to Ralph. "Thanks for taking a minute to talk."

Ralph looked at him, face bone-weary. "Spit it out Chad. I'm about to fall asleep on my feet."

"Boss, can you keep Rowan away from the airport for a couple days? The airlines out there are like one big dysfunctional family and they're all pissed off. The agents are in an uproar because apparently it's the first time in airline history that one person caused three flights to cancel, one right after another. The rumor mill is in full swing too, and the big news is that he's Middle Eastern. They don't understand how he can be an FBI special agent and part of an Anti-Terrorism Task Force."

Sniffing as the cold air stung his nose and eyes, he continued. "If you can offer some explanation to management, the info will trickle down to the masses, and they'll move on to the next big issue. From what I've gathered, these folks have a short attention span. One of United's customer service reps told me all this crap."

Ralph's shoulders sagged. "Nothing surprises me anymore, especially not when Rowan's involved. Don't worry, I'll tell him to lay low. He could use a couple days off. Besides, I need to establish a relationship with local Law Enforcement and the Assistant Federal Security Directors assigned out there and meet with airline management." Ralph gave him a tired smile and patted him on the shoulder. "Relax special agent, I'll pave the way. Now, I've got to get some sleep. See you in the morning, eight o'clock sharp in the restaurant here."

Watching as Ralph headed into the pool of light and warmth beyond the revolving door, he heaved a sigh. He'd done as much as he could. Sliding behind the wheel of the Lincoln, he headed for home, the stupid *Mandy* song still playing in his mind. His mother had been a hopeless romantic, collecting sappy love songs from the seventies and eighties and playing them endlessly while he was growing up. As a consequence, one of the silly songs always popped into his mind at odd times and places.

Like tonight, he thought as he drove through the snow-covered streets. He hoped that his mother, trapped in the alternate universe that Alzheimer's had relentlessly tugged her into, still enjoyed the music. Just like he hoped things would quiet down now so he and his colleague and boss could get serious about their assignment.

Absorbed in paperwork, in the midst of her shift as evening manager at the Sheraton, Jennie Kelly didn't want to deal with the late arriving guest blowing in through the revolving glass doors. Bracing herself for one more in a long line of disgruntled travelers, she looked up with a forced smile. Gazing at her with inscrutable black eyes was one of the sexiest looking men she'd ever seen. Yikes. A trip wire went off in the back of her mind, telling her to proceed with caution. He was good looking, but something about him scared her and she felt the tingling rise of the hair on her arms. Dry-mouthed, unable to stop staring at him, she felt like an idiot. "Um, good evening sir, do you have a reservation?"

To her utter surprise, he held out his hand and smiled. "Special agent Rowan Milani, FBI and yes, I have a reservation."

She shook his hand and wondered if she had to let go. With shaky fingers she flipped long black hair behind her shoulder, pushed up her glasses and tapped the keyboard, finding the information she needed to process the check-in. She handed him a key card and treated herself to another look at his indecently sensual face. "Is there anything else you need this evening, Mr. Milani?"

"Please call me Rowan, and yeah Jennie, is there any way to get a sweater and jeans washed before morning? Does your overnight staff do laundry?" He looked embarrassed. "My suitcase got lost today, and all I have with me is what I'm wearing. You couldn't find me a bathrobe anywhere, could you?"

In the Presidential Suite they had all kinds of supplies, and the suite wasn't booked. Tugging on the name tag he'd obviously read, she made a snap decision and looked up at him with a smile. "That's no problem, Mr., ah, Rowan. I'll have room service bring you a robe, and I'll be glad to take your clothes." Face reddening, she floundered on. "I mean, we can take your clothes and have them cleaned for you. We'll hang them on your door when they're ready, so you won't be disturbed."

He rewarded her with a wicked smile and a second, even bigger surprise. Pulling a worn wallet from his back pocket, he peeled five one hundred-dollar bills from it, folded them carelessly and shoved them across the counter while she gaped. "Thanks, Jennie, I appreciate it a lot. Would you divvy that up with your night staff? Oh, there's one last thing." He jerked a thumb over his shoulder. "Does that Starbucks open early?"

Looking past him to the Starbucks kiosk, she nodded. "Yes sir, they open at six o'clock every morning."

He smacked the counter with his hand. "Fantastic. Would you mind leaving them a note to bring a carafe of Italian Roast up to my room around eight?" When she nodded mutely, he pulled another hundred from the wallet and handed it to her. "Please make sure the wait staff gets this. You guys are great." With one last killer smile he turned, stuffed the wallet back in his pocket and walked off, following the signs to the Executive Wing. She was sure she heard him laughing.

A hot shower and Jack Daniel's whiskey worked miracles for his attitude. Rowan sat on the edge of his bed in a warm velour bathrobe that was purple, for God's sake, and wiggled his toes in heavy black socks. Chad was a godsend, and he'd already called him to say thanks. Of course, his friend blew it all off and asked him how much he'd paid to get his clothes washed.

Downing a shot of whiskey, he thought wryly that Chad knew him too well. Thanks to his clandestine activities on behalf of his country, he earned a lot of money, and one of the few things he enjoyed was spreading it around to people he knew worked their asses off for low wages. So some poor old lady stuck washing his clothes got a gift. Big deal, it was the least he could do.

Sloshing more whiskey in the cup, he stood up and stepped around the bed to look out the window. Cold air radiated from the glass. Gazing down, he saw snowflakes, still falling, glittering in the lights of the parking lot and flailing in eddies around the corner of the building. How did people live in this godforsaken state? The weather was even worse than he'd imagined. The cable TV channel posted the temperature at ten degrees, and the wind chill made it an even zero. With a shiver, goose bumps forming all up and down his arms and legs he stepped back to the bed, punched a couple pillows into shape against the headboard and crawled under the sheets and down comforter.

Yawning so hard he spilled the drink, he wiped his hand on the sleeve of the robe and thought back on the day. It had been long and ugly, harboring the potential to destroy his career and maybe even his life. Taking a gulp of the potent whiskey, he tipped his head back and swallowed, hating to think what would have happened if Ralph hadn't appeared when he did. How many days would he have sat at the Federal Building in downtown Denver, being interrogated by the likes of special agent Banks, Fred Ralston and God only knew who else?

His career as an FBI special agent would not have survived the ordeal. The aftermath of that kind of scrutiny would leave him on the wanted list of more than a few foreign governments. Not to mention the wish lists of a bunch of pissed off holy warriors who'd seen their plans uprooted and their martyrs sent to paradise early.

He'd like to know who had made the anonymous phone call – and how they knew about the jihadists he'd killed along the border. The list of people involved in the Mexico operation was extremely short, and he couldn't imagine any of the other participants making that call. But someone *had* called. And now according to Ralph, the poison had spread to Sioux Falls. Massaging drowsy eyes, he thought righteously that it wasn't his fault any of those three flights had canceled. And anyway, if he hadn't been detained in Denver, none of this would have happened.

Tossing back another mouthful of whiskey, he relished the burn down his throat and felt the warmth spreading. Now he had two days off, and Ralph had been adamant. *Stay away from the airport.* That was all right with him, because he didn't think the focus should be on the airport anyway. He'd like to head for the local mosque. If he could keep a low profile and get acquainted with the faithful, he'd be another step closer to uncovering the invisible leader of the secret jihad working to undermine the country. All he needed was time to let his beard and already shaggy hair grow even longer.

His head dipped as his eyes slid shut. The whiskey had warmed him nicely. Downing the last swallow, he pitched the cup and hit the switch on the bedside lamp before pulling off the robe and tossing it to the floor. Flat on his back with hands clasped on his belly and feet crossed at the ankles, he could sleep undisturbed – at last.

CHAPTER THREE

He heard the planes. The horrendous fireballs seared his soul. As he staggered up the stairs, caustic, ash-laden smoke filled his nostrils and caked his throat. Choking, coughing, lungs on fire, he knew he had to keep going, he had to find her. Then the tower imploded, the stairs disappeared and he fell through space, arms clawing the air, legs pumping in vain. Rowan jerked awake in a tangle of sweat soaked bedding, heart slamming in his chest. Gray light leaked from the edges of the curtained window and he slung an arm over his eyes and lay there, waiting for his heart rate to slow.

After all the intervening years, the nightmare still plagued him. On the evening of September 10, 2001, his fiancée had been in New York City for a job interview. She'd called to tell him that she planned to have breakfast at Windows on the World the next morning. On assignment in Ohio, he'd been drinking coffee with Ralph in his hotel room when the first plane hit. His sweet Michelle, with honey-blonde hair and kind blue eyes, didn't answer her cell phone. It wasn't until he traveled to the city to collect her things that he found it, with all his heartrending messages, on the bedside table in her hotel room.

For one precious month, his life had been perfect. Both he and Michelle were twenty-five and had grown up together in Carpinteria, CA, a sleepy town a few miles down the coast from Santa Barbara. Engaged on August 11, 2001, he'd been happy – delirious when she'd told him she was pregnant. Lying in bed together, they'd laughed and dreamed and he'd splayed his hand across her abdomen and closed his eyes, envisioning a family with the only woman he'd ever loved. One month later, she was gone. His family was gone. Forever. He still couldn't get his mind around the concept of that word. Shoving the rumpled blankets aside, he sat on the edge of the bed and rubbed his eyes viciously with the heels of his hands. But goddamn it, he'd tried.

He'd shown up at Ground Zero a week after the attack with his FBI credentials, grabbed a hardhat and a mask and stayed for six months, working alongside firefighters and volunteers, digging through debris by the bucket full. One afternoon, he taped their engagement picture next to the thousands of other pictures and letters on the fences lining the massive funeral pyre. Michelle's remains were never found and finally, despairing, he flung the platinum wedding bands that would never be worn as far as he could into the wreckage.

A threesome of volunteers from Lynchburg, Tennessee took him under their wing. They empathized, told him they were sorry for his loss and introduced him to Jack Daniel's whiskey. The potent elixir became his new lover, faithfully numbing his mind and allowing him the nightly relief of passing out. For that he would be eternally grateful.

Taking a call from Ralph one day, he'd agreed to join a low profile Anti-Terrorism Task Force his boss commanded under the loose discretion of the Director of the FBI. Whispers about black ops came soon after that, and his own personal jihad had given him a reason to continue living. Which brought his mind back to the present as he stretched, scratched himself and yawned, wondering if the wait staff had remembered his Starbucks. They had and he sipped the strong coffee, gazing with longing at the bottle of whiskey on the bedside table. Ralph had been right about him needing a couple days off.

Grasping the coffee cup in one hand, drawn back to the window, he shoved the drapes aside and gazed at the alien landscape four stories below. The trees looked like black sticks stuck in wads of grayish cotton. Low clouds blocked even the thought of sunlight and across the street, atop a pole a flag whipped back and forth in the unyielding wind. Still mystified that people chose to live in such misery, he turned away and decided to find something to do in the hotel. He remembered a sign in the lobby with directions to a work-out room and a pool. If he kept himself busy for the morning, he could spend the afternoon with his bottle of whiskey and by evening, he'd pass out and not wake up until the next morning. *Perfect.*

Jennie looked up at the sound of heavy footsteps and tried not to stare at the two hard-featured, big men approaching her podium. "Good afternoon, how may I help you?"

One of them had close-set blue eyes and buzz cut black hair. When he smiled at her, she felt uneasy. "We need to check-in, one room. I'm Seth Hancock." Tipping his head toward the other man, who was taller, he continued. "And this is Lucien Talbot. Say, a buddy of ours is staying here – Rowan Milani. Can you set us up with a room somewhere close to his?"

Just looking at both men made her skin crawl and she could hardly believe either of them had anything in common with the sexy man she'd checked in the night before. "OK, let me see. I can't give out special agent Milani's room number. Um, he was here a while ago, playing pool in the work-out room with our maintenance man, but I'm not sure where he is now. Did you want to leave him a message?"

The taller one had blond hair and bulging muscles. When he smiled, all his teeth showed, and she shrank back. "Nah, that's all right. We want to surprise him."

Three Days Later
Rowan tipped the shuttle driver and climbed out the sliding door of the hotel van, stepping carefully through the half-frozen slush. Bracing against the never-ending wind, snowflakes falling thick and fast on his head, in his eyes and down his shirt, he made his way into the airport. Stamping his feet and brushing snow out of

his hair, he clutched his coffee mug and muttered vile epithets. His jeans had absorbed the cold and felt like sheets of ice against his legs. Shivering and thinking he should have worn an overcoat instead of his leather jacket, he looked around, expecting to see crowds of people. But the wide hallway stretching from baggage claim at one end of the airport to the ticketing area at the other end was empty. None of the baggage belts were moving. Three car rental agencies sat vacant with not an employee in sight. Didn't people fly into or out of Sioux Falls at eight o'clock in the morning?

Heading toward ticketing, the hallway opened to his left and he spotted Chad and Ralph sitting in the airport restaurant talking to an African American police officer. Veering inside, he coasted into the remaining chair at their table. It was warm in the restaurant, and his body stopped shivering. The aroma of frying bacon made his mouth water, but he didn't have time for breakfast. Ralph had something for him to do. Otherwise he'd still be at the hotel enjoying room service.

Chad smiled and lifted his coffee cup. Ralph frowned at his Starbucks to-go mug and the police officer held out a hand. "Good morning, I'm Jax. You must be the third member of this special team we've got helping us out."

Taking in the curling black hair shot through with gray and the muscular body tucked into the chair, he shook hands firmly and smiled at the police officer. "It's nice to meet you, sir. I'm special agent Rowan Milani, and yes, I belong with these two, more or less."

Ralph snorted. "Face it Rowan, if it weren't for us, God only knows where you'd be. And what's the matter with the hotel coffee that you have to drink that damned crap? It's a wonder you have a stomach lining. Wait, maybe you don't, and that's why you have such a stellar personality."

Ralph loved to give him a hard time, and his boss did have a point. Without his two colleagues, there was no telling where he'd be. But he was dead wrong about the coffee. "Aw hell boss, you know how much I enjoy it. The Starbucks girls at the hotel bring it up to my room every morning, and they gave me my very own to-go mug."

Chad replied. "By the time we're finished with this assignment, the Starbucks girls will probably be able to attend whatever college they want, from your tips alone."

Mouth opened to retort, he frowned when Ralph spoke before he had the chance. "I'd like you to make nice with a few airline agents and scope out the security here. Jax tells me there are some holes, but he thinks the airline folks can give us specifics. Consider it your opportunity to gain a semblance of redemption in their eyes."

Oh hell, he'd love to make nice with the people who blamed him for canceling three flights. Knowing he was screwed, he took a long drink of coffee before replying. "OK boss, whatever you want. Guess I'll get started."

Ralph leveled a knowing grin in his direction. "You can report what you find out tomorrow morning, because that's when you, special agent Cantor and I will have our next meeting. Seven o'clock sharp at the hotel. By the way, where's your weapon?"

He looked Ralph in the eye and smiled. "You'll be happy to know the Glock is secured. It's in the safe in my room." In certain situations, Ralph worried that he'd lose his temper and shoot someone, but that wouldn't happen today. And he hadn't lied – his Glock 22 service weapon was in the safe. But he never went anywhere without the Glock 36 holstered inside the waistband of his jeans, in front of his left hip for easy access. He also wouldn't mention his favorite knife, the lethal, folding Karambit he'd meticulously cleaned after the Mexico op and had just that morning stashed in the inner pocket of his jacket, along with a couple extra mags of forty-five caliber ammo for his pistol.

Ralph chuckled. "That's smart thinking, special agent Milani. Have fun with the folks. You'll find they're a decent bunch. I explained to management that a case of mistaken identity caused the problems in Denver and consequently with all the flights here. But Rowan, be careful how you conduct yourself."

Shoving back the chair, he winked at Ralph and sketched a wave at Chad and the police officer. Sauntering across the two-story tall, main entryway of the airport, he wondered why his boss was sticking him in an awkward situation like this. Because Ralph knew he didn't want to interact with these people, professionally or otherwise. Irritated with both his boss and the cold air flowing nonstop from the front entrance, he set his jaw for the distasteful task ahead.

Clusters of people stood at the Delta kiosks, and United had a crowd, but no one was checking in at Legacy. Leaning against the wall across the broad walkway from Legacy Airlines ticket counter, he scanned the area and sipped his coffee. Boarding announcements overlaid the hubbub of passengers, and the old Elvin Bishop song, *Fooled Around and Fell in Love* echoed throughout the airport as part of the rendition of seventies songs airport management must think represented easy listening. At least it was warm where he was standing.

While he lounged against the wall, a guy in a red shirt, gray uniform pants and a worn *NWA* ball cap stepped out of Delta's back office doorway and surveyed the passengers milling in front of the counter. Then the door to Legacy's back area opened and a woman looked around, waved at the man and walked over to stand next to him. God, she was sexy. Dressed in black airline-issue sweater and pants, she had long legs and breasts that would more than fill his hands. Her hair, just past shoulder length, was luxuriously thick and dark, almost burgundy red. Her confident *don't mess with me* aura turned him on. Talk about a challenge.

Lured irresistibly, he found himself walking toward the couple who stood talking like they were comfortable with each other, probably good friends. The woman turned, met his eyes, and went perfectly still. Not sure what he was going to say, he reached

Legacy's ticket counter and stopped, conscious of sweaty palms and his pulse ticking erratically. She stared at him. He couldn't take his eyes off her.

While he waited, she left her companion and walked to the computer terminal in front of him. Looking carefully at her face, he saw something secretive in her eyes. Then she smiled and he lost himself, his gaze lingering first on her mouth and then sliding down to the inviting V-neck of her sweater. Arousal rolled over him in an intense, uncontrollable wave, and he rocked back on his heels.

Tucking strands of hair behind her ear, she tilted her head and kept staring at him. "Sir, may I help you with something?"

Tamping down the voracious desire, he dragged his eyes back up to hers and hoped he could keep his mind on the job. Trying to be unobtrusive, he sat his coffee mug on the counter and wiped sweating hands on his jeans. "Is the Legacy manager available?"

This time her smile dazzled him. "My name is Danielle Stratton, and I'm the Legacy station manager. What can I help you with?"

It had only been three days since the flight debacle he'd been blamed for, and he wasn't sure he wanted to tell her his name. Hesitating for only a second, he stuck out his hand. "It's nice to meet you Danielle. Rowan Milani is my name. I'm a special agent with the FBI and need an escort to show me the airport, inside the sterile area."

Incredulity widened her eyes and her lips parted. "Oh my God, it was you. I should have guessed." Then she blinked and took a hold of his proffered hand with a quivering one of her own. The dampness of her palm matched his. The touch made him want more.

Extricating his hand from hers, he attempted a smile. "Could one of your agents escort me through the security checkpoint and show me around the sterile area? I'd be especially interested in hearing insider thoughts and opinions about security or the lack thereof." If he kept strictly to business, maybe he could forget about the soft warmth of her hand in his. Doubtful, but hell, what choice did he have?

Practically giving him heart palpitations, she leaned closer. Voice low, she spoke conversationally. "Special agent Milani, none of my employees have gotten over your involvement in those three canceled flights. But I'll give you a tour."

The tour he'd like involved his hands and her body. Clenching his fists, he took a deep breath and held it. For God's sake, he needed to get a grip. Letting the breath out in increments, he forced himself to focus on her face, instead of the tantalizing V-neck. "That would be fine and please call me Rowan. Do you have time right now to show me around?"

Nodding enthusiastically, she waved an arm. "Sure, let's go. I'm assuming you have your official ID? You'll need it at the checkpoint, unless you want to access the sterile area from outside." Before he could answer, she looked toward the man she'd been talking to, who was watching them. "Hey Derek, catch you at home if not before."

Glancing to where the guy stood, he raised a brow, surprised at the animosity emanating from her friend. Giving the man a nasty smirk, he turned away. A moment later the door to Delta's back room slammed with an echoing thwack, rattling the wall. He jumped and then snickered. Danielle looked puzzled. "Good grief, what got into him?"

He shrugged. "Who knows? Hey, I'm not crazy about going back outside, so I need to leave my coffee mug here and touch base with the security supervisor at the checkpoint. I should be on their list."

They stashed the mug in her office and headed up the escalator toward the security checkpoint and the concourse beyond. An hour later, he'd seen the entire sterile area of the airport. Danielle spoke intelligently and with passion about what she considered flaws in airport security at Sioux Falls. Her personality, as dramatic as her hair, had him enthralled, and he wanted to spend more time with her. Tagging along behind her down narrow stairs and a grungy hallway, mesmerized by her hips swaying back and forth in the snug pants, he kept walking when she stopped and bumped into her. "Oops, I'm sorry."

Looking up, he saw that they'd reached a dented, gray metal door. Placing his left hand against the wall, he thought he should back up, but didn't want to. Danielle turned and looked up at him with an enticing smile. They were only a few inches apart, but she didn't seem to mind. "This is the end of my tour. This door takes us into Legacy's operations center. It's always locked."

Touching her had become an all-consuming need. But he wondered about the man he'd angered on the Delta side of the counter. Searching her eyes, he saw only anticipation and felt his willpower slipping away. "Ah, that guy from Delta, is he your boyfriend?"

Danielle chuckled. "Derek? We've been housemates for almost four years, ever since his divorce. He's a great guy and a close friend, but he's not my boyfriend." When she lifted a hand and ran feather light fingers along the sandpapery stubble on his jaw, he drew a sharp breath. Gazing steadily at him, she said, "I don't have a boyfriend."

Reaching out slowly, he touched her hair. "OK, good." Done talking, desire surging, the look in her eyes finished him off. Wrapping his arms around her, he bent his head to her mouth, half sighing, half groaning in pleasure when his lips touched hers. Soft and willing, they responded with an eagerness that stoked the fire she'd already lit for him, deep inside. Her hands slid beneath his jacket, clung to his back and then drifted downward to settle around his hips. The Glock pressed between them and he felt for it with his hand. Muttering "just a second," he fumbled beneath the polo shirt, grabbed the holstered pistol and shoved it deep into his jacket pocket.

Sometime he'd have to stop kissing her, but not yet. When his tongue touched hers, she moaned softly. His hands smoothed down to caress her firm backside and she followed suit, laughing into his mouth before pulling him tight against her body. Breathing unevenly, heart pounding, he knew he needed to stop, but wondered instead if she'd drop down on the filthy cement floor with him and finish what they'd started. He wanted to, desperately. But a long time ago his father had drilled the importance of respecting women into his hard head. And he planned to give this woman the utmost respect.

That single thought jolted him. What the hell was he thinking? Nothing. That was the problem. He'd quit thinking when he started kissing her and been carried away by her incredible body. In a matter of weeks or a couple months he'd be gone, back to another third world shithole or a Task Force assignment somewhere else. His lifestyle didn't tolerate the entanglements of a relationship. Besides, she wouldn't want a man who had cold-bloodedly killed more people than he could count, even though they were terrorists. No, he needed to get out while he still could.

He knew Danielle sensed his disengagement, because she pulled away from his lips and lifted her hands to his shoulders. Leaning against the wall, he blinked his way back to reality, reading the confusion on her face. Now he felt like a jerk. Hell, he was a jerk, for leading her on and for leading himself on. He pulled her hands from his shoulders, running the back of one along his jaw before giving it a kiss. Then he let both hands go and looked at her. "Danielle, I'm sorry. This shouldn't have happened. I'm not conducting myself professionally at all. I hope you can accept my apology."

The two bright spots of red that appeared on her cheeks should have forewarned him. When she crossed her arms and glared at him, he felt the heat. "Of all the arrogant things to say. You're not behaving professionally? What does that make me, the local airport whore? Please. Accept my apology for being attracted to you and thinking you felt the same way." While he watched open-mouthed, she put a hand over her eyes. "Oh my God, I've never been so embarrassed."

Stung by her words, not sure what to say, he stuffed his hands in his jacket pockets. *Fuck her.* Well yeah, goddamn it, he'd like to. "Wait, you don't understand. It's just that I don't usually do this when I'm on an assignment. I didn't mean to imply anything. You're beautiful and I was, I mean *I am* attracted to you. Oh hell, forget this."

Shoving off the wall, the familiar emptiness settled around him, but it was nothing a bottle of Jack Daniel's couldn't fix when he got back to the hotel. Retrieving the holstered pistol from his jacket pocket, he lifted his shirt and stuck it back inside the waistband of his jeans. He yanked the shirt down and shrugged, doing his best to feign nonchalance. "Like I said, I'm sorry. I'll pass your security concerns along to my boss and I'm sure he'll want to talk to you as well. You've got some valid issues and good ideas." For a fleeting second he wondered what Ralph would think of this conduct.

Danielle stared at him and laid a hand on his arm. While he watched, she closed her eyes and opened them, then took a deep breath and exhaled, words coming in a rush. "Look, I'm sorry too, and I don't usually do this either. I know you're probably here on a short-term assignment, but neither of us knows what the future holds."

What she did next surprised him, but he liked it. Placing trembling hands on either side of his face, she pushed her fingers into his hair and drew his head down. Taking her time, she kissed him, lips tender at first, then more demanding until he put his arms back around her. When she finally stopped, dragging his bottom lip between her teeth, he was damn near gasping for air, all his reasons for walking away burned out of his mind. Swallowing hard, he gingerly probed the inside of his lip with his tongue.

Attempting to regain his thought processes, he realized that for a man who'd spent years perfecting the art of what he liked to call incidental sex, she created a hell of a problem. Once involved, he knew instinctively that he wouldn't be walking away after a night of fun. That revelation left him unsure of how to proceed. From the moment he'd laid eyes on her, feelings he wanted no part of had been clamoring for attention, trying to stage a comeback in his heart. That couldn't happen to him. It had been too many years and it hurt too damned much for him to ever go down that road again.

Still inside the circle of his arms, Danielle gave him a captivating smile. "When I saw you step off that plane a few nights ago, I knew you were someone special. No one has ever affected me like that before, and I don't want to lose what we haven't had the chance to have. So please, can we start over? Maybe we could go out for dinner and just talk?"

He needed to walk away, but he wasn't going to because he didn't want to. And she sure as hell seemed to know what she wanted. Closing his eyes in surrender, he crushed her close and murmured into the thick hair. "OK, let's start over. How about tonight? Just tell me where you want to go and what time. I can even pick you up." He wondered if he could talk his goofy colleague into playing driver for a night.

Wishing they could forget dinner and go to his room at the Sheraton instead, he took a deep breath, inhaled the strawberry scent of her hair and stepped back. His thoughts echoed her words – how could she affect him like this when he'd only met her a couple hours ago? Nothing like this had ever happened to him before. Well, maybe it had, many years and another lifetime ago.

Giving him a carefree smile, Danielle grabbed his hand. "Tonight works for me. We'll go to one of my old favorites, if that's all right with you. It's a restaurant called Minerva's. They have great food and cozy booths. We can talk about whatever you want. How does seven o'clock sound? Do you want me to make the reservation?"

The more she talked, the more animated she became, and the more he wanted her. Raising her hand, he grazed it with his lips and watched, smiling at her reaction. It wouldn't take much for her to lose interest in talking. "Don't worry about the reservation, Danielle. I'll take care of everything. We'll pick you up at seven."

Brow furrowed, she looked at him as they started walking back the way they'd come. "What exactly do you mean when you say *we'll* pick you up?"

Derek Norris sat on a sofa in the living room of the house he shared with Danielle. A tall glass of Bacardi and Coke in one hand, he scratched his head with the other and stared at his housemate. The black dress, shot through with silver threads clung to her body. Silver earrings sparkled through the dark red hair floating around her shoulders. Slender legs in black heels completed the image and took his breath away.

She would have an even more deleterious effect on Rowan Milani, he thought, feeling churlish. "Please tell me you're not getting involved with that guy. Hey, do you want to know what my buddy at United Operations in Denver told me? The FBI called them; the *FBI,* Dani. They said he was dangerous, and that's why the captain kicked him off the plane. Then he deliberately implied that his luggage was a problem, too."

The blissful look on her face irritated him. "Oh please, Derek. You're overreacting, just like everyone else at the airport. Rowan is with the FBI, and besides, his boss explained to all the station managers how he'd been mistaken for someone else. You know as well as I do how easy it is for misunderstandings to occur, especially for someone who's Middle Eastern."

How could he explain the alarm bells going off in his mind? Watching Rowan Milani zero in on Danielle at the airport that morning had scared him to death. That the man was a ruthless predator had been obvious to him, and he couldn't figure out why she'd be interested in someone like that. "All I'm saying is that you don't know anything about the guy. Why would you go out to dinner and spend time with him after what's happened? He's a dangerous man who caused major problems for all of us and that concerns me, a lot."

When she sat down beside him and ruffled his rusty brown hair and kissed his cheek, it took all his willpower not to kiss her back. Knowing she wouldn't understand that either, he gave up and took another swallow of his drink. Intoxicated as much by her perfume as the rum, he thought that if she knew what was good for her, she'd move to the other sofa, but instead she patted his knee and stayed unbearably close. "Derek, you're my best friend, and I know you care about what happens to me, but you have to trust me on this. I like him. Believe me, when I'm with him, I'm safe. I just know that."

Thinking she was acting deliberately naïve, he started to speak, but stopped when her one hundred-twenty pound Rottweiler stood and growled at the door. Danielle squeezed his knee and jumped eagerly to her feet. The excitement in her eyes and the color in her cheeks told him he'd been on a futile mission. "Shasta, who's here? C'mon girl, let's go see."

Planning to head upstairs so he didn't have to meet Rowan Milani, he stood up. But he was too late. Danielle opened the door, and the man stepped into the house, shivering inside an overcoat, brushing snow out of his hair and off his shoulders. Watching Rowan lean close to give Danielle a private smile and a kiss didn't do anything for his humor, and Shasta committed the final insult, leaning into the disturbing man's legs and woofing until he bent down and scratched her head. When Rowan Milani's gaze flicked over him, the hair on the back of his neck stood straight up. The man had the coldest eyes he'd ever seen.

Of course, Danielle remained oblivious. Grasping Rowan's hand, she smiled at both of them. "Rowan, this is my friend Derek Norris. He's a supervisor for Delta. Derek, this is special agent Rowan Milani."

Watching the two of them together was pure hell and enough to send him deep into the bottle of Bacardi. While he stood there feeling like an overprotective father, Rowan grabbed Danielle's long, down coat from where she'd laid it across the table and glanced at him as he helped her into it. "It's nice to meet you, Derek. Well, we better get going."

Trying to cover his increasing antipathy, he gave the man a grudging smile. "Yeah, it's nice to meet you, too. Have a good time. See you later, Dani. I'll get the door." Pausing on the threshold, he watched Rowan put his arm around Danielle and walk close beside her down the snowy sidewalk to a waiting Lincoln Town Car. Shaking his head, wallowing in private misery, he saw a tall man open the back door of the car for the two of them. Frustrated because he knew he could never compete with Rowan Milani, and irritated at his inability to tell Danielle how he felt about her, he slammed the heavy door and leaned against it. Shasta moved close and sat on his foot, gazing up at him with a tongue lolling, doggy smile that pissed him off. "You're as smitten with that guy as she is, you worthless mutt. What kind of protector are you, if you can't tell a creep when you see one?"

Grunting with the effort, Seth finished screwing the heavy-duty eye bolt into the stud he'd painstakingly located in the wall. Teetering on the slippery seat of a metal folding chair, he gave the meat hook attached to the eye bolt a perfunctory yank and stepped down. Wiping his forehead, he glanced at Lucien. "Think that eye bolt will support his weight?"

A sneer twisted the lips of his muscular cohort. "It'll work just fine." Mashing wide hands together, Lucien looked at him. "I can't wait to get a hold of this raghead poser and teach him a lesson."

He nodded. "That makes two of us. That guy is the worst of the worst, born and raised here, benefiting from all this country has to offer and then selling it and all of us down the river. But this time, he's not going to slip through our fingers like he managed to do in Denver. I'm going to make sure of that. When we get back to the Sheraton, we'll set up a surveillance schedule, so we can track his movements. I want him bad, Lucien. Not just for the money, either."

After fighting along with Lucien as a young Marine in the first Gulf War, becoming CIA field agents enabled him and his friend to play an ongoing role in defending their country. Apprehending a clever traitor like Rowan Milani would be a feather in both their caps. Their other employer, the mysterious Egyptian Muusa Shemal had offered $250,000.00 apiece for their assistance in bringing an end to Rowan Milani's deception. Instead of handing him to the FBI for federal prosecution, they planned to transport the miscreant directly to Tora Prison in Egypt.

But first, he and Lucien intended to separate their prey from his colleagues and conduct their own private interview. The small warehouse they'd rented on the north end of Sioux Falls had a back office with no windows, deep inside the old building. No one would see or hear them. By the time he and Lucien finished with Rowan Milani, the man would understand that betraying the United States of America would not go unpunished.

CHAPTER FOUR

Head throbbing, Danielle tried to focus on making coffee. Squeezing her eyes shut and then blinking, she hit the switch on the coffee maker. The clock on the wall in her kitchen said three-thirty in the morning. Her employees would be expecting her in exactly ninety minutes, and it was going to take some serious coffee drinking to make that happen. Why had she kept saying yes to the wine? Because she'd never been with a man so solicitous to her every need.

After spending the evening, well, most of the night with Rowan, she had fallen hard for him. None of the men she'd dated over the years had ever treated her the way he did. From the moment he put his arm around her when they left for the restaurant until they came back at midnight and snuggled up together on the cozy love seat in her living room, he'd been focused on what she wanted.

At the restaurant, he'd flashed a thousand-watt smile at the maitre d' and acted like they were old friends. A mixed bouquet of red roses, white carnations and stargazer lilies waited at their table. The wine was the best she'd ever tasted, a 2007 Italian red, Bolgheri Sassicaia, that he'd picked it out at The Market, down the street from Minerva's, just for her. How had he known she'd like it? Their server had been tongue-tied when he pulled five one hundred-dollar bills from his wallet and handed them to her, because he'd reserved the booth for the entire evening.

She could barely recollect the meal. They'd talked about security and decided to work together. Beyond that, she only remembered staring at his lips, thinking how much she wanted them pressing against hers. How much she wanted to explore the athletic body beneath the black Armani suit, white shirt and silver striped silk tie. And the way he looked at her; the overt, untamed desire in his eyes should have given her pause, but instead anticipation left her breathless. When he smiled at her, she melted.

The aroma of French roast drew her back. She poured a cup and pulled out a chair at the kitchen table. Her thoughts continued to meander, and she closed her eyes, remembering how she'd finally had a chance to check out the hard body beneath his clothes. She giggled, thinking about how much fun she'd had loosening his tie and unbuttoning his shirt while he tried to concentrate on her dress. Good Lord, how could she handle working with him in her office all day?

Brisk footsteps on the stairs woke Shasta, who'd been snoozing next to the patio door. The big dog growled and then woofed when Derek, dressed in his Delta ramp uniform, strode into the kitchen. "Morning, Derek. Hey, can I catch a ride to the airport with you when you leave?" Watching while he grabbed a cup of coffee, she couldn't miss his frown of disapproval. Oh geez, what was that about?

Derek plopped down across from her at the table and sipped his coffee. "Sure I can give you a ride, no problem. Is something wrong with your Explorer?"

Taking a hefty swallow of coffee, she looked at him, wondering if he could smell the wine. Twirling strands of hair between her fingers, she smiled artlessly. "No special reason I guess. Well, I did have more wine than I should have last night."

Derek frowned again. "Have you even been to bed yet?" His voice turned bitter. "Or maybe I should be asking, did you get any sleep?"

The heat crawled up her face. He was way out of bounds. Why was he being such a pig? "You know, Derek, I don't think you've ever asked me anything like that before. Really, it's none of your business whether I've been to bed yet or whether I've slept. And you know what else? You can forget about the ride. I'll take a cab."

Her irritation seemed to cut through his angst. "Whoa, wait a minute, Dani. You're right and I'm sorry. It's just, I don't know. Rowan Milani seems to bring out the worst in me. I think it's because I get so worried about you. But don't call a cab. I'll give you a ride whenever you're ready."

Rowan stared at Ralph. "What?" He couldn't seem to please his boss. Ralph should be applauding his efforts, not doubting his motives. At least he'd made it to the seven o'clock meeting.

"Rowan, you're telling me you went out to dinner with the Legacy station manager, that classy red head I met? And now you're going to work together? God almighty son, that's great. I think." His boss shot a suspicious glance at Chad. "Special agent Cantor, were you at this dinner party?"

Chad looked up with bleary eyes and smiled at Ralph. "Yes boss, I drove to the restaurant and hung around for a drink, and then I left so Rowan and Danielle, I mean Ms. Stratton, could talk privately. You know my efforts are best utilized on hacking. Once Rowan gathers some names, I'll be in business. Digging into travel records via the airline is a brilliant idea. Oh, and of course, I drove them home. Uh, I mean we dropped Ms. Stratton off at her house."

Rowan gave Chad furtive thumbs up around the corner of the table and sneaked a glance at Ralph, who chewed on a slice of toast while he listened, a skeptical look on his face. Did their boss know about Mandy, for God's sake? Not that it mattered. The Denver incident had hyped Ralph's instincts about every feasible or infeasible ramification of his behavior, and there wasn't a damned thing he could do about it. In short, his boss cared way too much about his special agents and about him in particular. "Ralph – boss, don't worry about it. We had a nice dinner, and Ms. Stratton offered to open up the airline's passenger records."

Pausing to yawn, he stared at his hands and thought about the three hours he and Danielle had spent in her living room after dinner. That had been fun. At the end, he'd stood and kissed her and then twisted away laughing, trying to button his shirt while batting away her persistent fingers. Slipping his tie around his neck, he'd given up and left the shirt half buttoned and the tail hanging out when he'd said good-bye on her doorstep at three o'clock.

Throwing on his overcoat and skidding down the icy sidewalk to the waiting Lincoln, he'd chuckled at Chad's only comment when he slid into the warmth of the front seat. *Man, you didn't waste any time with her, did you?* It was none of Chad's business, so he didn't bother to tell his colleague that when he and Danielle made love for the first time, it wasn't going to be on a sofa in the same house where her jerkwad friend was sleeping. It dawned on him that he'd left his suit jacket on the coffee table between the two sofas in her living room. *Damn it.* If her badass dog didn't trash it, Derek sure as hell would.

Lost in the private thoughts, unsure whether Ralph had said something else, he looked up. "I'm heading to the airport as soon as we're done. Ms. Stratton told me she would compile a list of Middle Eastern travelers in and out of Sioux Falls. What I'm going to look for is a pattern of movement around the country. I'd also like to work on a plan for infiltrating the mosque in town. It's entirely possible that whoever is traveling in and out of Sioux Falls is networking with a radical element in the mosque, but I won't know for sure until I'm in there."

He sat back and watched as Ralph guzzled coffee and patted his mouth with a crumpled napkin. Chad covered a yawn behind his hand. In the kitchen someone dropped glassware. The tinkling crash turned heads across the busy dining room. Tucked into a far corner of the dining area, the cacophony of voices and clanking silverware sheltered their conversation. In spite of that, Ralph leaned forward and lowered his voice. "All right Rowan, what's your timetable for this project?"

First scratching his fingers through the burgeoning whiskers on his jaw and then tugging on his hair, he gazed at Ralph. "It's going to be a couple weeks or so before I'll look the part. In the meantime, I can put together a lot of information from the airline records. Chad can help me with that as I collect names." Pointedly ignoring the concern in Ralph's eyes, he shrugged. "You know how it works, boss. I like to get in and out, but it takes as long as it takes."

Marta Pinella couldn't take her eyes off the man sitting in her manager's office, poring over the passenger itineraries she'd printed at Danielle's request. This was the kind of man she dreamed about doing kinky things with – the kind of things that got the juices flowing down low inside and made her all hot and horny. Drawing glossy, ebony hair through her fingers and letting it cascade down her back, she thrust her boobs forward in her black and white gate agent uniform and slipped around the desk.

Leaning against it, planting her body directly in front of his chair, she ran her tongue around her lips when he glanced up. "Hi, I'm Marta. If you tell me what you're looking for, I can help you. I've been an agent here with Legacy for over five years. Are you looking for a certain passenger?"

Impatience flickered in his face, and the sexy man leaned back in the chair, perusing her body with his eyes before speaking. "Hello, Marta. It's nice to meet you. I'm special agent Milani, with the FBI. If I need any help, I'll be sure to ask. Thanks for the offer."

When he bent his head back to the papers in his lap, obviously not interested, she could only stare in rage. What an arrogant man. Fingers clenching the edge of the desk, she blinked green eyes and took a deep breath. Maybe he'd respond to a more direct approach. "It's nice to meet you too, special agent Milani. Do you have a first name?"

This time the dark head jerked up and he looked at her with an insolent smile curling his lips. "Special agent Milani works just fine. Now, if you don't mind, I've got quite a bit of information to digest."

Furious, wishing she could slap the sneer off his face, she leaned forward and lightly touched his shoulder, eyes widening when he looked at her again. Oh yes, he had a temper and that was the biggest turn-on ever. "You know, if you're looking for information on Middle Eastern people traveling to Sioux Falls, I can help you. I'm familiar with most of our frequent travelers." Giving him a lascivious smile, she continued. "A special friend of mine comes every few months to teach at the mosque. His name is Muusa Shemal. I could introduce you the next time he flies in, if you're still around."

This time she saw a glimmer of interest in the seductive eyes. When he stood up in front of her, ditching the papers he'd been examining into the chair behind him, she turned so he could see her profile. Did he finally get it? Would he kiss her now? When she looked at him again, the contempt she saw on his face surprised her. Reaching out to touch his arm, she gasped when he grabbed her wrist. Wow. He was quick. His hold was tight and his eyes were cold. "Like I said, thanks for the offer, Marta, but I'm not interested."

How had she misjudged him so completely? Almost all of the hot men she ran across liked her, wanted her and had no qualms about a night in the sack. But she appeared to have no effect on this one. He'd better rethink, because she didn't like rejection. The last man who'd ignored her advances, a fellow Legacy gate agent in Chicago, had learned the hard way. His career lay in ruins after she was finished. This man had no idea how creative she was – or how vindictive. When he let go of her wrist, she massaged it and stared at him, hoping he couldn't see the malice she felt. "That's OK, special agent Milani. But if you want some help later on, let me know."

Danielle stepped into the office and Marta knew instantly why he'd blown her off. His whole attitude changed, and she watched with envy at the way he looked at her bitch manager. Danielle gave her a warm smile. "Hey, Marta. I was wondering where you'd gone. The inbound Chicago flight is running late, so I'd like you to take over at gate seven, because nobody rebooks passengers better or faster than you do."

Faking a friendly smile for both her manager and the stupid special agent who would never know what he'd missed, she turned to leave the office. "No problem, Danielle. I'll head up there right away." Her eyes slid from one to the other, and she thought about how much fun it would be to fuck up their lives. Maybe she would spend some time figuring out how to do just that. And wouldn't her sometime lover, Muusa Shemal, like to know that a special agent from the FBI was messing around in Sioux Falls, digging through the travel records of Middle Eastern passengers? Yes, as a matter of fact, she knew he would.

Seth slammed his phone shut and turned to Lucien with a sly smile. "That was Shemal. He's getting antsy for us to nab Milani. I told him he's always with either his boss or that tall kid or else out at the airport. You want to hear his orders? He's ready for us to snatch him from his hotel room in a damn raid. He said we should bring in a couple more agents and take out his friends if necessary, and that he'd fix it with the higher ups."

They were sitting in their hotel room, taking turns with the binoculars, waiting for their quarry to return. Slouched in a chair, feet up on the end of the bed, Lucien looked at him and grinned. "I'm all for it. For crying out loud, the guy doesn't have a routine as far as I can tell. It seems like he's in and out at all hours. At least we have his room number, and we know he dinks around with that Mexican maid and her husband. Hey, maybe we can grab him after a pool playing session."

He nodded at Lucien as an idea crystallized in the back of his mind. "You know, I think you've hit on something." Rubbing thick hands together, he chuckled. "Yep, I think we've got him now. But, it wouldn't hurt to bring Jackson and Campbell in for this. Especially since the son of a bitch is so good at falling through the cracks. Here's what I have in mind."

CHAPTER FIVE

Three Weeks Later – First Week In March
Leaning back in the uncomfortable chair, Rowan squinted at the computer screen on the desk and stretched, then smiled and turned his head as Danielle leaned over him from behind, sliding her hands from his shoulders down the front of his shirt. If he didn't stop her, she'd start on the buttons. She was already kissing the side of his face, and he turned further to find her lips, reveling in their gentle, insistent touch.

It was almost six o'clock in the evening. They'd been in her office with the door locked since noon, sneaking in and out for bathroom breaks and to grab hamburgers from the airport restaurant. Locking the door was the only way to keep assorted employees and friends from barging in with a burning question or to ask what in the world they were up to.

For the past three weeks he'd been digging through itineraries of Middle Eastern travelers going from Sioux Falls to damn near everyplace on the planet and back again. No patterns had emerged until he examined Muusa Shemal's records. If not for that horny slut Marta, it would have taken much longer to find that particular man. Grabbing Danielle's hands, he stopped the progress that along with her lips already had his heart rate ticking up and his palms sweating. Damn she was nimble with the buttons. "Danielle, let's fly to Chicago for the weekend. The Four Seasons is a great hotel, and I know a few Italian restaurants you'd like." If she said yes, he hoped she wouldn't mind room service instead.

Resting her chin on his shoulder, she nipped the side of his neck and thrust her tongue in his ear. Twisting away from her eager mouth, he almost fell off the chair. Struggling to regain his balance, he swore, which made her laugh. *"Ouch. Damn it.* That hurts and it tickles."

Still laughing, she pulled her hands out of his and squeezed his shoulders. Half scared of what she might think of next, he flinched when she dug her fingers into his hair. "That's a fantastic idea. I'd love to fly to Chicago for the weekend. Let me check the flights and I'll get you a buddy pass."

Her hands were a constant distraction. Now her fingers scraped through the prolific whiskers he hated. If he didn't stand up, the whole process would start over again and drive him right over the edge of reason. Ducking out of her reach before she could delve into the hair on his chest, he stood up and turned to face her, buttoning his shirt while she grinned at him. Dressed in the same black sweater and pants she'd worn the first time he saw her, she had shoved up the sleeves like she was ready to dive into something, most likely him.

No matter what she wore, he had a hell of a time concentrating on the job when he was with her. But that was as much her fault as it was his. "Will Legacy sell me a ticket? I know better than to try at United, but if I can buy tickets for both of us, you won't need to worry about the flights."

Danielle raised her hand and lowered it. "Gosh, I haven't flown on a purchased ticket in years, but sure Legacy will sell you a ticket. Heck, I'll sell you a ticket."

Already thinking about what they could finally do in complete privacy in a suite at the Four Seasons, far away from the assignment in Sioux Falls, he chuckled at the interest on her face. "OK, great. Sell me two first class round trip tickets to Chicago for you and me this weekend. I need to head back to the Sheraton to set up a meeting with Ralph and Chad for tomorrow morning."

Disturbed by Muusa Shemal and the pattern of his travels around the country, he'd finalized a plan that included Chad, so he needed Ralph's blessing. Digging his wallet from the back pocket of his pants, he pulled out the platinum American Express card and held it out for her.

Smile turning to a frown, Danielle stared at the credit card and then at him. "Do you have any idea how much two first class tickets cost, especially on only a couple days advance purchase? I can't let you do that for me. Plus, the Four Seasons has to be outrageously expensive."

What could he say? That he had more than enough blood money lying around in his two offshore accounts? Shrugging, he tried for a nonchalant demeanor. "No worries. I've made some extra money over the years and invested it well. It's been a long time. Besides, you and I need some time alone, with no distractions. For a couple days we can forget about my colleagues, your friendly housemate and these damned airline records."

The uncertainty lingered in her eyes, but she took the credit card from his hand. "Are you sure? You spend way too much money on me, and sometimes I feel bad."

If only she knew how alive he felt when he was with her. "You don't have to feel bad. Let's just go away and have a nice weekend. C'mon, it'll be fun."

The emotions playing out on her face were an accurate harbinger of her moods and always entertaining. Now her look was shy, which surprised him. She gave him a tentative smile. "Oh, all right. I'll do the tickets now, so you can get going."

Wanting to see the return of the fierce independence he liked so much, he decided to tweak her. "That's my girl. You do your ticket thing and I'll take care of everything else."

Mouth wide open, hands on hips, challenge replaced the shyness. He snickered while he watched her. "You know, Rowan, I've traveled all over the world, and I don't need you to take care of me. I've probably been to Chicago a hundred times in the last thirteen years. And I am not a girl."

That she was not a girl hadn't escaped his notice. And he would never have been interested in a meek woman who wanted to be taken care of or dominated. Nope, she was damn near perfect, as far as he was concerned. Raising his hands in a backing off gesture, he gave her a conciliatory smile. "Hey, I hear you, loud and clear. You can lead me all over Chicago, and I won't complain."

Her eyes narrowed and her lips formed a thin line. Batting his credit card back and forth against her fingers, she stared at him. "You said that stuff to me on purpose, didn't you? Oh my God, you are such a jerk sometimes."

When she stepped in front of him, he put his arms around her and pulled her close before she could smack him. Murmuring into her hair, glad she couldn't see the smirk on his face, he gave her a quick squeeze. "Aw hell, I'm sorry. Sometimes I forget that you're as independent as I am."

Still clutching his credit card, she pushed on his chest with her hands. She was close enough for him to see into the depths of her eyes. He loved the intense, deep blue color and the fringe of black around the edges. Thankfully, they held no anger, just humor. "Rowan, you're so full of crap. But I still like you. I can't seem to help myself."

The length of her body pressed against his was too much. Fighting the inevitable arousal, he swallowed and took a deep breath, letting it out slowly. Wishing they were anywhere else, he planted a quick kiss on her lips. "Yeah, I like you too. At least we can agree on something. But I need to get going, so let's take care of this ticket purchase, OK?"

Following her out of the office and through the cluttered back room, he didn't miss the speculative glances and sly smiles on the faces of the agents lounging around the room. Slipping into his leather jacket, he ignored them and stepped through the door leading to the ticket counter where Danielle was already busy at a computer. He noted with irritation that Derek stood at his usual spot with Marta beside him, the two of them deep in conversation, slinging snide glances at him and Danielle. Sioux Falls felt claustrophobic. Chad harassed him for details about Danielle all the time, and Ralph was on him constantly, finding fault with every move he did or didn't make. Rubbing weary eyes, he wondered what his boss would say about him leaving for the weekend. Not that it mattered, because he was going.

The Next Morning
Ralph couldn't believe what he was hearing. But he could damn well see the stubborn set of Rowan's jaw and the mutinous look in the black eyes. It was blatantly obvious that no matter what he said, Rowan was flying to Chicago for the weekend. Lifting a shoulder and letting it fall, he shifted in the chair next to the desk in his hotel room. Gazing at his subordinate, he smiled benignly. "Sounds like a great idea. When were you planning on coming back? Sunday or Monday?"

Rowan leaned against the wall next to the window and frowned at him. "We're flying out tomorrow, Friday, mid-morning and coming back Sunday afternoon. Don't worry. I'll be here for the meeting you'll want to have Monday morning. And of course, I'll have my phone with me."

What was going on with his special agent? He'd give his left nut to know, because in all the years Rowan had worked with and for him, he had never gotten involved with a woman on an assignment. So much for the platitudes he'd heard for the past three weeks about working together. Absently fingering the cup of coffee that had gone cold, he fixed the younger man with a hard stare. "You don't have the best track record flying commercially. As a matter of fact, you've got a nasty habit of pissing people off with your charming personality. Don't get yourself kicked off a plane at O'Hare. Leave your weapon here and be careful. You got all of that, special agent Milani?"

The look on Rowan's face made him chuckle. Evidently his subordinate didn't always say what he was thinking. "Yeah boss, I got that."

Glancing at his watch, he slapped his knees with his hands. "All right, I'm glad we cleared that up. Your cheery colleague should be here any minute. I'm anxious to hear what you've come up with as far as a plan regarding this Egyptian national and the airline agent you've been telling me about. Oh, and Rowan, let's you and me meet for dinner Sunday evening, after you're back. By then you should be able to give me some sort of explanation of what you're getting into with Ms. Stratton." Waving an index finger at the immediate hostility in his subordinate's glare, he continued. "What I need and what I expect are the facts germane to our assignment."

It pleased him to see his recalcitrant special agent forced to acquiesce. Rowan gave him a stony look. "Fine, let's meet at seven o'clock in the hotel restaurant."

A brisk knock signaled the arrival of the other half of his team, and he let Rowan step away from the wall and open the door. Chad swept into the room jingling a set of car keys, oblivious to the lingering undercurrent of tension. "Looks like I'll be retiring the Lincoln for a while. Wait until you two see my new wheels."

Some days Ralph felt like he had no control whatsoever over the two men who called him boss. According to their track record, they were two of the most accomplished special agents in the field. Yet he'd been forced to handle the insurrection of one, with finesse he thought, and now the other one showed up with a new car before eight o'clock in the morning. Maybe it was his age.

Managing Rowan's dark persona required an iron will, or he'd be flattened, like road kill. Chad had a sunny personality and was usually an easy agent to oversee. He shook his head and sighed. God forbid they deal with a serious terror threat. Feigning interest, he smiled at Chad. "What's this all about, special agent Cantor? How'd you find the time for a new car?"

Chad grinned like a twelve-year-old. "My high school friend Chris Kelly has a car dealership, Premier Motorcars. He built it from nothing and mostly deals in exotics – Lamborghinis and Ferraris. Once in a while he gets something else in on trade and I've been after him to sell me a car. He called me yesterday about a red 2010 Shelby GT500 Mustang convertible with hardly any miles and in mint condition. And now the baby is mine."

Ralph stared. "That's great. Just great. You can drive us to lunch. For now, pull up a chair or park yourself on the bed, because Rowan has some ideas we need to bat around." Feeling as though his patience and good grace had been tried to the limit, he gestured at Rowan. "All right, let's hear what you've got on your mind."

Three hours later, Ralph sat back, pleased with their progress. Rowan had laid out the travel records of Muusa Shemal, the Egyptian national who resided in the UK and according to Chad's research was also a surgeon. The man traveled with regularity to the United States, spending three to four weeks on each trip, crisscrossing the country, hitting numerous cities. Shemal did not appear on any watch lists and had been traveling back and forth between London and the US for a number of years.

That he supposedly taught at the various mosques had raised an instant red flag in Rowan's mind. According to his special agent, Shemal fit the profile of someone operating under the radar, with the ability to foment the poison of jihad and recruit homegrown terrorists. The thought that the man may have been engaged in that process for years left him with a hard, cold knot in the pit of his stomach.

Looking at both Rowan and Chad, he could tell their appetites had been whetted. Finally they had something more than amorphous theories to work with. Considering Chad, sitting cross-legged on the bed, deep into his laptop, he was grateful for the young man's hacking abilities. If a system needed penetrating, Chad always found a way. That he was tall, blond and what the women called cute was an asset as well.

Chad's assignment now included making nice as he liked to say, with Marta, the resident airline hussy. He'd love to be a mouse in the corner for that. Once Chad cajoled the woman, he'd hack her computer and send all her correspondence to his own email in-box. They could only guess at what her emails might reveal about Muusa Shemal. It had been fortuitous that the salacious woman had come on to Rowan and blabbed about her supposed friend.

Rowan had outlined a web of personal subterfuge that left him less enthused, although he knew his cold-hearted subordinate thrived on it and had the President's go ahead. It was Rowan's intent to infiltrate the local mosque as an unhappy, first generation son of an Iranian immigrant who had joined the FBI but rediscovered Islam and now saw his pathway leading to jihad. As Rowan explained it, they couldn't pretend he wasn't part of the FBI. Averse as he was to deliberately positioning his special agent in harm's way, he too, couldn't deny the rising anticipation of outsmarting a clever enemy at its own game, devising a plan as close to flawless as possible, and launching it fearlessly. It was, after all, what they did best.

Friday Afternoon
Standing at the window of their Executive Suite on the fortieth floor of the Four Seasons, Danielle gazed at the dizzying view of the Chicago skyline below and felt like pinching herself. Had she and Rowan really escaped the entanglements in Sioux Falls that had kept them apart? From the moment she settled into the first class seat to Chicago, sweet, agonizing anticipation gripped her. She could barely imagine two days and nights alone with the man who stood behind her now, his warm breath, teasing mouth and prickling whiskers on her neck doing crazy things to her body.

The shivery sigh slid from her lips unbidden and she heard Rowan's quiet chuckle. When he lifted his head and gently turned her to face him, she couldn't stop trembling. His smile was tender and so were the fingers that brushed her cheek. "What's the matter, Danielle?"

What would he say if she told him that he was her problem? That she had rashly, intentionally fallen head over heels in love with him? She'd known him for not quite a month, yet it felt like forever. Not trusting herself to speak coherently, she gazed into his dark eyes. Concern overlaid the intense desire she'd come to expect. Trusting him instinctively, she decided to be honest. "Remember what I told you when we first met? When I saw you walk off that jet I knew you were someone special. That hasn't changed. All I want is you."

Rowan placed his hands on either side of her face and kissed her. The voracity of his lips and the dampness of his palms made her smile and he drew back. "What is it now?"

Pulling him close, giddy at the feeling of his warm, hard body in her arms, she murmured into the crook of his neck. "Nothing. What did you want to do this afternoon?"

He stepped back, holding her at arm's length, his look playful. "You're asking me what I want to do?"

Snickering, she nodded. "Uh huh, because I know what I want to do, but I don't want to be selfish."

When he grabbed her hand she followed him, padding barefoot across the deep carpet as he led her through the opulent sitting room and into the bedroom. Making a sweeping gesture at the king-size bed, he flashed the sexy smile that always left her weak-kneed. "This is what I want to do this afternoon and tonight and tomorrow and well, you get it. I hope you don't have any other plans, because once we land in this bed, I don't think we'll be leaving."

The look in his eyes sent a zing of desire through her body and she shivered again. Before she could say anything, he worked his hands under the bottom of her sweater. "May I?"

Dry-mouthed, she could only nod. Rowan tugged the sweater over her head, and she helped him pull it off. Once he'd smoothed the static electricity from her hair, he fiddled with the front fastening on her bra and gently freed her breasts. Goose bumps covered her body, but she couldn't help a smile when he tilted his head and stared. "Wow."

When his agile fingers unbuttoned her linen dress pants and dropped them to the carpet, she sucked in a breath. He paused. "You OK with this?"

Chuckling at her quick nod, he slid warm hands beneath her panties and they followed the dress pants to the floor. Gripping her fingers in his so she could step out of the pile of clothes, he pulled down the covers with his other hand. Sliding between the cool sheets and pulling them to her chin, she tried to keep her teeth from chattering.

Watching his boyish enthusiasm made her giggle. Rowan yanked the crew neck sweater over his head, kicked off his shoes and unzipped his dress pants, letting them drop to the floor. Clad only in boxers, he dragged back the covers on the other side and bounced into the bed next to her. "OK, since I took your pants off, turnabout is fair play."

Thrilling at his wild grin, she wished her fingers weren't so cold. His body felt hot next to hers, and she shivered again. When she couldn't maneuver under the waist band of the boxers, he folded her chilled fingers inside his. "How about we get you warmed up? C'mon, let me help."

Snuggling close, he wrapped an arm and leg around her. Starting at her forehead and working his way down, he covered her face with soft kisses, interspersed by the brush of rough beard. When he nuzzled her neck and dipped lower, teasing with his tongue and teeth, she felt the heat enveloping her body, starting at the center and radiating out. Back arching, she gasped at the sensations. Every touch turned to liquid fire and pulsed through her, clear to the bottoms of her feet.

Bolder now, she tugged on the boxers as he wiggled around, helping her pull them down. She couldn't get enough of his body, from the spicy scent he wore, to the taut shoulder muscles, the hard abs that rippled beneath her fingers and the sinewy, hairy legs that kept hers captive. Dragging her fingers through his hair, she pulled his head up. Kissing him was something she couldn't live another minute without. Black hair a mess, he smiled down at her. "This is fun, Danielle. And you're beautiful. You're perfect. I..." Pain shimmered through his eyes and he bent his head to her lips. For an instant she wondered if he'd almost said *I love you*. But why would that elicit the depth of hurt she'd seen for a single, quick second?

Then his tongue touched hers and she gave herself to the mutual exploration. Moaning with the sheer pleasure of intimate contact, she wanted, needed all of him. Head thrown back, breath coming in quick gasps, she could only whisper. "Oh please Rowan, let's do this. I can't wait any longer."

Sunday Afternoon

His room at the Sheraton felt especially cold. Rowan smiled at Danielle, hit the thermostat and rubbed his hands together. "Sorry it's so chilly in here. Guess the maid turned down the heat. But it won't take long to warm up."

He watched while she grabbed pillows and shoved them against the headboard before kicking off her shoes and arranging herself cross-legged on the bed. The grin she gave him was teasing. "It's OK. I'm used to the cold. Not like some people I know who don't believe in wearing socks. Thanks for bringing me here. I don't think I could face Derek's grouchy attitude. Geez, he's been such a bear, and I don't know why."

Unable to help a snort of disbelief, he sat down next to her and loosened his tie. "Much as I don't want to waste time talking about your housemate, you gotta be kidding me, right? The reason Derek is in a perpetual bad mood is because he's deep in love with you and you're with me. He hates my guts, has since the first moment he laid eyes on me. Tell me you don't know that."

Danielle twirled hair between her fingers and stared at him. "You think Derek is in love with me? Nah, he's had darn near four years to say something, and he's never intimated that he cared about me that way. The reason he doesn't like you is because an old buddy of his works for United Operations in Denver, and he told Derek the FBI called and said you were dangerous. He gets worried about me and thinks I'm not safe with you."

Hell, the airline grapevine was nothing if not efficient. Unbuttoning the top two buttons of his white dress shirt and pulling off his tie, he gave her a wry smile. "Think what you want, but I know Derek has the hots for you, big-time. How about some wine? I could use a shot of Jack Daniel's. Talking about that jerk makes me want to drink."

Danielle giggled and reached out to pat his whiskered cheek. "You poor baby. I'd love some wine. Don't worry about Derek. He'll come around, you'll see."

Thinking he didn't give a rat's ass whether Derek ever came around or not, he grabbed her hand and kissed it. "Screw Derek. Did you have fun in Chicago? Want to go again sometime?"

The look that crossed her face made him smile. "I've never had such a wonderful time. I'd love to go again, but it had to be incredibly expensive."

He dropped her hand and stood up. Spending a miniscule amount of his hard earned money didn't bother him at all. "Let me get your wine." Shrugging out of his suit jacket and draping it over the desk chair, he dug in the dresser drawer and pulled out the corkscrew and bottle of Bolgheri Sassicaia he'd purchased with this afternoon in mind.

Seeing a curious look on Danielle's face while she watched him uncork the bottle, he raised a brow. She tilted her head and smiled. "I love that wine. Did you plan all along for us to come back here together after the weekend? You're almost diabolical sometimes, you know?"

Frowning, he handed her the glass of wine. "You make me sound evil. I'm always thinking ahead." The cold reality was that he hated being without her. The emptiness he lived with hovered around the edges of his consciousness, and he couldn't bear that after the weekend.

Danielle sipped and closed her eyes. "Mm, that's delicious. Thanks. You know, I'm not sure I can handle it when you have to leave."

Sloshing whiskey into a glass, he spilled on the desk. "Damn it." Giving her a sideways glance he wondered, had she fallen as hard for him as he had for her? Tossing back the shot, he inhaled the pungent fumes, coughed and poured again, this time filling the glass halfway. After unbuttoning his shirt cuffs, he pulled the holstered Glock from inside the waistband of his suit pants and laid it on the bedside table. Grabbing a pillow, he slung it against the headboard and slid down beside her. "I'm not going anywhere. I mean, not for a while, anyway."

Seeing the glimmer of hurt in her eyes, he stroked the side of her face. "I'm sorry. I shouldn't have put it like that. Besides, wasn't it you who told me that neither of us knows what the future holds?"

Now he thought she looked sad. She took another sip of wine and gave him a knowing smile. "I did say that, didn't I? And I meant it, but I also know you're committed to your career. I've learned that much about you. In the end, you'll go." Her voice softened to a whisper. "It's just that I'll miss you so much."

Gathering his thoughts seemed hopeless. He couldn't think past the next hour, let alone days and weeks. Nothing made as much sense as being with her. After a hefty swallow of whiskey, he sat the glass on the bedside table, took her glass and sat it next to his, then sidled close and put his arms around her. "I don't have any answers as far as the future goes Danielle, except that I can't imagine being anywhere without you. We just have to take it one day at a time."

Her arm went around him like a vise and she buried her face in his shirt front. They sat in silence for a while. He smoothed a hand over her hair. Keeping one arm securely around her, he reached for his drink with the other and downed the rest, enjoying the accompanying warmth and heaviness in his arms and legs. Placing the glass on the bedside table, he put his arm back around her and yawned.

Danielle raised her head and gazed into his eyes. "I can't imagine not having you in my life either. Please promise me one thing."

He returned her gaze, hating the reticence he felt. The trust he saw scared him. "OK." Now he'd blown it. Clearly she sensed his reservation.

She pushed her way out of his arms and turned so she was facing him. "You know, I get it that you can't tell me much about what you're really doing here. We've been through a lot of records of Middle Eastern passengers, and obviously the focus has become Mr. Shemal."

Danielle paused and he opened his mouth to speak, but she put a finger on his lips. "Let me finish. You've been growing a beard you don't like and your hair gets longer by the day. You look like," she chuckled, "well I'm quite sure you know what you look like. Other people notice too, I saw that in O'Hare. Doesn't that get to you sometimes? It seems so unfair for you to be judged totally by your appearance. That's why you wore a suit on the flight home, isn't it?"

Now he wished he'd held off on the whiskey, so he could keep up with her. So far she'd nailed everything. Hating to think what she might say next, he tried to intervene. "I, well, you're right, I guess." Feeling like an idiot, he simply stared at her.

Clasping her hands in her lap, Danielle continued. "You don't have to say anything. I'm not going to ask you to betray a loyalty that obviously goes way beyond your job. Just promise me that when you have to leave, you'll tell me good-bye before you go."

Her words touched him and made him feel guilty about the secrets he could never share with her. Scratching the beard and then stopping, he knew it was his turn to talk. "All right, I promise to tell you good-bye if I need to leave."

She looked so forlorn, he cringed. "Not if, Rowan. *When.* I'm not that dense." Tossing her hair behind her shoulders, she gave him a tremulous smile. "I can't talk about this anymore. And you were right, we need to take one day at a time." She paused to yawn. "How about a nap?"

Relieved that the conversation appeared to be over, he nodded. "Yep, a nap sounds great."

Ralph swirled the ice in his Glenlivet and looked at his watch. Rowan was fifteen minutes late for their seven o'clock dinner meeting. Surveying the restaurant, he craned his neck to see down the hallway toward the Executive Wing. Thinking how he'd rag on his subordinate for keeping him waiting, he sipped the scotch and then smacked the crystal tumbler down on the white table cloth. Damn it, what was Rowan's problem? His attitude and behavior on this assignment were not up to par. Something was going on, presumably involving the red-headed Ms. Stratton, and he didn't like not knowing. Normally cold and calculating, all business and never late, Rowan had been behaving out of character practically since the get go.

When his subordinate's phone went directly to voice mail, he downed the last of the scotch and stood up. It was time to find

Rowan and have a chat. One way or another, he would get to the bottom of whatever was eating his special agent. Then Rowan had better fix it, or he wouldn't be infiltrating a mosque, where he'd need to be focused, with all his faculties at one hundred percent. While he strolled to the elevators in the Executive Wing, he called Chad. But his blithe operative hadn't seen or talked to his colleague since Thursday evening.

Stepping into the elevator, he hit the button for the fourth floor. Plucking the key card for Rowan's room out of his billfold while the elevator whisked him upward, he thought about how the two of them had decided to share key cards, in case they encountered an unforeseen problem. This situation qualified, he thought sourly.

A few minutes later he stood outside Rowan's room and knocked. When his special agent didn't respond, he pulled the Glock from its holster and slid the key card. The tiny light blinked green, but the deadbolt prevented the door from opening. Well damn it, Rowan had to be in there. Why didn't he answer the door? Knocking again, harder, he waited. "Rowan, its Ralph. Are you there?"

The deadbolt turned and the door opened. Rowan stood looking at him, barefoot with tousled hair and a rumpled white dress shirt hanging out over suit pants. "What do you want, boss?" His subordinate's eyes drifted down to the Glock, then back up. "What the hell's going on?"

Annoyed that Rowan had forgotten their dinner meeting, he waved an arm. "Let me in and I'll explain."

Irritation changed to anger when Rowan smirked at him and said, "OK boss, come on in." He shouldered past and stepped into the room. When he saw Danielle, fully clothed and sitting up sleepily in bed, eyes widening at his gun, he sighed and shoved the Glock back in its holster.

Rowan shut the door and yawned, then stuffed his hands in his front pants pockets. "Guess I forgot about meeting for dinner. We fell asleep a while ago. Sorry."

Rowan knew he wouldn't say anything in front of Danielle, which explained the smirk. But he had to say something. "Good evening, Ms. Stratton. Sorry to bother you. Rowan and I were planning to meet for dinner. I was concerned when he wasn't on time and didn't answer his phone."

Danielle smiled at him, seeming unconcerned that he'd discovered her in bed with his subordinate. "That's all right, special agent Johnston. I'm sorry if I caused Rowan to miss your meeting."

He'd never understand young people these days. At least she was dressed, in a sexy white sweater, and that was all he could tell. For all he knew, she was stark naked under the covers. Pissed off at the heat he felt in his face, knowing it was red, he kept his eyes resolutely on hers. "Don't you worry, Ms. Stratton, this isn't your fault."

Turning to face Rowan, he shot his special agent a grim smile. "Tell you what. Let's forget dinner and meet at the restaurant in the morning. Seven o'clock sharp. No, wait. I'll meet you here at six-thirty. That way you won't be late."

Grinding his teeth at the impenitent look on Rowan's face, he wanted to tell the younger man how close he was to utter insubordination, but knew it wouldn't do any good. Rowan was as stubborn as a mule. But he'd be in for a surprise in the morning. This shit was going to end. While he glared, Rowan yawned again. "OK boss. See you in the morning."

Unable to think of a decent reply, Ralph turned and left.

CHAPTER SIX

Monday Morning
The first gray light of approaching dawn had appeared around the edges of the drapes by the time Rowan kissed Danielle and closed the door behind her. It was time to get out of his clothes and hit the shower before Ralph got there. He was in deep shit and didn't want to anger his boss more than he already had. A knock on the door sent his coffee cup, halfway to his lips, clattering back onto the table. *"Damn it."*

Squinting through the peephole, he cursed and opened the door. Ralph glared at him. "Come on, Rowan, not again. What's the matter with you?"

Knowing Ralph was going to chew his ass and maybe even lay down some kind of ultimatum, he flung the door wide. "Come in before you wake up the entire floor. Ten minutes and I'll be ready."

Head beginning to pound from the bottle of Jack Daniel's he'd finished while Danielle slept, he headed for the bathroom as Ralph stepped inside. He'd never seen his boss so angry. "Make it quick, Rowan. I'm done fucking around with you."

Hung over and exhausted from not sleeping all night, he felt ill-prepared to handle a session with the Navy SEAL persona exuding from Ralph. And he had no idea how to explain, as his boss expected, what was *going on* between him and Danielle. He'd spent the night sipping whiskey and watching her sleep while he tried to figure out what to do. Over and over he'd told himself that he had no business leading her on, that he had an assignment to complete. He needed to dive into infiltrating the mosque and most of all, he had a clandestine life he couldn't walk away from. But he couldn't walk away from her, either. And goddamn it, he didn't want to.

Fingers poised to unbutton his shirt, he stopped when he heard another knock on the door. Stepping out of the bathroom, he gave Ralph a questioning look, but his boss just shrugged.

Feet shuffled outside the door and someone knocked harder. A woman's strained voice called out. "Mr. Rowan, are you there? Mr. Rowan, its Rita. My Javier, he's in trouble. Can you help me? Are you in there Mr. Rowan?"

His hand went instinctively to his side. His Glock 36 lay on the bedside table. He'd retrieved the Glock 22 from the safe and loaded it during the night, thinking he could never have too many weapons available. What had he done with it? Ralph whispered, "One on the desk, one on the bedside table. Take your pick." What was wrong with him? Grimacing, he stepped to the desk and grabbed the Glock 22.

Blinking and wiping his eyes, he squinted through the peep hole and saw Rita, the young Hispanic maid who brought him room service every morning. She stood in front of his door sobbing, hands clutched together in front of her. Dressed in her gold and black uniform, she must be there to work the early shift.

Suspicious by both nature and years of practice, he hated to open the door. But he couldn't leave her standing out there bawling. Javier was her husband and a maintenance man at the hotel. He'd played pool with him off and on and let him win so he could give the couple money he knew they needed. He looked back at Ralph, who stood ready with his own pistol. His boss nodded decisively.

Taking a steadying breath, wishing he wasn't so damned hung over, he turned the deadbolt and opened the door, weapon ready. Rita stood as if paralyzed, tears gushing down her face. He reached to draw her into the room, glancing down the empty hallway as he did. "Oh Mr. Rowan, I'm so sorry, so sorry. They made me come up here." When he heard *they made me,* he cursed again. As he shoved her past him into the room, the door across the hall burst open. Four massive men armed with guns and wearing dark blue jackets, poured from the room.

Taking split second aim, Rowan fired two rounds into the chest of the first man rushing through the doorway, the report from the gun reverberating throughout the pre-dawn quiet of the hotel, leaving his ears ringing. The huge man grunted and kept coming. Were they wearing body armor? He backed into the bed, lost his balance as he fired again, and the bullet meant for the man's head entered his shoulder. The big bastard grunted again and lurched into the wall, but didn't fall down.

As he fired at the next man, he tripped over his shoes. The shot exploded into the mirror, sending shards of glass crashing to the desk and floor. At the same time a stocky figure roaring obscenities plowed into him, spun him sideways and sent him toppling face first onto the floor next to the bed. A heavy knee bored into his lower back while rude hands skillfully twisted his arms backward, cuffed his wrists together and took his gun.

Rowan turned his head in time to see a booted foot coming his way. It slammed into his ribs, left him gagging and gasping. Big hands wrenched him up, forcing him into a sitting position on the bed.

"That's for shooting my agent, you worthless son of a bitch." Sweat beaded on a jutting forehead and close-set blue eyes stared into his. This was a Marine, and in charge of the ugly operation, he was certain. Taking quick breaths, the man turned, waving his pistol and barking commands. "Campbell, hurry up. Call an ambulance. This fucking traitor could have killed Jackson."

When he saw *Federal Agent* emblazoned in yellow on the back of the leader's jacket, he swallowed hard. Both he and Ralph were federal agents, so why had these men attacked? Why hadn't they identified themselves as feds from the get go? And what did they want with him? Wishing he could wipe the sweat out of his eyes, he tried to make sense of the nonsensical, but his fuzzy brain couldn't reason it out.

Across the room the situation didn't look promising. Ralph sat on the floor with his hands behind his head, looking mad as hell. Rita stood still as a statue, eyes widened in stark terror. A blond behemoth of a man held her with one giant hand, a pistol shoved against the base of her skull.

Angered that they would mistreat someone so innocent, he glared at the agent holding her. "For God's sake, stop terrorizing her and let her go. Rita, you're going to be OK."

The burly leader sneered. "Look what we've got here. What a prince." The man threw back his head and laughed, spittle flying everywhere. "It's the fucking prince of darkness." The agent's fist shot out, crashed into Rowan's jaw and cut the inside of his mouth. Head reeling, he tasted blood and felt it dripping down his chin, beneath the whiskers. The pain of the blow on top of the blossoming hangover left him completely vulnerable.

Facing him, still breathing hard, the man thrust an ID and badge in his face. "Seth Hancock, CIA." Wielding a stainless steel Sig P226, keeping it trained on him with one hand, the agent pillaged his briefcase with the other. First waving the Iranian passport he used when traveling covertly and then thumbing through the print-out of Muusa Shemal's travel records, Seth stepped back to the desk, grabbed his wallet and taunted him with a fistful of one hundred-dollar bills, a few of them fluttering to the floor. "Why don't you tell us where this money came from? Never mind, we already know. It's what you've been paid to betray your country."

He ignored the barb, still sickened by the man holding onto Rita. The black-haired man dumped his wallet back on the desk. The agent named Jackson, a monstrous jerk with a shaved head and wire rimmed glasses stepped back in the room. "Sir, I called an ambulance for Campbell and took him downstairs. They're taking him to one of the local hospitals."

Seth nodded and pointed at Ralph and Rita. "Good job, Jackson. Stay here and keep an eye on those two. Lucien, let's go." The agent twisted back to face him. "We need to question you, special agent Milani. Care to come quietly, or are you going to continue to resist arrest?"

Without warning, the big man stomped on his left foot. He heard the distinct crunch of bones breaking as a blinding flash of pain engulfed his foot and streaked up his leg. While his eyes watered, he concentrated on not passing out. Swallowing bile, he squeezed his eyes shut and then opened them, blinking at the brute still gloating in front of him.

Ralph blustered from across the room. "That's my subordinate you're abusing, agent Hancock and we happen to be federal agents as well. You better have a warrant for special agent Milani, or you better remove those cuffs and damn fast."

The ugly man pointed an index finger at Ralph. "When it's all said and done, special agent Milani will be declared an enemy combatant." Patting the front of his jacket, the agent smirked. "The warrant for his arrest is right here. And now, your special agent is coming with us. We've got a private interrogation planned for him, which is none of your concern."

Seth yanked him to his feet and propelled him to the door. Every step brought excruciating pain in his foot. The agent banged him purposely into the door frame and shoved him down the hall toward the elevator. A panic-stricken security guard and Jennie, the friendly hotel manager he enjoyed kidding with raced around the corner and skidded to a stop. Round-eyed, Jennie looked first at him and then at the two men gripping his arms. "What's going on here? We heard shots and called the police. Rowan, what happened to you? Are you all right?"

The blond agent pulled an ID and badge from beneath the blue jacket. "Nothing is going on. You can tell the police that the CIA is in charge, and it was a false alarm. Now, excuse us, please."

The two agents dragged him to the elevator and down to ground floor, then out the side door of the Sheraton to a waiting black Suburban. After opening the back end, one grabbed him under the arms while the other wrapped a thick arm around his legs. Together they heaved him inside the cargo compartment. His teeth rattled when his head whacked the wheel well and bounced off. Then everything went black.

Calloused hands slapped his face. Rowan opened his eyes and the nightmare began again. The two agents dragged him from the cargo compartment as he watched a huge overhead door grinding closed. The door settled against the ground and yellow light from the Suburban's headlights pooled in the pitch darkness. His nose tickled as he breathed through a cloud of dust and exhaust fumes. As far as he could tell, they'd taken him to some kind of warehouse. Seth poked the barrel of the Sig into the small of his back, above his cuffed wrists. "Move it, special agent. We're ready to interrogate you."

His breath rose in white clouds and he shook with a terrible sense of foreboding as he limped in the semi-darkness of the headlights across the filthy floor, the frigid concrete burning the bottoms of his feet. *He'd shot a federal agent.* The two men would make sure he paid for that decision.

Seth kept a tight grip on his arm, yanked him toward a battered wooded door marked OFFICE, pulled it open and shoved him into the room. He staggered and half fell against a cold wall. When Seth flipped on the fluorescent lights, he saw a scarred wooden table and two metal folding chairs. Someone had recently installed a large meat hook in the puke green wall, just below the ceiling. Bits of plaster and dust were scattered across the grimy tiled floor below it. His sense of foreboding expanded, along with the first whispers of terror.

Seth grabbed his arm, slammed him against the wall face first and held him there with a knee jammed against his legs. The agent removed the cuff from his left wrist, but before he could react, big hands spun him around and the handcuff sliced into his wrist again. This time his hands were in front of him. Closing his eyes and clenching his jaws, he waited. With an iron grip on both his arms, the agent grunted and lifted his bloodied wrists over the hook, leaving him twisting on tiptoe.

His bulky tormentor looked at him and leered, grabbed his shirtfront and ripped it open. Buttons flew. Precarious balance lost, his body hung suspended on his cuffed wrists. Tearing pain shot from his shoulders up his arms, blending with the agony exploding in his wrists. While Seth laughed, he floundered against the wall, desperate to regain his balance. The door opened and the blond agent brought his briefcase and laptop in and dumped them on the table. Muscles bulged in the man's biceps and forearms when he removed his jacket. This agent had the same cocky bearing as his companion and stared at him with unadulterated loathing as he shut and locked the door.

He gritted his teeth to keep from groaning out loud, teetering on tiptoe while blood from his lacerated wrists oozed down his arms. Observing helplessly while the agent opened his briefcase and rummaged through his things, he hoped they wouldn't find the flash drive stashed in a hidden pocket. Next the agent booted up his laptop. Did the men think he was naïve enough to keep anything of value in his computer files or that he'd tell them the password to access those files?

Seth held up the key to the handcuffs and waved it in front of him. "Just tell us what we need to know special agent, and here's your key to freedom." Laughing again, the agent slapped the key down on the front corner of the table, slid into the other chair, opened a folder and pulled out what looked like bank records. Damn, they'd been thorough. "We've gathered quite a bit of information about your operations." The big man picked up his passport, opened it and read the name. "Mr. Ismail Hassani. That's your real name, isn't it?"

While he watched, Seth wiped sweat off the thick forehead and fixed him with a caustic glare. "We've been tasked with apprehending you and turning you over to your own employer, the FBI, for federal prosecution. But see, both Lucien and I served in the Gulf War, and we've got buddies serving in Iraq and Afghanistan now, some of whom have lost their lives because of miserable ragheads like you who help make that happen." The agent tossed his passport back down on the table. "On behalf of our fallen brothers, we decided to conduct our own private interrogation first and give you our version of justice. And then," Seth paused to smile at him, "you don't need to concern yourself with your final destination."

In a moment of terrifying insight, he realized that the two agents thought he'd betrayed his own country. How had they learned about his clandestine activities? Who had twisted his service into treason? It didn't matter now, though. He could see the lust for revenge in their eyes. These two didn't want to interrogate him. They planned to punish him for every jihadist who'd ever killed an American soldier. If only he could think through the waves of agony rolling from his wrists to his shoulders and down his back. His left foot throbbed mercilessly, and so did his head.

The monstrous blond started in. "How long have you been committing treason? Long enough to accumulate a large amount of cash in a couple offshore accounts, I see. Who's paying you?" Waving the bank records, the agent scattered them on the table and picked up his passport, paging through it with stout fingers, reading the time stamps as he went. "Let's see. Afghanistan, Pakistan and Iran."

Lucien stopped reading and looked at Seth. "This piece of shit has been to Iraq, Lebanon and Syria as well, such interesting venues for travel these days." The big man's face turned red and he waved the passport. "You were probably involved in planning 9/11, too." Slinging his passport on top of the papers, Lucien leaned forward, thick hands planted on the table. "So, Mr. Hassani, what do you have to say for yourself?"

The agent's last comment pushed him over the edge. That the stupid bastard thought he of all people would be complicit in 9/11, the day that had destroyed him, brought the submerged rage roaring to the surface. They would never listen and never believe in his innocence, so he'd say what they were determined to hear. Glaring from one to the other, affecting a look of pure hatred, he spat out the phrase. *"Allahu Akbar, kafir."*

The men exploded from behind the table as though he'd lit them on fire. Seth steadied him against the wall while Lucien applied a one-two punch, first on one side of his ribcage and then the other, leaving him gasping. When the gargantuan fist slammed into his unprotected belly for the first time it took his breath away. Wheezing, voice rasping, he managed a jeer. "You hit like a CIA girlie man." A paroxysm of coughing gripped him. Thick blood leaked out the corners of his mouth.

The men laughed and Lucien jerked his chin up, forcing him to stare into challenging brown eyes. "That would be Marine to you, raghead. You're looking at the heavy weight boxing champ, three years running."

He did his best to sneer. "Well, semper *fucking* fi." Seth pulled the Sig and whacked him on the back of the head. Lucien dealt a jarring blow to his jaw, drawing a black curtain over his eyes. Sharp slaps to his cheeks brought him back.

Still gripping the pistol, Seth tapped him on the temple with the cold steel slide. "How about we just shoot you right now? We'd save the taxpayers a shitload of money."

Lucien's purposeful eyes stared into his. "Nah Seth. This traitor deserves everything he's got coming to him." This time when the big fist rammed his belly, something tore inside, and he couldn't stop groaning as he struggled to breathe, nearly passing out as searing pain in his abdomen overlaid the agony consuming the rest of his body.

Seth slid the pistol back in its holster and twisted thick fingers in his hair, dragging his head up. "All right special agent, are you ready to tell us why you have Muusa Shemal's travel papers in your briefcase?"

Blood and sweat stung his eyes and he blinked at the two men. He could only manage a whisper. "Why those papers are in my briefcase is none of your business. Go *fuck* yourselves."

The big blond cracked bloody knuckles and turned to his companion. "That's all I needed to hear."

Seth let go of his hair and his head drooped. The agent's voice mirrored the malevolence he'd seen in the close-set eyes. "Teach this fool a lesson."

Lucien began plying rhythmic blows from all angles with his oversized hands. Blood leaked copiously from the cuts on his face and dripped steadily down his arms, soaking the white shirt and turning it crimson, while sweat poured down his back. Every blow slammed him against the wall and knife sharp pain accompanied every groaning gasp. The beating went on and on, until his tormentor staggered back, drenched in sweat. Through burning eyes swollen almost shut, he glimpsed the two agents nodding at each other, satisfaction written on their faces. Lucien smiled at Seth. "Justice served, at least for now."

Both men grinned at him while Seth grasped his jaws between rough fingers and turned his head from side to side. "You're not so feisty now, are you, special agent? You've got a lot to answer for, but we'll take up where we left off after you think about all this." The final humiliation came when the agent spat on his face and gave him a shove. Balance lost, he hung freely, his full weight once again supported only by his wrists. He ground his teeth to keep from screaming.

Head hanging, body shaking in agony, he heard the two men chuckling as they shuffled his papers on the table and snapped his laptop shut. Seth turned the deadbolt and opened the door. "Let's get cleaned up and find some breakfast while our special agent thinks things through. We'll just have to beat that badass attitude out of him this afternoon."

Lucien grunted his agreement. "The stubborn jerk isn't leaving this room until we get some answers. I want to know why he has Muusa Shemal's travel itinerary in his briefcase, for one thing. And so help me – he's going to admit to what he is by the time we're done."

The light went out, the door closed and the lock turned. Only his wheezing groans punctuated the silence. Consumed by unrelenting pain, he knew with certainty that he wouldn't make it to the afternoon. Wobbling on tiptoe with one foot and quivering legs, he tried to use the wall behind him to relieve his wrists. Helpless to stop the process, he groaned as the muscles in his shoulders and back seized over and over, sending him into a spiraling torment of spasms, spattering blood and sweat on the floor and walls.

He passed out and came to, heard himself moaning. Would the country condemn him, call him a traitor? Would he be executed? And oh no, what about Danielle – would he ever see her again? *He'd promised to say good-bye.* Half-conscious when the spasms returned, he fought to breathe, tried to resist the slide toward oblivion. A shimmering golden light enveloped him, and the pain drained from his body. A soft voice caressed his mind and whispered to his tortured psyche – *Rowan, come with me.* It pulled him into peaceful darkness and claimed him completely.

Agonizing consciousness returned when the wooden door splintered and fell with a resounding crash. The pitch darkness changed to blurry light and he heard loud voices, thought he recognized them, but slipped back into unconsciousness. Then he came to again and felt hands on his body, slippery with blood, lifting him off the hook. Big arms drew him close and shaking fingers grappled with the handcuffs. The voice he heard held bitter rage, undercut with grief.

"*Sweet Jesus, God almighty.* Rowan, can you hear me? There will be hell to pay when I find those bastards." The voice broke into a sob. "Get an ambulance. *Hurry.*" A set of feet raced from the room. With consciousness came unbearable pain and when the darkness called, he went willingly.

Ralph sat on the floor with Rowan cradled in his arms. Tears streamed from his eyes as he took in the battered face, bludgeoned body and for the love of God, the mangled wrists. Holding his friend's limp body close to his chest, certain he was dying, he rocked him gently back and forth, murmuring "Oh God, oh God, oh God," until the paramedics charged into the room behind Chad. They lifted Rowan capably out of his arms while he stayed on the floor in a shocked daze, staring at the blood on his hands and clothes.

Chad gave his shoulder an urgent shake and he looked up, tears burning his eyes. "I'm not sure Rowan's gonna make it."

His special agent's face twisted in a grimace. "We need to find those agents and make sure they don't get in the ambulance with him."

The specter of Rowan in their brutal hands again galvanized him, and he staggered to his feet. The overpowering stench of his friend's blood and sweat turned his stomach. Stepping out of the room, he bent over, hands on his knees, and took deep breaths. Recovering his equilibrium, he tore after Chad, through the cavernous warehouse into the melee starting outside. The ambulance sat across the parking lot, blue and red lights flashing, while the paramedics made their careful way toward it with Rowan on a stretcher. "Chad, get the car, pick me up, I'm going to make sure those bastards aren't with him, else I'll be in the ambulance too. Just look for me."

Chad was already pelting around the corner of the warehouse. They'd parked behind the dilapidated building in the alley, hoping to surprise the CIA's thugs. Looking down at his bloodied clothes and hands, he clenched his fists in renewed rage, but fright overcame him as he remembered how limply Rowan had lain in his arms. How much blood had he lost? What had turned an interrogation into such a brutal attack? Wiping sweat and tears out of his eyes, he peered across the parking lot and sure enough, there were the two CIA agents. He pulled his weapon and broke into a run. They weren't going anywhere with his special agent, he'd see to that.

CHAPTER SEVEN

Danielle sat at her desk, resisting the urge to check her watch again. Where was Rowan? When she left the hotel, he smiled and said he'd see her in a couple hours. The file he'd asked about lay on the chair he should be occupying. When she tried calling, his phone went directly to voice mail, and her texts went unanswered. Feeling uneasy, she wondered if she should call his boss. Derek stuck his head in her office. "Dani, you need to see what's on TV, right now. I swear you are not going to believe what's happening. Come with me to the restaurant, quick."

Danielle made her way to the airport restaurant and sank into a chair beneath the flat screen on the wall. She stared at the headline and gasped. **Suspected Terror Mastermind Apprehended in Sioux Falls, SD.** Still staring, she listened in numb disbelief as the news anchor spoke. "A CIA undercover operation carried out in Sioux Falls, South Dakota has yielded the arrest of FBI special agent Rowan Milani. Milani, who has been an FBI agent since 1998, has most recently been on assignment with an Anti-Terrorism Task Force and is suspected of operating as a double agent, recruiting for terror organizations globally."

Head reeling, she put a hand to her mouth when Rowan's official FBI photo flashed on the screen and the anchor continued. "It also appears that Milani violently resisted arrest and was injured before being subdued by four CIA agents during the early morning takedown. Reports confirm that an agent involved in the arrest was shot and later transported by ambulance to Avera McKennan Hospital in Sioux Falls, where he remains in stable condition. We now go to live video coverage from South Dakota."

Unable to stop shaking, Danielle stared at the TV and felt Derek's hands on her shoulders. Waves of shock rolled over her as she watched paramedics swarming around a stretcher being rolled out the door of a warehouse. Two huge men milled around waving guns, trying to get as close as they could to the stretcher. Then she saw Ralph Johnston, covered with blood. Was he with the two men?

An oxygen mask covered Rowan's face. One of his arms hung over the side of the stretcher and bright red blood leaked through a bandage that covered the lower half of his arm. As she stared in horror, one of the paramedics noticed, grabbed Rowan's dangling arm and laid it across his chest. Shoving back the chair, she stood up, stomach heaving and turned to head for the restroom across the hall. Ignoring Derek's surprised "Hey," and with a hand plastered tight over her mouth, she barely made it into the stall before losing her breakfast. Collapsing to her knees, she covered her face with her hands. Who could have done this to Rowan? Would he live? Could she see him? She had to see him.

Ralph waited until he was certain the CIA agents weren't riding in the ambulance to the hospital. While he stood doubled over, trying to catch his breath, he watched the two men sling Rowan's laptop and briefcase into a black Suburban; leap in and speed off. Frantic honking caught his attention and he turned to see Chad braking to a stop at the edge of the parking lot in the red Mustang. Media vehicles poured into the already cramped parking lot, disgorging reporters lugging cameras and microphones, making navigation nearly impossible. A mixture of city police cars, Minnehaha County Sheriff's vehicles, highway patrol cruisers, a fire and rescue truck and unmarked patrol cars clogged the lot as well.

Racing to the Mustang, he dove in. Chad hit the accelerator and almost instantly the brakes, turning hard to avoid a reporter, a blonde woman, dressed in black and carrying a microphone.

Uttering a sharp "fuck this," Chad gunned the car across the snow at the edge of the parking lot, weaved between a tree and lamp post, jumped the curb and screamed into traffic, spewing gravel and sliding with shrieking brakes around the first corner, against the light. A white Honda minivan heading through the intersection slammed on its brakes, almost broad-siding them, horn blaring as a blue Ford Focus rear-ended it with a loud bang and the tinkling crunch of breaking glass.

Digging his phone from his jacket pocket, Ralph hit number one on his speed dial. "Listen, Operator, I don't care about protocol, I don't give a rat's ass about what meeting he's in. Get me through to the President, right now. No, I'm not joking. You tell him its Ralph Johnston calling regarding Rowan Milani, and it's a matter of national security." Near to hyperventilating, heart hammering, he laid a hand on his chest.

Suddenly pressed against Chad's shoulder, he read the speedometer, realizing with widening eyes and a dry mouth that he hadn't known a car could take a corner at that speed. The Mustang clunked down hard, and he was thrown against the passenger side window with the sure knowledge that they'd been on two wheels. Chad blew through the Monday morning back-to-work traffic in Sioux Falls, passing cars impressively, leaving screeching tires and honking horns in their wake.

It was his good fortune that the CIA goon left guarding him at the hotel was an arrogant son of a bitch looking for bragging rights. Remembering the man strutting back and forth made him sick. *Yeah, we got a room all set up for your special agent. He's gonna be interrogated and then it's straight to an Egyptian prison for that traitor.* When the foolish agent shoved Rita into the hallway, threatening her with deportation if she didn't forget about what she'd seen, he took the opportunity to grab his Glock. When the agent came back in the room, he told the moron to tell him where they'd taken Rowan or he'd shoot him. The coward folded instantly and told him the address of a rented warehouse.

The morning meeting he'd set up for Chad, Rowan and himself was one more stroke of luck. Chad had been en route when he called him. The kid loved to drive fast, and they reached the warehouse on the northeast edge of Sioux Falls in law-breaking as well as speed-breaking records. The agents hadn't thought to lock the overhead door, and their frantic search of the dark interior revealed nothing except a locked wooden door marked OFFICE. An abandoned, solid oak coat rack stood outside the door. It made a superlative ramming bar. Queasiness gripped him again as he saw Rowan in his mind's eye, bloodied body hanging by his wrists on a damn meat hook. It took a certain kind of animal to do that to another human being and then walk away.

Chad slammed the car into park at the Trauma Five emergency entrance of Sanford Medical Center, practically sending him through the windshield as the White House operator came back on the line. "Special agent Johnston, I have the President." Ralph held his breath while the President said good morning.

"Good morning, Mr. President, and thank you, sir, for taking my call." He noticed Chad out of the corner of his eye, staring at him with a curious frown. "This is a matter of utmost urgency. I believe you are quite familiar with FBI special agent Rowan Milani. Sir, I am not in a position to provide you with the details at this time, but the integrity of the missions you have sent him on and our national security are in grave danger of being compromised. He is not, I repeat – *not* a double agent. I will stake my career and my life on that. I am asking, Mr. President, that you personally remand him from CIA custody into my protective custody, immediately."

Pausing to let the President absorb what he'd said, he waited, short of breath. When the President spoke, he blinked back tears of relief. "Thank you, Mr. President. You won't regret the decision sir, and I will keep you informed. Thank you again Mr. President. Good-bye, sir."

He flung the passenger door wide and scrambled out. "Come on, let's go." Chad already waited outside the car and they ran with weapons in hand, into the Emergency reception area. The young police officer assigned to patrol the ER had seen them coming and stood with pistol gripped tightly in both hands.

Swearing softly, Ralph wiped sweat from the side of his face, holstered his Glock and addressed the young man. "Officer, it is imperative that we access a patient in your emergency room. My name is Ralph Johnston and I'm the Special Agent in Charge of an FBI Anti-Terrorism Task Force." Tilting his head at Chad, he continued. "And this is FBI special agent Chad Cantor. Time is of the essence. I'm going to show you my badge and ID, so take it easy." Reaching slowly into his inside jacket pocket, he pulled his ID and badge for the police officer to see. "Now, unlock the door, please."

The officer holstered his pistol and complied, pushing a button that released the lock, sending them through the door into the emergency treatment area. Luck or God was on their side one more time. The ambulance team had just brought Rowan to a cubicle and were milling around inside the curtained opening, rushing between the cubicle and the central Nurse's Station in the middle of the room. Flashing his credentials, he took in the frantically working doctors and nurses.

Motioning to Chad, he stationed his subordinate on one corner of the cubicle entrance, while he took the other. They stood, weapons at the ready, Chad watching a long hallway with double doors at one end, while he kept the door they'd entered in his sights. It was only a few minutes before the two CIA agents burst through the double doors and pounded down the hallway, skidding to a stop when they saw Chad.

Chad stepped to the center of the hallway and aimed his Glock unerringly at the chest of the black-haired agent who'd manhandled Rowan at the hotel. "Drop your weapons where you stand, or I will shoot you." His special agent's face wore pure intent and the stocky black-haired man dangled his gun by one finger and laid it on the floor. His partner, the tall, muscle bound Neanderthal with blond hair did the same.

Chad advanced slowly, weapon still aimed. "Is that the one, boss?" He nodded, wondering what the kid was up to. Chad nodded back, his mouth a grim line. Then his special agent shrugged his shoulders, twisted his neck and without warning executed a flawless roundhouse kick that connected with the black-haired man's left cheek, snapping his head to the right. The CIA agent fell like a pole-axed bull. Ralph nearly laughed out loud when his subordinate looked at the other agent. "Wanna go next?" The big man backed against the wall and raised his hands.

Chad confiscated the discarded weapons, giving him an idea. "Special agent, lock their guns in the trunk. We may need them later for leverage, and they sure as hell don't need them in here."

Danielle splashed cool water on her face and grabbed a paper towel to dab at the wetness while she stared at herself in the mirror. She took a deep breath and stepped out of the bathroom, holding one hand on her still rolling stomach. Derek waited, eyes narrowed, a frown etched on his face. "Are you OK? Is there anything I can do for you?"

Hoping she could talk, she shook her head. "Yes, have they said where they're taking Rowan? You can give me a ride to the ER. I have to see him and make sure he's going to be all right."

Derek nodded. "Yep, they took him to Sanford Medical Center. Are you sure you want to go to the hospital? You don't want to be linked to him, especially not now. I told you he was dangerous. You should have listened."

Scorching anger blotted out her thoughts. "How can you say that? Just get away from me. I'll drive myself." Intense grief crushed the anger and hot tears spilled down her cheeks. Leaning against the wall, she covered her face and sobbed.

A firm hand gripped her arm and an authoritative voice spoke quietly in her ear. "It's all right, Dani. I'll take you to the hospital and make sure you find out what's going on."

Lowering her hands, she sniffed and wiped at the tears, trying to compose herself. Jax stood next to her, dark eyes compassionate. "I'm sure Ralph Johnston will be there and I'll have access. If I can arrange for you to see Rowan, I will." Jax wrapped comforting arms around her, and she buried her head in his shoulder. That was all she needed; to see Rowan and make sure he was going to live. Then she could tell him how much she loved him.

Ralph looked up to see Chad striding through the door, an angry look on his face. "Boss, the media have arrived. I got back inside before they could get to me and instructed the police officer to send them away. The guns are in the trunk, and I moved the car to the parking lot."

The media was another complication they didn't need. Shaking his head, he placed a hand on Chad's arm and drew his subordinate close. "I'm going to take those two thugs to a conference room and have a chat. Sometime soon they're going to get the message that Rowan's our boy now, and I don't think they'll be too happy about it. Stay right here, and don't you let anybody take him out of the ER until I get back, unless it's to emergency surgery. If that's the case, let me know."

When Chad nodded his assent and stepped back to his vigil beside the cubicle, Ralph turned to the loathsome pair of agents, massaging his neck in a vain effort to relieve the tension. "Gentlemen, we need to chat. I believe there's an empty conference room down this hall, if you'll come with me." He waggled his pistol and the two men followed him. As he'd thought, there was a small room a short distance down the hall, with a table and chairs.

Waving the two agents into the room ahead of him, he shut the door and leaned casually against the wall with his Glock cradled in the crook of his arm. "Sit, please." Both men just looked at him. Gazing from one belligerent face to the other, he scratched his chin. "I could call my special agent in, if you'd like. I'm sure he'd enjoy having another go with either one of you."

The black-haired agent touched the fresh bruise on the side of his face. "Bring it on. Your special agent won't surprise me again."

He decided to ignore the bullish man. "Here's the thing. The man you abducted this morning is now in my custody, by order of the President. We don't need your services any longer."

The two agents glared at him, and the ugly blond cracked thick knuckles before speaking. "Rowan Milani is a bona fide terror suspect and belongs to the CIA now. He is our prisoner and will be transported out of here on an agency jet. You can't do anything to stop us."

Approaching the thickset agent, revolted by the bloody cuts on the man's knuckles, Ralph decided he'd had enough. "Let me tell you two torture-for-hire thugs something. I spoke with the President less than an hour ago. If you think you're taking special agent Milani anywhere, I can guarantee you with absolute confidence that you will not walk out of here."

Standing in front of the towering man, he poked him in the chest with the barrel of the Glock and looked up into angry brown eyes. "Rowan Milani isn't going anywhere, except probably to emergency surgery to repair what you did to him. Now, I am done with this pissing match. I'll make you a deal. We'll exchange special agent Milani's laptop and briefcase, including contents, for your weapons. As a matter of fact, let me be more specific. Neither of you is leaving until I have possession of the items I mentioned." Glowering from one to the other, he added,

"Don't bother telling me you don't have them, because I saw you stash them in your Suburban at the warehouse."

Before either man could answer him, the door opened and Chad appeared. "They're taking him for a CT scan, boss. The doctor would like to speak with you."

Ralph nodded. "Thanks, special agent. Stay with these two, but don't hurt them. If they're so inclined, we'll make an even exchange of their weapons for special agent Milani's laptop and briefcase, contents included. Manage the transaction as you see fit. I'll let you know where we are."

Chad gave him a quick nod. "That'll be my pleasure boss."

A harried looking physician with shrewd eyes behind glasses, wearing a white coat with blood on the front met him in the hallway. The doctor looked like he wanted someone's butt. "Are you responsible for the patient I've been working on for the last hour?"

He nodded. "Yes sir, my name is Ralph Johnston, Special Agent in Charge for the FBI." Attempting a smile, he showed the doctor his badge and ID.

The physician glanced at his credentials, didn't appear impressed and didn't return his smile. "I'm Doctor Anderson, head of the ER team at Sanford. Step in here, please." The man gestured toward an open door. Stepping obediently inside, he sank into a chair facing a desk and watched as Doctor Anderson slid around to his own seat. The room was cramped, the walls crowded with varying photos, degrees and awards, all bearing either Doctor Anderson's likeness or his name.

The doctor leaned back in his chair, folded his hands in front of him on the cluttered desk and gazed at him with stark contempt. "Special agent Johnston, perhaps you can clear something up for me."

Ralph leaned forward. "Anything doctor, shoot."

Doctor Anderson waved his arm vaguely. "Well, correct me if I'm wrong, but I was under the distinct impression, from recent publicity on various news programs that our country does not torture terror suspects. Was I incorrect in that assumption?"

Sitting up straight, feeling his face reddening, he fought the urge to tell Dr. Anderson the whole sordid story. "You are correct in that assumption."

Dr. Anderson glared at him. "That's all you've got to say? Did you happen to notice what your agents or whatever you call them did to your prisoner? I saw the news shortly before he arrived in the ER. It's great that he was apprehended. But that man was tortured. I can't sit by and say nothing."

He opened his mouth to speak but the doctor barged on. "That man may never have the use of his hands again." Doctor Anderson looked at his own hands and flexed them. "I have never seen such severe, deliberately inflicted injury from handcuffs. The soft tissue trauma is almost more than I can get a handle on. The radial, ulnar and median nerves must be tremendously damaged, and there are fractures in both wrists. The damage will most likely be long-term and might even be permanent."

The doctor gave him a grim stare. "We are also dealing with what I suspect is a torn or ruptured spleen, which a CT scan will confirm. Depending on the extent of damage, he may need immediate surgery. He's already received a blood transfusion." Doctor Anderson threw both hands in the air. "Maybe all this is superfluous to you. This is a terrorist after all. Was the intent merely to destroy his ability to shoot a gun, or say, feed himself?"

Although well-schooled in managing situations requiring his utmost discretion, not responding as he wanted to the doctor's information was excruciating. Knowing he would be grossly misinterpreted, he soldiered on, thinking that at some point, he needed to develop a closer relationship with the bottle of scotch in his dresser drawer. "Your concern is noted, doctor. You are of course free to make whatever reports you feel are necessary. My main concern is that you and the other doctors in this hospital make my prisoner as healthy as possible, as quickly as possible, so I can transport him out of here." Well, that was the truth, as far as it went.

The phone on the doctor's belt rang. Ralph listened anxiously as the doctor spoke. "Yes? That's what I suspected. Prep him for surgery. I'm on my way." Dr. Anderson stood up. "Special agent Johnston, the CT scan revealed a torn spleen and we're proceeding to surgery. And you can rest assured, I will be making multiple reports. You can also be assured that every effort will be made to show this man compassion and create the most favorable environment for complete healing, whatever his final destination may be." The doctor stepped around the desk and opened the door. "I wish I could say it's been a pleasure to meet you."

With that, the doctor strode out of the office. Drooping in the chair, staring at the man's receding back a moment before following, he muttered to himself. "God help you. I hope you can do everything you've said, doctor."

Dr. Anderson reluctantly led him through the hospital to the one-way locking doors that led to surgery. After calling Chad and leaving him a message, Ralph settled into a molded plastic chair against the wall. His subordinate appeared within minutes, Rowan's laptop and briefcase in his hands. "Hey boss, the pussies," noting the expression on his special agent's face, he couldn't help a chuckle. Chad smiled weakly and tipped his head down at the booty in his hands. "The agents agreed to your exchange. They received a phone call shortly after you left. You were correct in assuming they wouldn't be happy about the change in their plans for transporting the, uh, Rowan."

Ralph scratched his head and stared at Chad. It left a nasty taste in his mouth to refer to Rowan as a prisoner. "I heard you the first time, special agent. Thanks for a job well done. Listen, stay here and keep me informed. The docs aren't close to being done with him. I've got some exceedingly unpleasant phone calls to make. Then I'm going to take a cab to the hotel and get cleaned up."

It was nine-thirty in the morning, Pacific Time, when Khalil Milani turned on the TV for the first time that day. It was a gorgeous, sunny day in Carpinteria, California, perfect for a walk on the beach. He and Janice, his wife of over thirty years had done just that. Now, while she made coffee, he grabbed the remote, plopped down contentedly in his favorite recliner and switched on FOX News. The first thing he saw was the red and yellow alert banner: **Alleged Terror Master Captured in Sioux Falls, SD.** Rowan's picture flashed on the screen. Then he saw the ambulance, and glimpsed his son on a stretcher, surrounded by paramedics and men with guns.

The anchor droned on and on about someone called Ismail Hassani. At first he thought they'd confused Rowan with another man. But no, the anchor said Rowan *was* that man. His son was being named an international terrorist. A roaring sound filled his ears and he felt lightheaded. Bending over, he put his head between his knees. The next thing he knew, Janice was next to him on her knees beside the chair. "Khalil, honey, are you all right? You're pale as a ghost, what's the matter?" She pressed one hand to her chest, gripping his forearm with the other.

Taking a shaky breath, he pointed at the TV. They both stared at the screen. The headline remained, but it couldn't be true, this couldn't be happening. Rowan, his son, would never betray his country. Janice put her hands over her face and began weeping quietly.

The phone rang and he clambered up, answering it automatically. "Hello, Milani residence." Perched on the edge of the chair, he put a hand on Janice's shoulder. Ralph Johnston's voice answered his hello and he wanted to respond, but felt like he was in some kind of trance. Placing a hand over his eyes, he tried to concentrate. "Ralph, it's good of you to call. Yes, we're just seeing it now." He listened intently as Ralph described the whole situation as a mistake that would be sorted out soon and apologized for not calling earlier. Ralph paused and he interrupted. "What happened to Rowan? The TV says he violently resisted capture." His gorge rose at the words. "How badly was he hurt, and where is he now?"

Caution and hesitation came across clearly in Ralph's voice. His hearty assurance that Rowan would be fine sounded hollow. Concern for his only son constricted his chest. If Ralph had trouble lying to him, Rowan must be in bad shape.

The front door slammed, he heard running footsteps and his daughter Bettina shouting. "Mom, Dad, did you see the news?" She appeared in the living room, fluffy black hair whispering around her face. Khalil watched his daughter kneel and take her mother in her arms. They clung together crying until Bettina looked up. "Who's on the phone Dad, it's not Rowan, is it?" The desperate hope in her eyes nearly killed him.

He smiled kindly at her. "It's Ralph Johnston, Rowan's boss."

"I want to talk to him." Handing her the phone, he sank back into the chair, watching her determination take over. "Mr. Johnston, I want to talk to my brother. What do you mean? I understand he's in the hospital, but can't I talk to him? He's not a prisoner, is he?"

Khalil watched as tears gathered in her eyes. "He's unconscious? I want to know what happened to my brother. Please tell me he's OK."

When she collapsed, shaking with sobs, he gently retrieved the phone. "I'm sorry Ralph. I guess we're all taking this pretty hard. Thank you for calling, and I trust you will keep us informed?"

Bettina wrenched the phone from his hand. "Mr. Johnston, where is my brother? Sioux Falls, South Dakota? He's still on assignment there?" Her voice wavered. "He's in the hospital there, right?"

Bettina wiped away her tears and he marveled at her fortitude. "Mr. Johnston, I am going to see my brother." Her face scrunched up with fresh pain. "I will be in Sioux Falls, South Dakota, wherever that is, tomorrow."

Ralph stared at his cell phone, a mixture of consternation and disbelief rolling through him. Snapping the phone shut, he blew out a heavy sigh. What in God's name were they going to do with Bettina Milani? He kneaded his forehead and considered. How would she handle being told Rowan was his prisoner? He'd barely left Chad outside the doors to surgery when his boss, Rodney Ainsley, the Director of the FBI, had called. Although Ainsley proclaimed outrage over what had happened to Rowan, he detected a subtle resistance in his boss's voice about whether it was a mistake.

To top it off, his boss insisted on knowing how he was so connected, that he'd gotten the President out of a meeting. He'd been forced to admit that a very long time ago, as a Navy SEAL on leave, he'd happened to be in the same hunting party as a certain businessman turned politician. They'd bonded over guns, fighter jets and scotch, remaining clandestine friends over the ensuing years.

Rubbing tired eyes, he relived the revolting conversation. Ainsley had insisted that the prisoner remain secured and under guard. Special agent Milani had shot a federal agent, so they could do nothing less. How would anyone know, he'd countered? It was non-negotiable, his boss replied. The conversation had become acrimonious at that point and he'd launched a full-scale assault – ranted, raved and threatened to resign. Ainsley remained unmoved and in the end, he'd said *Yes sir, I'll see to it,* and hung up.

It had taken steely resolve, but he'd called the county sheriff's office and made the request. They'd already delivered leg irons, since handcuffs were out of the question. As soon as Rowan was out of surgery and transferred to a room, the deputy assigned to guard him would place them on Rowan's legs and lock them there, keeping his special agent, his friend, the man he thought of as a son, secured to a hospital bed with a chain. He'd sat on the bed in his hotel room and held his head in his hands as tears like he hadn't experienced in years poured down his face, and gut wrenching sobs wracked his body. All he could think about was the terror Rowan would feel if he woke up alone and realized he was a prisoner. That broke his heart and he didn't give a damn who knew it.

CHAPTER EIGHT

Early Tuesday Morning

While Ralph snored in a chair and Danielle dozed next to the hospital bed on a cot, Rowan's tortured mind floated through layers of trauma and sedation toward consciousness. *He'd promised to tell her good-bye, but he couldn't, because they'd taken him. Somehow he'd been betrayed and now he was lost.* As he blinked in the semi-darkness, awareness crept into his mind. He stared at the ceiling, felt the IV in the crook of his elbow and smelled strong antiseptic. Turning his head a fraction, he saw machines with blurry neon numbers and drapes pulled shut across a window. He tried to move his hands but couldn't. His feet were bandaged. He felt cold metal above his ankles.

When he moved his leg, a chain clanked. His eyes widened as everything came rushing back. There were leg irons above his ankles and a chain that kept him secured. *Oh no, oh Jesus, they still had him, he was their prisoner.* His heart pounded, his breath came in labored gasps and sweat drenched his body. Someone coughed and he waited in abject fear and terrified helplessness to see his monstrous captors, but saw Ralph instead, looking down at him with a sad, haggard face.

Ralph leaned close. "Hey Rowan, it's me. We've got you now and you're going to be all right. You're safe." He winced, eyelids fluttering, expecting a blow as Ralph reached down and touched his forehead. "You feel hot, son. I think you've got a fever."

Moving restlessly, he felt the cold metal again and moaned in raw despair, the sound barely audible. Ralph moved out of his line of sight, and then he saw her. Danielle hovered over the bed, clutching the rail with her hands. "Rowan, I'm so sorry. I wish I could help you." Her fingers skimmed his hair. "I love you and

I'll be here, no matter what." And then she was gone. Had he imagined her standing there? God, he hoped not.

A nurse appeared. He watched her professional concern as she checked his vitals, frowned at the thermometer, and made a note. Desperation washed over him in crashing waves. He'd never confess to being a terrorist. They couldn't make him do that. Closing his eyes, he turned his back on consciousness, following the darkness to the place where he was no longer in agony.

Later Tuesday Morning
Ralph woke with a start to his ringing cell phone. Fumbling, he pulled it out of his pants pocket and dropped it. The damn thing kept ringing. Grunting, he strained to reach it, feeling like he was eighty years old. Another night in a chair would be the end of him. Grabbing the phone, he sat up and smacked it resoundingly against his ear. "Ouch, damn it. Johnston."

"Morning, Ralph." What could his boss want at this hour? Twisting around, he swatted at the closed drapes. Weak sunlight filtered into the room, but he had no idea of the time. Scratching his face, he realized his boss had continued talking in his calm, unhurried way. "The upshot of all the information I've been provided with, from sources I trust, is this. Our intelligence shows credible evidence that special agent Milani has been playing us very cleverly."

Not believing what he'd just heard, he interrupted. *"What?"* But his boss continued before he could say anything else.

"It's going to be difficult for you to accept that, Ralph. After all, you've worked with special agent Milani – or perhaps we should accustom ourselves to his real name, Ismail Hassani – closely, but oftentimes that puts a good agent in the position of not seeing the forest for the trees. We've all been there. Don't beat yourself up. The fact that he shot a federal agent, who is now hospitalized, doesn't help the situation."

As usual Ainsley had succeeded in pissing him off. He knew his agents, and he hadn't, by God, been played by Rowan. A thorough, diabolical betrayal of his special agent was rapidly unfolding, but he'd be damned if it would succeed. Someone, or more likely some entity had invested considerable time, resources, and manpower in the endeavor. It made no sense, but one thing was glaringly obvious: they'd managed to co-opt his boss.

It was time for serious subterfuge. Taking a deep breath, he marshaled his thoughts. It would be his best performance, because it had to be. Rowan's life hung in the balance. Allowing a dry chuckle for Ainsley's benefit, he began. "Your point is well taken, sir. In the interests of national as well as local security, considering the danger inherent in housing a terrorist in a regional medical center, I believe it would behoove us to move him to a more secure facility. The only drawback is his physical condition, but I will confer with the doctor in charge and determine a plausible date for transfer."

Ainsley became animated. "Yes, yes, I'm glad you understand. We need to transport our prisoner as soon as possible. Please meet with the doctors there. Perhaps they can liaison with the medical team at Quantico, which is the facility I prefer. I want this man in shape for interrogation, and I don't want anything to interfere with that happening as expeditiously as possible."

Ralph pulled the phone away from his ear and stared at it. The urge to throw it as hard and far as he could was beyond strong. Finally, he simply released his fingers and let it clatter to the floor. Ainsley kept talking in a tinny voice. "Are you still there? Did I lose you?" Next he resisted the desire to stomp the phone to pieces. Grunting in irritation, he bent over and picked it up.

Faking a chuckle, he addressed his boss. "Sorry sir, butter-fingers this morning, I dropped the damn thing. You were saying?" He'd find a weakness in whatever blighted plot Ainsley came up with. His boss wouldn't be moving Rowan anywhere, anytime. It would be, he decided grimly, over his dead, stinking carcass.

Ainsley continued. "Sounds like I caught you off guard this morning. It's still early there, only eight o'clock here." *You jerk*, Ralph thought darkly as he sat hunched in the chair, chin in one hand, elbows boring into his knees. His boss never did anything without a reason. The conniving man had every intention of taking him by surprise, but two could play that game.

He sat up. "Well sir, if you can ready things on your end, I can make the arrangements here." Hoping his utter disgust wasn't evident in his voice, he glanced at Rowan and almost dropped the phone again. His special agent laid in the bed staring at him, listening to him.

Ainsley sounded relieved. "It's good to hear you're onboard with this situation. I'll begin making arrangements for secure transport. Keep me informed of what's happening on your end. Have a good day, Ralph."

Snapping the phone shut, he slung it away, watching as it skittered across the floor and out the door. "Yeah, I'm onboard all right, but it's a different fucking train. You just don't know that yet." He looked down at Rowan again. His prisoner gazed back at him. Despite the situation, he had to smile. With his disheveled, coal black hair and ragged beard edging his bruised face, Rowan looked like the real deal.

Taking a moment to stand and stretch, he walked out of the room to retrieve his phone. Danielle stood outside the door sipping coffee from a Styrofoam cup and held it out for him. Giving her a gruff smile, he grabbed it from her hand. "Thanks, Danielle." At some point during the long night, she'd asked him to call her by her first name. "Rowan's awake." Seeing the eagerness in her face, he smiled again. "Just give me a couple minutes to talk privately with him and then he's all yours."

Stepping back into the room, he stood by Rowan's bed and looked down. "Rowan, you can hear me, can't you?" His friend's dark head moved fractionally on the pillow. "Can you speak at all? Because son, we've got to do some strategizing. We've got a big problem, you and I." He worried it might be too much for Rowan to absorb, and he didn't want to push him.

Rowan angled his head, his swollen lips moving slowly. Dipping his head low and close, he felt warm breath on his cheek, bringing an unexpected lump to his throat. His friend could only whisper. "They found out about the black ops somehow. Someone betrayed me, twisted everything."

Thunderstruck, he stepped back and stared at Rowan. "Sweet Jesus." With sudden, stunning clarity he realized that the time was fast approaching when he'd have to count the cost and declare his allegiance. Would it be to the nation he'd served throughout a lifelong career or to the younger man lying in the hospital bed, who he loved like a son? He shook his head. The answer lay staring up at him, bruised and broken but *thank God, still alive.*

Leaning close to Rowan once more, he whispered. "I will do everything in my power to keep you safe. The President put you in my hands, and I won't betray you. You have to know that."

What Rowan did next buoyed his spirit as much as it wounded it. Moving his legs enough to make the despicable chain clank against the leg irons, his friend stared at him and whispered fiercely. *"Why?"*

Mouth twisting in revulsion, he replied, "Ainsley." Rowan struggled to lift his head, and he looked into the tormented eyes. "What is it?"

Sweat stood on Rowan's forehead as his face strained with the effort to speak. *"In my briefcase, hidden pocket, tell Chad."* His special agent sank back into the pillow, closed his eyes, and slipped away.

He needed to find Chad pronto and get into Rowan's briefcase. What in the world was his special agent talking about?

Rowan must have known Chad could find and decipher what he'd hidden. He sighed. They'd soon find out.

Tuesday Afternoon

Chad waited inside the front entrance of the airport, shifting impatiently from one foot to the other while he inspected the bronze statue of Joe Foss, South Dakota's very own World War II hero. Ralph had sent him to pick up Rowan's sister. Her plane had taxied in twenty minutes earlier. She should be coming down the escalator, now. Not having a clue what she looked like, he hoped he hadn't missed her among the crowd that had already straggled past him. Ralph had smiled and said he'd recognize her and not to worry. What was that about?

Scowling, he looked up at the lone woman riding down the escalator. From that point forward he, FBI hot shot special agent and hacker extraordinaire, second degree black belt and confirmed bachelor, became a convert to the religion of *Love at First Sight*. His mouth hung open, and he tried to find his voice. The woman, and there was not a single doubt in his mind that she was Rowan's sister, looked around tentatively and walked toward him.

Dressed in a form-fitting white suit with a slim skirt, barelegged and wearing tan leather heels, she had Rowan's olive complexion, hair that was black as onyx and short, curling seductively around a face with delectable red lips. But it was her eyes that got him. There was no mistaking the family resemblance. A woman goddess version of his colleague had entered his life. Shaking himself mentally, he hoped he never let any of those thoughts slip out. Wiping sweaty palms on his pants he stepped toward her, hoping he could form a complete sentence. "Ms. Milani?"

She turned toward him, relief evident in her face. Then she smiled and rocked his world. He smiled back, surprised his face worked. Head tilted, she looked at him. "Um, are you special agent Cantor?"

Reaching out, he hoped he could handle the touch of her hand in his. "Chad, yes, that's me." His voice sounded like he was in seventh grade and he cleared his throat. "It's a pleasure to meet you. It's Bettina, correct?" Giving him another smile, she grasped his hand. He survived first contact, staring at their hands clasped together. Would she say yes if he asked her to marry him?

When she giggled, he looked up and released her hand. "Rowan told me you're kind of quirky, but in a good way." It hurt him to see sadness overtake the smile. "How is Rowan? It's been horrible, wondering what's going on." She tapped the handle of the black carry-on bag next to her. "This is all I brought with me, so we don't have to collect any luggage. Can we go straight to the hospital? That's all I want to do, and of course see Mr. Johnston."

Her dark eyes entreated him, and he knew he would take her anywhere she wanted to go, lay his coat over the proverbial puddle for her to step on. No, he'd lay down in the mud so she could step on him. Grabbing the handle of the carry-on bag, he put a hand lightly on her back. "Car's right this way, I can have you next to your brother's bedside in about thirty minutes."

They walked outside to the red Mustang where she stopped, looking from him to the car and back. Watching her brows climb her forehead, he read the disbelief in her eyes. "Since when does the FBI provide Mustangs – red ones and convertibles no less, for their agents? The last time I talked to Rowan on the phone, he griped about the Lincoln you drive." Then she shivered and wrinkled her nose. It was all he could do not to bend down and kiss it. "He also talked about how cold and barren it is here. *Brrr,* he was right." Rubbing her arms vigorously, she looked up at him with inscrutable eyes. God help him. He'd fallen for the female version of Rowan Milani. His life would never be the same.

* * *

Wednesday Afternoon

The next time Rowan drifted awake, he thought the world seemed brighter. His eyes followed the numbers on the machines tracking his status among the living. He noticed the beige drapes pulled back from the window, a TV mounted on the wall, the cluttered countertop, and small cabinet beneath it. An opaque white curtain obscured his view of the rest of the room. Ralph must be taking a break because he wasn't in the chair at the end of the bed. Had he imagined Danielle being there? He moved his legs, rattling the chain. The cold metal above his ankles fostered ripples of panic through his gut.

Then there was the pain. Clearing the fog in his brain was one thing, but with it came the grim awareness of how much damage his body had sustained. Swallowing convulsively, he remembered the huge hands and how he'd enraged the man they belonged to, egged him on and been severely punished for his efforts.

Quick footsteps trod into the room, the curtain flew open, and a nurse with a mask of professional concern covering her features hovered over him. Long blonde hair dangled in a ponytail over her shoulder and she assessed him with kind, blue eyes. "I see you're awake, sir. Can I get you anything? Are you in pain?"

When he managed to nod, she reacted immediately, eyes roaming over the flasks of fluids attached to the IV pole. "Oh dear, this is empty, it should have been replaced. I'll be right back. In the meantime, let's sit you up for a bit. You seem a lot more alert this afternoon, which is a good thing." She patted his shoulder, and he drew a quick breath at the stinging pain in her simple touch. As the bed hummed, he found himself more or less sitting up, with a view of the doorway on one side and out the window on the other.

Finally he could look at his hands, but there wasn't much to see. Thick bandages covered all but his fingers, and went well past his wrists. He tried to move his fingers, concentrated hard, felt sweat bead on his forehead. The index finger on his right hand moved a hair, and he detected faint movement in the fingers on his left hand. What the hell was wrong with his hands? Sweating in earnest now, he felt the thin hospital gown sticking to his body. Panic set in and he told himself to suck it up and calm down.

The nurse reappeared with a bulging flask of clear fluid that he hoped was pain medication. She also had a needle and syringe and smiled at him as she removed the empty flask and replaced it. "That will help manage your pain, sir. I also brought something that will take the edge off. It looks like you're hurting." Pulling the plastic cover off the needle, she inserted it into the IV in his right arm. "There you go. You should get relief right away."

She took his pulse and frowned, checked his temperature, and watched him with a practiced eye. He felt the sting of fluid flowing into his vein, then soothing warmth spreading through his body. Grateful, he looked up and managed a whisper. "Thank you."

"You're welcome. It's nice to hear your voice. You've come a long way in two days, and we expect to see continuing improvement. Your vitals are strong and steady, which is a miracle considering everything." Looking embarrassed, she didn't finish the sentence, just smiled and gathered her things from the bedside table. "I'll come back in a little while to lower your bed. I think a change of scenery will do you good." She turned, pulled the curtain shut and was gone.

The tension fled as the medication did its job. Drifting toward darkness, he remembered the blood dripping down his arms and the unending agony when his legs gave out. Wishing the ugly memories would go away he turned his head to the right, closed his eyes and slipped into unconsciousness.

When he woke up again, he saw Danielle, asleep in the chair at the end of the bed. Hesitant footsteps approached. He turned his head, watching as the curtain slowly moved aside to reveal the anguished face of his sister, with Ralph and Chad trailing in to stand beside her. Bettina was trying not to cry, tears gathering in her eyes as she clenched and unclenched her fists. "Oh Rowan." She choked up and stood staring at him while tears slipped down her cheeks.

He closed his eyes. If his mother and father walked in next, he'd kill Ralph with his bare hands. Anger burned hot with the dawning recognition that he may never be able to do anything with his hands. Opening his eyes, he glowered at Ralph, felt rage building and then spilling over, but he didn't care. Feeling anything besides desperation and terror was invigorating and made him feel alive again. He welcomed his old familiar state of being. At least he hadn't lost that. Damn near everything else that mattered was long gone, and maybe he'd add his hands to that list too, but by God, nobody could take away his rage.

Ralph watched Rowan with interest, noting the full bore return of his special agent's forceful personality. It fascinated him to see the rage light Rowan's eyes and gave him hope that his special agent's razor sharp mind was on the mend as well.

Gazing at Chad, he smothered a snicker behind a cough into his fist. As far as he could tell, Cupid's arrow still resided in his special agent's back. Apparently Danielle noticed too. He saw her looking with lively interest from Bettina to Chad. Catching her eye, he raised a brow, and she grinned. Bettina appeared oblivious to the stir she'd created, with eyes only for her brother. Rowan had been unconscious the day before when she'd arrived and again in the morning. The poor thing had sat for hours by his bedside, finally taking a break to eat in the hospital cafeteria.

He'd had a hell of a time explaining to her why Rowan was restrained to his bed with a guard at the door. She'd finally calmed down when he told her that because her brother had shot a federal agent, he simply hadn't been given a choice about the restraints. It was great to see Rowan awake and more alert, so Bettina could talk to him and satisfy herself that he was on the mend. Then, hopefully, he could get her to leave.

Watching his special agent carefully, Ralph frowned. Rowan stared with narrowed eyes at Chad, trying to say something. His voice was scratchy, barely more than a whisper, but still managed an undertone of menace and must have taken colossal effort. *"Stay away from my sister."*

He guffawed and smacked Chad on the back. "Way to go special agent." Still chuckling, he plucked his phone from the cluttered countertop and stuffed it in his jacket pocket. "You three stay here. I need to talk with someone. I'll be back in an hour or so."

Heading for the elevators, he yawned. Chad falling for Bettina was one more thing he hadn't seen coming. Maybe he should consider retirement. Adding to his darkening mood, the two nurses he entered the elevator with didn't respond to his polite "Good afternoon," but glared at him and turned deliberately away. It seemed that the entire nursing staff in the enormous medical center thought he was personally responsible for Rowan's injuries. He set his jaw and ignored them. He couldn't do anything about the nurses, except maybe shoot them. Sadly, that wasn't an option, but thinking about it lightened his mood.

Exiting the elevator on ground floor, he looked around in confusion. He had to find the Emergency Room and Doctor Anderson. If the man would speak to him, which was admittedly doubtful, he was sure the doctor could help him thwart Ainsley's scheme to move Rowan to Quantico. Fifteen minutes of aimless wandering and wrong turns later, he saw the double doors that said TRAUMA FIVE EMERGENCY and pushed through them. The hallway looked familiar and then he remembered, it was the same one the two CIA thugs had come running down, and where he'd met Doctor Anderson. Continuing along, he saw the doctor's office. The door was open. Glancing in, he was relieved to see the doctor at his desk, talking on the phone. It appeared he'd gotten lucky and caught a lull in ER activity.

Taking a tentative step inside the door, he raised a hand in greeting. Doctor Anderson saw him and scowled. "Say, John, a moment please." The doctor held the phone in his hand and gave him a cold stare. "I'm involved in an important conversation. What do you want?"

Hoping his voice conveyed adequate deference, Ralph gave the doctor a brief smile. "Doctor Anderson, I apologize for the interruption, but it's imperative that I speak with you."

The doctor stared at him for a moment longer, shrugged in acquiescence and returned to the phone. "John? I apologize, something's come up that needs my attention here. How about day after tomorrow at noon, does that work for you? Great – we'll continue then. Thanks, John."

Doctor Anderson laid the phone in its berth and looked up at him, gesturing at the empty chair across from the desk. "Close the door and sit down – Special Agent in Charge Johnston, isn't it? My time is limited, regardless of how important your problem may be." The doctor's voice dripped with sarcasm. "Is your prisoner in need of my services? Are you unhappy with the room location? Or are you just concerned about his injuries and how to most quickly get him healed for more interrogation?"

Closing the door, Ralph sat down, ignored the jibes and leaned forward, hands clasped in his lap. What he had to say was deadly serious, and he hoped to God the doctor would be able to appreciate that. Looking intently at the adversary he desperately needed as an ally, he began. "Doctor Anderson, I appreciate your time and let me get straight to the point. The man you treated here is my friend. He is most certainly not a terrorist, although someone has gone to great lengths to create that impression. I was able to circumvent what would have resulted in his death, by obtaining personal custody of him from the CIA by order of the President."

Gathering his thoughts, he focused on the doctor's unfriendly eyes. "Now, my superior has apparently bought into this cabal and is intent on moving Rowan to a military prison, as soon as possible. If he accomplishes that, gets the ear of the President and I lose custody, Rowan will be lost forever. And that, Doctor Anderson, is not going to happen. I intend to take whatever steps are necessary to protect my friend's life."

Various emotions played over the doctor's face. Would the man help him? In a moment of panic he saw himself shooting his way out of the hospital, Rowan tossed over his shoulder. Shaking his head to rid his mind of the bizarre image, he knew he needed a decent night's sleep.

Doctor Anderson still looked skeptical and opened his mouth to speak. Ralph held up both hands to stop him. "No doctor, please. I know how things looked that morning, and I didn't do anything to dispel your concern or redirect your thoughts. What I've told you now is privileged, sensitive information, and I may have put you in danger by asking for your help. Quite honestly, I don't know where else to turn."

Doctor Anderson adjusted his tie, which he noticed was imprinted with tiny American flags. Next the doctor took off his glasses, wiped them absently on the sleeve of his white coat, put them back on, and gazed at him pensively. "Special agent Johnston, please try to understand my concern. It's all well and good that you're telling me this now, but I remember that morning clearly, and your hands and clothes were covered with blood. Call me a cynic, but I can't think how you'd get blood all over you without somehow participating in the damage to Mr. Milani."

Impotent anger coursed through him. He felt the heat rising from his neck to his cheeks. God almighty, he couldn't believe what he was hearing. Taking a measured breath, he decided to drop the formal, polite routine and tell Dr. Anderson just exactly how he'd found his special agent, and let him decide if he'd been complicit in his injuries. Looking up, he spoke in a low, tense voice. "Doctor Anderson, let me tell you what happened to special agent Milani as best I have been able to put together, before he arrived at the hospital."

The good doctor leaned back and folded his hands in front of him on the desk. "Please do."

Seeing the skepticism in the doctor's eyes, he decided not to soft soap anything. "The CIA had evidently been planning, for a period of time, to abduct special agent Milani. They took him to an office tucked away in an old warehouse and placed his cuffed wrists over a sturdy meat hook on the wall, near the ceiling. It was high enough that he must have been on tiptoe. They beat him, ostensibly I believe, to obtain a confession. Rowan's tough and he'd die before confessing to anything, but of course they didn't know that."

Doctor Anderson grimaced, and Ralph noted the revulsion in the man's eyes with satisfaction. Good, he thought savagely, maybe he was getting through to him. Slowly rubbing the stubble on his jaw, he smirked at the doctor. "I know my special agent extremely well and trust me, he didn't take what they were doing quietly. I can only imagine what he may have said and as I'm sure you know, he also shot and injured one of their agents earlier at the hotel. It's a given they'd punish him for that. It's my opinion that after they beat him, they thought he'd come around to their way of thinking if they let him hang for a while. The floor and the wall behind him were splattered with blood, so I know he must have struggled."

Watching the doctor's face, he finished the gory account. "That's how we found him, unconscious and covered in blood, hanging by his wrists. It took both me and special agent Cantor to lift his body off the hook. I held him." He stopped talking and cleared his throat to erase the hoarse emotion from his voice. "I held him in my arms until the paramedics arrived. And that is how I came to be covered with my friend's blood that morning." He blinked once to clear the wetness from his eyes and gazed at the doctor, taking petty pleasure in the horror on the other man's face. Silence filled the office and he could hear the clock on the wall behind the desk ticking away precious seconds.

Doctor Anderson lifted a hand and let it drop back to the desk. "I'm sorry special agent Johnston. I had no idea. Listen, call me Steve. Let's forget the last forty-eight hours and start over. What can I do to help you?"

Relief washed over him in a warm, reviving wave. Thank God he'd gotten through the suspicions and found a reasonable man. "Well, doctor – Steve – I need a reason to insist that my special agent requires care at your medical center, that his condition is too fragile for him to be moved, something I can take to the President to buy me time to figure out what to do," he finished lamely.

The doctor shoved his glasses up and rubbed his hands together. "My main area of concern is his wrists. The soft tissue damage is extensive, he sustained significant trauma to the nerves as I mentioned to you before, and each wrist has several fractures. He has at least a couple fractures in his left foot, also." Ralph watched as his new ally looked at his watch and continued. "One of the most prominent orthopedic trauma surgeons in the country has already looked at his X-rays and is going to be here later this afternoon.

This doctor is a longtime personal friend. I called him immediately after I evaluated Mr. Milani. I've never seen trauma like that and wanted expertise I could count on. He managed to clear his schedule and make travel arrangements. Your friend needs surgery as soon as possible if he's going to regain the use of his hands, and Byron Williams is the best in the country. If anyone can work a miracle, it's him." Steve hesitated and then said, "You can take that to the bank and to the President."

He sagged weakly in the chair. "Thank you, and please, call me Ralph. You know, this could make all the difference. It gives me the time I need to make other arrangements."

Steve smiled. "Don't mention it. I decided to personally manage your special agent's case as soon as I saw him. What you've told me is extremely disturbing, but if there's one thing I've learned over the years, it's the importance of absolute discretion and confidence. I'll help you and Mr. Milani any way I can. We'll come up to examine his wrists as soon as Dr. Williams arrives." The doctor gave him a dark look. "It's hard to believe we could do something like what you described to one of our own citizens. I find that very troubling."

Ralph stepped off the elevator in a more sanguine frame of mind, with renewed energy and determination. Spotting the deputy guarding the door, he pulled the young man aside and sent him home for the rest of the day. Chad sat in the small waiting area at the end of the hall, poring over Rowan's laptop. He found Bettina and Danielle conversing quietly in Rowan's room. They both looked up and smiled as he walked in.

Stepping next to the bed, he looked down at his friend. Rowan's head was turned to the right, which seemed to be his preference, and his eyes were closed. The bruises on his face were cast in sharp relief by a shaft of sunlight, but at least the swelling had gone down. Someone, most likely his nurse, had lowered the head of the bed. Reaching down, he smoothed the black hair and spoke softly. "I bought us more time today, but I need your help, so come on back to me." He turned and left the room, grabbing a cup of coffee from the pot that was always on in the waiting area and snagging the last chocolate chip cookie from the plate food service brought each morning.

Chad glanced up from the laptop with an incredulous look. "Boss, you are not going to believe all the information Rowan had stored on the flash drive I found hidden in his briefcase."

He eyed Chad and munched on the cookie, then took a sip of coffee. "Is there anything we can use to help him or have you gotten into it deeply enough to know?"

Chad shook his head. "Yeah boss, we need to meet privately somewhere. This is an accumulation of extremely sensitive information. If this flash drive had been found, a great amount of intelligence and covert activity would have been compromised, but you know, Rowan said someone betrayed him. It's possible that this information has already been gleaned by whoever's doing this to him, although I can't think how."

Glancing at his watch, Ralph saw that it was four o'clock. "We'll talk more about this later, special agent." The doctor Steve had mentioned would be arriving before long, and he wanted to get the two women out of the picture for a while. Bettina and Danielle agreed to grab a pizza and wine, and camp out at Danielle's house for the evening. They'd only been gone about twenty minutes when the two doctors appeared at the doorway to Rowan's room. The man with Steve had tightly curled gray hair and bright blue eyes. The renowned Doctor Williams, he presumed.

Wiping errant cookie crumbs from his sweater, Ralph approached the two men with a smile. "Hello Steve." Turning to the other man, he held out his hand. "You must be Doctor Williams. I can't thank you enough, sir, for making this trip. My name is Ralph Johnston, and as far as I know, I am still the FBI Special Agent in Charge of this mess."

Doctor Williams gripped his hand and gave it a firm shake. "It's my pleasure to make the trip, nice to meet you and please, call me Byron. Sorry to hear about your man here. If you don't mind, I'd like to make my evaluation of Mr. Milani's injuries and schedule surgery as soon as possible."

Relieved, he waved them through the door. "That would suit me to a T, gentlemen. Please, right this way."

* * *

Rowan watched Ralph and the two doctors warily, wondering what they wanted. The one in the white coat with graying hair and kind eyes behind glasses smiled at him. "Mr. Milani, my name is Doctor Anderson. I treated you when you arrived at the hospital. This is my colleague, Doctor Williams. He specializes in orthopedic injuries. With your permission, he would like to evaluate the trauma you sustained to your wrists and schedule surgery to correct the problems." The doctor turned and fussed with the bed controls. "Let's raise this up a little more so we can have a conversation. Are you able to talk yet?"

Swallowing and trying to clear his throat, he could only manage a scratchy whisper. "Can't move my fingers, because of wrist injuries?" Sweating again, determined not to fall into the abyss of fear and despair, he found himself teetering on the edge. Without the use of his hands, life stretched ahead endlessly with no meaning.

Doctor Williams seemed to sense his distress and spoke soothingly. "Mr. Milani, let's not jump to any conclusions. I'm anxious to take a look at your injuries and do whatever I can to correct the problems we find. I'd like to proceed immediately with my own examination and evaluation, if you feel up to that."

Closing his eyes, he nodded. "Please." Bettina's tearful face swam into his thoughts along with Danielle's strained visage. Opening his eyes, he focused on Ralph and whispered again. "Are Bettina and Danielle gone?"

Ralph looked proud. "I sent them off for an evening of pizza and wine at Danielle's home."

"Oh great." He'd have no more secrets. Bettina would tell Danielle the sordid story of his entire life, or at least the parts she knew about.

Doctor Williams inserted himself back into the conversation. "Mr. Milani, are you in a great deal of pain right now?"

Gazing at the doctor's sympathetic countenance, he didn't know how to describe the depth of the pain, both physical and mental. After a moment of reflection, he whispered. "Some."

Doctor Williams frowned and met his eyes. "Why do I get the feeling you're not telling the whole story? It would probably be best if you were sedated for this evaluation. It will most likely be very painful." The doctor looked at his colleague. "Steve, if you can get his nurse, I'd like to sedate him, add morphine to the mix and take a look right here."

Rowan had to agree with the doctor. Deep sedation was his preferred state of existence. Somehow, surgery on his wrists with no anesthesia didn't compare to the anguish he'd experienced while hanging from the hook. But how could he explain that to the doctors? Their minds couldn't grasp that kind of brutality. Well, his mind was having a hell of a time with it too, and he watched with relief as the nurse inserted the needle into the IV. Feeling the burn of the drugs, he closed his eyes. The darkness welcomed him like an old friend and whisked him away, into peaceful unconsciousness.

Ralph remained at his chosen vantage point, the chair at the end of the bed, head in his hands while the doctors unraveled the carefully bandaged wrists and conferred quietly. Steve began. "The major issue we dealt with was an injured spleen and a tear we found in the diaphragm muscle. We were able to repair both and control the hemorrhaging in order to get him hemodynamically stabilized."

Byron spoke with appreciation in his voice. "You've obviously got a great team here. I can see that the flexor and extensor tendons are involved, unavoidably, I'd say. These nerves received a good deal of pressure, too. It's going to take some time for them to recover from the shock. You've created the best conditions for regeneration, but we need to proceed to surgery right away."

The final comment brought Ralph's head up. With aching sadness he gazed at Rowan again. His tough special agent looked broken and desolate, but at least the anxious tension that inhabited his features had been drugged away. God only knew the nightmares that must occupy his mind, and he wondered if

Rowan would ever recover from the wounds left on his battered psyche. He looked from one sober-faced doctor to the other. "Special agent Milani is an honorable man who has sacrificed generously on behalf of his country. I want to be certain he is well cared for and remains safe. I'll be right outside. This time, when you take him, I'll be with him."

CHAPTER NINE

Ralph gazed tiredly at Chad as they sat in the surgical waiting area for the second time in two days, while Byron Williams turned his phenomenal expertise to saving his special agent's wrists and hands. He hoped the doctor was as good as Steve had assured him he was, because he'd seen the look in Rowan's eyes. His friend wasn't willing to accept a future that didn't include the use of his hands. A tremor fluttered through his body. Pushing the unruly, frightening thoughts away, he tried to focus on his other special agent. "Tell me about the flash drive, Chad."

Chad yawned and blinked at him, fidgeting in the molded plastic chair. "From what I've gathered, Rowan's been living another, completely clandestine life. You know boss, I always joked about his dark personality, but I had no idea he was an assassin. You sure we should be discussing all this stuff here?"

Yawning because his subordinate had and also because he was exhausted, he wiped burning eyes before looking blearily at Chad. "I know about Rowan's covert activities. And I don't know where else to talk. There's no one besides us in here, and I doubt the waiting room is bugged. I don't know about you, but I'm not comfortable with both of us leaving the hospital." He shrugged. "Just give me the essentials of what you found."

Chad leaned back and stretched long legs. "The drive provides a detailed description of literally hundreds of Islamic radicals; background, location and terrorist activities, along with the dates of their elimination. I found another list of names that I've surmised are Rowan's contacts. It's possible, I suppose, that one of those people betrayed him."

Ralph gaped at Chad, suddenly remembering what he had called the *Denver debacle*. "God almighty. I think this whole thing started last month, in Denver."

Chad peered through bloodshot eyes, brow furrowed. "You mean when Rowan got kicked off the plane? I thought that was because of his appearance, as usual."

The rush of adrenaline fired the synapses in his fatigued mind. "Oh no, he got taken off that plane because of an anonymous phone call made to Fred Ralston, saying Rowan had killed two men on the Mexican side of the border, which he had, as part of a black op. I got him the hell out of there before someone higher up decided to investigate."

Chad whistled softly. "I had no idea. Wait, didn't you tell me that the jerk holding you at gunpoint in the hotel said they were taking Rowan to an Egyptian prison?"

Eyes wide, he wondered why he hadn't remembered that. But there'd been no time to sit and contemplate anything. "Yes, he did. The son of a bitch told me Rowan was headed straight to an Egyptian prison. But what does that say about Ainsley, wanting to move Rowan to Quantico? Is he involved in this? I'll never trust that sucker again."

Chad clamped a hand on his arm. "Boss, we've got to do something. We've got to get Rowan out of here. If you lose custody of him for some trumped up reason, he'll be gone. We won't know where he is or what they've done with him. For all we know, Ainsley could send him to Quantico, only to have the CIA rendition him from there. We can't let that happen."

Washing a hand over his face, he stared at Chad. "I know. But we can't do anything until Rowan's out of the woods. I bought some time today with Doctor Anderson, but we need to be prepared to act as soon as we can. Until then, one of us has to be here, armed and ready for anything. I have no idea how long it'll be before Rowan's recovered enough for us to move him. And I have no idea where on God's green earth we can take him."

Wondering if Chad had considered all the angles, he captured the younger man's gaze. "Son, there is one more thing. If we do this, you know we're going to be wanted for aiding and abetting.

We'll be hiding right along with Rowan. We're saying good-bye to our careers if we continue along this path."

His subordinate's response pleased him mightily. "You know that Rowan means more to me than my career ever could." Chad stretched and yawned again, then gave him a sad smile. "My mother's been in an Alzheimer's facility in DC for going on seven years and my father spends all his time lobbying. First, it was from Pierre, but he lives in a condo in Georgetown now. I'm not sure why he even keeps the house in Sioux Falls anymore. Maybe for me . . . In a way it's still home. But anyway, you and Rowan are as much my family as my parents are. And Bettina's going to be my family too, eventually."

Nonplussed by Chad's final statement, he scratched his chin. "OK, I guess congratulations are in order. Does Bettina know this?"

Color crept up Chad's neck and stained his cheeks. "She doesn't know yet, but I fell in love with her the instant I laid eyes on her. Rowan would have my ass if he knew, but one day he'll understand."

Chuckling, he patted Chad's shoulder. "Don't worry. Rowan knows. Why do you think he gave you the evil eye and told you to stay away from his sister? You've got to understand, Rowan's trying to protect Bettina from the likes of you, the guy who got the scoop, so to speak, from Mandy and who went out with that crazy bitch from the airport. What was her name? Oh yeah, Marta."

Chad stared at him. "Uh, how did you know about Mandy?"

Still chuckling at his special agent's discomfiture, he stood up. "You two guys think I'm old and senile, but I get around, son. Not much got by me, until now. I could never, in my worst nightmare, have imagined this scenario."

Chad crossed his arms and frowned. "I did get into Marta's computer like we planned and set it up so I'd receive her emails on my system at home. It might be worthwhile for me to check those out. And for the record, I did not sleep with her. She's creepy and I'm not into that."

In the middle of a stretch, he smiled. "Good for you. If you want to, head home tonight and take a look at her emails. They're probably worthless to us, but hell, you never know. I don't want to take anything for granted."

Chad exhaled heavily. "Me either. Things spun out of control so fast, I don't know if we're coming or going. All I've thought about is Rowan, and Bettina." Chad looked at him, mouth and eyes round. "Boss, we can't have Bettina and Danielle up here all the time. If something goes down, we can't be responsible for the two of them and Rowan and ourselves. Now that I think about it, Danielle shouldn't be here at all. The last thing she needs is to be identified with Rowan."

Hands on hips, he gazed at Chad. "For now, I think we're all right with Danielle being here. She's damned important to Rowan. God knows he's lost everything, so let's not take her away from him, too."

Chad's kind face drooped. "Yeah, OK. I'll talk to Danielle and let her know we may need to pull her access to Rowan on short notice so she'll be prepared. And much as I hate to say it, Bettina should go home."

Nodding at Chad, he slumped back down in the uncomfortable chair. "It sounds to me like you've got things well in hand, so I'm going to lean against this nice wall and take a nap. Wake me when the doc comes out."

Chad grunted his assent, so he leaned back and closed his eyes. A huge yawn overtook him. He covered his mouth with his fist, twisted uncomfortably and settled in to wait.

Chad unlocked the door and stepped inside the house. Weary and ready to sleep, he decided he'd better take a quick look at Marta's emails before he went to bed. Trudging into his office and sliding into a chair at his desk, he yawned and touched the mouse, bringing the screen to life. Forty-five minutes later he stared transfixed at the last of the damning emails, flickering in front of him.

Muusa Shemal, the Egyptian national, the man Rowan had been suspicious of had put the wheels in motion. It had to be the tip of an iceberg. And why had Muusa Shemal zeroed in on Rowan? The emails Marta had sent and the replies from the man made his blood run cold. The wily jihadist considered Rowan his *prize* and must be insane. He thought to turn on the printer and begin making hard copies of the emails. Ralph needed to see them and so did Rowan.

Fresh enthusiasm fired in his weary mind. This could be the lifeline they needed, to begin figuring out why his friend had been targeted for destruction. In the morning he needed to call his father. The conversation with Ralph had spawned seeds of a solution to their problem, had reminded him of a place that existed, where he hadn't been in years. He'd never wanted to go back, not after Alzheimer's claimed his mother. The memories were too painful. But now, he leaned back in the chair and sighed. It would take some time to open the place up and check it out. It might need repairs, but the secluded spot he had in mind would be a perfect place to hide not just Rowan, but all of them, if necessary.

Janice Milani threaded her way carefully along the beach to her favorite spot, a broad igneous rock that stood watch at the edge of the Pacific like a massive sentinel. She liked to think of it as her hiding place and had spent many hours seated on its table-like top thinking and praying through whatever life cast her way. Reaching the rock, she sidled onto it and sat with hands flat on the warm surface, knees bent as she gazed across the water to the horizon.

Being here calmed her troubled mind like nothing else. And Lord knew it needed calming today. Wiping away the tears sliding down her cheeks, she leaned forward and wrapped her arms around her knees. With thick, curling black hair and a smooth face, everyone said she looked younger than fifty-five, but every year was showing today, of that she was sure.

She'd grown up a good Catholic girl and then totally blown it, at least according to her raucous, opinionated Italian family by first marrying, of all people, Khalil Milani. Secondly, she'd ditched Catholicism for personal salvation and a relationship with Jesus. That had likely been harder on her family than marrying an immigrant from Iran. Sitting back and lifting her head to the sun she smiled, thinking back to the first time she'd taken her handsome Iranian boyfriend home with her for a weekend. That he had stayed after that experience attested to the depth of his commitment and love for her.

While Khalil attended college and pursued a career as an electrical engineer, she poured her creative energy into growing flowers, tending the Iranian style courtyard garden they built in the backyard of their home, and raising their two children. The four of them had always had so much fun. Bowing her head, she closed her eyes, willing her mind to quietness. The waves rushed, broke and roared, gulls called, and she felt occasional spray on her cheeks, mingling with the tears she couldn't stop.

She pictured Rowan in her mind's eye as she'd last seen him, the summer of 2001. He'd stopped by the house with secret happiness spilling over, thrilled to show them his fiancée's engagement ring. It had been breathtakingly beautiful; a square-cut diamond that sparkled with deep fire, a full two carats atop a platinum band inset with sapphires.

She'd never seen her son so happy and to her sorrow, she had never seen him since. After 9/11, he refused steadfastly to come home, and it was her fault. Striving to be a good Christian, she'd told him that God would punish him for living in sin with his fiancée. Covering her face, unable to believe the horror she'd perpetrated on her son, she despaired of the cutting, self-righteous words that still echoed in her mind. *Remember Rowan? I told you, you can't mock God. This is your fault. You reap what you sow. If you hadn't chosen to break His laws, God wouldn't have allowed Michelle to die on 9/11.* All her regret couldn't heal the pain she'd caused and the chasm she'd created between them.

Thankfully, she'd grown beyond the insidious, blinding, self-righteous pride. But it was too late. Rowan had never been home again and only spoke to her when necessary. She smiled sadly. When she spoke with him on the phone he treated her with kindness, which was more than she deserved, but it was the distant, empty sort he'd give a stranger. But that was the past. She couldn't change it and needed to concentrate on today. Even though her son rejected her, and with good reason, she still needed to pray for him.

Muusa Shemal slammed his phone shut and tossed it on the table, cursing. The stupid swine, greedy for their own revenge, they'd nearly killed Rowan Milani. Clenching his fists, he fought to control his fury. That was to be his privilege. His alone. Striding angrily to the kitchen of his London flat, he lifted the teapot from the stove, added water, and lit the flame beneath it.

Reaching for a cup, his moist, shaking fingers couldn't hold onto the fine china. The cup clattered noisily to the countertop. Wiping his hands on a towel, he sat it upright and dug a tea bag from the collection he kept in a bowl. Eyes narrowed, mouth a grim line, he stared at the rain spattering the tiny window behind the sink.

Somehow, the ghost agent had learned his identity and had his travel records, going back several years, in his possession when he was captured. Rowan Milani was diabolically cunning, more than even he had realized, which only increased the great respect he had for the man who was now his captive, unaware that though he lay in an American hospital, the shackles on his legs were at his insistence.

He had made it unalterably clear that when Rowan Milani was apprehended, he must be secured. The man had a preternatural ability to slip away, and he wanted to be sure that the crafty jinn would not somehow escape. He lived for the coming day, when he'd gaze into his prisoner's kafir eyes and see terror burgeon and flourish as he taught him about retribution for all the warriors he'd slaughtered.

Raising his hands to Allah, he marched to the cramped front room and watched the traffic on the street outside the rain streaked window. If the ghost agent had studied the pattern of his travels, who knew what else he may have surmised? The Brotherhood's *Project*, centered in the sleeper cells he'd worked so diligently to plant, nurture and teach for many years, was at risk as long as Rowan Milani remained in the United States.

Shaking his fist in frustration, he considered the two men he'd hired. The CIA fools were his errand boys, sent to procure and deliver his prisoner, nothing more. And now their misguided zeal threatened his entire plan. He tugged at his shirt collar and opened another button. The heat of anger left him sweating, heart palpitating crazily in his chest. As the teapot whistled, he returned to the kitchen, switched off the flame, and poured boiling water over the tea. Inhaling the wafting steam, he hoped the jasmine would calm his mind.

He'd given his life to Allah, recruiting, teaching and preparing for jihad across the heartland of America, the death blow that would slice the belly of the Beast and bleed it to death. The Brotherhood had worked quietly for many years to achieve their goals. Nothing would deter them. Rowan Milani's activities had only increased his sense of urgency. The ghost agent must be renditioned to Egypt, before the clever man could prove his own innocence, and indict him.

Stroking his black hair with one hand, he carried the delicate cup in his other as he continued his restless march around the flat. An extensive trip was in the offing, to rejoice with the faithful around the country. Sitting at his desk, he leaned back and closed his eyes, willing his quivering muscles to stillness. *All praise to Allah, forever.* It would be as he intended, the conqueror and the vanquished, together for as long as he, the conqueror, wanted the vanquished to live, and suffer.

Opening a battered tin on his desk, he scooped from the mound of Turkish tobacco, carefully rolled it in thin parchment, licked the fragile paper and gently pinched it closed. Striking a wooden match, he lit the fragrant tobacco, inhaling deeply. He burned the life from the crackling leaves, just as he would extinguish the life of Rowan Milani. Closing his eyes, he smiled as Allah's peace entered his soul at last.

Chad looked down into the inscrutable eyes and thought he'd die. Saying good-bye to Bettina hurt more than he'd ever imagined possible. Feeling guilty because her brother needed to be his first priority, he wanted more than anything to board the plane with her and fly away from every responsibility. At least he'd been able to spend one night with her. They'd had dinner at the same restaurant Danielle had recommended to Rowan. And it had been marvelous. He didn't have the flair for special effects that his colleague possessed, but he and Bettina sat for hours in the cozy booth. Afterward he'd taken her to his home and into his bed. They'd enjoyed each other's bodies, made love and to his utter delight, agreed to begin a long-distance relationship.

Bettina reached up and cupped his cheek in her warm hand. At five feet six inches, she wasn't exactly short, but he was almost a foot taller. Her red lips quivered. "Thanks for caring so much for Rowan. It helps to know you're with him. And uh, I can't, I mean, it's hard to say good-bye."

Bettina sniffled, her eyes filling with tears as he folded her into his arms. Overcome with a fierce desire to protect her, he closed his eyes, held her tight and bent over to murmur into her hair. "I know. I don't want to say good-bye either. But you can

144

call me anytime. And I'll let you know how Rowan's doing every day. Maybe in a couple months I can fly out to California, or you can come back here."

Releasing her just enough to kiss her, he concentrated on the soft fullness of her lips. When she slid her arms around him beneath his jacket, he shivered with pleasure. Deepening the kiss, trying to mold her body to his with his hands, he forgot where they were until the overhead announcement of United's arrival from Chicago brought him back to reality. Whoa, he'd better cool it before someone told them to get a room, and that would be all right with him.

Bettina had a dreamy expression on her face that pleased him, made him feel like he'd accomplished something. She gazed up at him. "Oh Chad, I don't want to go. This is too hard."

Looking into her dark eyes, he remembered how he'd always laughed at the maudlin, teary-eyed couples mooning around airports. Remaining footloose and free, he'd thought of himself as the superior being. Not anymore. "Bettina, this is it. I'm going to miss you, but we gotta do this. Good-bye, honey. I love you. Now go, before you miss your plane. Call me when you land, so I know you're home safe." He gathered her in his arms one last time, kissed her hard, and let her go.

Before she could react, he stuffed his hands in the pockets of his bomber jacket, smiled at her stricken face, and walked away. He heard quick footsteps and felt a hand on his arm. Bettina pulled him around. "I love you too, Chad. Bye." Tears streaming, she fled to the escalator. As he watched her ascend, she wiped her cheeks and waved. Then she was gone, drawn into the crush of people making their way through the security checkpoint.

Feeling desolate, he slouched through the main entryway and out the double doors. Even the red Mustang didn't lift his spirit. Until Rowan recovered and they'd taken down Muusa Shemal and whatever organization had targeted his friend for destruction, none of them could relax or even consider a normal existence.

Not for the first time since the nightmare had begun, he felt weary, exhausted and at his wits end.

CHAPTER TEN

One Month Later – First Week In April

Ralph woke with a start. His left foot had slipped off the narrow cot and was dangling in the chilly air. He pulled on the blanket, uncovering his other foot. Rubbing gritty eyes, he decided to get up since he needed to use the bathroom anyway. The cold floor made him shiver, but at least he was smart enough to wear socks, he thought righteously, glancing at Rowan's bed. Sunlight poured into the room, making a shiny pool of light on the tiled floor, but it held no warmth. It must be the gray walls, or maybe the absence of pictures. The dry erase boards covered with writing and numbers didn't do much for the ambience in the cluttered hospital room.

Scratching his belly, he thought about standing up. Every morning found him so stiff he could barely move until he'd hobbled around for ten minutes. He scowled and planted his hands on the edge of the cot, grunting his way to an awkward, standing position. At least he'd made it out of the cot without upending the damn thing, like he'd done the day before. His right hip bone still hurt from that escapade. His wife Marion had laughed out loud when he'd told her. He'd spank her sweet behind for that, if he ever got to go home again.

Still sore, he stepped over to check on Rowan. The surgery had been successful and Doctor Williams had told both him and Rowan in great detail what he'd done. How much his friend had absorbed was debatable, but he'd taken extensive notes and Doctor Anderson checked in every day to answer his questions. The best news was that both doctors agreed that with proper rehabilitation, Rowan would regain most if not complete use of his hands. The relief in his special agent's eyes was overwhelming and he was relieved too, more than he'd ever admit.

He looked down at Rowan again, sleeping with his head turned as usual to the right. The bruises on his face and body had faded. Still, he'd lost weight and looked like hell. Leaning on the cold bed rails, Ralph ruminated over his special agent for a moment longer, marveling at how the younger man maintained a cold, distant demeanor, day after day. For someone like Rowan, with towering self-assurance and more than a smidgeon of arrogance, it must be hell to depend on nurses for everything he needed. That wasn't about to change either, because the casts on both arms started at his fingers and went damn near to his elbows. His left foot was encased in a cast as well. The CIA bastard had fractured three bones in the foot he'd stomped on.

The shrill ringing of his phone shattered his melancholy reverie. Limping to the cot where he'd left it lying on the floor, he bent painfully to retrieve it. He'd be damned if it wasn't Ainsley. What did he want at eight-thirty in the morning? "Johnston," he answered tersely.

"Good morning, Ralph. How are things in South Dakota? How's our prisoner coming along after a month of recovery?" Ainsley's voice held an undertone of urgency, which raised his suspicions.

"Well, good morning, sir. It would appear we're going to have spring in South Dakota. It's a balmy morning, and we've got a good weather forecast for the entire week. And our prisoner is progressing quite well."

Ainsley laughed. "That's great news. We have nothing to prevent us from moving Hassani to Quantico, where he can be safely incarcerated."

The bottom fell out of his morning, and he hadn't even made it to the john. Ainsley's voice held a temerity that made him uneasy. Clearly, his boss thought he had one up on him. "You might be rushing things, sir. The surgery went well, but rehab is going to take some time with this. We're talking months." He stopped abruptly, with the ugly certainty that he was speaking to a brick wall.

Ainsley's voice turned hard, edged with a cruelty he'd never heard from his boss. "Now Ralph, let's speak candidly. Rehabilitation is not our first priority with this man. This isn't the special agent you thought you knew. This is an international terrorist. Screw the suspected shit. I've had confirmation of that from intelligence the CIA gathered independently of my sources. I don't give a good goddamn whether he recuperates or not, and frankly, neither should you. I've spoken to the President about this Ralph. He concurs."

Ah, the one up. Barely holding his temper, he pinched the bridge of his nose. How could he make Ainsley think he was still onboard his fucked up train? He had to be extremely careful. After speaking with the President a week ago, they'd decided to wait and see about moving Rowan anywhere. Now it appeared that Ainsley had weaseled his way in and convinced the President he knew what he was talking about.

"Well sir, since you put it like that, what can I say?" He affected a hearty chuckle. "Honestly, it would be a tremendous relief for both me and special agent Cantor to wash our hands of this entire operation. We have apparently apprehended the terrorist masterminding the operation we were here to circumvent. The fact that he so effectively infiltrated the FBI explains why we had such a hard time making any headway." Waving an arm wildly, he rolled his eyes. "All in all, sir, I believe you are quite astute in your perceptions, and I think we've effectively cut the head off the snake." Sweat soaked his armpits. How had he done?

Ainsley spoke decisively. "Let's get this done. Much as it pains me, the CIA wants the glory. They've been extremely upset that you had the ear of the President and were able to transfer custody. In two days, the team of agents that apprehended

Hassani in the first place will arrive in Sioux Falls and make the transfer via an Agency jet. That way, they get the media splash they crave, while you and special agent Cantor get to go home for a month's leave. How's that sound to you?"

Suddenly dizzy, he lurched across the room. His mouth went dry, his heart pounded, and he wasn't sure he could speak. Spying a half glass of water on the bedside table, he tossed it back like scotch and spawned a coughing fit. Sputtering, he wiped his streaming eyes and dripping nose on the back of his hand. "Sorry, sir," he managed to rasp. "That's the best news I've heard in months. Your assistance in resolving this once and for all is greatly appreciated by both special agent Cantor and me."

His boss chuckled. "Great Ralph, you get to work pacifying the doctors. Make them think we'll be following up with rehab on this end. Keep Hassani secured and you'll be relieved of the whole mess in a couple days. Bye now, I'll be in touch."

Ralph barely spoke to the deputy standing guard as he stepped out the door. He and Chad needed to act. Now. The aroma of fresh coffee got his attention, but when he poured from the pot his hands shook. Feeling dazed, he took a slurp of the hot liquid and wandered back into Rowan's room. Slouching into his usual spot at the end of the bed, he sat the coffee cup on the floor and bowed his head, covering his face with his hands. How in the hell were they going to stop the CIA from taking Rowan? This time they had the President's go ahead. The sequence of events he and Chad had discussed over and over again was about to overtake them.

He heard Rowan stirring and looked up. The nurses had already raised his bed so he was sitting up partway and his eyes were open. "Morning, Rowan, how are you feeling?" His endangered special agent appeared to be thinking it over. Think fast, he wanted to say, because we're running out of time. Not waiting for an answer, he took a gulp of coffee. "Rowan, we have a big problem. I am going to get dressed and call special agent

Cantor. The three of us are going to have a meeting, and we are going to end that meeting with a plan to get you out of here, within the next twenty-four hours. I'll explain why when he gets here. If you have any ideas son, we need them now, or your world is going to turn to big-time shit. I'm leaving now so your nurses can get you all prettied up for our meeting." He smiled at Rowan, knew that would piss him off, then turned and walked out.

Rowan watched his boss's receding back and frowned. Something must have upset Ralph acutely, because he was pale, for God's sake. They were going to have a meeting. What had Ralph said? His world would turn to big-time shit? Could it get much worse? Running his right foot along his left leg, he nudged the ever present leg irons and the chain, which remained padlocked to the bed frame. He hated the constant reminder that he was a prisoner of his own government, enmeshed in a cleverly woven web of lies, all playing on the subterfuge he'd committed for that same government, enhanced and made believable because of his Iranian heritage.

During the last month, as he'd reluctantly left the beguiling peace and darkness of unconsciousness and been dragged back into the land of the living, he'd tried to come to terms with his situation. Shifting around on the bed, he wiggled his fingers and wished he could scratch himself. But lifting either of his arms hurt like hell. Giving up on getting comfortable, he sighed and thought about the endless nights. The beating he'd endured had done a number on him. At least once every night he woke up sweating and shaking, the leering faces of the two CIA agents swirling through his mind.

Sometimes when he woke up he smelled blood and felt it, thick and warm on his arms. And every day he dreaded the humiliating therapy that involved removal of the leg irons so a physical therapist could make him exercise his legs while the guard stood in the room with his pistol drawn. When they finished, Ralph would step forward, heave a deep sigh, and place the shackles back on his legs. The sound of the cold metal clicking closed around his ankles left him panic-stricken, filled with helpless terror.

Then there were the nurses. Their cheery familiarity grated worse than anything. They had to do everything for him, and goddamn it, they seemed to enjoy it. At first he refused to eat, but they badgered him, wore down his resistance until he gave up and let them feed him, brush his teeth and bathe his body. But it killed him inside.

Gazing out the window at the grayish brown terrain and still dead trees, he thought about Danielle. He hung his head and closed his eyes as a wave of longing rolled over him. It was time for him to say good-bye, like he'd promised. She wouldn't want to hear that, but he had to do it. Associating with him was detrimental to her future. His life had come to an abrupt halt, but hers stretched ahead, and hell, maybe she'd learn to love that jerk she lived with. The last thing she needed was him.

His thoughts turned again to the two CIA thugs and Muusa Shemal, the Egyptian man who seemed to be the linchpin in the organized effort to destroy his life. He had reasoned, during the long nights, that it must be because of the jihadists he'd killed. The canny Egyptian had obviously purchased influence high up in the Intelligence agencies because Ainsley remained convinced that he was a double agent.

Surely the President knew he would not betray his country. But the President couldn't intervene, because there were too many sovereign foreign governments involved and too much intelligence that would be compromised. Besides, the world could never know that America's President had sanctioned all the assassinations he'd carried out on foreign soil in the name of national security.

Now that he could think with a semblance of clarity, he knew he had to act – and quickly, to get himself out of the FBI's custody and out of the reach of the CIA. Hopefully he hadn't waited too long. His two most trusted friends, Gabriel Hernandez and Michael Cristo, former Army Rangers, part of the black ops team sworn to serve along with him, were his only hope for rescue. It was essential that he call them, right away.

Thinking about the two men made him smile. Michael was the taller, stretching north of six feet by several inches, catlike and graceful with black hair, blue eyes and a reckless grin often fatally mistaken for a lack of discipline. Gabriel, by contrast, was a solid six feet of brute strength. Brooding and intense, he was a first generation American from south of the border. Brown-eyed with thick black hair curling beneath his ears and sporting a thin moustache, they called him their Mexican Muscle.

Two nurses walked in and he sighed. Eyes closed, jaws clenched, he steeled himself for the morning ritual, trying to send his mind elsewhere as they began his care. Without warning he saw Danielle the first time he'd met her, wearing those damned black pants and sweater, looking so sexy it drove him crazy. Swallowing hard, he tried desperately to think of something, anything else. After what seemed like an eternity, the nurses were finished. When he opened his eyes, Chad was walking in, with Ralph on his heels. Looking at his boss, he read the concern and alarm on his face and wondered again what the hell was coming.

Staring at him, hands on hips, Ralph waited until the nurses had left, shutting the door behind them. "All right, here's the thing. Ainsley called this morning, and he is handing you back to the CIA. The same agents that abducted you are flying here in two days to transport you to Quantico."

Stark terror reared its ugly head. He felt like he'd been sucker punched. Taking a deep breath, he knew it was past time to act. "I do have a way out of this." He hesitated, looking from Ralph to Chad and back again. "Since shortly after September 11, 2001 I've worked with two men. We've been together in some tough places. We all know how the political winds blow. Times change and because of that, we put a plan in place to deal with a situation like this." Considering for a moment, he shrugged. "Not exactly like this, but close enough."

Ralph looked at him, waving a hand in his direction. "Would you please tell us what this plan entails?"

The rapidly escalating situation would soon be out of his friend's purview. Looking at Ralph, he spoke resolutely. "A phone call from me will put an extraction plan into motion. The two men I mentioned will arrange transport to a secure, secret location within forty-eight hours. They will control the scenario. We'll just play along. Neither you nor Chad will have knowledge of the location or the identities of either man." Looking from one to the other, he tried to smile. "It's that simple, problem solved. I can make the call right now."

Ralph frowned. "That's it? You fall off the face of the earth, and we have no contact and no way of knowing where you are or what has happened to you?"

Frustration rising, he tried to explain what he thought his boss should already understand, that it was imperative he disappear. "Come on Ralph, you know as well as I do, we can't have it any other way. My colleagues are professionals, they know what to do, how to handle this."

Ralph stared at him. "Are you damn certain you trust these two, that they aren't going to transport you right back into the loving arms of the CIA?"

Gazing at Ralph, he could see that his plan was tearing his friend apart. "Boss, let's face reality." Giving Chad a quick look and then turning back to Ralph, he laid it out for them. "My career as an FBI special agent is over. My name and face have been plastered on every cable station and network on the planet as an international terrorist. Frankly, I don't see any other solution to the problem. I've put my life in the hands of these two men on a continual basis for most of the last ten years. There's no one I trust more."

Immediate hurt appeared in Ralph's eyes as the older man sat down heavily in his usual chair. Glancing again at Chad, who stood listening silently with arms crossed, Rowan continued. "I would trust either of you with my life. You know that. The two of you saved my life in this godforsaken place, and I owe you both a debt of gratitude I may never be able to repay and will damn sure never forget. But can't you see? I don't want to take you two down with me. If there is any whiff of involvement by either of you, your careers are as dead as mine and I won't let that happen." He gave each one a grim stare, hoping they'd realize that their reality was the same one in which he'd been so artfully ensnared. "Let me make the call, and I'll fill you both in on the details."

Catching the look on Ralph's face, he raised a brow, gave his friend an arrogant smirk and loaded his voice with sarcasm. "Boss – well, not anymore. You're the one who keeps talking about how much you need my fucking input, so take it."

His words and tone had the desired effect. Ralph slapped his hands on his knees and jumped up from the chair at the end of the bed. "Come on, special agent Cantor. Let's find some breakfast while this plan gets put into motion." Ralph turned on his heel and walked out of the room. Chad shrugged at him, mouthed *thanks a lot,* and followed Ralph from the room.

Heaving a ragged sigh, he let his head sink into the pillow and closed his eyes, weary of the exchange, wondering where Michael and Gabriel would take him and wishing he could somehow escape the never-ending nightmare his life had become. Opening his eyes, looking from the phone on the bedside table to his hands, he managed a bitter laugh. He couldn't make the call, because he couldn't pick up the phone. As soon as Ralph quit pouting and came back to the room, he'd put the next chapter of his ruined life into motion.

The door opened and closed and he looked up, expecting Chad and Ralph, but it was Danielle and his heart sank even further.

Her cheeks were pink, and she'd stuffed the long red hair he loved into a ponytail. She carried two covered cups of Starbucks coffee and sat them on the bedside table while she slipped out of her light jacket. "Hi Rowan. It's a gorgeous spring day and I brought you some coffee. Are you all right?"

The smile faded as she stared at him and he hated what he had to do. He'd been a fool, or too drugged to figure it out earlier, but now he needed to get her out of danger. "Thanks for bringing coffee." How could he tell her that after today she'd never see him again?

Giving him an uneasy smile, Danielle held the cup to his lips while he took a long swallow. It had cooled off, but still tasted great. And now he'd better get on with it. "Ah, I needed that. Danielle, do you remember when you asked me to promise to say good-bye when I had to leave?"

Pausing mid sip, eyes huge, she nodded and he watched the ponytail bounce up and down. "Yes, of course I remember."

Agonizing pain gripped his chest while he gazed into the depths of her worried eyes. "Well, unfortunately, I have to tell you good-bye and I can't, I mean I don't know." God, he was such a coward.

Danielle's face paled and her hands shook, holding the coffee. "Rowan, just be honest with me. Please tell me what's going on."

He swallowed and tried to breathe through the pain in his chest. He owed it to her to be strong. "OK, it's like this. I need to disappear before the CIA or FBI hauls me out of here for prosecution. Sometime in the next day or so, I'll just be gone. You'll hear about it on TV. Even I don't know where, but it'll be a safe location." There, he'd said it. Would she get the finality?

Instead of talking, Danielle gave him another swallow of coffee. Then she sat down beside him, leaned over and kissed him, lips so tender he forgot, for a couple minutes, about the direness of the situation confronting him. When she pulled away, he wanted to beg her not to stop. She smiled at him, fingers gentle on his cheek. "Rowan, take me with you. I'll be happy anywhere, as long as I'm with you. There's nothing to hold me here. I've been thinking about leaving the airline industry anyway."

That was the very last thing he'd expected her to say. Seeing the despair in her eyes made it damn near impossible for him to keep talking. "The thing is, I can't. It'll be dicey at best to get me out of here, and I can't put you in that kind of danger. The bottom line is this. When you walk out of here today, we'll most likely never see each other again. And that's for the best, for you. Trust me, I'll never forget you. And you'll be free to move on with your life, whatever you have in mind." Looking at her face, he knew he'd gotten through, in a big way.

Danielle sat hunched over on the edge of the bed next to him, her body trembling. When she looked at him, he could see determination mingling with terrible pain. "You can't tell me I'm never going to see you again. Oh my God. I hate this so much. I know it's stupid for me to ask you to take me with you. But all I want is to be with you. And someday, I will be. I refuse to believe anything else." Putting her hands over her face, she slumped over onto his chest. Then she wiggled around until she was snuggled up next to him with her head beneath his shoulder, one arm holding him tight.

The warmth of her body next to his took his breath away. He wished he could tell her how much she meant to him, but the words wouldn't come. The lump in his throat hurt, and he could only whisper. "I'm sorry. It's just, there's no other way."

She sat up, stared at him and spoke in a brittle, emotionless voice. "Let me give you another sip of coffee before I go. Oh, and I brought you something. It's nothing really, just a gift I wanted you to have." Her voice cracked, but her sweet lips made a hard line as she continued. "I'll leave it here for you to open later."

He gulped the coffee she held to his lips, unable to think past the pain of losing her. Nodding, he attempted a smile, a mistake. Clenching his jaws to keep from breaking down, he took a deep breath and held it. His eyes were wet, but he couldn't do anything about that. Letting the breath out slowly, he gazed at her. "Thanks, I'll have Chad help me with it when he comes back."

"OK, that will work out just fine." All business, she stood up, pulled on her jacket, took a small, wrapped package out of one of the pockets, and placed it on the table. "It isn't much, but I thought you might like it." Her face a hard mask, she looked him in the eye. "Good-bye for now, Rowan. I love you." Before he could answer, she left, even flinging the curtain closed so he couldn't watch her leave the room.

He closed his eyes as the pain and desolation washed over him. "Good-bye, Danielle. I love you too." Now he didn't care what happened to him. The CIA or FBI could have him, interrogate him until hell froze over and then execute him and put him out of his misery. He'd never felt more like dying, not since September 11, 2001.

Chad wandered back into Rowan's room. Tugging the curtain open, he looked at his colleague, and thought he was sleeping. Rowan's eyes were closed, but when he coughed discreetly, they flew open. They were red-rimmed and he saw deep sadness for an instant, then the cold, distant look took over, and Rowan raised a brow. "Is Ralph still pouting?"

Chuckling, he took a seat in what he had come to think of as Ralph's chair. "You hit him damn hard. I thought he was going to break down and cry after we left. But you made him so mad all he could do was cuss."

Rowan looked at him and sighed. "He'll get over it. But hey, Chad, I have a favor to ask."

Hands clasped together between his knees, he gazed down the length of the bed. "What do you need? You know I'll do anything I can."

Rowan wiggled his fingers and stared at them while he spoke. "I'd be indebted to you for life if you would dial the phone for me and hold it to my ear so I can talk."

He chuckled again. "Shit, Rowan, we walked right out of this room an hour ago, and it never occurred to either of us." His voice trailed off at the look on his friend's face. Jumping up, he stepped to the bedside table and grabbed the phone. "What's the number? Are you sure you want to use this phone?"

"No one can trace the number or the phone I'm calling." Rowan recited the number in a monotone voice as Chad punched the key pad. Giving his friend a perfunctory smile, he held the phone and waited silently. Finally Rowan spoke. "Ghost Rider." An animated voice responded and Rowan frowned with concentration. One brow went up, his mouth opened and closed and he said, "All right, sounds good."

Chad waited a few moments, watching the changing emotions, still holding the phone at his friend's ear. "You finished?"

Rowan dragged empty eyes to meet his and replied in a weary voice. "Yeah, I'm sorry. Thanks for your help. If you don't mind, I'm going to check out for a while. It's been a long day already." With that, his soon to be ex-colleague closed his eyes and appeared to drift immediately to sleep.

Doctor Steve Anderson sat in his tiny office, gathering his file on Rowan Milani. His sister Georgia had called from northwest South Dakota. She lived with her husband Frank on a 20,000 acre, windswept ranch abutting the Cheyenne River Indian Reservation, where they raised cattle and buffalo. Shaking his head, he smiled to himself. To him, it was the middle of nowhere, but they called it God's Country and loved it. A couple times a year he visited, usually for a prairie dog shooting party, but only in the summer. Winters were brutal.

Georgia was a registered nurse and Frank a retired surgeon who'd served as an Army doctor in Desert Storm. Now they operated a medical clinic on the edge of the reservation. Georgia wanted copies of all the information he had, all the tests they had done, as well as the CT scan on special agent Milani. In addition to nursing, his sister freelanced for a disparate group of magazines. She planned to research what had happened to his patient while in CIA custody for a possible magazine article.

The CT scan results lying on his desk caught his eye and he lifted the top film to the light, squinting at the images. No, it couldn't be, they wouldn't have missed that, would they? He shoved his glasses up and concentrated, realizing with dismay that according to his own CT scan, Rowan Milani had torn rotator cuffs in not one, but both shoulders. Why hadn't he complained about the pain? It had been over a month and the man had to be suffering. Clutching the film in his hand, he headed out the door.

Rowan lay with his eyes closed, body rigid. When he'd told Ralph and Chad it would be forty-eight hours before he could be extracted by his colleagues, he hadn't known what had already transpired. Michael had been beside himself. *Why the hell haven't you called? You have no idea the mess you're in. The Imams on the Islamic websites are issuing fatwas calling for your public beheading. Muusa Shemal has those two CIA agents in his back pocket. They're going to execute an extraordinary rendition right here on American soil and send you to Tora Prison in Egypt. Then the Muslim Brotherhood plans to auction your sorry ass to the highest bidder.*

We're already in Sioux Falls. We've been here for three days getting organized and it's going down tonight. The CIA is going to take you, but we'll be there. It won't happen like they think. We've reconnoitered and we have our own plan in place, so be ready, my brother.

While he lay there sweating and thinking about extraordinary rendition, Egyptian prisons and beheading, he shivered. What if the CIA agents got there before Michael and Gabriel expected them? Ainsley had told Ralph the CIA planned to move him in two days, but he must have been lying. Was Ainsley in collusion with the CIA or with Muusa Shemal? He didn't know and he'd never been more frightened at his complete helplessness.

A hand touched his shoulder and he started violently, opening his eyes to see Doctor Anderson frowning at him. Concentrating on getting a hold of his crashing emotions, he deliberately slowed his breathing and hoped he could speak. "Doctor Anderson, I'm sorry, I have nightmares sometimes. Did you want something?"

The doctor looked relieved and then disturbed. "Mr. Milani, I have discovered something we regrettably missed on our first examination the morning you were admitted." Flourishing what looked to him like some kind of X-ray, Doctor Anderson continued. "You have torn rotator cuffs in both your shoulders. The tear is worse on your right side and it requires surgery. You must be in terrible pain. Can you move your arms or are they too weak?"

The kindhearted doctor was a distraction he didn't need. He'd suspected from the stinging pain and the increasing weakness in his arms that he'd injured his shoulders while hanging from the meat hook. "Yes, the pain is noticeable. My arms are fairly weak, but I figured it would diminish over time."

Doctor Anderson shook his head. "Unfortunately, this pain is not going to diminish. I'd like to schedule surgery for tomorrow morning to repair the tear on your right shoulder. We should have caught this much earlier and I apologize."

Gazing with no interest at the doctor, he nodded. "Tomorrow morning sounds fine and no apology is necessary." Affecting a tired smile, he closed his eyes, not caring whether the doctor stayed or left.

With burgeoning dread, Rowan watched as Ralph and Chad walked into his room late in the afternoon. Ralph looked at him and frowned. "You look like you've seen a ghost. What's going on? Care to enlighten us?"

He shot them both an implacable stare. "Here's what's going to happen tonight. I don't know what time, but probably when the hospital calms down, when they think we'll be most vulnerable."

Ralph interrupted querulously. "What are you talking about? I thought it would be forty-eight hours before your boys showed up."

Frustrated with his friend, he took a breath and started again. "Things have changed. My colleague informed me that Shemal is planning an extraordinary rendition, with complicity from his two thugs. They will deliver me to Tora Prison in Egypt and then turn me over to whichever organization can pay the most. I guess beheading is their goal." Gazing from Ralph to Chad, he stopped talking. Under other circumstances he would have laughed. Ralph sat in his usual chair, slack-jawed. Chad leaned against the window, his mouth a perfect O.

"We have to wait and let them take me." Sweat trickled down the side of his face and his stomach rolled. Grimacing, he continued. "We'll let them take me, but my colleagues are in place. They won't get far. I've been assured of that."

Ralph responded first. "Rowan, there is no way I will sit by twiddling my thumbs while all this happens." The older man paused, an expression of utter horror on his face. "I have seen and felt the results of letting those thugs take you."

He looked at Ralph, irony twisting his lips. "I feel your pain, but there isn't any other option. We'll play it cool, let them haul me out of here, and my guys will intervene. They're already in town. They have a rendition of their own all set up."

Chad coughed quietly, cleared his throat and added his two cents. "Rowan, with all due respect to what you've been through, what Ralph means is this. We've lived through the horror of finding you, afterwards." Chad looked at him, revulsion darkening his face. "Neither of us can allow you to be placed in those same hands again without being involved."

Shaking his head, he looked helplessly from Chad to Ralph. "We don't have any other option. As we covered earlier, I will not allow your careers to be shafted on my account."

Chad snorted. "Again, with all due respect, my career is mine to manage as I see fit. Let me second my boss here." Chad tilted his head in Ralph's direction. "We *will not* allow you to be hauled off by those two, ever again." His friend shoved off the window where he'd been leaning, pulled his cell phone from his jacket pocket and flipped it open. "Give me the number and let's call your colleagues. We've just joined their team and its best we let them know, before all hell breaks loose around you again."

Ralph sent him a triumphant smirk. "You taught him well, Rowan. Now don't start your stubborn shit with us. Give him the number. We don't have a minute to waste."

Enraged, goaded beyond reason with his inability to make them listen and understand, he shook his head again. They would sacrifice themselves and their careers, and he couldn't do a damn thing about it. But then, there wasn't much he could do about anything. He closed his eyes. If anything happened to either one of them, he couldn't live with it.

A feather light hand touched his shoulder. He opened his eyes and looked up into Chad's hard face. "The number Rowan, don't waste time. We're in this with you whether you like it or not."

Staring intently at Chad, he repeated the number and watched him punch it in. "Just say Ghost Rider, that way they know you're with me. Then say whatever the hell you want."

CHAPTER ELEVEN

Derek stood outside the Operations office of Legacy Airlines on the far side of the airport ramp, enjoying the unusual spring warmth and sharing a smoke with Marta while they watched a glistening white jet taxi noisily down the runway. Turning onto the taxiway, it headed toward the Fixed Base Operator, connected to the commercial area of the airport by a paved one lane road meandering past the control tower to the section of tarmac reserved for private passenger craft.

He couldn't help admiring the jet. Its aerodynamic lines and big engines bespoke power and prestige. Who in the world with a jet like that was flying into Sioux Falls, South Dakota? Marta gave him a quizzical look. "What kind of jet is that? It's gorgeous, and I bet it's a fast sucker."

He nodded. "You bet your butt it is. That's a brand new Gulfstream G650 and she is damn fast. That baby hits mach point nine-five at full throttle." He stubbed out his cigarette with his steel-toed boot and wiggled his eyebrows at her. "Want to get a closer look?"

Marta tossed him a seductive smile, took the last drag on her cigarette and pitched the butt off her fingers. "I thought you'd never ask."

He laughed. "Let's go. I was on my way to baggage claim, but that can wait. Lost bags don't hold a candle to that." He jerked his thumb at the jet, which had been parked and chocked, the fuel truck already making its way toward it.

Marta tapped her watch. "We gotta hurry, though. I've got an hour before the next turn gets here. I'm training a new gate agent, so I need to walk him through our procedures before that aircraft arrives."

"Sure, that sounds good to me." Grinning at Marta as they roared and bounced across the tarmac on an ancient tug, minus the baggage carts he'd unhitched, he pulled up and parked next to the main hangar. Gazing reverently at the jet, he watched as two crew members, uniformed in pristine white stepped carefully down the aircraft steps, met by two tree-trunk sized men strolling toward them from the main entrance of the customer lounge.

Marta gripped his arm and stared at him, eyes wide. "Those two men, see their jackets, can you read the backs? They say Federal Agent, right? I saw them on TV, the morning they took special agent Milani out of that warehouse. I think they're the CIA agents who arrested him. I remember, because they're so big. It didn't make sense that he would give them much trouble."

Adjusting the NWA ball cap, Derek squinted at the two men walking across the tarmac. "Yeah, I saw that too. I bet they're here to transfer him. Wasn't there an uproar about taking him to DC, but they couldn't because of how badly he'd been injured?"

Marta nodded and gave him a sly smile. "It's been all over the local news. Does Dani know about this?"

"Heck if I know. Ever since I told her she shouldn't be associated with Rowan Milani, she's given me the cold shoulder. Besides, she spends every spare minute at the hospital."

Michael Cristo looked at Gabriel Hernandez and nodded. Gathering the brochures they'd been gazing at unseeingly in the customer service lounge, he stood up and stretched. Dressed in casual attire that implied affluence, from the soft, battered leather jackets to the large gold watches and Gucci loafers, he and his colleague appeared as nothing more than two businessmen collaborating on the flight services offered to well-heeled travelers. Sketching a vague wave at the customer service staff, he and Gabriel headed out of the building to the parking lot and into their rented Dodge Durango.

One hand on the wheel, he kept the Durango at a controlled distance as they followed the black Suburban in late afternoon traffic. The two men in the front seat dwarfed the two sitting in the back. No wonder Rowan had been on a stretcher. Watching the debacle on TV, he'd known that his friend was in deeper trouble than if he'd been in a hostile country. Shaking his head, he glanced at Gabriel. His companion looked grim. "So what do you think? Those two are the jerks who damn near killed Rowan."

Gabriel stared at the black Suburban for a moment longer and then turned his way. "Amigo, don't let me get carried away tonight, eh? After what they did to Rowan, in my book they don't deserve to live. It will be difficult *not* to break their necks."

He scratched the back of his head and gave Gabriel a sideways glance. "And therein lies our problem. Some enemies, you just can't kill to get away from, and that kind usually has considerable reach, such as the CIA and FBI."

Gabriel frowned, but didn't reply. Instead, he cracked his knuckles and slid lower in the seat. Smiling to himself, he hoped Gabriel got the chance to mete out some justice to the two CIA agents. But now, he needed to concentrate. They were here to deliver Rowan out of the hands of the FBI, CIA and the crazy Egyptian who'd started the whole mess, and they would accomplish that, no problem.

Waiting for his friend to call, he and Gabriel had grown frantic, compiling damning information and intelligence from numerous sources inside and out of the country. Muusa Shemal intended to remove Rowan permanently and had expended great effort and many dollars in the insane venture. Well, they'd make damn certain their friend disappeared. He snorted softly. The crazy bastard would never find Rowan and they'd make sure he remained safe.

Digging in his jacket pocket, he retrieved his phone. He needed to call their flight crew to tell them about the jet they'd be piloting later in the evening. Jerry Reynolds and Bryan DeMuth would be ecstatic. The two pilots, along with him and Gabriel comprised the elite support team that backed Rowan on covert assassinations. Together the five of them had safely completed many clandestine operations.

Jerry and Bryan had served together in the Air Force and were still partners, sharing ownership of a company they called Business Jet Express. The two men had flown thousands of hours in Gulfstream and Learjet aircraft and he knew they'd have a blast flying the aircraft he'd just seen. The Gulfstream G650 was the crown jewel of the CIA's fleet. He figured the jet would be a nice gift to Rowan from the CIA for their complicity in destroying his life.

Ralph looked up as Doctor Anderson stepped into Rowan's room. The doctor looked uneasily from Rowan to Chad and then focused on him. "Ralph, I received a disturbing phone call just minutes ago. Do I understand correctly that Mr. Milani is going to be transferred to Quantico Marine Base this evening by the CIA, at the request of the President?"

Casting a sardonic glance at Chad, Ralph addressed the doctor. "Steve, nothing surprises me anymore. We've been laboring under the apparently false assumption that transport would take place later in the week."

The doctor stared, a look of dismay on his face. "I spoke with Mr. Milani earlier. We discussed the fact that he needs surgery, soon."

Ralph raised his hands. "What? Another surgery? Did I miss something here?" What a surprise that Rowan would keep quiet about something he needed.

Steve nodded at him, urgency in his eyes. "Yes, he tore both rotator cuffs during the, uh, accident and he needs surgery right away."

He shot the doctor a rueful look. "I'm sorry, but that's not going to happen. My hands are tied on this one."

Steve appeared nonplussed, frowned at him and then turned to Rowan. "Mr. Milani, it has been my pleasure to treat you and help in even a small way with your recovery. I hope for the very best for you in the future." Before any of them could reply, the doctor turned and walked out the door.

Rowan closed his eyes as the doctor left, the kind words only increasing his frustration. Ralph and Chad were stupid and stubborn. They had no right to endanger their lives and careers on his behalf. He'd never been angrier at either of them. This kind of situation often spun out of control, and anything could happen. He needed to prepare his mind, but he was consumed with worry for his colleagues. Ralph and Chad conferred quietly and then he heard them leave and shut the door.

As the door closed, he opened his eyes and gazed bleakly out the window, catching the glow of the sinking sun and wispy clouds tinged pastel pink and blue. Turning away, he coughed. His chest hurt and chills wracked his body. In spite of his rage, or maybe because of the energy it drained from his body, he drifted off to sleep. When he woke, street lights gleamed in the darkness beyond the window. His chest hurt worse, he was sweaty with a fever, and his teeth chattered.

Lying helpless in the hospital bed, he waited with shivering apprehension until he heard heavy footsteps approaching. The door opened and closed, the light switched on and the two hulking agents grinned at him. They wore their navy blue Federal Agent jackets, CIA credentials prominently displayed. Fierce hatred overwhelmed him as he struggled with the specter of the two men who had cost him so much. Lucien stood next to the bed, resting massive hands on the railing, making him shudder.

Towering over him, the big man glared, malevolence in his eyes. "I hear you need shoulder surgery after our last chat. My

168

colleague needed surgery too, after you shot him." Lucien reached out and grabbed his right shoulder. Frowning with the effort, the agent prodded until he found the spot he wanted and then dug in hard with strong fingers. Fiery pain shot down his arm. Dizzy, Rowan drew a sharp breath and closed his eyes, back arching as he clenched his jaws to keep from crying out.

Seth watched, hands on hips. "You can't seem to get a rise out of him today. Let me give it a try."

Breathless with fresh agony, he wondered what had happened to Ralph and Chad. If his tormentors thought he was alone and unprotected, there was no telling what might take place. He forced himself to remain still, trying to control his harsh breathing as Seth slid around the end of the bed and maneuvered next to him on the other side. Goddamn it, they were going to manhandle him again, and he couldn't do anything but endure it.

The agent grabbed him by the chin, turning his head, first to the left and then to the right. "Hey Milani, you look like a regular raghead now, and I see your face recovered nicely from our gentle persuasion."

The simmering rage boiled over. He didn't care anymore what they did. Let them get it over with and put him out of his misery. Smirking at Seth, he said what he was thinking. "Fuck you and this big-assed horse you rode in on." Jerking his head away from the heavy hand, he turned toward Lucien. His next words should get the ball rolling. They had sure as hell worked the first time. "Allahu Akbar, kafir." *Like a charm* was his last thought, before the monstrous fist smashed into his jaw and brilliant stars streaked behind his closed eyes.

Consciousness washed over Rowan in a slow wave, dragging him away from peaceful black waters. He tried to stay, but the water shoved him back, leaving him lying on the cold sand of wakefulness. The familiar tang of blood lingered in his mouth, and he knew the side of his face was already swollen. Both eyes still opened and closed. That was something, although the lights above him were too bright. His head throbbed, his right shoulder burned, and tight straps kept him secured to a stretcher. They'd wrapped him in a heavy, rough blanket, and the leg irons remained above his ankles.

Ralph's face, taut with anger and fear appeared above him, blocking out the bright light. "Are you all right? What do you say to these jerks, that they can't stop themselves from beating you every time they lay eyes on you?"

Managing a half-assed smirk, he coughed and tried to speak, voice croaking in a hoarse whisper. "It's like you always say, boss – I've got a charming personality. Where did you and Chad disappear to? And where are we now?"

Ralph snorted and shook his head. "Rowan, this is serious. You could be dead. That son of a bitch really laid you out. We're waiting for the elevator, next stop the airport. Your CIA escorts are trading papers with the charge nurse. And Chad and I got our wires crossed and dropped the ball. I am sorry."

He coughed again, squinting up at Ralph. "Tell Chad, there's a small, wrapped box. Danielle left it for me. Can you make sure it comes with me?"

Ralph nodded. "You got it. We'll make sure your friends have it, before you leave." The older man choked up on the last, but there was nothing left to say.

Seth's insolent voice intruded. "All right, let's go, he's been released to our custody, and we have a plane to catch." The stretcher moved. Rowan closed his eyes with a terrible feeling that the transport they were going to use was one he'd already enjoyed.

They'd no sooner stepped outside at the delivery bay on the back side of the hospital than he felt the straps being loosened and pulled off. Ralph swore. "What the hell is this shit?"

Neither agent paid any attention, shoving him carelessly into the back of the same black Suburban he'd ridden in once before.

His head missed the wheel well this time and he was conscious for the next humiliation, as he was jerked forward, a heavy length of duct tape plastered rudely over his mouth and a black hood pulled over his head. The hood smelled musty. He sneezed and struggled to breathe through his nose. While he coughed into the duct tape, they pushed him backward and slammed the doors, leaving him in silence.

The Suburban tilted back and forth when the two men climbed in. He heard the ignition and felt the vehicle jerk into motion. Familiar tendrils of terror snaked through his mind and wound around his heart. What if Michael and Gabriel weren't at the airport, what if their timing was off, what if they'd been purposely misled or delayed? Disoriented and helpless in the claustrophobic darkness, his body listed from side to side as the vehicle accelerated and then slowed and turned, stopped and started.

The rumbling engines of a nearby jet aircraft let him know they'd arrived at the airport. The vehicle stopped again. The doors opened, big hands dragged him unceremoniously out of the SUV and carried him, one with his feet and the other with a massive arm around his upper body. They trotted along and then slowed. The screaming engines deafened him and the smell of jet fuel permeated the hood. When his head tipped up, he guessed they must be ascending the steps into the aircraft.

Utter terror overtook him as he wondered what had happened to his colleagues. One of the men grunted and dropped his feet. Seth spoke, "What the fuck?" and let go of him. His body slammed face first onto the floor of the aircraft. Nose stinging, he lay inert, the breath knocked out of his lungs. The crash that followed rocked the cabin.

Gabriel's voice bellowed, "Stay on the floor motherfuckers and don't move," followed by a solid thud and a grunt of pain. His friend yelled again. "I said don't move. What's the matter, you bastards don't know fuckin' plain English? You move again, I'll shoot your fuckin' balls off."

Quick hands flipped him to his back and ripped the black hood off his head. Michael's wild, blue eyes and grinning mouth appeared through holes in a black ski-mask, the rest of his face obscured. "Holy shit Rowan, how you doin'?" Michael yanked the duct tape off his mouth, and he dragged in precious air. "Damn brother, you look like you've been out in the field somewhere mean, not in the good ol' USA. Let's get you moved to this bed we made up for you."

He pulled in another ragged breath but couldn't stifle a moan as Michael pulled him to a sitting position. His colleague paused and gripped his right shoulder, making him gasp. "I'm sorry, Rowan. Look, we gotta hurry. Jerry and Bryan created a distraction. We've only got a few minutes to get these jerks out of here without being seen. Gabriel has the divan all ready for you, and I need to make sure he doesn't kill those two before we finish up. Then we're out of here."

Eyes closed, he nodded and coughed as blood trickled down his throat. Michael lifted him as Gabriel's voice began again. "Get up slowly ladies and walk like you want to live, right down those steps and back to your Suburban." He heard the dull smack of pistol on flesh, and another grunt as Gabriel continued his badass routine. "Give me a reason, and I'll end your stories right here motherfuckers, because I want to, very, very badly."

Michael deposited him on what seemed like a bed and disappeared. Time slowed. He felt woozy again from the pain all over his body, but at last he was in the hands of people who could take him away from the pervasive evil that wanted so badly to destroy him. He shuddered at how close he'd come to annihilation.

A gentle hand touched his face, and he opened his eyes to see Gabriel bending over him like a dark angel. "Hola, my brother. Michael says you need some relief. Let's see what we got going on, eh?" Gabriel pulled away the rough blanket, took in the casts on his arms, moved down and whistled when he saw the leg irons. "Holy Mother of God, we gotta get you out of this shit, yes we do." Disbelief and anger burned in Gabriel's eyes. "What's up with this, Rowan? You really fell into it this time. I'll be right back. Don't you go anywhere."

"No worries," he whispered. Relief and pain blurred into one as he drifted on the edge of consciousness. Gabriel reappeared over him, brandishing a key. Did that mean Ralph and Chad were at the airport? He frowned, couldn't sort it out. Gabriel slid the shackles off his legs and rubbed with warm hands where they'd dug into his skin. It felt good to be free of the cold metal and the chain.

Gabriel waved something above him and he tried to focus. "Are you still with me? This will take your pain far away and let you go to sleep." He felt the prick of a needle and instant heaviness in his arms and legs. Drifting into familiar black waters, he heard Gabriel's voice close to his ear. "You're safe Rowan, and we'll keep it that way. This shit is all over. Buenas noches. Sleep well."

Michael bounded up the aircraft steps and yanked the black ski-mask off his face. Making a quick search, he found the correct button to activate the hydraulics and lifted the stairs. Then he turned the handle and secured the door. Stepping to the entrance of the flight deck, he listened as Jerry and Bryan discussed the specs of the powerful aircraft, conferring cheerfully while they waited. He chuckled. Those two were having a ball.

Bryan twisted around and smiled at him. "All set? We're ready anytime you are. How's Rowan?"

Wiping sweat off his forehead, he nodded. "We're good to go, the sooner the better. Rowan's OK, but he got knocked around. Gabriel doped him up for the trip. Hey, your distraction worked perfectly. We didn't see a soul when we needed to move those two jerks. Everybody was with you on the starboard side. What did you do?"

Both Bryan and Jerry snickered. Bryan gave Jerry a quick wink and looked back at him. "Yours truly here moved one of their tugs and parked it about a foot from the wing. Then I raised holy hell and demanded that management, customer service and every damn line tech get their asses over there. I took pictures with my phone and threatened to publish them and expose their incompetence. I told them we'd see to it that every government contract they ever dreamed about would go somewhere else. The line supervisor and customer service rep were shitting their pants. I lectured them about safety and the proximity of ground equipment to aircraft like they were kindergartners. It was great."

While he chuckled, enjoying the story, Jerry addressed the Sioux Falls control tower. "Sioux Falls Ground, Gulfstream November 275 Whiskey Tango at the General Aviation Ramp, ready to taxi."

The controller replied. "November 275 Whiskey Tango, Sioux Falls Ground, I don't have a clearance for you. Say your destination."

As the impressive engines revved, Jerry spoke calmly. "Ground, November 5 Whiskey Tango departing eastbound VFR."

The controller responded. "November 5 Whiskey Tango, Roger. Taxi runway 33. Squawk 0245. Verify you have ATIS Papa."

While Jerry continued conversing with the tower, Michael turned and navigated through the galley, glimpsing Gabriel fussing over Rowan in the mid-aft cabin. Watching for a moment, he gave his colleague quick thumbs up and slid into his forward cabin seat. He tightened his seat belt and folded his hands in his lap, thinking about his unconscious friend, safe at last under their auspices. Remembering the tiny, wrapped box Rowan's tall colleague had thrust into his hand, he pulled it out of his pocket and examined it. *Something for Rowan* had been the hurried explanation. Well, Rowan would have it, as soon as they got him settled.

Jerry and Bryan had told him they'd take off and head east. When they were twenty miles or so away from Sioux Falls, which he figured should take about three minutes, they could terminate radar service. After they'd done that, Jerry would turn off the aircraft's transponder and head back west. No one would notice them, as long as they stayed at approximately 10,500 feet and avoided either Rapid City or Ellsworth Air Force Base on the western end of the state. Locals in central and western South Dakota often saw military aircraft flying lower than normal. And they had the added benefit of darkness.

Gazing out the window, he watched the runway lights flicker by, disappearing as the big engines sent them thundering down the runway and screaming into the sky. He shared the unspoken sentiment and admired Jerry's skill as they climbed precipitously fast into the empty blue-blackness. Smiling in satisfaction, he leaned back in the luxurious seat and closed his eyes. Just as he'd planned, they'd completed another successful extraction of Rowan Milani, delivering their friend from monstrous evil at just under the speed of sound.

Jerry contacted the tower again. "Sioux Falls departure, November 5 Whiskey Tango with you, climbing through 3000 to 4500, VFR eastbound."

Sioux Falls departure responded. "November 5 Whiskey Tango Sioux Falls departure radar contact. Did you want flight following with Minneapolis Center?"

Giving Bryan a quick smile, he replied. "Negative departure. We are going to be maneuvering out here."

He rolled his shoulders while he listened to the controller's response. "November 5 Whiskey Tango, Roger. Radar service terminated, squawk 1200. Frequency change approved."

Nodding decisively, he completed the conversation. "November 5 Whiskey Tango, Wilco. Good day. *See ya.*" He banked the powerful jet in a lazy arc, reached for the transponder switch and flipped it off. Away from radar contact, they were ready, as he'd informed the tower, to *maneuver* Rowan out of danger. Grinning, he applied the throttle and sent them howling back the way they'd come. God, he loved this airplane.

Chad stood quietly beside Ralph in the shadows next to the black Suburban and watched the jet as it roared into the sky at hellacious speed, climbed at a jaw dropping rate, banked sharply east and blinked out of sight. He looked at his boss, brows rising as his breath coalesced in a cloud. "Damn. They didn't waste any time getting him out of here, did they?"

Ralph just looked at him, wiped his face with the back of his hand and gestured toward the Suburban. "Let's finish up with these two and get the hell out of here."

Taking a deep breath, he grabbed the handles and opened the back end of the SUV. The two men sat quietly, hands cuffed behind their backs, ankles cuffed as well. Black hoods covered their heads, and he knew Rowan's cohorts had covered their mouths with duct tape. Hidden from sight, watching Rowan's colleagues handle the two CIA agents with ease had given him bitter pleasure.

And now he would complete their participation. He grabbed the stockier man by the arm, dragged him forward to the edge of the floor above the bumper and shoved him face down. Bending over, he whispered. "This is for Rowan Milani." Pulling his pistol, he looked at the black hood and groped with his fingers until he found the man's ear. Estimating carefully, he delivered a punishing blow behind the ear with the steel slide. The son of a bitch groaned as his body went limp. *That's not nearly what you deserve*, he thought savagely as he shoved him back.

Lugging on the taller agent, the one who'd beaten Rowan, he grabbed him by the jacket and yanked the huge man toward the door frame. First tapping the side of the agent's head through the hood with the barrel of his gun, he poked it against the man's temple. Leaning close, he murmured intimately. "If you ever lay a hand on Rowan Milani again, I will hunt you like the animal you are and kill you myself." First holstering his pistol, he drew back his arm and smashed his fist into the black hood with all the power he could muster. Cracking his knuckles in satisfaction, he watched the massive man topple over.

Ralph whacked him on the shoulder and closed the cargo doors of the Suburban, motioning him away. "Rowan would be indubitably impressed, special agent. Now, take me back to the hotel, because the shit is going to hit the fan when the media and Ainsley get a hold of this." Chuckling along with his boss, he shivered as they tromped back to the red Mustang.

CHAPTER TWELVE

Ralph climbed stiffly out of the Mustang and waved as Chad drove away. They'd agreed to meet at eight-thirty the next morning at the hotel. The South Dakota assignment had officially ended. Snorting, he trudged into the Sheraton and headed for his room. It wasn't over by a damn sight, but they'd been effectively shut down, and he couldn't do anything about that. Now he planned an intimate affair with his bottle of Glenlivet, and no one could do anything about that, either.

Arriving in his room, he laid his Glock on the bed and stripped down to his t-shirt and boxers. Smiling sadly as he looked at his stocking feet, he fumbled for the bottle of scotch in the drawer and commenced the affair. He made strides and settled back on his bed with the TV tuned to FOX News, eager to hear the first Breaking News Alert about the duplicity of their evening activities.

Drinking alone always made him nostalgic, and his thoughts wound their way back to the first time he'd met Rowan. Remembering the young hotshot special agent with an ego to match, he shook his head. That was nearly twelve years ago. His hand quivering as he poured more scotch, he sighed, unable to get his mind around the fact that his friend was gone. "Poof," he muttered, and snapped his fingers. "End of story." As he stared blindly at the TV, he wondered where Rowan's colleagues had taken him and whether he'd be well cared for. He raised his glass in tribute to his absent friend. "Godspeed, Rowan. I hope we meet again someday." Wiping the wetness out of his eyes, he tossed back the rest of the Glenlivet and poured again.

* * *

Michael stood and stretched as the jet banked and continued to rumble across the sky. He bent over Rowan, frowning as he watched him cough and turn his head to the right. Placing a hand on his friend's forehead, he felt the heat and noticed the color in his cheeks. Rowan was tough, but a man could only take so much. It was time to bring them all home and get his friend started on the road to recovery.

Stepping to the flight deck, he listened to Jerry and Bryan, quietly discussing the conference they were both due to attend in Atlanta the following week, hosted by Gulfstream. "Hey guys, we should be seeing the signal sometime soon."

Jerry twisted around and smiled. "Yeah, we've been waiting for radio contact from your dad. You said it's a two-lane road, right? And we can taxi right into the storage facility or warehouse, whatever it is you guys have out here?"

He nodded at Jerry. "I gave him an approximate time, so he should be making contact soon. When he calls, will you please tell him that we need medical attention?"

The flight deck radio crackled to life as he finished speaking. "November 275 Whiskey Tango, this is Ghost Rider. Do you copy?"

Bryan turned to give him a worried smile and then went back to his controls. "Right on time Ghost Rider; this is November 275 Whiskey Tango, awaiting your instructions."

"Good evening, November 5 Whiskey Tango. See the signal. I repeat, see the signal." All three of them strained forward, looking out the windscreen into the empty blackness below. His father had managed to string blue lights along either side of the deserted blacktop road that ran through a section of their property. It looked like a damned lit up runway.

Bryan chuckled. "Ghost Rider, November 5 Whiskey Tango sees your signal, and we are proceeding. Request medical attention, do you copy?"

Michael heard the concern in his father's voice. "Ghost Rider copies, November 5 Whiskey Tango. Medical attention is standing by. Evaluate urgency, please."

Bryan looked at him, questioning. He considered. "Tell him we need transport to the medical clinic, ASAP." Bryan repeated his words.

"Ghost Rider copies, November 5 Whiskey Tango. We'll be ready."

Jerry and Bryan sat the ostentatious aircraft down sedately and taxied along the bumpy roadway. Squinting out the windscreen, he could see the cavernous warehouse doorway at the end of the drive off to his left, light spilling out onto the cement and the old ambulance sitting on the edge of the apron, lights doused and exhaust spewing. Within minutes they were inside the massive building, the roaring jet engines whining to an echoing stop.

When he opened the door and lowered the stairs, his father's face, etched with concern was the first thing he saw. His mother was right behind him, standing next to a stretcher with her arms full of blankets. Michael unbelted Rowan from the divan and roused Gabriel, who'd snored loudly and serenely since shortly after takeoff. "Gabriel, wake up, we have to move Rowan out of here."

While Gabriel stretched and rubbed his eyes, his father stepped aboard the jet. "Welcome home boys. It looks like 'mission accomplished' to me. What's up with your friend here?"

Yawning hugely, he slid into a seat, watching while his father stuck a thermometer in Rowan's ear and placed a stethoscope on his chest, frowning as he listened. "We'll transport him to the clinic right away. Sure sounds like he's got pneumonia."

Stifling another yawn, he nodded. "OK Dad. Has Mom gotten Rowan's medical records from Uncle Steve yet?"

His father slumped into a seat across the aisle and looked at him. "Not yet. He was going to overnight all the records today, I mean yesterday." The older man shrugged. "So, by sometime later today, we should know what's going on. I was hoping you would know what had happened to him."

"Gabriel checked him over before we left. All I know is he's hotter than hell and has been coughing. Oh yeah, something must be wrong with his right shoulder, because I just barely touched it and he practically jumped out of his skin."

His father stood up. "Help me move him and we'll get him settled in and start an IV. I'm sure you want to secure this aircraft and get some sleep."

He shoved himself out of the seat and faced his father. "Sleep is the farthest thing from my mind right now. Once we get Jerry and Bryan settled in, Gabriel and I will be over to the clinic to see how he's doing." Grasping his father by the shoulder, he captured the tired blue eyes that mirrored his own. "Dad, Rowan means a lot to all of us. We appreciate you and Mom getting involved. Somebody went to a lot of trouble to destroy not just his body, but his entire life. We're going to help him put it back together again."

Ralph's cell phone rang and vibrated on the bedside table, startling him awake. He glanced at his watch, wondering how long he'd slept. Eyes too blurry to read the time, he frowned at the TV and flipped his phone open. "Ralph Johnston." A FOX News correspondent he knew from DC, where it was five o'clock in the morning, jabbered excitedly about the breaking story. "Jack, I have no knowledge of what you've described. We released Mr. Milani, or Hassani, if you insist, to CIA custody around nine o'clock last night. That is the last we saw of him. Uh huh, well Jack, I'd have to say, on behalf of the FBI, no comment at this time. If anything comes to mind, anything new here, I'll make sure you get the exclusive as usual. You bet and thanks for calling. Good luck with this one."

He yawned and put his hands behind his head. Now it would begin. How long would it be before Ainsley called? His eyes had barely gone shut when his phone rang again. He stared blearily at it, saw it was his boss and punched talk, lips twisting in a sarcastic smile. This would be fun. "Ralph Johnston."

"*RALPH.* What happened in Sioux Falls last night?"

He pulled the phone away from his ear and glared at it. *Fuck you, Rodney.* "Sir, you want to clarify for me? I don't know what you're talking about. Did something happen here? Just a minute, let me grab the remote."

"What do you mean, Ralph? Don't you know what happened, haven't you seen the coverage or gotten any other calls?" The outrage and frustration in his boss's voice gave him immense satisfaction.

"Well sir, I've been sound asleep, so I expect you know more than I do. We were surprised, to say the least, when the CIA arrived last evening to transport Mr. Hassani, but they had the appropriate paperwork in hand. I inspected it myself. Dr. Anderson had been informed, and we released the prisoner to their custody at approximately nine o'clock." Making Ainsley squirm was the most fun he'd had since the whole mess began.

"Ralph, are you telling me neither you nor special agent Cantor accompanied Hassani to the airport?"

"No sir, we did not." Sliding off the bed to fiddle with making coffee, he continued with a grin. "To be perfectly honest, I was pleasantly surprised and relieved to release Hassani to their custody. I went to the hotel for a well deserved night's sleep in a real bed. Have you ever stayed at a Sheraton, sir? If you haven't, you really should. The beds are excellent. OK sir, I have FOX News tuned in. Ah, let me see. *Holy shit.* Hassani was the victim of an extraordinary rendition? Or he escaped? I'll be damned. Sir, do you have any idea why that would happen or who was pulling the strings? Were the agents we released him to culpable? Or do you suspect that he orchestrated his own escape?"

Ainsley was beside himself. "Ralph, those agents were overpowered by someone and left in their vehicle. The pilots of the aircraft were detained in their hotel rooms. And the jet they were using for transport to Quantico has disappeared right along with Hassani. That aircraft was brand new with a sixty-five million dollar price tag."

Why did he believe the CIA would never see that jet again? "Well sir, our hands are certainly clean, but it will be interesting to get the story from the CIA agents who were here last night. Anything we can do along those lines?" He paused, waiting for Ainsley's reply.

"The CIA can clean up its own mess. Frankly, I can't fathom how they allowed this to happen. But I will tell you this. If Hassani somehow managed to orchestrate his own escape, I'll find him, wherever he is, and I'll prosecute him to the fullest extent of the law."

He sneered at the phone. Ainsley always made him want to toss the thing as far away as possible. "I'm with you on that, sir. And I am more than happy to allow the CIA to take care of its own problems. Special agent Cantor and I should be finished up here by day's end."

"Sounds great, Ralph. Call if you need anything. Otherwise, I'll see you in DC in a month. Bye now."

Snapping the phone shut, he refrained from tossing it, laid it on the desk instead and poured coffee from the tiny pot. "Don't worry asshole. There isn't one damn thing I need that involves you."

Danielle stared at Derek as he plopped down on the adjoining sofa. Her face felt hot and her eyes were scratchy, the lids swollen. How long had she lain, curled up under the comforter on the loveseat in the living room? "What do you want? Need a moment to gloat? Want to tell me I told you so?"

Derek's eyes held only kindness, laugh lines crinkling in the corners when he gave her a sad smile. "No, I don't want to tell you anything. I just want you to know I'm here if you need to talk. I'm worried about you, Dani. It's four o'clock in the morning and you've been down here since yesterday afternoon. Will you at least tell me what happened?"

Gazing at his anxious countenance, her lower lip quivered. "Rowan's gone. He said he had to tell me good-bye." It was no use. Raw pain overwhelmed her, hot tears spilled down her cheeks, and the lump in her throat choked her voice. Shaking, she covered her face with her hands.

Derek sank down next to her and put his arm around her shoulders. Drawing her close, he patted her head while she sobbed. "I'm so sorry it worked out this way. I know you cared about him."

Pushing out of his embrace, she shredded a crumpled tissue and hiccupped through the tears. "He told me I'd never see him again, and I was free to move on. But I can't do that. I don't want to do that. All I want is to be with him. That's all I'm ever going to want."

Derek tipped her chin up with a forefinger. "You may not believe me, but I do know how you feel. Whenever you need to talk, you just let me know. But kiddo, I gotta go to work. You want me to tell your agents that you're not coming in today?"

Rowan's words about Derek whispered through her mind. *He's deep in love with you, and you're with me.* Oh God, if only. Blinking back tears again, she tried to read his face, but saw only compassion. "Thanks, the airport is the last place I want to be today. If you don't mind telling them I don't feel well, I need some time to think things through."

Derek patted her knee. "Good idea. I'll call you later, but if you need anything, let me know, all right?"

Danielle managed a nod and a murmured, "OK." Closing burning eyes, she listened to Derek tromping through the house, gathering his jacket, keys and coffee. The door slammed and the house grew quiet. Shasta's furry bulk pushed against her knees. The big dog whined and she opened her eyes. "What's the matter, baby? I bet you need to go out, don't you." Shasta sat staring at her and then woofed, placing a monstrous paw carefully in her lap. Smiling in spite of her sadness, she stood up, shoved the comforter aside and walked with Shasta padding beside her to the patio door.

Watching the dog bound away into the darkness, she slid the door shut and locked it, then grabbed the last cup of coffee from the pot and wandered into the study where they kept the TV. Rowan had said she'd see news coverage about his leaving. Spotting the remote, she perched on the edge of a chair and hit the power button.

Sure enough, the red and yellow FOX News Alert banner flashed importantly on the screen. **Suspected Terror Mastermind Rowan Milani, Victim of CIA Extraordinary Rendition or Daring Escape?** She drew a sharp breath as Rowan's now familiar FBI ID photo appeared, juxtaposed next to video of a powerful looking jet. A blonde anchorwoman spoke. "Federal authorities are beginning an investigation early this morning to determine whether suspected terror mastermind Rowan Milani has fallen victim to Extraordinary Rendition or managed to orchestrate a daring escape. According to employees at the airport in Sioux Falls, South Dakota, a private jet landed there yesterday afternoon and took off again last night. Sources at Sanford Medical Center in Sioux Falls, where Milani was being held pending transfer, confirm that he was released to CIA custody sometime last evening.

However, the two CIA agents were found, bound and gagged in their SUV, behind the airport. The agents were accosted by black-masked gunmen when they boarded the jet with Milani. The pilots of the aircraft were also found bound and gagged in their hotel rooms. They tell a similar story of being detained by black-masked gunmen. Both the CIA and the FBI have declined comment."

She slumped in the chair, shut off the TV, and closed her eyes.

Georgia and Frank Cristo stood looking at their new patient, settled into the one bed in the isolation room of their medical clinic. It was the only room in the clinic with a lock on the door, ensuring that none of their daily patients would inadvertently wander inside. Georgia tucked her arm into Frank's and looked up at him. "He's one sick man, Doc. Somebody sure smacked him around before he got here."

Her husband stirred beside her and patted her arm. "He's going to be in a lot of pain for a while. We need to get this pneumonia resolved before we can take care of whatever else he needs, after we get Steve's records and examine him ourselves. What do you think, honey? Can you manage? We don't know anything about his personality and he may be difficult to handle."

Contemplating the deep set eyes in the face she'd always found so handsome, she nodded. "You're right about all that, but I'll talk to Michael and find out everything I can about him. Besides, once he knows he's safe and in good hands, he'll respond to kindness, I'm certain of that."

Frank put his arm around her. "If anyone can relate to him, I know you can. My main concern is the level of pain he's going to be in once he wakes up. But we can keep a close eye on that, too."

She nodded again. "When he comes around, I'll make sure he sees Michael and Gabriel and knows he's safe, and I'll have pain meds ready for immediate injection." Gazing again at the bruised face, shaggy black hair and rough beard of their new patient, she was reminded of when Michael was a boy, bringing home wounded animals for them to fix. They'd faithfully healed every furry patient over the years and they'd do the same for this poor man who meant so much to their son.

* * *

As the last vestiges of the drug Gabriel had given him faded from his mind and body, Rowan heard his own strained breathing and felt knife-sharp pain in his chest. He opened his eyes and saw Michael and Gabriel, smiling down at him. A woman he didn't recognize appeared next to them. Instinctively rubbing his right foot against his left leg, relief swept through his mind. The hated leg irons were gone. He was no longer a prisoner.

He tried to speak, but couldn't. Shallow, painful breaths were all he could manage. While he blinked at his friends, Michael spoke. "Rowan, you're safe. No one can find you here, and we'll be with you every step of the way to recovery. You've got pneumonia, but we'll take care of that. We're going to let you sleep now, brother."

The woman bent over him and the familiar, slow burn of drugs into his vein brought relief from the pain and slowed his mind. Eyes heavy, he wondered for an instant where he was and then slid back into unconsciousness.

Chad rubbed gritty eyes and stared vacantly at the French doors opening onto the patio from the family room, wishing he'd slept, now that the sun peeked in behind the drapes. But he'd been too wired. With a disconsolate sigh, he hunched forward on the sofa, thinking about his career, no longer sure he belonged in the Bureau. Smiling to himself, he admitted that Bettina had unwittingly thrown a monkey wrench into his future as well. Besides that, he'd made another decision during the night.

Mouth stretching in a gaping yawn, eyes watering, he blinked to ease the scratchiness. Leaning over and grabbing his phone from the end table where he'd dumped it along with his car keys, he flipped it open. He'd saved the number Rowan had recited, and he intended to call Ghost Rider and tell them he wanted in. Startled when the phone rang in his hand, he fumbled it onto the table and picked it up again, frowning at the screen. Oh hell. He punched talk. "Hey, Bettina," was all he said.

She replied, voice high pitched and filled with anguish. "Chad, I had to call. Do you know what happened to Rowan? We saw on TV . . . Is he really gone?"

He slumped back on the sofa, a hand over his face. The thought of deceiving her twisted his gut, but he had no choice, and she'd never know it was for Rowan's sake. "The President transferred custody of Rowan to the CIA, and they showed up at nine o'clock last night. We had to release him. This morning, we were surprised to hear that he'd been taken by someone else."

Gazing between his fingers, he cringed at her next question. "What does extraordinary rendition mean? CNN said maybe he'd been kidnapped. It doesn't make any sense. Why would someone want Rowan?"

He closed his eyes, left his hand on his face. "Well sweetheart, extraordinary rendition is when the CIA plucks up a foreign national and takes them someplace secret, out of the country, for interrogation."

"Oh no, they'll torture him." Her words dissolved into ghastly cries. The whole exercise wrung him out, and he knew it had to be a hundred times worse in her shoes.

Lowering his hand, listening as Bettina's heart wrenching sobs subsided, he glanced at his watch. He needed to meet Ralph. "I'm sorry, I have to go." Grabbing his keys and wallet, he slipped out the door. "I'll call you in a couple hours. Can you hang in there?"

Sliding into the Mustang, he started the powerful engine, wondering if she'd hung up. "Sweetheart, are you there?" He pulled out of the driveway and roared onto the street.

Bettina sniffed. "Chad, you be careful with that Mustang. I don't want anything to happen to you." Her voice wavered, but he was proud of her courage. "Please let me know if you find out anything. I love you."

* * *

Staring at the TV in his Portland, Oregon hotel room, Muusa Shemal clutched his head in his hands, crying out in guttural, shrieking rage as he listened to CNN's coverage of the extraordinary rendition of his prisoner by someone else. By all that was holy to Allah, he would murder the ones with the audacity to take what was rightfully his, what he had bought and paid for at an exorbitant price. His hands shook as he watched video of the powerful jet aircraft he had paid to use. It had disappeared, along with the ghost agent, the man who managed to usurp him at every opportunity. He had never dealt with such an opponent. The face of Rowan Milani; his prisoner, his rightful prize, appeared again on the screen, and he pointed an index finger at the picture of the man he so desperately wanted to kill.

"I will have my day of vengeance. You will be mine. By Allah it will come to pass." Wiping spittle off his chin, he grabbed the remote and punched the power button. He could no longer stomach the endless story of the man who belonged to him, but was once more tantalizingly out of his grasp. Smoothing his disheveled hair, he struggled to regain his composure. Drawing in quick breaths, he thought about how much he loathed the United States with its precious democracy, spawning undisciplined, incompetent fools with no accountability to anyone. A fiasco such as this would never have been allowed in his homeland. When this despicable country and its immoral, filthy culture fell to Islamic rule, on that day, he would rejoice.

Michael looked at Gabriel's brooding face as they walked toward the vast warehouse that housed and concealed the covert accoutrement of their lives. "You know Rowan will pull out of this, Gabriel. Once he's up and around, he'll be his old self again, you'll see."

His phone rang and he stopped, looking at the unfamiliar number in surprise. "This is Ghost Rider. Identify yourself, NOW." He listened intently. "What do you want, special agent? You aren't supposed to have this number, and I don't appreciate you calling."

Poised outside the yawning door that opened into the interior of the warehouse, Michael leaned against the warm steel wall, shaded his eyes from the sun with one hand and gripped the phone with the other. Gabriel looked at him expectantly and he put a hand over the phone. "It's that FBI special agent, the younger one, Chad."

Scowling, he listened as Chad started talking again. "What do you mean? How did you figure that out? Tell you where he is?" He slammed his fist against the steel siding and stabbed the toe of his boot into the ground. "I don't think so. Listen to me. You want to help Rowan? You let us take care of things and stay the hell out of this."

Gabriel put a hand on his arm and mouthed, *what's going on?* He snorted and covered the phone again. "Chad insists he can help us because he's such a great hacker. He's being a real prick about it too."

Gabriel shook his head, gesturing with his fingers across his throat. "Michael, tell the special agent you'll call him back in five minutes."

Much as he hated to admit it, when Gabriel called him Michael instead of amigo, he needed to listen. "Special agent, give me five minutes and I'll call you back." He stuffed the phone in the front pocket of his jeans and glared at his colleague. "What? You think we should let him help us?"

Gabriel sighed in what he could only guess was irritation. "Michael, think about it. It's just you and me. We can't bring in a nurse's aide to help your mother and we can't hire any kids off the rez to paint the jet. We can't because nobody can find out that we're harboring a man wanted by the FBI, CIA and every Islamic organization on the planet. I think maybe we could use some help from Chad and the other guy, Rowan's boss." Gabriel rolled his eyes. "C'mon Michael. So the gringo's a prick. I'll be damned. No wonder he got along with Rowan."

Managing to set his anger aside, he shrugged. "I hate it when you're right and I'm wrong. His attitude got to me, you know? But I'm not going to tell him where we are. He can help from Sioux Falls for now. Later, if it becomes necessary, we'll tell him. Sound all right to you?"

Gabriel nodded and punched him lightly on the arm. "You're a smart man, Michael. Call him back and let's get started, because it's going to take a hell of a lot to sort this out and put it right."

CHAPTER THIRTEEN

Two Weeks Later – Third Week In April
Marta smiled, placing the phone gently in its cradle. What she'd done would nail Danielle. And maybe Rowan Milani would suffer more because of it. He should have known better than to blow her off. Now all she had to do was wait to see what happened. And she must call Muusa. He'd be so happy and proud of her. Besides, he might be able to use Danielle to get to his prize, as he liked to call Rowan Milani.

She giggled as she walked down the concourse. Lots of things could come from her simple phone call to the FBI Regional Office. They'd been extremely interested to know that the missing terrorist had a girlfriend, someone who'd spent every spare minute with him, even after he ended up in the hospital. Remaining anonymous by calling from the phone at gate six, she'd told them about how much time he'd spent digging through Legacy's passenger records and how he'd seen the sterile area of the airport. Of course, she'd told them about the trip to Chicago, too. She rubbed her hands together. This would be fun.

Clifton Cantor, III, frowned and scribbled notes as he listened to his only son. At fifty-eight, he took care of himself and knew he still looked good. With blond hair going gracefully to silver and the same clear blue eyes as his son, he maintained a trim six foot two inch frame. After devoting his life to the quiet acquisition of wealth and influence, he enjoyed the effective wielding of both in the causes, political and otherwise, that he deemed worthy. Most people called that lobbying, but he called it getting things done in a civilized manner.

Chad sat across from him at the massive desk in his Georgetown office, rubbing bloodshot eyes. "You know, Dad, things fell apart so fast we didn't have time to plan. One day we were waiting while Rowan recuperated and the next, all hell broke loose. But I'm telling you, I had to resign. Something's not right at the Bureau. Somebody somewhere got a lot of money to hand Rowan over to Muusa Shemal, and I'm hoping you can make some inquiries. I'm determined to get Rowan out of this, and I'm going to marry his sister."

Chad paused to yawn and then continued. "Thanks for getting things rolling at the estate. If only we could have completed the repairs before all this happened. And I know we've covered this, but you're absolutely certain tracing us to Kauai would be impossible?"

Steepling his fingers in front of him, he contemplated his son. "You've got a lot on your plate, Chad and I'm happy to help you and your friends. As a matter of fact, I'm having dinner with the President next week. I'll start there with some discreet probing and work my way down the chain of command. As far as the estate, I've hired independent investigators on several different occasions. None of them have been able to find any hint that the property exists. It is deeded in your mother's grandmother's maiden name, in case you've forgotten. What's your timeline for moving your friends out there? And do tell me about your fiancée. I'm most interested in that, I must confess."

It relieved him to see Chad smile, some of the strain dropping away from his son's worried face. "Her name is Bettina and you know what? I saw her and fell in love." Chad snapped his fingers, making him smile, too. "It happened that fast. We decided to work on a long-distance relationship, but I know I'm going to marry her. She's beautiful and smart, and I miss her terribly."

Chad leaned forward, his face hardening. "Anyway, regarding the estate, the repairs you requested are progressing. Ralph contacted Rowan's parents and they've finalized their affairs.

Ralph's wife Marion can't wait, and Bettina is ready as well. I haven't had a chance to talk to Danielle yet, but that's my next project. Once we've removed every possible lever the FBI or CIA could use to force Rowan out of hiding, I'll talk to his colleagues about moving him. They won't tell me where he is, but that's fine." Chad looked at him and smirked. "If I don't know, I can't be forced to tell anyone. When I get everything and everyone in place, we can focus our resources and energy on taking down Muusa Shemal and clearing Rowan's name."

Amazed at the enormity of what his son proposed to do for his friend, he nodded slowly. "Are you confident of the team you've got in place to accomplish all this?"

Chad smiled and Clifton could see the enthusiasm in his son's face, despite the obvious weariness. "I couldn't have a better team, Dad. Ralph's in for sure and so are Rowan's colleagues. No worries on that end. I appreciate whatever help you can give us."

Giving Chad a sharp nod, he glanced at his watch and stood up. "You can count me in with whatever you need. Stay in touch and keep me informed. Right now, unfortunately, I've got to attend a hearing on the Hill. But we'll talk soon. And son, it's good to see you."

Danielle rested her chin in her hands, elbows on the table as she sat in the kitchen with her second cup of coffee. It was ten o'clock in the morning, warm sunlight poured in through the patio door and just like every other morning, she couldn't get moving. The inescapable, brutal fact that Rowan was gone left her drifting and apathetic. Despite her brave words to him at the hospital, reality had crashed through the hope in her heart and she knew – she would never see him again.

Shoving the coffee cup aside, she laid her head in her arms. Legacy had reluctantly accepted her resignation, and she'd forced herself to clean out her office, relieved that she could get away from the airport and its memories of the man she'd loved so briefly. *Still loved*, she thought fiercely. Sitting up, she laid her hands flat on the table and took a deep breath. What if she called her parents? Then she remembered the day she'd told Rowan the story of how her mother met redheaded Dr. Charlie Evans while working part-time as a college student at Seattle's first Starbucks. He'd laughed with such pleasure. Oh God, her parents would have loved him too.

Grabbing her coffee, she took a long swallow and resigned herself to the painful memories. He'd asked her one day, dark eyes curious and playful, why her last name was Stratton instead of Evans. Embarrassed, she'd stuttered and blushed and finally admitted that she'd been married once for six months, ten years earlier, to a Legacy captain named Jeffrey Stratton, who flew Boeing 777's on an overseas route between Chicago and Amsterdam.

The brief whirlwind of romance and marriage had ended when she flew to Amsterdam to surprise him, only to find him bedded down with the lead flight attendant. They divorced and she'd never bothered to change her name. Rowan had kissed her, told her he was sorry. Goose bumps rose on her arms as she remembered him asking whether Jeffrey had ever hurt her. For a few moments he'd become a different man, one she didn't know, with ruthless eyes and a hard face. Inexplicably frightened, she'd rushed to assure him that Jeffrey's only sin was infidelity and that he'd never laid a hand on her.

Rubbing the chill from her arms, she decided to take Shasta for a walk and then call her mother. After retiring, her parents had sold their house and began wandering the country year-round in a huge motor home. Tugging on her ponytail, she thought about how happy they were. Always encouraging and unfailingly kind, they'd been her biggest cheerleaders. They'd be ecstatic if she wanted to travel with them for a while.

If she asked, they would help her sell the house. Or, if Derek was interested, he could buy or rent it. She sighed. One day, maybe she would be able to put her life back together and move on, like she knew Rowan wanted her to. But she would never love anyone else, and the emptiness would be with her forever.

A sharp knock at the front door shattered the silence, and she jumped, sending the coffee cup wobbling. Shasta commenced barking and she sighed again. She didn't want company. Another knock, louder than the first dragged her out of the chair and to the front entryway. Hanging onto Shasta's collar, she pulled open the door. Jax stood on the front step looking unhappy, along with a man in a black suit, white shirt and black tie, holding out an FBI ID and badge. She squinted in the sunlight. "Good morning Jax. Um, hello sir, did you want to come in? Can I help you with something?"

The two men stepped inside, and she apologized for Shasta's curiosity. The antsy dog snuffled and growled while she yanked on her collar. "Let me put her in the backyard. I'm sorry, she's not usually so naughty. She needs a walk. Shasta, come on."

Both men followed her into the kitchen, and she noticed the FBI agent motioning to Jax, who shook his head. What in the world was this about? Jax caught her eye as she shut the door behind the excited dog. "I'm sorry Dani, but we need to ask you to come down to the police station with us."

The front door slammed and she heard brisk footsteps. Derek strode into the kitchen in his dusty uniform, sweat marks under his armpits. The acrid scent of jet exhaust clung to his clothing. Removing his cap and thrusting fingers through his flattened hair, her friend glared at the two men. "Jax, what's going on? I heard the FBI was out at the airport looking for Dani. Tell me this doesn't have something to do with Rowan Milani."

Jax grimaced. "Dani, I apologize. This is FBI special agent Gary Hawkins, who usually works out of the FBI Regional Office in Minneapolis."

The man offered her his hand. "Hello, Ms. Stratton. The FBI would like to question you concerning your association with

Rowan Milani. We understand that the two of you were quite close."

Derek started cussing under his breath, and she tossed him a frown of irritation as she grasped special agent Hawkins' hand in a quick grip, then let go. "Yes, we were very close. I'll be glad to answer any questions you have, especially if it will help Rowan."

Special agent Hawkins gave her a shrewd look. "This is about helping yourself, Ms. Stratton. We'd like to leave now, if you don't mind."

When the special agent pulled handcuffs from his belt, she gasped and sat down. Shoving aside instant panic, she looked from Jax to special agent Hawkins. "Am I in some kind of trouble because of being Rowan's friend?"

Jax scratched the graying stubble on his cheek before responding. "Dani, there's no easy way to say this. After you're questioned today, the FBI does have the authority to detain you if they deem it necessary. I'm afraid your association with Rowan has left you in a precarious position."

Derek spoke before she could respond, staring with hands on his hips at Hawkins. "This stinks. I knew that guy was big trouble. Special agent Hawkins, she wasn't involved with the crap Milani was into. I've lived with her for four years, and I've known her for over ten. She worked for an airline. We went through 9/11 together. There's no way she'd ever betray her country."

Derek's outburst had given her a chance to regroup. Hoping she looked and sounded convincing, she lifted her chin and stood up, holding out her hands. "OK, I'm ready, let's go. Arrest me if that's what you need to do. I'll be happy to answer any of your questions. I have nothing to hide. Derek, please keep an eye on Shasta for me."

CHAPTER FOURTEEN

Three Months Later – Third Week In July
Rowan sat cross-legged on a grassy bluff near the edge of a ravine. Gauging the depth of the brush covered slope that dropped almost like a cliff in front of him, he estimated it must be at least several hundred yards to the bottom. Rolling up the sleeves of his blue work shirt, he wiped sweat off his forehead even as it trickled down his chest. Hot and sticky at midmorning, the simmering threat of thunderstorms built steadily in the western sky.

Laying his hands in his lap, he contemplated the scars on his wrists. He hated looking at them, almost as much as he hated the two men who'd caused them. Flexing his hands and then rubbing them vigorously together, he grimaced. Sometimes his fingers tingled and didn't always work the way they were supposed to. But at least he hadn't lost the use of his hands entirely.

Eyes closed, head flung back to embrace the sun's rays, he breathed in the aroma of warm grass and prairie soil. At first he'd thought he was losing his mind, because he relived the trauma of hanging from the meat hook by his wrists every night. The faces of the two agents haunted him when he woke in the darkness, heart pounding while he waited, straining to hear heavy footsteps coming down the hall.

Georgia Cristo had noticed the dark circles under his eyes and explained Post Traumatic Stress Disorder. Of course she wanted to help him. But nothing could make him tell her about his experience at the hands of the two men. As far as he was concerned, once he killed them, the nightmares would end and so would the stress.

Thinking about Georgia, his lips twisted in a rueful smile. She was a good woman, a good person, and had persisted in calling him Mr. Milani from day one. Earnest brown eyes boring into his, she'd told him that she didn't want him to lose his dignity. He'd laughed and she'd been offended. No matter how many ways he tried to explain it, she couldn't understand that he'd already lost so much more than his precious dignity.

Georgia had fed and bathed him while his wrists and foot healed inside the casts and while his right shoulder was immobilized in an awkward sling. She encouraged him, got him to laugh once in a while and offered uncomplicated friendship. At the direction of her doctor husband, he worked on endless therapy for his hands, wrists and shoulders, walked everywhere to strengthen his left foot and hoped he might walk without a limp someday. The couple had devoted their time and resources to saving his life. He could never repay them.

Picking up a stick, he stabbed it into the dirt. Distant thunder rumbled and he looked up, saw dark swaths of rain dipping from low black clouds. It still looked miles away, but he could smell it on the light breeze. Flinging the stick over the edge of the ravine, he let his head hang and closed his eyes. A thin line of sweat made its way down the side of his face. Hopelessness settled over him like a suffocating cloud.

Everyone and everything he loved and valued was gone. The future, bereft of purpose or meaning, stretched ahead as empty as the grassland where he'd been hidden. Living on the ranch with Michael and his parents appeared to be the only option left, if he wanted to remain safe, free, and most of all, alive.

Pain slanted through his chest when he thought about Danielle. Leaning back, he dug in the front pocket of his jeans and pulled out the gift she'd given him. Michael had plopped the tiny wrapped box in his lap while he lay in the hospital bed in the medical clinic. He'd waited until the casts came off so he could open it himself, alone in the small bedroom that was his in the back end of the clinic. Danielle may not have thought it was much, but it meant the world to him.

Pulling the oversized coin out of the box, he'd read that it was minted from World Trade Center steel and then plated with gold from the vault beneath the wreckage. On one side of the coin, the twin towers were etched in sharp relief. On the other side, in flowing script were the words: *We will never forget. 9/11/01.* On a piece of paper, Danielle had written a simple note. *Rowan, I'm sorry for all you've lost, and I'm grateful for all you've done. Love, Danielle.* He kept the note in a drawer with the few items of clothing Georgia had gotten for him. But he carried the coin with him all the time.

Glancing around, he wondered when Gabriel and Michael would appear. They watched him every day with their binoculars, thinking he didn't know. The two men treated him like a child, hovering over him, warning him about rattlesnakes, telling him to be careful not to trip and fall into a ravine. How many years had he navigated, without any help, through the dangerous back country of hostile nations? He wasn't an idiot, for God's sake, just because he limped. Heaving a sigh, he tried to tamp down the angry thoughts and ignore the ever present humiliation. Without Gabriel and Michael, he'd be in an Egyptian torture prison, lost forever.

The breeze kicked up and he felt a spatter of rain. He stuffed the coin back in his pocket and looked up. Fast moving, low clouds scudded across the sky ahead of towering thunderheads. Staggering to his feet, he brushed dirt, grass and a crushed pink prairie flower off his jeans before starting the slow trek back toward the clinic. Michael and Gabriel would pick him up before he'd gone very far, he knew that.

Gabriel prowled restlessly around the rusted blue Ford Ranger pickup while Michael perched on the hood with binoculars, watching Rowan. Waving an arm wildly, he strode to the front of the truck. Somehow, he had to make his loco friend understand. "Michael, you know that all the shit he went through screwed him up. *Listen to me.* Rowan's not right, he isn't the man we used to know, and there isn't a damned thing we can do about it."

Michael smirked at him and gestured toward the grassy bluff where Rowan sat, then started in with a familiar argument. "You sound like my mother and I get it, he's suffering from post traumatic stress. But still, we have to tell him. He has a right to know what's happening to someone he cares about. Who knows, maybe it'll jolt him back to reality."

Wiping at the sweat on his face with a tattered red handkerchief, Gabriel stared at his colleague. "But can he handle knowing about Danielle? It'll kill him to think that she's been detained because of him. And you know he'll want to do something to get her released. Doesn't that concern you, Michael? He's not fit, either physically or mentally to do anything, but that won't stop him from trying."

Michael shrugged and didn't look at him, just adjusted the binoculars and kept watching Rowan while he answered. "We have to tell him."

Gazing at Michael, he felt only trepidation. *Compassion* was not in his friend's vocabulary. Michael would tell Rowan the unvarnished truth, with no consideration for their friend's troubled state of mind. And nothing he said would make a difference. Throwing up his hands in defeat, he blustered, "OK, I give up. Let's go get him. It looks like we could be in for a hell of a storm. If Rowan walks back in the rain, he'll catch pneumonia again."

Climbing into the ancient truck, he slammed the door and watched uneasily as Michael lowered the binoculars and jumped from his perch on the truck to the ground. Fat drops of rain fell on the pickup and ran in rivers across the dusty hood. Michael slid into the driver's seat and turned the key in the ignition, fixing him with a grim look as he yanked the truck into gear. "You know I think of Rowan as a brother, and I don't want to cause him more pain. But he needs to know what's going on. Tell you what – we'll have this conversation with him in the conference room on the lower level of the clinic. If we have to, we'll lock him in there while he thinks it through, so he doesn't go off on some tangent."

Back in his room, Rowan watched out the windows as the sky turned from rainy gray, to green, and then to black. The security lights came on in the clinic parking lot, and the day turned pitch dark. Thunder like he'd never heard before rolled in booming echoes across the prairie, accompanied by crackling lightning that seemed to gobble up the sky. Then the rain came hard, pounding the windows while the wind howled. The storm possessed magnificent power, but it left an aura of instability in the air that he didn't like.

He finished rubbing the dampness from his hair and slung the towel on his bed, gazing without interest as Gabriel and Michael walked into his room. They'd pulled up as he trudged along the gravel road in the rain, just like he'd known they would. "What's up, what do you want?"

That was as far as he got. Michael clamped a hand on his arm. "Rowan, we need to have a talk." Michael sounded hell-bent on something, but he wasn't in the mood for talking.

Trying to yank his arm out of the tight hold, Rowan stared into his colleague's eyes and felt a frisson of unease. "What's going on?"

Michael didn't answer. When he looked at Gabriel, his stocky friend started muttering in Spanish and walked out of the room. His foot hurt, he was cold and tired and didn't want to play stupid games with either of them. "Look Mike, whatever you want, I'm not interested. Just leave me alone, OK?" He yanked his arm harder, but it didn't do any good. Michael pulled him out into the hallway.

Frustrated with his ruthless friend, he stopped walking and braced himself, forcing Michael to pivot around him. "What's the matter with you? I said *I don't want to talk.*" His friend, inches taller and pounds heavier, ignored him, dragging him down the hallway and into the elevator. Once inside, Michael punched the button for the lower level, maintaining the grip on his arm. Gabriel slid in before the door closed, still muttering. Twisting his head around, he scowled. "Gabriel, what is going on? Why are we doing this? Has he gone nuts or something?"

Gabriel glanced at Michael and then fixed him with an unreadable stare. "Rowan, we need to talk to you."

Thoroughly disquieted, looking first at Michael's hard face, then the strong hand gripping his arm, he had a terrible feeling of déjà vu. These were his friends, so why did he feel like he was being forced to walk a familiar pathway to destruction?

The elevator opened and the three of them walked down the hall, stopping in front of a doorway. Gabriel opened the door, hitting the light switch as they stepped inside. The room had a feeling of disuse, like a dank cellar, with a musty odor that made him want to sneeze. Several wooden chairs and a sturdy, rectangular wooden table were the only furnishings and a single window sat up high near the ceiling. Lightning flashed on the rain spattered panes, but the thunder was muted. Glancing up, he halfway expected to see a meat hook hanging from an eye bolt drilled into the wall. Michael kicked a chair away from the table, let go of his arm and pointed. "Rowan, sit down."

Used to following directions without question, he sat. Looking up, he rubbed his arm and tried again to reason with his friend. "OK, enough. I'll *talk*. What do you want?" He leaned back in the chair, massaged his eyes and gave Michael a bleak look. "Let's get it over with."

He watched as Michael pulled out a chair, sat down, and addressed Gabriel. "All right, help me out here?"

Gabriel flopped down in a chair at the other end of the table. "Michael, settle down. You're making way too big a deal out of this by dragging us all down here."

Thinking his friends must have lost their minds, he gestured impatiently at both of them. "Do either of you want to tell me why we're doing this? Is there some reason we have to talk here instead of upstairs in my room?"

Michael clasped his hands together on the table and looked at him. The wariness he saw in his friend's eyes only increased his edginess and he stood up. "Start talking, one of you, or I'm out of here."

Michael sighed heavily. "Rowan, we need to tell you something and to be honest, we're not sure how you're going to take it. And just so you know, if necessary, I *will* lock you in this room."

Sweat breaking on his forehead and in his armpits at Michael's words, he sank back down on the chair. *"Fine.* Do whatever you need to. Just stop screwing around and tell me what the hell is going on."

Gabriel rested his elbows on the table, put his chin in his hands and blinked at him. "Rowan, I want you to know, this conversation was not my idea. In my opinion, you need to continue healing, both physically and mentally."

Michael ignored Gabriel and stared at him, his mouth a firm line. "All right, I'll tell you what's going on, but take it easy. A couple weeks after we got you out of Sioux Falls, the FBI brought Danielle in for questioning. They interviewed her several times over the course of a month or so and then detained her. They're still holding her in Sioux Falls."

Stunned to silence, he stared back at Michael, pain tightening his chest at the thought of her being all alone in a cell. Not Danielle. And he hadn't known. They'd kept him in the dark while she suffered because of him. Anger fired deep inside. He stood up and limped around the table, glaring at first Michael and then Gabriel. "How could you keep this from me? Did Ralph sanction this?" He tapped his chest with a forefinger. "This is my responsibility. *She* is my responsibility. Goddamn it, I had a right to know."

Michael raised his hands and let them fall. "You were in no shape to be told, at least not right away. You needed to focus on healing, like Gabriel said. And no, Ralph didn't have anything to do with this. But Rowan, there's more. The Bureau has decided to charge Danielle with aiding and abetting. They're going to move her from Sioux Falls to a women's prison somewhere in the DC area to await trial. Ralph told us that Ainsley is expediting the process, planning a major, public announcement, hoping to bring you out of hiding."

Bending his head, he closed his eyes and tried to breathe evenly as visions of CIA thugs, Egyptian prisons and unspeakable torture slithered up from the depths of his mind. Swallowing hard, he opened his eyes and looked up, gazing coldly at first Michael and then Gabriel. "It looks like Ainsley wins this one. Get me a phone. I have to call Ralph. I'll surrender to him if the Bureau will agree to drop all the charges against Danielle and let her go." He glowered from one man to the other. "That's the only solution, and don't think you're going to tell me no, either of you."

While he continued staring at his colleagues, Gabriel crossed his arms and smirked at Michael. "I tried to tell you this would happen, but you wouldn't listen." Gabriel's gaze slid his way and his friend looked sad. "Rowan – amigo, we can't let you turn yourself in to the FBI. Don't you remember what they want to do with you? Besides, there are other forces at work here, and you know that. Muusa Shemal has paid off too many high level intelligence sources. If you turn yourself in, you'll be taken to a prison in Egypt. How will that help Danielle?"

Wiping sweaty palms on his jeans while his heart hammered, he tried to quell the terror winding through his mind. Once they had him in captivity, they could do anything they wanted with him. "No. I can't hide like a coward while Danielle is prosecuted for something she didn't do. My life is over. It ended when Muusa Shemal put a price on my head." Stabbing an index finger at his friends, he spoke forcefully. "You can lock me in this room for as long as you want, but it isn't going to change my mind. Just get me the phone."

Michael drummed his fingers on the table and looked at him from under dark brows. "What about rescuing Danielle? We could plan an operation the way we always have and keep both of you safe and free. You know Ralph and Chad would help us. I vote for that."

Why couldn't they get it? The discussion was over. His decision had been made, and it wasn't up for a vote. "Mike, these people are diabolical. If I don't turn myself in now, maybe they'll up the ante and let Muusa Shemal take Danielle to Tora Prison in order to bring me out of hiding. I can't let anything else happen to her now that I know what's going on. Once she's out of danger, if you can find a way to stop the FBI and CIA before they hand me over as Muusa Shemal's *prize*, I'm all for it. Now get me the *goddamned* phone."

One Week Later – Fourth Week In July – Sunday Morning
Ralph kept his hands at ten and two on the steering wheel of the white Chrysler 300 he'd rented at the Sioux Falls airport. Reflecting morosely that it was a nice day for a drive, he barreled west of Sioux Falls on I-90 at eighty-five miles an hour. He barely noticed the gently rolling fields of corn and beans interspersed between pastures populated with scrub trees and cattle that were either glossy black or burnt orange-red. God almighty. How could he deliver his friend into custody? Taking one hand off the wheel to massage the tension in the back of his neck, he wished for any other option.

Ainsley had been giddy with excitement over the prospects of capturing America's most wanted homegrown terrorist. Unfortunately, that didn't bode well for Rowan. Once they had their coveted prisoner, the FBI, or possibly even CIA interrogators would waste no time breaking him down to get a confession. Of course, according to Rowan's colleague, his friend had been mulishly stubborn, unwilling to consider any option besides surrender. He sighed. Rowan hadn't changed.

Squinting at the mile marker flashing past, he looked for his exit. Michael had explained that he and his cohort would be waiting with Rowan at a rest area overlooking the east side of the Missouri River. The man remained tight-lipped throughout their conversations setting up the details of his friend's surrender, offering no hints about where Rowan had been hidden.

Ainsley had balked at first, saying *No way,* when he'd explained that Rowan would only come forward if he kept the operation low-key and managed it alone. Oh no, his boss had wanted a splashy, public Bureau arrest. Then the greedy jerk wanted to figure out a way to hang on to Danielle. But in the end, Ainsley had agreed to Rowan's demands. And hell, why shouldn't he? The bastard was getting what he wanted.

Pulling off the interstate, he headed up a hill following a road that curved back across the four lanes of traffic. Cresting the long incline, looking west, his mouth fell open. The Missouri River sparkled at the bottom of the hill with the town of Chamberlain nestled on its banks. Lofty, untamed bluffs shimmered in the heat on the west side of the river. Compared to the pastoral fields on the east side, his first view of West River, as he'd heard the locals call it, looked like an entirely different country.

Cruising slowly through the rest area looking for a parking space, he saw a South Dakota Highway Patrol station. The actual rest area building, a Tourist Information Center was further along and had scattered white picnic tables separated with stone walls and cement overhangs. A huge teepee made of cement poles sat adjacent to the building.

He pulled into a parking spot and shut off the car. Glancing out the window, he saw Rowan, almost unrecognizable with shoulder length hair and a sparse beard, lounging at one of the picnic tables between two men sporting ball caps and sunglasses. Together they made a menacing trio, and he felt the hair on his arms rising as he watched them.

Climbing stiffly out of the car, he winced for the first few steps until his joints limbered up. Despite the situation, a smile creased his face. It was good to see his friend in one piece instead of lying in a hospital bed. Raising a hand, he waved. Rowan stood up, nodded and walked toward him with a slight limp.

Not sure what to expect, he faced the younger man on the cement walkway. "It's good to see you, but I wish the circumstances were different."

Rowan stared at him, eyes cold. "Let's get this over with, Ralph. Do you need to cuff me here?"

How had he forgotten what a jerk Rowan could be? "Aw come on, don't pull this shit with me. Not now, not this time. And no, I don't need to cuff you here. We'll stop a few miles from Sioux Falls and take care of that."

Rowan gave him an indifferent shrug and looked past him. "All right, let's get going. I don't want Danielle to be detained a minute longer than necessary."

So that's how Rowan wanted to play it. Turning on his heel, he intended to wave at the other two men, but stopped short. They had disappeared. He headed back toward the car, walked to the passenger side and opened the front door, before Rowan could climb in the back like a prisoner, which was exactly what the damn idiot would do.

Amazed at how quickly he'd become irritated, he frowned. This time he wasn't going to put up with his friend's rotten attitude. Sliding into the driver's seat, he watched Rowan get in the car, glimpsing raised scars on the younger man's wrists beneath the long-sleeved shirt. "Look, I know I can't make this any easier for you, but damn it, you're like a son. It's killing me to do this."

As they pulled onto the eastbound lane of I-90, Rowan turned sideways in the seat, his face a hard mask. "I'm sorry. I hate that Danielle's been detained because of me and I just, I don't want to think about what's coming my way. Michael and Gabriel insist they've got a plan in the works to pull me out, but I can't depend on that. You know as well as I do that once we arrive wherever Ainsley wants me, it's over. Who knows what will happen?"

Ralph took another quick gander at Rowan and clamped his hands tighter on the wheel. Now that his friend had opened up, there wasn't much he could say to help him. "Your colleagues are experts at getting you out of dangerous situations, and you know Chad and I will help in any way we can. We've got a strategy in place for removing Danielle from harm's way. Your parents and sister are already safe. I won't tell you about it. That way, no one can get any information out of you."

It pleased him to see a spark of hope in Rowan's dark eyes. "Thanks, Ralph. I need your help with one other thing. Do you still have my briefcase?"

Nodding, he frowned at his companion. "Yeah, I've got your briefcase, but there's nothing in it. The contents had to be turned over to the CIA."

Rowan's shoulders drooped. "If they didn't already find it, there's another hidden section in the briefcase and it holds an ATM card for a Wells Fargo Money Market account that I set up years ago, under the name of James Hawthorne." Rowan paused and slanted a pensive smile his way. "I used to play a drinking game I called *What If* and one night I came up with the idea for an assumed name and identity, just in case." The smile vanished. "I want you to give the card to Danielle. Michael is creating the paperwork necessary to add her to the account as Mrs.

Hawthorne. Over the years I managed to stash over a million dollars in that account, and I want her to have it. And, can you take this for me?"

Glancing surreptitiously from the two lanes of summer traffic surrounding them, he watched Rowan dig in the front pocket of his jeans. Pulling out what looked like a gold coin with the twin towers etched on it, his friend laid it on the console between the seats. "I'd like you to give this to Danielle the next time you see her. She gave it to me last spring." Rowan looked at him again, the façade shifted and he saw the naked desperation on his friend's face. "Please tell her I treasured it, but I can't keep it now. It'll just get taken and have its meaning misconstrued somehow. Ask her to keep it for me, OK?" The mask slipped back in place and Rowan turned, faced forward in the seat and closed his eyes.

They drove on in silence. He wanted to tell the younger man so many things, but none of them seemed appropriate given the situation, so he stayed quiet. Rowan eventually dozed and he let him sleep until he noticed the green *Sioux Falls, 12 Miles* highway sign. He gently touched his friend's arm. "Rowan, we're getting close to Sioux Falls. Let me brief you on what's going to happen. We'll go directly to the private side of the airport. The Bureau has a jet standing by." Rowan nodded, eyes bleary with sleep.

Gripping the wheel harder, hating what he had to say, he continued. "Sioux Falls SWAT will be there, thanks to your penchant for escaping from custody. By early afternoon, you'll be in the brig at Quantico. I'm sorry, once we arrive there, I'm afraid you'll be out of my reach." He glanced from the road to his friend. "You need to know this. Ainsley thinks you're a fertile source of terror-related information. He intends to break you down fairly rapidly."

Rowan rubbed his eyes and looked at him, the hard mask of stubborn defiance firmly in place. "Ainsley's in for a big surprise."

When Ralph swung the Chrysler off North Minnesota Avenue and down the long drive to the private side of the airport, Rowan drew in deep breaths, trying to slow his pounding heart. Overwhelmed by unreasoning panic, he looked at the steel handcuffs enclosing his wrists. Every time he moved, he felt the weight, saw the padlock, and heard the clanking from the other chain that attached to leg irons. They'd parked at a truck stop near the airport so Ralph could lock the restraints around his waist, wrists and ankles. Closing his eyes, he tried to shove the invading terror aside. He'd made his choice and accepted the consequences.

The car stopped and he opened his eyes. A Sioux Falls armored SWAT vehicle sat next to the massive hangar. The back end opened while he watched, disgorging six men in full combat gear, carrying rifles. For God's sake, did they think he was a one-man terror organization? His heart sank when he looked further and saw three news vans and reporters with microphones trailed by camera lugging companions on the other side of the chain link fence that surrounded the airport. Ralph touched him and he jumped.

The older man gripped his arm. "I'm sorry, Rowan, but it's time. As soon as we're airborne, I'll get you out of the restraints. Unfortunately, right now I have to play my role, as much as I detest the whole process."

Breathless, he jerked his head up and down. "I understand. Let's just get it over with."

Ralph swore, swung open the door and clambered out of the vehicle. The SWAT team closed around the Chrysler, rifles aimed. He pulled in another quick breath as Ralph opened the passenger side door. His ex-boss had assumed the hard-boiled

Navy SEAL persona, eyes hidden behind sunglasses. "Step out of the vehicle please, Mr. Hassani."

Not sure how his body would respond, he squinted up at Ralph. His legs moved and he shifted around, swinging them awkwardly to the pavement, leg irons scraping the skin above his ankles. Ralph reached in, took a firm hold on his arm, and spoke in a low voice. "Easy Rowan, I've got you. Let me help you out of the car."

He didn't know if he could stand up and walk to the jet. The cuffs, the clanking chains, and the leg irons sent his mind into a tail-spin. Shaking, panic-stricken and powerless to defend himself, he knew he needed to get away, before the two CIA agents came to hang him by his wrists again. But he couldn't, he'd made his decision. This was what he had to do.

Ralph pulled him upright and he stood next to the car, swaying back and forth. When the SWAT team slid closer, rifles poised, ferocious rage swept his errant thoughts aside, and his lips twisted in a sneer. What was wrong with them? Couldn't they see he was trussed up like a goddamned animal?

Ralph shoved his sunglasses onto his forehead and looked at him, eyes widening in alarm. "Rowan, son, you gotta shitcan the attitude. Walk with me to the plane, right now. Come on, let's move."

Body rigid, breath coming in short gasps, he glared at Ralph. "Get those bastards out of here. What the hell do they think I'm going to do, call down jihad from the sky?"

Ralph didn't let go of his arm, but he swung around. "OK gentlemen, back off. You heard me. Roll back, right now. The situation is under control."

Jaws clenched, he watched the six men move reluctantly toward their vehicle. Next to him, Ralph sagged and let go of his arm. Sketching a wave at the men, his friend turned to look at him, sweat dripping down the sides of his face. "All right, let's go. You need to take short steps and let me help you."

Rage dissipating as quickly as it had surged, he saw the concern in Ralph's eyes. He took one step, then another, until they reached the aircraft stairs. Helpless, he stopped and looked at Ralph again. "It's my foot. It doesn't bend very well and the chain's too short. The cuffs; I can't reach the railings. I'm sorry."

Ralph pulled keys from his pocket and crouched down beside him. "Don't apologize, Rowan. I'll fix it." The leg irons fell off his ankles and Ralph stood up. Giving him a gruff smile, his friend unlocked the cuffs and the chain, pulling the clanking restraints away. "There you go. Now take your time and be careful with that foot."

Grateful for the simple kindness and humiliated beyond measure, he could only whisper. "Thank you."

Ralph squeezed his shoulder. "It's all right. Now let's do this before those SWAT boys have a conniption fit over a loose terrorist."

Seated across the table from Rodney Ainsley, Muusa Shemal rejoiced. Squeezing his hands together in triumph, he smiled at the televised images of Rowan Milani, in custody again because of his efforts. Let Allah be forever praised. It was a good day for the cause of jihad. Once more the man who had eluded and frustrated him was within his grasp. This time, by Allah's gracious favor, he would not escape.

Elated at the ease with which he'd worked his way into Rodney Ainsley's confidence over the last five months and how quickly it had paid off, he decided a celebration was in order. Fortunately, the Wynfrey Hotel in Birmingham, Alabama offered an array of dining options that met his epicurean standards. His celebration would commence immediately following his arrival and meeting with the faithful. One of the most intensely devoted groups in the country, the assembly in Birmingham always energized him with their fervor for Allah and jihad.

Now he could begin the next phase of his plan. Once Rowan Milani had been transferred to his custody, the ghost agent would make his final home in Egypt, where he would pay for his crimes against Allah for many years. The anticipation of such a richly deserved retribution left him breathless with desire. He gazed for a moment longer at the humbled man. The Brotherhood would have its vengeance, at his hand, as Allah's chosen instrument. It would be his honor to fulfill that destiny.

Hearing Ainsley clear his throat, he turned his thoughts back to the present and gazed at the man seated across the table in an impeccable black suit and gray silk tie. His manicured hands and bony face with its receding hairline and carefully combed blond hair made Shemal want to laugh out loud. Creating doubts about Rowan Milani in this kafir's mind had been ridiculously easy. But he tolerated the man, because of his groveling, subservient attitude.

Even now, he spoke like a true dhimmi. "Mr. Shemal, I can't thank you enough for bringing this treasonous man to our attention last winter and assisting with his capture. It will be my pleasure to remand him to your custody, courtesy of the CIA, once I've gleaned the information I need. I don't expect that to take longer than a week. A close colleague of mine in the CIA will conduct his interrogation at Quantico."

Shemal smiled indulgently at Ainsley. "Give me Rowan Milani for a day, and you'll have whatever information you require. The sooner he becomes my possession and resides in my country, the sooner your Intelligence Community will be free of the blight his presence has created."

The FBI's Director smoothed the silk tie and chuckled. "You've never met Senior CIA Field Agent Sal Capello. He's well respected in the Intelligence Community, and I've arranged a dinner meeting for the three of us later this week, if you'll be available. At that time, he can provide an update on how his interrogation is progressing and finalize plans for transport. If the two of you can come to agreeable terms, he's indicated that he'd be interested in accompanying Hassani to Egypt as a CIA handler."

He continued smiling at Ainsley, but in his heart he felt only revulsion. The Americans were all the same. Dollars always mattered more than honor, and for the right price, he could purchase anyone. But so be it. He'd offer the CIA agent more dollars than the kafir would see in a lifetime, if it would ensure that the agent would trust him completely and not listen to anything Rowan Milani might say about his and the Brotherhood's activities. It was imperative that he gain custody of the crafty jinn as soon as possible. He nodded. "Mr. Ainsley, allow me to speak personally with agent Capello. I will reward him generously, of course. And I will make our dinner a priority. But now, I must continue my travels. Allah has given me many opportunities to reach out to his faithful in this great country."

Danielle stared in disbelief at special agent Hawkins, sitting across from her at the beat up metal table in the interrogation room. "You mean I can go? It's all over and you don't want me anymore?"

Hawkins mopped the hair off his forehead in a gesture she'd become familiar with. His smile seemed genuine. "That's correct, Ms. Stratton. You are free to go, no strings attached."

When he pushed back his chair and closed the file with her name on it, she stopped him. "Wait. How did this happen? I thought you were charging me with aiding and abetting a terrorist. How can you just suddenly change your mind? I don't understand. And what's to stop you from changing your mind again, later?"

Avoiding eye contact with her, the special agent stood up. "That information is classified, Ms. Stratton. We determined that your connection with Rowan Milani was innocuous. Let me escort you out. I'm sure you want to collect your things and begin enjoying your freedom."

Fighting rising anger, she stayed sitting, staring at the FBI special agent who'd grilled her over and over, asking the same questions in endless combinations, changing obscure details to confuse her and trip up her answers. "Special agent Hawkins, I could have told you, well I did tell you, many times, that my connection to Rowan Milani was as innocent as he is. You ignored me, accused me of lying, and practically of treason. Don't tell me that the explanation for my release is classified. Just tell me the truth, like I've been telling you."

Watching the red creep up Hawkins' neck, she felt some vindication. But when he smiled at her, his mouth had a sarcastic twist. "All right, Ms. Stratton, come with me. I'll show you why you're free to go." He waved her out of the chair and opened the door.

Following him down a hallway, her trepidation grew. Why had she argued? Why hadn't she accepted her freedom and left? Hawkins opened a door and motioned her through. Stepping into a small room with a TV on a cart, she turned to look at him. "What's this about?"

Grabbing the remote, Hawkins punched buttons. "You might as well see it here. I recorded this just an hour ago." A video started and she stood, arms crossed, watching a gleaming white Learjet land on what looked like a military base. The jet taxied to a stop and soldiers armed with huge rifles surrounded it. The camera panned closer as the door to the jet opened and the stairs lowered. A man appeared in the doorway, and she gasped. Was that Rowan's boss, Ralph? It was, and he gestured to the men with rifles. Two of the armed soldiers ascended the stairs and disappeared inside the aircraft.

Hand over her mouth, she watched wide-eyed as Rowan stepped into view at the top of the air stairs, flanked on either side by a soldier. Unwanted tears filled her eyes as she remembered

---

Mary Yungeberg

the first time she'd seen him, standing in the doorway of a private jet. But this time, he was restrained and the soldiers held onto him as he took halting steps down the stairs, head bowed.

Once on the tarmac, he never looked up and the two soldiers hustled him into the back seat of a black Suburban. It drove away fast, followed by another Suburban. The camera shifted and she saw Ralph standing alone in the doorway of the aircraft, looking forlorn. Wobbly with shock, she leaned against the wall and wiped away the tears that strayed down her cheeks.

The screen turned to snowy static, and special agent Hawkins stepped in front of the TV. "Well, Ms. Stratton, now you know. Rowan Milani purchased your freedom. Apparently he had an attack of conscience when he heard you were going to be prosecuted. He surrendered in exchange for your release."

Staring at the abominable man, she wanted to slap the smug smile from his face. But he wasn't worth the effort. Rowan had traded his life for hers. How much would he suffer? Swallowing past the hard lump in her throat, she looked at Hawkins. "I'm ready to leave. Can you show me the way out of here, please?"

Thirty minutes later, clutching the meager belongings she'd relinquished nearly three and a half months earlier, she stood outside, blinking in the sunshine. Looking across the parking lot, she stopped, thoughts swirling. It felt so strange to be free of special agent Hawkins and the endless questions, free to walk home and curl up in her own bed, free to cry her heart out over Rowan.

A movement caught her eye and her mouth dropped open. In the far corner of the parking lot, Chad leaned against the red Mustang he'd been so proud of last spring. Smiling, he waved her over. "Hi Danielle, how are you holding up?"

The kindness in his voice had her blinking away fresh tears. "Hello Chad. I'm afraid I'm not doing too well. What are you doing here? I thought you'd be gone. Didn't you resign?"

217

Chad gave her a quick hug and opened the passenger door. "Climb in and let's talk. I've got a proposition for you. And don't worry. We're going to get Rowan back, just as soon as we finish putting our plan together."

After she slid into the car, Chad slammed the door and sprinted around to the driver's side. Observing how he folded his long frame into the low-slung Mustang, she smiled sadly. Rowan had told her how much he liked Chad, and she could see why. His sunny personality must have been a constant uplift. "I'm dying to hear your proposition. But I'm worried sick about Rowan. How can you get him out of this mess?"

Chad shot her an enigmatic smile as he swung the car out of the parking lot onto Minnesota Avenue. "How'd you like to relocate with Rowan to a secluded beach estate on Kauai?"

CHAPTER FIFTEEN

Sunday Afternoon
Sitting slumped over on the narrow bed in the eight-by-eight foot cinderblock cell, Rowan wondered when the interrogation would start and what would happen to him. His uneasy gaze wandered from the small steel sink and toilet in one corner, then up to the tiny black camera high in the opposite corner. He twisted around, trying to reach a spot between his shoulders. The orange jumpsuit with *Quantico Brig* stenciled across the back scratched him in all the wrong places.

Succumbing to rising panic, he stood up and limped to the door, the slam and clank still echoing in his mind. Constructed of solid steel, the only openings were two sliding metal plates inset at floor and waist levels so the guards could cuff and shackle him before he left the cell, and release him after locking him inside. Sitting again, he closed his eyes, propped his elbows on his knees, and rested his head in his hands. Waiting was part of the hell.

A blaring whistle pierced the silence, and a disembodied voice instructed him to approach the door. Heart slamming against his chest, he thought, *fuck them*. If they wanted him, they could come and get him. The voice repeated the instructions, but he didn't move. The door swung open and two guards, weapons drawn, strode into the cell. In the hallway outside the door he saw another guard standing with his gun drawn. The spectacle brought the indiscriminate rage bubbling to the surface again. What did all these people think he could do to them?

The taller of the two stern-faced men barked commands and kept a pistol aimed at his chest. "Stand up. Move over here.

Now." He stared at them, breathing hard. The guard repeated the commands, and then both of them stepped in front of him.

The shorter of the two rolled his eyes at his companion, holstered his pistol, bent down and got in his face. "Hey, *raghead*, we're talking to you." Rage overflowing, he balled his fist and smashed the man in the mouth as hard as he could.

Chaos ensued as the man fell backward, cursing, blood gushing from a split-open bottom lip. The other guard pounced, rolled him over, and cuffed his hands behind his back. Lifting him upright, the guard turned him around and shoved him back down on the bed. He watched helplessly while the guard who'd stood in the hallway slapped on leg irons. Both of the men were red-faced and out of breath. The other one sat on the floor, a hand over his mouth, blood dripping down his arm.

Glowering at him, the guard from the hallway spoke. "What are you trying to pull? You can't get away with assaulting federal agents. You're going to make things a lot more difficult for yourself."

Jaws clenched, he focused his attention on the grimy cinderblock floor. The barrel of a pistol tapped the side of his head. "Hey, look at me." Sullen and subdued, he stared at the angry young man. "When you are asked, step to the door and place your hands and feet in the appropriate sliders. That is the procedure at Quantico, and you're expected to follow it to the letter. Do you understand?"

They could do all kinds of things to him, and they could keep him from doing anything, but goddamn it, they couldn't make him talk. The two guards looked at each other and the taller one shrugged. "Maybe he doesn't speak English."

While he sat on the edge of the bed, his nose started to run like it always did, and he sniffed. The other guard frowned at his companion. "Don't you know who this guy is? He's the FBI double agent who turned himself in this morning. I'm sure he knows exactly what you're saying. He's just stubborn. But that'll change. It always does. C'mon, we've got our orders, so let's get to it."

The other guard nodded. "Fine, let's take care of this."

Certain he'd earned a beating, he watched the men warily. Each one grabbed an arm and yanked him off the bed. Pulling him toward the door, they waited until their injured colleague scrambled to his feet and stepped ahead of them into the hallway, a white handkerchief plastered to his mouth. The three guards walked him down the hall, around a corner, and then down another hall. After turning yet another corner, they stopped while the injured guard pulled keys from his pocket and unlocked a steel door.

They entered a chilly, cinderblock cell like the one they'd dragged him from, except this one didn't have a bed, sink or toilet, just an eye bolt drilled into the ceiling and a corresponding one in the floor. What looked like sprinklers were set at intervals in the ceiling and a black surveillance camera with a winking red light was mounted high in a corner of this cell also. Along one wall sat a metal step stool with a thick silver chain draped over its top.

After positioning him in the middle of the room, one guard squatted down and snapped the chain on the leg irons to the eye bolt. The tall guard grabbed the foot stool and chain, snapping the weighted links to the cuffs holding his hands behind his back. While his companion offered a hand for balance, the young man stepped on the stool and snapped the other end to the eye bolt in the ceiling. As simple as that, he'd been rendered completely helpless to do anything but stand in one spot.

The three men surveyed him, hands on hips, except for the one he'd punched, who still clutched the bloodied handkerchief to his mouth. The tall guard stepped forward and smacked him on the back of his head. "Have a nice day, jerk. We'll see if this improves your attitude and your ability to answer questions." The three men filed from the cell and slammed the door. He heard the lock turn and hung his head. His left foot ached and he realized that his enervated mind hadn't even reacted when the cuffs went on his wrists. The fluorescent lights burned bright. He closed his eyes.

CIA agent Sal Capello chewed on a toothpick while he watched Rowan Milani on the monitor from the observation room in the maximum security wing of the brig. Over the course of his career he'd dealt with hundreds of detainees, and he couldn't wait to get started on this one. He chuckled. The noble fool had surrendered to the FBI to save his girlfriend, but Rowan Milani didn't know that Rodney Ainsley had already turned the tables and agreed to remand custody of him to the CIA.

The girlfriend had been tagged for pick-up by Seth Hancock and Lucien Talbot. Eager to exculpate themselves, they'd asked for the assignment. Taking a last look at his prisoner, it pleased him to see the man standing with his head down. Grunting in satisfaction, he turned to the agent on duty. "Here's what I want you to do."

Stepping carefully down the aircraft steps, Danielle marveled at how quickly they'd arrived on the island of Kauai. Nearing sunset, the fragrance of fresh flowers hung on the light breeze. The quick good-bye to Derek, the hair-raising drive down I-29 with Chad in the Mustang, and meeting Rowan's colleagues seemed like a dream after the months of interrogation and detention. Hurrying across the tarmac on the private side of Omaha's Epply Airfield and onto the waiting jet had left her breathless.

In the midst of her chaotic departure, she'd never felt more certain of the *rightness* of what she was doing. But her heart ached, knowing that Rowan had surrendered to secure her freedom. Michael and Gabriel had been friendly and solicitous, getting her blankets and a pillow, and offering drinks and food, which she couldn't stomach. Jerry and Bryan, the same pilots, they told her, who'd flown Rowan to safety last spring, had treated her kindly. But none of them could fix the devastating emptiness that overwhelmed her.

Michael stepped to her side and touched her elbow. "We've got a vehicle waiting in the parking lot, Danielle. Once we get to the estate you can settle in, see Bettina and meet Ralph's wife, Marion. Did you know that Rowan's parents are here, too? If you feel up to it, I know they'd love to meet you."

Responding as gamely as she could to his kind demeanor, she nodded as they walked. "That sounds fine. I did know Rowan's parents were here, but I hadn't thought about meeting them." Michael stopped in front of a shiny, black Cadillac Escalade and opened the passenger side door for her. Gabriel, Jerry, and Bryan stowed the bags and piled into the back seat.

Closing her eyes, she tipped her head back and half listened to the quiet conversation around her. She wondered what time it was in Washington, DC and what was happening to Rowan. Thinking about him, at the mercy of people who'd never believe he was innocent, who'd hurt him to get the answers they wanted, brought stinging tears to her eyes. Feeling a hand on her shoulder, she blinked the tears away and turned. Gabriel smiled sympathetically from the back seat. "Honey, don't you worry. We'll get Rowan out of this mess. After you get settled I'll tell you some stories about how many times the four of us have pulled his nuts out of the fire."

When he rolled his chocolate-brown eyes dramatically, she couldn't help smiling. "Thanks, Gabriel. I would love to hear your stories about Rowan. It's just, knowing they'll hurt him is so awful."

Gabriel gripped her shoulder. "Danielle, honey, the first thing you have to remember is that Rowan is one tough hombre. He knows how to handle himself. The second thing is this: we are very good at what we do. Failure isn't an option for us. When we go after Rowan, we *will* succeed. You just think about that. And tonight, if you want, I'll give you something so you can get some rest."

Telling herself to buck up, she managed another smile. "I'll try to think positive. And if you can give me something later, after we talk, I'd like that."

Monday Morning
When a loud knock on the front door alerted Shasta, Derek glared at the big dog as she barked and growled. Following her, he muttered to himself. "It figures, now I'm stuck with this mutt for good."

Opening the door, he grabbed Shasta's collar and looked questioningly at the two men standing on the front steps. Recognition dawned and he felt a shiver of fear. He'd seen the stocky black-haired man and his muscular blond companion at the airport meeting that fancy CIA jet. Shasta growled again and practically dragged him out the door. "Shasta, sit." The big dog sat, but the hair stood up all along her back. "Sorry. Can I help you?"

The men pulled out ID's and flipped them open. He couldn't read the names, but he couldn't miss the letters in bold print. These men were CIA agents. The taller of the two, the blond, smiled at him. "We'd like to talk to Ms. Stratton. Would you mind if we came inside?" The man sidled toward the door.

Shasta bared her teeth and snarled. Holy cow, was the guy nuts? Tilting his head at the dog, he said, "Uh, I don't think coming inside is such a good idea. I can't always control her like Dani, I mean Ms. Stratton. But anyway, she's not here. She left and I don't know when she's coming back or where she went." Chad had given him a cell number, *just in case,* but neither Danielle nor Chad had told him anything, and for once he was glad. Looking from one man to the other, he doubted they would buy his story, even though it was the truth.

The black-haired agent stared at him with hard, disbelieving eyes. "Ms. Stratton left without telling you when or even *if* she's coming back, and you're stuck with her *dog?*"

Smiling weakly, he looked from one man to the other. "Sucks to be me, I know. Can you leave me a card or something? If I hear from her, I could have her call you."

The two agents looked at each other. Then the shorter man frowned at him. "We'll check back in a couple days. You don't have any plans to leave, do you, Mr. Norris?"

How did they know his name? Swallowing, hoping he could talk, he answered. "Nope, I'm a working stiff, stuck here for the foreseeable future."

The blond agent looked pointedly at Shasta. "When we come back, you'll have to do something with the dog." With a final smirk, the tall agent turned and walked down the steps and his companion followed.

Michael looked up from the deck chair, watching as Gabriel stepped off the brick walkway onto the sugary white sand. After shedding his shirt for an impromptu swim, he'd retreated to the deck chair to clear his mind and assess their options. Now the light breeze made him shiver and his saltwater soaked shorts weren't helping. "How's Danielle doing? Did she settle in all right last night?"

Gabriel flopped down next to him on a matching chair. "I gave her one of my special pills so she could get some rest, but she's so sad. I tried to cheer her up, but all she can think about is how much Rowan is suffering, and she blames herself."

Momentarily captivated by the sunlight sparkling on the waves, he nodded. "The sooner we get Rowan out of Quantico the better. But fuck me, we have another problem."

Gabriel looked at him, alarm written on his face. "What now? What else could possibly go wrong?"

Waiting for his friend to finish, he grimaced. "Are you done whining?" He stared pointedly at Gabriel, and then continued. "Here's the thing. Danielle lived with a guy. His name is Derek. He's been approached by those two CIA assholes we dealt with last spring. They came to the house, looking for Danielle. Derek called Chad. Chad called me and then I called Derek. The poor guy is scared shitless of being taken in for interrogation. The last thing we need is another lever in the hands of the CIA. The way I see it, our only option is to fly back to Omaha today and haul his sorry ass out here, too. What do you think?"

Gabriel stared anxiously at him, making the sign of the Cross as he began to speak. "Sweet Mother of God, what else can we do? You know as well as I do that Rowan would never let the gringo be incarcerated because of him. You want me to fly back with Jerry and Bryan? Or do you want me to stay here with the women?"

He shrugged. "You stay here and keep an eye on Danielle. I'll call Derek and make arrangements. It's five hours later in South Dakota, and he needs to get ready to leave." He scowled at Gabriel. "And here's the frosting on the cake. Danielle has a dog, a freaking Rottweiler. I don't know what to do about that. We can't waste time making arrangements for a dog." He stood up, reluctant to leave the soothing waves.

Gabriel pursed his lips and raised an index finger. "Wait a second. What about sending the dog to the ranch? We could send Derek there, too."

Why hadn't he thought of that? "You know, that's a damn good idea, at least for the dog. But Derek, I don't think so. The guy's too much of a wild card right now. When I talked to him on the phone, he sounded badly shaken up. I think we better bring him out here and let him chill." Taking the time to rub his jaw, he squinted at Gabriel, wondering where he'd left his sunglasses. "Then we can help him decide what he wants to do with the rest of his life. It hasn't dawned on the poor bastard yet that he's another victim of the Rowan Milani saga." Starting up the brick pathway, he stopped and gestured to his stocky colleague. "You better come help me with these phone calls. I've got to reach my mother and have her meet me in Sioux Falls, and I need to rent a car at Epply. We'd better get on this before it turns into a *real* pain in the ass."

Janice Milani sat comfortably in the cheery sun room off the kitchen, sipping a cup of tea and enjoying the tropical breeze. Outside the screened windows an overgrown tangle of flowers, shrubs, and deep grass spread across the wide lawn. The house itself was nestled in a semi-circle of tall trees with a brick walkway that cut through the lawn and led directly to the beach. Now that she and Khalil were settling into their new life, she planned to revamp the gardens and landscaping around the estate. The satisfying task would take her months, if not an entire year. Happy to have something productive to occupy her time, she looked forward to creating a new look for the sprawling property.

Working with the soil and the plants distracted her mind from the latest catastrophe involving Rowan. Although Khalil had cautioned her against watching the news footage of his surrender, she couldn't help herself. Hungry for a glimpse of her son, she'd been shocked at the hard-faced man with a beard and hair that grazed his chin. Watching had left her in tears, but she'd needed to see him.

Glancing up, she saw a slender woman with dark red hair pouring a cup of coffee in the kitchen. Oh dear Lord, that had to be Rowan's friend. Hurrying in from the sun room, she stopped and smiled as the woman fixed her with a desolate gaze. "Good morning. You must be Danielle. I'm Rowan's mother, Janice. It's nice to meet you. Welcome to Kauai."

Danielle smiled back at her. "Hello Mrs. Milani. It's very nice to meet you. I have, I mean Rowan has mentioned you." As she watched, Danielle sat her coffee cup on the kitchen counter and took a deep breath.

The raw ache in the younger woman's eyes moved her. "Oh my dear, I know it's hard. Believe me, I do. Come and sit down. You can tell me everything and we'll say a prayer for Rowan to remain strong and be released quickly. And I would love to hear all about how you and he met. I'm sure it's a beautiful story."

Monday Afternoon
Sitting in a booth at the busy deli not far from his father's office, Chad sipped iced tea and gazed out the window. His father crossed the street with long strides, impeccably dressed in a dark blue suit, white shirt and snazzy tie. The oppressive heat and humidity of the District during the summer never fazed his father. He always looked cool and refreshed. Sliding into the booth across from him, Clifton Cantor smiled. "It's great to see you again, Chad."

Eyeing the older man's tie, a bold paisley print in lemon, navy and white, he had to chuckle. Only his father could pull that off. "It's good to see you too, and that's a great tie. You want some lunch? It's on me."

Clifton shook his head. "I'm meeting a client for an early dinner. That iced tea looks good, though."

After the harried waitress slammed a tall, dripping glass of iced tea in front of his father and refilled his, he ran an index finger up and down the glass, turning the condensation into rivulets of water. "Thanks for meeting me here. I hope you can fill me in on what, if anything, you've learned from your inquiries on Rowan's behalf. And Dad, I just got in. Would you have a problem with me staying in the Georgetown condo?"

Clifton sipped the tea and glanced casually around the noisy deli, then regarded him solemnly. "What I found out is disturbing, to say the least. The President wants to believe your friend is innocent, but he's been pressured by the Directors of both the FBI and CIA, as well as foreign sources. Besides, if the President were to speak out, he'd divulge his own hand in the violation of numerous sovereign governments."

His father stopped talking and ran two fingers around the inside of his collar in a subconscious concession to the weather. "I'd be almost certain Mr. Milani is cognizant of the fact that any admission or support from the President would undermine national security. If the situation hadn't become a media firestorm and if he hadn't been influenced by so many powerful sources, I believe the President would have stopped the whole thing."

The older man shrugged. "Now, of course, the media and the entire country are enamored with the story of Rowan's disappearance, surrender on behalf of Danielle, and his incarceration at Quantico. Despite the domestic and foreign pressure, the President is not planning to aid the investigations of the FBI or CIA in any manner. As I said, he wants to believe Rowan is innocent of the allegations against him."

Shaking his head in frustration, he frowned at his father. "That makes me sick. For the President to be co-opted enough to doubt Rowan's innocence bothers me, a hell of a lot." He sighed and rubbed his forehead. "Look Dad, I know you're busy, but did you have a chance to make inroads on any other levels?"

His father's face turned grim. "You were on target when you said something wasn't right at the Bureau. Rodney Ainsley is taking directions from Muusa Shemal, the Egyptian national you told me about."

Thinking his jaw would hit the table, he stared open-mouthed at his father. "*What? * Ainsley is working with the man who orchestrated the destruction of Rowan's life and wants to take him to an Egyptian prison?"

Looking sickened, Clifton continued. "That's the way it appears, and he may very well get that done, sooner rather than later. Mr. Shemal has cleverly presented himself as a moderate, dedicated to educating the faithful in the pursuit of a jihad-free version of Islam. Along with that, he has taken great pains to paint Rowan Milani as the worst kind of traitor. And he's succeeding, magnificently, in both endeavors. Both Ainsley and his cohort in the CIA, a senior field agent named Sal Capello, are convinced that Shemal is above reproach."

Clifton fiddled with his straw. "The other thing I've learned is that Mr. Shemal is paying an exorbitant amount of money to Ainsley and Capello for the privilege of hauling your friend to Tora Prison in Egypt. The Muslim Brotherhood and Shemal have expended a mind-boggling amount of money to engineer the betrayal of Rowan Milani."

His father paused and swirled the ice in his glass of tea. "I believe Shemal and the Muslim Brotherhood must have discovered the extent of Rowan's subterfuge on behalf of the United States, and they've taken it upon themselves to exact retribution. Your friend has angered the powers that be in the Islamic world in a very big way, and they're slobbering all over themselves to get their hands on him. Shemal has first dibs, but even he may have to forego custody if the Brotherhood insists."

The sense of urgency to rescue Rowan had become unbearable. Trying to get a grip on his thoughts, Chad shoved his fingers through his hair, which refused to do anything but droop in a disheveled mess atop his head. "Dad, we've got to get Rowan out of Quantico. What about the condo, can I use it as a base of operations? We need to move on this situation."

Clifton looked around the bustling eatery once more and gave him a sly smile. "I'd love to have you at the condo, but I've got a better idea. For years I've kept an apartment near your mother's Alzheimer's facility. You know how I feel about security and anonymity. This apartment is leased to a corporation belonging to a friend of mine in Chicago and bears absolutely no connection to the name Cantor. I'll give you a key right now. In addition, the black Mercedes, which is registered to the same company in

Chicago, is yours to use as long as you want. It's parked in the garage at the office."

Dread for Rowan burgeoning out of control, he could barely speak. "Thanks Dad. We can trade cars. I've got the Mustang here. You can drive it if you want. But right now, I need to get going. I've got a lot to do, and apparently not much time. I can't tell you how much I appreciate your help."

His father nodded. "Be extremely careful. If there's anything else I can do, please call me. Otherwise, I know where you'll be, and I'll watch what happens on FOX and read about it in the Post." Clifton slid out of the booth and smiled again. "Let's go trade cars. I'm looking forward to this. A Shelby GT500 convertible, and red no less. I'll rediscover my lost youth."

Monday Evening
Lulled by the steady roar of the twin turbofan engines, Derek looked sleepily out the window of the Gulfstream G650, barely able to believe he was flying close to the speed of sound in a luxury jet. Striding across the tarmac in Omaha, he'd stopped and stared at the spectacular aircraft he'd watched land in Sioux Falls the previous spring. Of course, then it had been white. Now it was gleaming, metallic black. Feeling like an incredibly simple man living what had, up until a few days earlier, been a mundane life, he shook his head.

It was difficult for him to relate to men who could steal a jet like this from the CIA without batting an eye, actually have the balls to keep it, and then fly the thing all over God's creation. When he asked, Michael had blown off his curiosity, explaining that Chad had fixed everything with his hacking ability. The computer genius had created a bogus front company, a new tail number, registry of ownership, and blah, blah, blah.

The mess he found himself embroiled in was over his head. What could he do now that he'd been uprooted from his career, friends and family? Would he have to assume a new identity, like someone stuck in witness protection? How would he support himself? He'd always loved airplanes and had worked as a mechanic for Legacy before transferring to Northwest, now Delta, and eventually to the ramp side as a supervisor. Maybe he could take some classes and refresh his skills. Yawning and running a weary hand over his face, he wished with all his heart that he'd never, ever laid eyes on Rowan Milani.

Michael's sleek black phone, lying on the low table between the seats, started ringing. He looked anxiously at the soundly sleeping man across the aisle. Grabbing the phone, he looked at the caller ID and frowned. Where was the talk button? Taking a chance, he poked the phone and was relieved when he heard Chad's voice. "Uh, hey Chad, it's Derek. Michael is sleeping. Do you want me to wake him? We're on the way to Kauai in the jet."

Chad sounded confused and he couldn't blame him. "Derek? Oh *shit*. How did you? *You're* on the way to Kauai with Michael?"

Squirming in embarrassment, he answered. "Yep, after I talked to Michael about the CIA guys, he decided it would be best if I came to Kauai too. Anyway, hang on." Gently touching Michael's shoulder, he hoped the guy wouldn't deck him when he woke up.

Michael rubbed his eyes and glared at him. "What's going on? Are we getting ready to land?"

Shrugging, he held out the phone. "Sorry, it's Chad."

Michael snatched the phone with an irritated, "What now?" Curious, he settled back in his seat and watched discreetly as Michael stretched and yawned. "Hey Chad, what's up?" The man bent his head and gripped his forehead with one hand. "Oh no, we've got to move fast on this one. I'd say we better get in there within the next forty-eight hours. Those bastards are not going to cut him any slack. Call me as soon as you hack into the system at Quantico and find out anything at all."

As he watched Michael sling the phone on the table, lean back and close his eyes, he couldn't help but wonder at the crazy loyalty these people had for Rowan Milani. If it were up to him, he'd leave the jerk to rot. From what he'd seen of the guy, he probably deserved whatever he had gotten himself into.

CHAPTER SIXTEEN

Tuesday Afternoon
Teeth chattering, shivering uncontrollably, Rowan winced and tried to move, but it was no use. His feet and legs were swollen and numb. He had no idea whether it was day or night or how long he'd stood barefoot on the concrete floor. Shortly after the guards left, a fan started, blowing cold air over him nonstop and every once in a while the sprinkler system he'd noticed sprayed a fine mist of water from the ceiling. The temperature in the interrogation cell had fallen steadily.

The fluorescent lights stayed on and every time he closed his eyes, a shrill whistle blared. They needn't have worried that he'd fall asleep. Scared to death that he'd fall over and hang by his wrists, he remained wide awake. His stomach rumbled, but he craved water. No one had offered him anything to eat or drink since his arrival, and his mouth felt like it was full of sawdust.

The lock turned in the steel door and it swung open. A thickset man strode in and planted himself in front of him, smirking while he rolled a toothpick between his lips. "So, I finally get to meet the infamous Rowan Milani." The man's black hair and prominent nose took him back to when he was a kid, meeting his Italian uncles on a family trip to Chicago. Except this man had ruthless brown eyes and wore a lanyard around his neck with CIA printed in large letters.

Hands on hips, the man surveyed him. "Let me introduce myself. Sal Capello, CIA. Now, let me get right to the point. I've got a job to do and I intend to do it. The Agency and the Bureau want to know the details of the terror network you've built in this country and what you've been planning. But first, I've had a hankering, since last spring, to know how in the hell you managed to orchestrate your own disappearance, along with the theft of a *sixty-five million dollar* aircraft, the disabling of two CIA agents, and a flight crew. That impressed me." The agent cracked thick knuckles and smiled at him. "Here's the deal, Milani. You tell me where that jet is, and who helped you, and I'll make sure the rest of your interrogation goes easily."

He stared into the hard eyes. Curling his lips, feeling the sting as they cracked, he sneered at the agent. Did the arrogant prick really think he'd fold so quickly? Without warning, the agent's heavy hand struck his face with an open-handed whack that resounded in his ears. Balance lost on the slippery floor, he tipped over, excruciating pain exploding in his shoulders and wrists as his arms were wrenched upward. The chain and cuffs held fast and he hung there, bent double for endless seconds, feet sliding but hindered by the leg irons snapped to the eye bolt. The CIA agent cursed and yanked him upright.

Swaying back and forth, a guttural moan escaped from deep in his throat and he gagged, vomiting bile all over the surprised agent's shirtfront. Yelling for the guards, Capello shoved him. Unbearable pain took his breath away when he toppled over again. Two guards rushed into the room, grabbed his arms and pulled him into a standing position. Quivering with shock, he blinked through tears of pain that streamed down his face and mingled in a salty tang with blood from lips torn by the brutal slap. With shattering humiliation, he felt warm urine running down his legs. Face brick red, veins bulging in his neck, Capello screamed at the guards. "Get this son of a bitch out of here and somebody get me a towel. *Now.*"

Deftly freeing him from the leg irons, the guards released the chain from the handcuffs and pulled him from the reeking cell, dragging him between them to the infirmary, where a sober-faced doctor and nurse waited. The doctor snapped at the guards. "Get the handcuffs off, right now. We need to get him on a bed and get an IV started. Can't you tell he's dehydrated? Why wasn't this man given water?"

The cuffs came off, but searing pain streaked from his shoulders to his wrists. He couldn't move his arms. His gut tightened and he gagged and heaved, but nothing remained in his stomach. The guards lifted him to a bed and he laid there, eyes tightly closed while his body shook in agony.

Wednesday Morning
Marta rolled naked onto her back in the double bed and sat up, glancing out the window. It was another sunny day and she didn't need to be at the airport for a couple more hours. Troy sat up beside her and gave her a sexy smile. Long black hair hung in his blue eyes, and his smile turned her on. One of the Line Technicians and her favorite boy toy from the company that serviced both private and commercial aircraft, she'd enjoyed his hard-muscled body many times. Lots of women at the airport found a reason to be nearby when he drove across the tarmac with his truckload of Jet-A to fuel aircraft.

But right now she was curious, still obsessed with finding out anything she could about Rowan Milani. Gathering the sheets around her waist, she reached over and scraped long, red-lacquered nails through the hair on his chest. "Hey Troy, were you working when they brought that FBI agent to the airport?"

Troy shook his head and flopped down on his back. Putting his hands behind his head, he looked up at her. "Nah, I had the day off. But hey, you know what? I was working the night he first escaped, or disappeared, or whatever. And there was something weird about that, because I swear Marti-girl, the guys who helped him get away were FBI agents, too."

Eyes narrowed, she had been thinking of how she'd punish him for calling her Marti-girl, the nickname she despised. Reaching over, she grabbed him and started slow, rhythmic pulls, giggling when he jerked and started moving. "They were FBI agents? How do you know?"

She grinned at the breathless quality in his voice and kept her hand going. "Ohhh, uh, I saw them, ah, when I was over at the terminal, giving the Delta manager a copy of a missing receipt. Shit. I can't talk if you're gonna do that."

She stopped and he groaned. "Answer my questions, sweetie, and I'll give you the blow job of your life."

"OK, what else do you want to know?" Troy sounded so hopeful that she giggled again and squeezed him gently.

"What did the guys look like? Was one tall and blond?" She stopped squeezing and waited for him to respond.

Staring unblinking at her, he appeared to be thinking. "I don't know about being blond, but one of them was tall. They kept close to the building, and I wouldn't have seen them at all except that I lost my ID somewhere on the tarmac when the pilot and first officer threw a fit over a tug somebody parked too close to the wing of that jet." He paused to reach out and caress her breast. "And you know what? Nobody ever admitted to moving that stupid tug."

Leaning into his hand, she arched her back, felt her heart rate quicken. Troy grinned. "Anyway, I was out there in the dark with a flashlight looking for my ID where the jet had been parked, since all the management bozos make us turn off the lights as soon as a plane leaves. They are such morons, I can't believe it sometimes."

He scowled, let go of her breast and scratched his belly. "After I found my ID, I headed to the parking lot, because my shift was over. That's when I saw the two of them walking out from behind the building. They never saw me, and they drove off in a Mustang. Some of the guys at the airport were talking about that FBI agent and his car. The other guy was older and I know I saw him talking to my supervisor one day."

Straddling him, she smiled down at his handsome face, letting her breasts graze his chest when she leaned over to pat his face with her hands. "You ready for a treat?" She had to finish him off quickly, because Muusa needed to know what she'd found out. It was one more way for her to fuck with Rowan Milani and Danielle. She hoped it caused them both as much grief as possible.

Hands cuffed behind his back, Rowan limped between the two guards who'd taken him from the infirmary, concentrating on taking short steps so the leg irons wouldn't gouge his skin. When he looked up and saw the stocky CIA agent leaning casually in the doorway of his cell, his heart rate kicked up and his mouth went dry. The vile agent stepped away from the door and walked down the hall. The guards pulled him along, making their way to the same interrogation cell he'd been dragged from. Had it been the night before? He'd lost all sense of time.

Agent Capello waited, smirking at him, while one of the guards unlocked the door. Once inside, they positioned him over the eye bolt and he wondered what new misery they'd concocted. The guards held onto his arms while agent Capello poked him in the chest with a forefinger. "All right Milani, we're going to step it up a notch. But you know how it works, don't you? Unless you're ready to tell me where the Agency's jet is and who helped you steal it."

Not wanting to provoke the volatile agent, he kept his face neutral and stared through the cruel eyes. He'd never tell the bastard anything, no matter what he did to him.

Capello shook his head. "Let's try again. Maybe we should discuss the terror network you've built in this country and the jihadist recruiting activities you've carried out around the globe. You've been a busy man."

Anxiety had his hands sweating. The agent got in his face. He glimpsed flaring nostrils and frustration in the acrimonious eyes.

It wouldn't be long before the interrogation turned physical. When Capello took a step back and turned toward the door, his shoulders slumped in relief. But then the agent swung around and stepped in front of him again. The hard eyes turned crafty. "You had a problem with rotator cuff tears in your shoulders last spring, isn't that right? If I remember the doctor's report, you needed surgery. Did you recover fully from those injuries while you were hiding?"

Trepidation rising, he struggled to control his breathing and continued staring straight ahead. Capello sighed. "That tumble you took yesterday had to put a lot of stress on your shoulders. I'd sure hate to see them reinjured. But hey, have it your way. Guard, get your scissors and cut the jumpsuit off of him and the underwear too."

Clamping his jaws shut to keep his teeth from chattering, he closed his eyes when he felt the cold edge of the scissors and heard the blades chewing through the fabric of the jumpsuit. In a matter of minutes he stood naked and shivering in front of the despicable man. Capello stared at him, head tilted to one side. "On your knees Milani, right here in front of me."

Fearful of the agent's brutal hands, he sank to his knees and bent his head. One of the guards clipped the chain between the leg irons to the eye bolt in the floor while the other one snapped a chain between the cuffs and pulled. Gasping at the sudden tug on his tender shoulders, he managed to stifle a groan. Capello took a step back and addressed the guard. "Come on, what are you waiting for? I want that chain attached to the eye bolt in the ceiling."

As his arms were pulled relentlessly upward, he sank lower, sweat breaking out over his whole body. Finally he heard the snap of the chain and the tugging stopped. His face was inches from the floor. Squatting down beside him, Capello snickered. "Care to tell me who helped you escape? Want to tell me where the CIA's jet is hidden? Are you ready to tell me about the terror network you've built?"

Grunting with the effort, he turned his head and stared through clumps of hair into the sadistic eyes, speaking to his tormentor for the first time. "No." Closing his eyes, he let his head hang.

Capello's shoes scraped the gritty floor as he scrambled to his feet. "You think about it Milani, and we'll check on you later. The next step won't be so pleasant, so you may want to reconsider." Shuffling footsteps receded and the steel door clanged shut. His arms and shoulders burned and the cuffs bit into his bandaged wrists. Humiliation ran deep, like a black river through his soul, but nothing Capello did to him would ever make him admit to treason or betray his friends.

Taking short, panting breaths, he closed his eyes and clenched his fists, trying to resist the pain and withdraw. Desperate for refuge, his agonized mind focused on Danielle and the weekend they'd spent in Chicago. Filled with the fierce desire to know every part of her, he'd explored her body with his hands, mouth, and tongue. While she lay on the bed with her head flung back, he'd fanned her dark red hair across the pillow. He loved the color of her hair, eyes, and skin – so exotic, so different from his.

He'd kissed first her face, then her lips and neck. Moving lower, he'd marveled at her breasts, cupping them in his hands. Wanting to taste them; taste her, he'd covered first one and then the other with his mouth, ran his tongue around the pink nipples and scraped the tips with his teeth until she writhed and gasped at the sensations. Her face, dazed with pleasure, swam in front of him, and he wished he could touch it. Smiling sweetly, voice thick with seduction, she'd pulled him down on top of her, whispering. *Oh Rowan, let's do this. I can't wait any longer.* She'd been ready for him too, hot and slick when he slid inside her. When she wrapped her arms and legs around him, he'd made her body his own.

She was everything he could ever want. He stared at the concrete and watched drops of sweat from his face hit the floor, joining the pooling mess beneath his body. At some point he'd lost control of his bladder, and now the stench of sour sweat and urine stung all through his nasal cavities and his nose ran in a steady stream. The muscles in his back, arms and legs cramped continually and he couldn't stop trembling. Groaning, he closed his eyes again and gave in to the pain. She would never know how much he wanted her, how much he missed her, and how much he loved her.

Thursday Afternoon

Focused with total concentration on the lines of code flickering on the screen in front of him, Chad wondered if the dull ache that persisted in his head after six aspirin would ever go away. He'd been working nonstop on hacking into Quantico's computer system. The brig records were his primary target. He needed to make sure there was no imminent plan to transfer Rowan out of their reach.

The screen changed. Hot damn, he'd done it. Rubbing his palms vigorously, he surveyed the new information. Someday there would be someone, somewhere who would truly appreciate his hacking abilities. Now, hopefully he could decipher the brig records about his friend.

Oh *hell*. The FBI had transferred custody of Rowan to the CIA? Frowning, he kept reading. It was happening, just like his father had said. They were going to rendition Rowan to Tora Prison in Egypt. Grabbing his phone, he speed dialed Michael's number, wiping a sweaty hand on his pants while he waited. "C'mon Michael, answer your damn phone." Relieved to hear the tired, irritable voice, his shoulders sagged. "They're already planning to move Rowan. They're sending him to Tora Prison."

Michael's calm determination helped stem the rising tide of panic. "All right, now we have something to work with. Do they have a time frame yet, and if so, how detailed?"

Mind racing, he wiped his eyes and squinted at the screen. "Let me see. So far all they have is a seventy-two hour window, nothing about a specific time yet."

Michael cursed. "We have to go in now. Within the next twenty-four hours. Otherwise we risk losing track of him. And who knows, Ainsley may have smartened up since the last time and decide to transport him, somewhere else this time, by some other means. Bottom line, we move now."

Chad leaned back in his chair and twisted his shoulders, certain he'd never felt so dazed and ineffectual. "What do you need from Ralph and me?"

Michael sounded like a drill sergeant. "Keep hacking. Find out everything you can from Ainsley's records. When Ralph gets in, have him call me. We'll coordinate vehicles and other things we may need through him. Gabriel and I will head back to DC as soon as Jerry and Bryan get some rest. My rough estimate puts us back with you guys by sometime tomorrow morning. I'll keep you informed."

Chad snapped his phone closed and sat it on the desk. Pausing to crack his knuckles and yawn, he decided Ainsley's system would be his next goal. But first he needed to make some coffee. Hoping desperately that his brain would function well enough for him to accomplish what needed to be done, he stood up and headed for the kitchen.

Rowan lay back on the narrow bed. At some point the guards had come and released the chains, hauling him out of the interrogation cell and to the showers. Then they dressed him, because he'd been too weak to do it himself. Since he wouldn't move obediently to the door like they wanted, the cuffs and leg irons stayed on. And to make it more difficult, they used a waist chain, so he couldn't scratch himself or wipe his damned running nose. His teeth chattered constantly in the bone chilling cold.

He couldn't remember the last time he'd eaten, sometime before, but he didn't know how long he'd been in the brig. His existence had narrowed to panicked waiting, wondering, while his heart slammed against his chest, if the next time the door opened it would be Sal Capello or maybe the two CIA thugs, ready to finish what they'd started in the deserted warehouse in Sioux Falls. Closing his eyes, he laid there, unable to stop the quivering in his arms and legs.

The lock turned and the steel door swung open. Strong hands grabbed him and yanked him into a sitting position on the edge of the bed. Agent Capello paced angrily back and forth in the small cell while he sat hunched over, shoulders twitching in fiery agony. "I've had enough screwing around with you, Milani. I want some answers and you are going to give them to me. See, I just received a call. I still can't believe this."

Anxiety turning to panic, he cringed when the agent threw up his hands. "It seems that your family and your girlfriend have disappeared. And I'll be a son of a bitch, but your girlfriend's housemate or whatever the hell you want to call him, is gone too."

While the agent stared at him, he swallowed hard. Evidently Chad had been successful at getting everyone out of danger. But Derek? Capello whacked him across the face, knocking him to the floor. Lying on the cold concrete, he tasted blood from re-torn lips. The fall jarred his sore muscles and joints, leaving him gasping. The stinging slap made his eyes water and he blinked up at the red-faced man, waiting for the agent to kick him. But instead, two guards rushed in and jerked him to his feet.

Rage glowed in Capello's eyes. "Listen, you're going to talk to me. Do you understand? I've had it up to here with your stubborn, badass attitude. If I have to, I swear, I'll beat it out of you. Now, where the hell are these people?"

Searching for escape from the enraged agent, he closed his eyes. A blow to his solar plexus brought him back to reality and doubled him over, just as a blinding flash of insight told him where Danielle and the others were hidden. Chad had talked about an old family estate on Kauai, secluded and cleverly deeded in such a way that it could never be traced. He wished to God he hadn't thought of that and wondered if the cunning agent would be able to tell. The guards forced him upright, and he dragged in a choking breath.

Capello glared at him. "Still nothing to say? All right then, we'll move on." Gesturing to the guards, the agent turned and walked from the cell. Poker-faced as always, the men marched him along after the CIA agent, who strode purposefully down the hall. Capello stopped in front of a door, but it wasn't the usual interrogation cell. The guards unlocked it and pulled him inside. The smell of chlorine and a blast of humid air enveloped him. Oh no. He couldn't let them do this.

Bracing his body, he tried to resist, even though he knew it was futile. One of the guards buckled his knees, and together they laid him on a board. They strapped his legs tight and the board tilted down. The guards kneeled on either side, gripping his arms. A heavy black mask slid over his eyes, and Sal Capello's thick hands caressed his face.

The sound of cellophane tearing struck terror deep inside, and the CIA agent confirmed his desperate thoughts. "You ever been water boarded, Milani, maybe during your FBI training? We're through giving you a pass, so do you want to start talking to me? Tell me where your family and friends are hiding."

They couldn't make him talk, no matter what they did. Shaking his head between the massive hands, he waited. The cellophane covered his nose and mouth. When the water started, he sucked the plastic into his mouth, felt his back arching, his body bucking, trying to escape, and trying to breathe. Panic-stricken, he knew he was drowning.

The guards pushed down on his chest and forced his body flat. Twisting in agony, he thought he was screaming, but all he heard was pouring water and the thundering of his heart. It would never end, because he would never tell them anything. And then he was aspirating water and struggling to raise his head. Capello lifted the mask from his eyes and ripped the cellophane off his face.

Gasping, wheezing, he saw a blurred vision of the agent, grinning down at him. "All right, how about now? Are you ready to tell me about your foreign terrorist associations and your domestic terror network? What about your girlfriend and your family? Where the hell are they?" Shaking his head weakly, he wished he had the strength to say *fuck you.*

The agent cursed and slid the mask over his eyes again. The sound of cellophane tearing had him fighting, but he was no match for the guards. Once more it covered his nose and mouth and the water poured. Body wrenching in anguish, he fought until Capello ripped the plastic off his face and lifted the black mask.

Soaking wet, chest heaving, he blinked at the leering visage above him. The agent chuckled. "I'm late for a dinner engagement, but when I come back, we're going to have another chat. If I don't get any answers, we'll do this again, with my own twist. Guards, keep trying and see if you can convince him to talk." Capello chuckled again. "And make sure he's hydrated, so the damn doctors in the infirmary stay off my back."

Michael didn't think he had the strength to resist Danielle as she stood facing him just outside the front door of the house. But he had to try to make her see reason. Who knew what kind of shape they'd find Rowan in after almost a week in CIA custody? Would she be able to hold up or would she become a hindrance? This would be the boldest extraction of Rowan Milani he'd ever attempted, and the fact that they were conducting it more or less by the seat of their pants didn't help his frame of mind.

Danielle's eyes zeroed in on his like a laser, and she shook a finger in his face. "I am coming with you to Washington, DC, Michael. I'm not asking your permission, I'm informing you. When you bring Rowan to that jet, I will be waiting for him. There's no telling what he's been through or what he'll need."

Scraping his fingers viciously through the ragged stubble on his jaw, he hoped he could remain civil. She was an intelligent, beautiful woman and he respected her. "Danielle, please believe me, I am well-schooled in extracting Rowan from dangerous situations and am also well versed in what to expect. Gabriel is a medic and has treated him more than once. We will deliver him back here to you within the next twenty-four hours, safe and reasonably sound. Why can't you accept that? Leave the hard work to us and be ready to help Rowan once he's here."

But no, Danielle stood there shaking her head, a defiant, almost desperate look on her face and it dawned on him that she was just as damned stubborn as Rowan. "No, I want to, and I will be on that jet when he steps inside. That's the end of it. Please Michael, he's there because of me. I can't sit here and wait, I just can't."

When he saw the misery in her eyes and heard the note of entreaty creep into her voice, he knew he'd let her come with them. "All right Danielle, get whatever you need, because Jerry and Bryan will be ready to leave in thirty minutes." Angry with himself for giving in, he glared at her. "Remember, we don't know if he'll be injured or in his right mind or just exactly what will be going on. Now, when we arrive, you will not exit the aircraft. Do you understand?"

Waiting, brows rising until Danielle muttered a quiet, "Yes I do," he continued.

"And one more thing. If Gabriel and I don't come back after a pre-determined length of time, Jerry and Bryan have been instructed to get the hell out of Dodge. You will accept that and not interfere with their decision. Because if we don't show up with Rowan, it means we've failed and have been arrested. We're playing with our lives here, Danielle. That's why I'm not enthused about your company on this trip."

Danielle stared at him, arms crossed. "As long as I can be with Rowan, I can handle anything. Don't worry about me. I'll be just fine. I won't cause you any problems."

Throwing his hands in the air in defeat, he did his best to smile. "Get your stuff and meet me back here right away." Turning away, so dead-ass tired he could barely think, he wondered if the cluster fuck would ever be over. Once he deposited Rowan safely in this annoying woman's arms, he planned to crawl into bed and not come out for a very, very long time. And he didn't care if he ever stepped foot inside another airplane.

CHAPTER SEVENTEEN

Thursday Evening

Sal Capello laid the linen napkin on his plate and plucked a plastic wrapped toothpick from a small china container. Surveying the Egyptian man across the table in the dimly lit restaurant, he marveled at the fountain of information the man had been. Even Rodney had been slack-jawed at what Muusa Shemal calmly revealed over dinner. Tucked into an intimate corner of *Brabo,* Ainsley's favorite Old Town Alexandria restaurant, adjacent to the Lorien Hotel where Shemal was staying, the three of them had enjoyed a sumptuous meal.

Once they'd exchanged introductions and settled on a lucrative sum for his services as Rowan Milani's CIA handler, their Egyptian friend had pontificated nonstop about his experiences with the faithful throughout America. Only the arrival of his foie-gras-stuffed ravioli and seared turbot with gnocchi and artichokes had finally ended the man's diatribe. The steak Sal preferred had been delectable.

Chuckling sardonically, he worked the toothpick between his teeth. Ralph Johnston and Chad Cantor were in a world of shit. He'd nearly choked on his steak when Shemal announced that they'd been the ones to disable Seth Hancock and Lucien Talbot the night Milani disappeared. Aiding and abetting. What the hell had those two been thinking? Did they honestly believe their colleague was innocent? That they'd risked their careers and freedom gave him pause. Why would they do that if they didn't think Rowan Milani was innocent of the charges he faced?

With a faint smile for the two men chatting quietly across the table, he thought deliciously of the task he remained committed to completing. After they lingered over coffee, and the dessert Ainsley had to have, he was heading back to the brig. He'd instructed his agents to be ready. It was going to be a long night for Rowan Milani. How the man remained so pigheaded and defiant was beyond his understanding. But the next step would break him. The stubborn jerk would tell him everything he wanted to know after being water boarded with a cracked rib or two. Even the toughest ones always did. No one could handle that kind of pain.

Pausing in his quest to hack into Rodney Ainsley's personal computer, Chad rubbed his forehead and decided he needed a break. Dumping his cold coffee and refilling the cup, he wandered into the living room of his father's apartment. Grabbing the remote and switching on the TV, he sat on the edge of the sofa to peruse the headlines. With a hand over his mouth, he stared in disbelief as the anchor soberly related the latest FOX News Alert.

"Authorities in the Washington, DC area are seeking former FBI special agent Chad Cantor and Ralph Johnston, Special Agent in Charge of an FBI Anti-Terrorism Task Force, in connection with aiding and abetting terror suspect Ismail Hassani, formerly known as FBI special agent Rowan Milani, who escaped from custody last March. Arrest warrants have been issued for both Cantor and Johnston."

"Oh no. *Hell* no." This complicated things considerably. Jumping at the sound of the door, he looked up as Ralph entered the vestibule, arms full of the last minute medical supplies Gabriel had requested. Gesturing at his colleague, he turned back to the TV. "You're not going to believe this. I don't know how it happened, but we're on FOX News right now, wanted in connection with Rowan."

Ralph dumped the supplies on the sofa and stared, first at the TV and then at him. "Now what are we going to do? We can't pick up the rental vehicle Michael set up, or help them with any aspect of getting Rowan out of Quantico."

Standing still in the middle of the living room, gripping his cup of coffee in both hands, Chad tried to think coherently. "I've made excellent progress tonight. The prisoner transfer forms from Ainsley's office computer are printed, and a transfer request for Rowan is pending in Quantico's system. I even have the schematics showing camera locations so Michael and Gabriel can avoid being identified."

He took a gulp of coffee and continued. "Michael has a plan in place to get Ainsley out of town. It's time for me to give my father a call, because I'm at my wits end as far as getting agent Capello away from Rowan. If he can call in a couple favors, we may be in luck. The other thing we don't have is a transport vehicle of some sort, since we can't pick up the rental for Michael. Wait, I bet we can use the Mercedes."

His colleague stared transfixed at the TV. "God almighty, I never thought I'd see the day." Turning to give him a sad look, Ralph continued. "I'm getting a crash course in what Rowan must have felt like when he saw all the lies about him on TV. It's not a good feeling. You know what I mean?"

Attempting to shake off the mood, he stared grimly at Ralph. "I know, I know. Look, we're going to get this done. Twenty-four hours from now, it'll be over and we'll all be safe. Shoot, we can cook out on the beach tomorrow night if we want."

Swearing succinctly, gesturing in frustration at Gabriel and Danielle's concerned glances, Michael washed a hand over his face. Could anything else possibly go wrong? Peering out the window as the G650 banked gently, he saw only blackness. "I'm not sure where we are. But you said we have the use of your father's Mercedes? I have plates for it, so when all this is said and done and the security video is examined, they'll have a hell of a time tracing that vehicle anywhere."

Chad sounded as tired as he felt. "Sounds good, Mike. Give me a call when you're about two hours out of Baltimore, and we'll get underway. We've got everything you should need. You've got your ID's, right? Sorry, I know that's a stupid question, but I can't think straight anymore."

Shifting his weary body, he said a silent thank you for the luxurious seats in the aircraft. "Welcome to my world. This is the biggest *FUBAR* I've seen in a while. And we don't have any idea what's been happening to Rowan. I hope to God he can walk."

Chad didn't make him feel any better. "No shit. That CIA agent has had unlimited access to him for way too long. But hey, I've got a few extras that will help you once you get inside the brig."

Massaging his burning eyes, he hoped they could pull Rowan out of Quantico and not end up incarcerated with him. "Sounds great, Chad. See you soon."

Muscles tensed and throbbing, wondering what agent Capello had meant when he said, *we'll do this again with my own twist,* Rowan shivered while sweat trickled down his back and sides. The guards had stomped in and dragged him back to the interrogation cell, then strung him up on tiptoe, with his arms stretched uncomfortably above his head. Tipping his head back, he squinted into the fluorescent lights at his bandaged wrists, enclosed in the steel cuffs, attached to a chain that connected to the eye bolt in the ceiling. Clenching and unclenching his fists, he shuddered at his helplessness and let his head hang.

Eyes closed, his mind wandered to Danielle. He wished he could see her one last time, to tell her how much he loved her. But that was a dream, like his life before, just a dream. The cuffs jerked on his wrists, and his eyes fluttered open. Reality was here, with the vicious man determined to destroy his mind and body. Trying to relieve his always aching left foot, wincing at the unrelenting pain in his shoulders, he told himself again that no matter what Capello did to him, he would never tell the bastard anything.

The lock turned, the door opened, and the agent strode into the cell. "Well, well, well. I've had an interesting dinner with an old adversary of yours." The mention of dinner made his mouth water, and his stomach growled. Staring into the cold eyes, he swallowed. Capello slapped his cheek and he stumbled back, almost losing his balance. "You should cooperate with me, Milani. And really, don't you know by now that all I want from you is the truth?"

The slap, along with the agent's tiresome comment brought the remnants of his rage sputtering to the surface. "You want the truth, so here it is. I'm not a terrorist. I'd never betray my country. But you're too stupid, or blind, to believe me."

Standing back, arms crossed, Capello looked surprised. "I was starting to think you couldn't talk, Milani. All right. Maybe we can make some progress. For starters, where is the CIA's jet? The theft of an aircraft like that is about a lot more than money. Surely you understand that you poked us in the eye by taking the crown jewel of the fleet."

Still shivering, he gazed at Capello. The pain in his shoulders had turned white hot and stabbing. "I don't know where that jet is, and I don't even remember being on it."

The agent frowned at him. "Come on. Who helped you that night? Who really orchestrated your escape?"

Something tickled at the back of his mind. The crafty agent knew something. "I'm never going to tell you. It would violate a commitment I made a long time ago to a certain group of people."

Judging from the agent's flushed face, his answers weren't acceptable. Capello strode back and forth, glaring at him. "Eventually, you will tell me everything, Milani. But where's the truth you said was forthcoming? So far, what you call the truth, I call lying."

Seemingly out of nowhere, the agent's heavy fist slammed into his side and he flopped back and forth like a fish on a line. While he struggled to breathe, Capello shifted adroitly and steadied him long enough for the same fist to slam into his other side and he choked, while his eyes watered and his nose ran.

Inexplicably, the detestable man heaved a sigh and leaned against the wall, one ankle crossed over the other, rubbing thick hands vigorously while observing him with a sad smile. "Why are you protecting these people? You're such a stubborn fool. And besides, it's all over." Capello uncrossed his ankles, shoved off the wall and paced around the cell. "We'll take a short break while I tell you a story from dinner. You're going to love this story."

Sniffing at the stench of bleach overlaying the sour bouquet of sweat and urine that permeated the cell, he felt light-headed and nauseated. Capello stopped pacing and stood in front of him. "Does the name Muusa Shemal mean anything to you? If not, it should. That man is obsessed with you. Apparently he's been tracking you for years, accumulating proof of your terrorist activities. Unfortunately for your loyal colleagues, Mr. Shemal identified them both this evening and informed us that they were responsible for incapacitating the CIA agents assigned to escort you to Washington, DC."

Thick blood in his throat made him cough and gag. He spat on the floor and smirked at Capello. "How did someone with your IQ become a CIA agent? Muusa Shemal has been devising a terror plot against the United States for decades, with financial backing from the Muslim Brotherhood. You have to understand. It's not me who's the terrorist, it's Muusa Shemal."

Capello shook his head. "The evidence against you is rock solid. But let's get back to those loyal colleagues, Ralph Johnston and Chad Cantor. By now I'm guessing Rodney Ainsley is ready to arrest them. Who knows, he may bring them here. Aiding and abetting a terrorist is a serious crime."

Straining to think beyond the agony in his body, he closed his eyes. If Capello thought Ralph and Chad had disabled the two CIA thugs, did he know about Michael and Gabriel? If his friends were in Ainsley's custody, then he was lost in the hands of the people committed to his destruction. Blinking, he realized Capello was standing in front of him again. The man was quick for someone so blocky, and this time, the force of the blow knocked him off his feet.

Fists clenching as the cuffs dug into his wrists, he writhed in torment. The agent grabbed a handful of orange jumpsuit to hold him still and repeated the punishing blow on the other side of his ribcage. Sweat poured from his body while intense pain forced him to breathe in panting groans. The bastard had cracked his ribs.

The sadistic agent grasped his bearded chin, so he couldn't look away. "Tell me the truth. That's all I'm asking. After all Milani, I've given you an easy time. If you were interrogated in your homeland, my techniques would seem like a fun day on the playground."

The impotent rage fired again and he whispered between groans. "I am in my *homeland*, you moron. Goddamn it. I'm an American citizen, and we don't use enhanced interrogation techniques on our own people, or anyone. We're too civilized for that." He wanted to laugh, but could only manage a sneer. "I'm innocent until you find proof that I'm guilty." Wheezing, voice rasping, he continued. "Why won't you believe me, you stupid son of a bitch?"

Losing his train of thought, head drooping after Capello let go of his chin, he fought the fuzziness in his brain, couldn't ignore the knife-sharp agony accompanying every shallow breath. Coughing weakly, he spat more blood and struggled to lift his head. "Look, the truth is that I've been eliminating terrorists as part of a black ops team. That's who helped me and I won't give you their names. I won't tell you where my family is, and I don't know where that *goddamned* jet is. So do what you have to, but I'm finished."

The indomitable agent waggled a finger in his face and shot him a mocking smile. "Now that's where you've got it wrong, my friend." When Capello paused, he let his eyes slide closed. A stinging slap on the cheek brought him back. "You know you're headed to Tora Prison in Egypt, don't you?"

Capello chuckled. "I'll have more latitude as far as interrogation techniques in that facility. But we're not finished here quite yet." The door opened and two guards came into the cell. They undid the chain, lowered his arms and let him stand, swaying back and forth in front of Capello, who glared from one guard to the other. "Are you ready, your team assembled?"

Watching anxiously as the guards nodded, panic overwhelmed him when they yanked on his arms and had him staggering out the door between them. Oh Jesus, not again. As he stumbled down the hallway, he heard himself mumbling and hated the terrible desperation in his voice. "No, no I can't. You can't do this. Please don't do this, I can't do it." Of course they ignored him, and when they buckled his body onto the board and leaned on his chest, he groaned.

Agent Capello grinned down at him, holding the black mask. "Last chance, Milani. Who planned your escape? Where are your girlfriend and your family?"

Mindless with pain, he managed to whisper. "No, I'm finished." Then the mask covered his eyes and the cellophane clung to his face. The water poured and primal reactions took over. When his body heaved upward, the guards bore down and the pain went off the charts. From a long distance away he heard the guards swearing, felt Capello slapping his face, but he was gone.

Consciousness returned gradually, accompanied by stabbing pain in his chest. Turning his head slowly from side to side, he realized he was lying in a bed in the infirmary, restrained by leather straps and leg irons. Head lolling to one side, he closed his eyes. Capello was a fool. He would die before he told the son of a bitch *anything*. But once they had him in Egypt, Shemal would have his prize. He opened his eyes, felt them widen as despair mingled with sheer fright and slithered into his mind. The torture had yet to begin.

Incandescent golden light enveloped him and he remembered, he'd seen that light before. As the glow persisted, shimmering all around him, the monstrous pain receded and so did the fear, leaving him wrapped in peace. The radiance diffused throughout his wounded psyche, and a voice filled with kindness spoke. *If you'll only ask me Rowan, I will help you.* What the hell was happening to him? The gentle voice whispered through his tortured mind once more. *Ask me to rescue you.* As the golden light dissipated, the agony and terror roared back, leaving him groaning. Tears slid down his cheeks. "I give up. Rescue me, please."

CHAPTER EIGHTEEN

Early Friday Morning

The incessant ringing of the phone dragged Rodney Ainsley from the depths of sleep. He blinked in the pre-dawn darkness. Who could be calling at this hour? Murmuring a groggy hello, he was unprepared for the gracious, sympathetic voice. "Mr. Rodney Ainsley? This is Caroline Smith, the ER Charge Nurse at Roanoke Memorial Hospital. Your mother, Dorthea Ainsley, was transported here by ambulance approximately thirty minutes ago. I'm sorry to tell you Mr. Ainsley, she was hit by a car in front of her residence and sustained serious injuries. In addition to numerous contusions and a broken leg, we are concerned about internal bleeding."

Head in his hands, he could barely comprehend her words. Since his father's death the previous year, he had procrastinated on moving his mother to assisted living. "Ms. Smith, I will be there as soon as I can. Is there a direct number where I can reach you? I'd like to stay apprised of her condition."

Caroline Smith answered in a soothing, professional manner. "Absolutely, Mr. Ainsley, This is my personal number at the hospital. We're working on stabilizing your mother right now. Give me an hour before you call again. If anything changes, I'll contact you immediately."

His plans with Muusa Shemal and Sal Capello would have to wait. Personal matters forbade him from taking a Bureau aircraft, so he'd have to drive the almost 200 miles himself. "Thank you so much Ms. Smith. I'll be on my way shortly."

Georgia Cristo stuck out her tongue at the phone. "We'll take good care of your mother, Mr. Ainsley. Please drive safely. I'll speak with you again in an hour." Smiling at Shasta and scratching the big dog's head, she set down the satellite phone. Rodney Ainsley would waste most of the morning driving and then find out that a terrible mistake had been made. Leaning over, she gave the bulky Rottweiler a hug. "C'mon sweetie, let's go make some coffee. It's going to be a long day."

Rowan sat hunched over on the edge of the bed in his cell, still cuffed and shackled, unable to move or breathe without intense pain. When he heard the lock turn in the door, he panicked, breath coming in agonizing gasps. Hearing a familiar voice cursing softly in Spanish, he steeled himself. It couldn't be Gabriel, could it? Then a gentle hand touched his shoulder. Looking up, he gazed into Gabriel's concerned eyes and forced his face to remain blank. Had his tortured mind retreated into memories again? Not trusting himself, he waited to see what would happen.

Gabriel stayed beside him, but glancing out the door he could see Michael, conferring with a guard and handing him some papers. Both his colleagues wore official FBI gear, including ball caps and sported photo IDs and badges. The guard smiled at Michael. "He's all yours, special agent. And be careful, he's a tricky son of a bitch to handle."

Michael snorted. "Oh yeah, he looks tough to me. Don't worry, we'll exercise extreme caution."

Gabriel grasped his upper arm and he flinched. "Come along, Mr. Hassani. You're being transferred today. Cause any problems and we'll kick your ass."

Still thinking he might be hallucinating, he tried to stand, but couldn't. Michael and Gabriel pulled him up and he moved numbly between them, plodding through a maze of hallways and clanging steel doors that left him shaking in fear. Sweat dripped down the sides of his face and his chest heaved. At any moment he expected to see either Ainsley or Capello.

Bright sunlight blinded him when they stepped outside. Gabriel opened the back door of a black Mercedes sedan with smoked windows and shoved him efficiently inside. Panting, he leaned back and closed his eyes. The humid warmth inside the vehicle felt good after the cold, damp cell. A touch on his forearm made him jump and his eyes snapped open. Michael was already in the driver's seat and had twisted around. "Hey Rowan, we've got you. We're going to get the hell out of here right now."

Unable to respond, he closed his eyes again and took shallow breaths in a futile effort to alleviate the all-consuming pain. The car shifted smoothly into motion, and he felt Gabriel unlocking the cuffs and the waist chain and then the leg irons, talking at the same time. "It's all right now. You're out of that hellhole and we won't let them take you back. Are you with me, amigo? I need your help."

Still panting, he opened his eyes and whispered hoarsely. "What?"

Brandishing an electric razor and a pair of scissors, his friend replied. "How about a quick shave and even quicker hair cut? We don't want you to look anything like the pictures that are going to hit the cable news shows in a couple hours. Any number of people may see you walk to your jet. You need to look like a totally different person."

Exhausted, unable to stop shivering, he nodded faintly. "OK."

Gabriel smiled. "Here we go. After we get to Kauai, Marion can make your haircut perfect. But I can do a respectable job and no one will recognize you."

Flat against the seat with his head back, he couldn't answer. Closing his eyes, he listened to the clip of the scissors and felt the tug on his head. When the razor started, he clenched his jaws, expecting more agony on his bruised face. But Gabriel's touch was light. Lulled half-asleep by the low-pitched buzzing, he came to when the noise stopped.

Gabriel laid a hand on his arm and spoke quietly. "We're done with that part, but I need you to help me with one more thing. We need to get you out of this ugly orange shit."

Opening his eyes, he looked with trepidation at the pile of clothes in Gabriel's lap. "I don't think I can."

His colleague gave him an encouraging smile and waved the scissors. "No problem, we'll just cut it off. You know, Chad missed his calling. You couldn't find a better valet. He brought you a nice suit to wear, so you can walk to your jet like a big shot instead of a prisoner. Once we get you onboard, I'll hook you up with some badass drugs and before you know it, you'll be in Kauai."

Twenty minutes later, he tugged weakly on the jacket sleeves and adjusted his shirt collar with shaky fingers. The black Armani suit was the one he'd worn the night he'd taken Danielle to her favorite restaurant, and Chad had found a silver-gray shirt to go with it. He'd already soaked the shirt with sweat. The shoes were his old slip-ons and he didn't need any damn socks.

The biggest surprise came when Michael casually tossed a pair of sunglasses over the seat. "Chad gave me these, said he's been keeping them for you." They were his favorite pair and he needed them too, because he'd gotten a glimpse of his clean shaven face in the rearview mirror. He put the sunglasses on with trembling hands. Until the jet was in the air, he wouldn't be free of the horrific CIA agent and the terrifying specter of an Egyptian torture prison.

A slamming car door had him gasping in terror. He'd fallen sound asleep. Gabriel and Michael were already out of the car. Gabriel opened his door and leaned inside. "We're here Rowan. There's your jet. Are you going to be able to walk up the stairs?"

The sleek black jet crouched like a powerful bird on the tarmac. He nodded at Gabriel and lurched to his feet, hanging onto the door frame so he wouldn't collapse. By God, he'd make it on that aircraft if he had to crawl up the stairs. Chad appeared at his side, gave him an affectionate smile and held out an arm. He tried to smile back, but his swollen face hurt too much. Taking a hold of Chad's arm, with Gabriel on the other side, he managed to limp to the jet.

Pausing at the bottom of the air stairs, he saw Michael passing a wad of cash and the car keys to an attendant. Focusing on the stairs, he took one agonizing step after another, following Chad, with Gabriel supporting him from behind. Once at the top, he leaned against the wall, too weak to move any further. He pulled the sunglasses off and saw Ralph, buckled into a seat and smiling at him. "Welcome back, Rowan."

Chad placed a hand on his shoulder. "It's good to have you back, brother. Now let's get the hell out of here."

Gabriel tugged on his arm, pointing down the aisle. "C'mon Rowan, I've got everything set up back in the aft cabin. You can lie down as soon as I take a listen to your chest. Can you slide out of that jacket? And when's the last time you had food?"

Reality wavered and he frowned at his colleague. "Can I? What? I don't remember."

Gabriel shook his head. "We'll hook up an IV for the trip. I've got some meds too. You've got serious pain issues and I don't want you to suffer."

That someone didn't want him to suffer was a novel concept. As he staggered toward the back section of the large cabin between Chad and Gabriel, a movement caught his eye, and he saw the lavatory door opening at the back of the jet. Who else could be onboard? His mouth hung open and shock rolled over him when Danielle stepped through the door and smiled.

Michael's sharp voice intruded on the moment as he bounded into the aircraft. "All right, Rowan, we need you on that divan, and Danielle and Gabriel, you sit back there, too. Folks, we're ready to head west, at a high rate of speed." The aircraft door went shut with a muted thud, and the engines whined as they started to taxi.

Slumped on the soft leather, legs stretched out in front of him, he looked at Danielle, wondering again if he was hallucinating.

She sat cross-legged next to him and thankfully hadn't tried to touch his body. Gabriel plopped down on his other side. "I don't want to butt in here, but while we taxi, let me listen to your breathing and get you hooked up to these drugs. Danielle, you'll stay right by him, yes? Because your lover here, he got himself beat up and it's gonna be lights out until we get to Kauai. I think we better keep his head elevated too, so he can breathe easier."

Danielle reached for his hand, then stopped and looked at him. Grasping her hand, feeling the soft warmth, he closed his eyes. She was real. He heard the determination in her voice when she answered Gabriel. "Yes, I'm staying right here. We'll use this pillow. Rowan, you can lay your head in my lap." The jet engines revved and the impressive aircraft hurtled down the runway, taking off with a thunderous roar. The thrust of the engines pushed him back against the seat. Thank God, it was over. He was free.

Gabriel helped him lie down and he barely felt the IV needle sliding into a vein in his hand. Floating into pain-free unconsciousness, he sensed a presence with no beginning or end, overflowing with kindness, toward him. The last thing he heard was the gentle voice, whispering like a golden thread through his soul. *Rowan, you're welcome.*

As soon as she knew Rowan had lapsed into unconsciousness, Danielle let her smile fade away. She'd wanted to kiss him, needed to feel his arms around her, but it would be days or even weeks before he could comfortably do either. At least he was alive and safe. And after five dreadful months, she was with him.

Smiling through the tears glimmering in her lashes, she touched the bruises on his cheeks and slid her fingers into his shorter but still shaggy hair. A nagging fear tugged at her heart. Rowan had been withdrawn, in shock, and the way he breathed made her wonder if he had pneumonia. Would he be all right? Would she be able to help him? Looking up, she saw Chad coming and swiped hurriedly at the tears dripping down her cheeks.

Chad stepped into the aft cabin, glancing at Gabriel, who was already reclined and snoring in the single club chair across the aisle. He stopped, gazing down at Rowan with a sad smile. "I can hardly believe this is over. It's a good thing we got him out of there when we did. I'm not sure he could have taken much more."

She cradled Rowan's head between her hands and looked up. "I can't imagine what he's been through and I don't know how to help him get past the suffering."

Chad yawned and rubbed his eyes before responding. "I'm afraid it could be a long road back this time. I think maybe he's had one too many mind-blowing traumas, if you know what I mean."

Friday Afternoon
Staring in barely controlled frustration at the bland face of the Senate Intelligence Committee Chairman, Sal dabbed at the sweat on his forehead with a tissue. "Sir, am I free to go? It's been a most interesting day, but I have other commitments."

The chairman smiled benignly. "Thank you, agent Capello. You are free to go. Have a nice afternoon."

Without bothering to answer, he strode out of the room. The meeting he'd been forced to attend had absolutely nothing to do with his areas of expertise as a field agent. The wasted morning had granted his prisoner a brief reprieve, but now, he planned to meet Rodney Ainsley and Muusa Shemal at Quantico. The three of them were going to confront Rowan Milani one last time. If that didn't make his recalcitrant prisoner talk, he planned to water board the stubborn fool until he got answers. Chuckling as he slid into the back seat of the Yellow Cab Lincoln Town Car he'd reserved, he thought of the pleasure he'd take in making the obdurate man beg him to stop the procedure. Today, he would find Rowan Milani's breaking point.

His cell phone beeped with a message. Irritated after listening, he punched in his colleague's number. "Rodney, its Sal. Did you say something happened to your mother? Is there some way I can help you with that? Your message kept breaking up. Are you with Shemal?"

Ainsley sounded stressed out. "Damn it Sal, somebody set me up with a terrible, a monstrous prank. I've been in Roanoke all day. I'm just leaving now. Have you gotten any information out of Hassani yet? I'd like to have something for the President before you transport him."

It was nearly three o'clock in the afternoon. "Rodney, I was waylaid too, with a worthless Intelligence Meeting. I'm just arriving at Quantico now."

Listening to Ainsley expound on how he'd been fooled into thinking his mother had suffered a life-threatening accident, he made his way to the isolation wing of Quantico's brig. Stepping into the brig's observation room, he glanced at the monitor, expecting to see Rowan lying on the bed. Scowling when he saw that the cell was empty, he thought his prisoner must still be in the infirmary.

An agent stepped into the room. Interrupting Ainsley's diatribe, he muttered, "Rodney, hang on a sec." Turning, he addressed the man who'd just slid into the chair in front of the monitor. "Call the infirmary and tell them to move Rowan Milani back here ASAP. Get your team together. We're going to water board him again this afternoon and possibly this evening."

The agent looked up at him, confusion in his eyes. "The FBI transferred Rowan Milani this morning, agent Capello. I'm waiting for the arrival of a new prisoner."

Speechless, he stared at the man. Ainsley's disembodied voice crackling in his ear brought jarring clarity. He knew exactly what had happened. The sneaky motherfucker had done it again. But how, in broad daylight, had his prisoner walked out of the brig at Quantico? "Rodney. *Rodney listen to me.* Rowan Milani is gone.

Supposedly the FBI moved him out a couple hours ago. Tell me you approved that order."

Ainsley sounded apoplectic. *"WHAT?* I did no such thing. I'll be damned if that guy and his friends haven't fucked us over, Sal. Not only do we lose the intelligence, we damage our relationship with Mr. Shemal. Not to mention the incredible embarrassment of losing him again. I don't know if my career can survive this."

Willing Ainsley to shut up, all semblance of patience vanished as the enormity of the debacle settled into his mind, and he responded angrily. "Forget about the embarrassment, Rodney. Get back here as soon as you can. I'll check all the security cameras. They can't have been good enough to avoid getting their pictures taken.

Alert your people. I'll call the District cops and get them in the private side of Dulles and Reagan. The son of a bitch can't have gotten far, and if his buddies think they're going to get away with my jet again, they've got another thing coming."

A mind-boggling hour later, he realized that whoever had taken Rowan Milani had bested them on every level. It was almost as if the two men escorting him had known the exact location of every camera. At each juncture, he'd gotten either the back of a bent head or a face covered by a cap pulled low. The government license plate on the car traced to nothing. Black Mercedes sedans were common in the DC metropolitan area, creating another dead end. Although he thought his operatives should have questioned FBI agents arriving in a Mercedes to transport a prisoner, none of them had.

Even the camera at the gate into Quantico had left them with nothing more than a cap, once again pulled down. The man driving the car had known better than to lower his darkened window any further than necessary. The agents, his hand-picked men who'd transferred custody could remember only that both FBI special agents had proper ID and official paperwork that matched orders pending in the system. They also thought one of them was Hispanic.

The entire operation had taken expert planning, formidable hacking ability, and just plain balls. Much as he'd like to get his hands on each and every one of Rowan Milani's loyal cohorts, Sal had to admit, he admired their panache. They must care a hell of a lot for the stubborn man, because they'd risked everything to save him. And if they had the CIA's jet, they could be literally anywhere in the world. Grinding his teeth in angry frustration, he made himself a promise. If it was the last thing he ever did, he would track down and apprehend Rowan Milani.

Friday Evening

Danielle looked at Rowan, hunched over on the edge of the bed in their suite. His eyes still had a shell-shocked, remote look, and his face was gaunt. Watching him struggle to get up after they landed and then walk with help from Gabriel and Chad had been heartbreaking. Gabriel had promised to be back with another injection of pain medication, and she hoped he wouldn't be long. Sitting down next to the man she loved so much, stroking his hand, she wondered again if he was going to be all right. "Can you help me get you out of these clothes? You have to know I can't wait to get my hands on you."

Rowan turned toward her and she shivered at the faraway look in his eyes. Had he even heard her? Then he blinked and seemed to focus on her face. "I missed you, so much."

Squeezing his hand lightly, she smiled. "I missed you too and I'm glad it's all over. Let's get you out of this suit and into bed."

Rowan took a breath and winced. Watching him tug on the suit jacket with trembling fingers brought tears to her eyes. While he sat, shallow breaths rasping, she slid the jacket off his shoulders and gently down his arms. As she unbuttoned his shirt, she saw the sheen of sweat on his face and neck. The pain must be unbearable. She hoped again that Gabriel wouldn't be long.

Taking it slow because she didn't want to cause him even more agony, she peeled his shirt off, careful of the IV needle and the tubing taped to his hand. Blue-black, purple and angry red bruises covered his abdomen and ribs. The bandages on his wrists were rusty with patches of dried blood.

Gently skimming his arm with her hand, she smiled when he looked at her again. "Hey, Rowan, we're almost there. Can you stand, if I help you?" He gave her a faint nod, groaning when she helped him stagger to his feet. Flinging the covers back, she made short work of the suit pants and then stopped. God in heaven, he was wearing white briefs, and she knew how much he hated them.

"Oh my, let's get rid of this crap." Tucking her fingers in the waistband, she pulled the nasty *tightie whities* as he called them down his quivering legs. Even his knees were bruised and cut. Above his ankles, she could see where leg irons had scraped his skin. When he sank back down on the edge of the bed, she gave him the most encouraging smile she could muster. He stared right through her. Stifling a sob, she touched his shoulder. "OK, into bed you go."

Perspiring now, she lifted his legs into the bed and tugged the briefs off his feet. Pulling the covers to his chin, she made a face at the white underwear and tossed them in a waste basket in the corner. Where was Gabriel? Rowan was in far worse shape than she'd imagined possible. Could he recover from the trauma? Would he want to? Hearing the outer door open, she spoke, voice ragged. "Come in."

Gabriel burst into the room, bringing relief for Rowan in the syringe he clutched in his hand and the IV pole he dragged along with him. "Hi Danielle, we'll get the IV going again. I set up the machine in here before we left. In the morning we'll see about getting him to eat something." Watching him work, she fought to maintain her composure. But when Gabriel paused and gave her a kind smile, the fragile grip she had on her emotions crumbled, and she turned away. Warm hands on her shoulders gently turned her around. "There, there, take it easy honey. Rowan's going to be just fine."

Hiccupping through the tears, she heard the desperate fear in her voice. "No, you don't understand. It's like Rowan is *gone*. I don't even know if he realizes where he is or that he's safe now."

Gabriel tilted his head toward the door. "Come with me for a sec." Once they were out of the bedroom, he drew her close in a tight hug and then held her at arm's length. She sniffed and peered at him through burning eyes. Gabriel frowned ruefully and squeezed her arms. "I didn't want to say this in front of Rowan. On our way to DC, I researched the jerk who interrogated him. He's a well-known CIA senior field agent who is lauded all the time for his ability to get actionable intelligence from detainees."

Gabriel smiled, but she could see the sadness in his eyes. "The CIA says his techniques are incredibly effective. Rowan didn't give in. We don't know everything that happened, but obviously the agent worked him over hard. Handling that kind of barrage took everything he had. It's going to take him some time to recover, both physically and mentally. Just be with him. Trust me, honey, I know Rowan. He's very resilient, and he cares for you, more than you know. Being with you will bring him back and help him heal."

Taking a deep breath, she returned his smile, determined to keep her lower lip from trembling. "From the first time I ever saw Rowan, all I've wanted is to be with him. It's just, it hurts me to see him in such pain."

Gabriel nodded. "It's hard to watch him suffer, I know, but hang in there. I'll be back first thing in the morning. If you need anything during the night, call me and I'll come right over." After giving her a final hug, Gabriel left, shutting the door quietly on his way out.

She pulled off her jeans and t-shirt, peeled back the covers and crawled into bed. Scooting carefully, she worked her way next to

Rowan, until she could feel the warm length of his body against hers. Taking a hold of his hand, she closed her eyes and hoped to God that the man she loved would come back to her. Resisting the crushing grief, she took a deep breath and then another. Once he made his way back, she would make sure, somehow, that she would never, ever lose him again.

Chad glanced at Michael as they trudged through the moonlit semi-darkness toward the house, feet crunching on the powdery white, crushed shell driveway. Rowan's friend looked exhausted. "Well, it's over Mike, and we did it. Without you coordinating things, I'm not sure we could have pulled it off."

Michael stopped at the main entryway into the big home and gazed at him through bloodshot eyes. "I hate to turn this into a mutual admiration deal, but hell, without you hacking into those systems we'd never have gotten Rowan out of that brig. On the way back I caught a couple reports. More than one person in the media is calling this the hacking job of the century. Congratulations."

Chad grasped the knob and pulled the door open. "We each did our part. And right now, I know you want to get some sleep. Catch you in the morning, or maybe the afternoon."

Michael waved at him and headed down the hallway to the wing where he and Gabriel had their suite of rooms. "Give my best to Bettina. See you sometime tomorrow."

Lifting a hand in a weary wave, he headed toward the section of the house Bettina had claimed for the two of them. Now that the nightmare was over and Rowan was safe, he could relax for a few hours before he and Michael started the next phase of their plan. He heard a door slam and light footsteps running. Bettina flew around the corner and gasped when she saw him, hands at her cheeks. "Chad, you're here. You're finally here."

Bracing himself, he waited, staggering back a step when she flung herself into his arms. Bending down, he kissed her, losing his hands first in her hair and then reveling in the firmness of her body. After a few minutes, it dawned on him that they were still standing in the hallway. Lifting his head, he gazed down at her. "It's so good to be here, to see you."

Bettina reached up and stroked the side of his face, lips quivering, eyes filling with tears. "We were all so worried. How's Rowan? Can we see him tomorrow?" She smiled while the tears spilled down her cheeks. "Hey, I've got a bottle of Jack Daniel's for you." She stopped and looked up at him, brow furrowed. "Are you all right?"

Wiping the tears from her face with gentle thumbs, he sighed. "Rowan's had a rough time, but he's with Danielle and he's going to be OK. We'll talk more later about when everyone can see him, because he needs some time to recover." A huge yawn overtook him. Looking down at Bettina, he smiled. "I'm all right, now. Take me home, sweetheart."

Saturday Morning

Rowan woke with a start. Gazing at the unfamiliar ceiling, panic invaded his mind. *Had they transported him?* Taking a quick breath, he winced. His chest and his entire body hurt like hell. Awareness dawned. No leather straps held him down and no leg irons clanked coldly above his ankles. Cascading relief left him shaking. Lying with his eyes closed, he tried to remember what had happened. Gabriel and Michael had led him from the brig. The gleaming black jet had been waiting. He shuddered. Sal Capello had wanted that jet back in the worst way.

Another layer of fog shimmered away and he felt cool sheets, realized he was naked between them. Did he smell coffee? Turning his head, he squinted at dazzling sunlight pouring through big windows. Could he sit up? The pain wracked his body, but he needed to find a bathroom. Grunting with each tortured movement, he managed to inch his way up until he was sitting. Sweat ran down his chest and sides, and he wiped at the trickle making its way along his jaw. *Goddamn it.* Gasping in agony with each shallow breath, he wondered how he'd gotten to this room. Who had placed the IV in his hand, and who had taken off his clothes?

The door to the bedroom opened and he watched, heart pounding. Expecting hard-faced guards or Sal Capello, he saw Gabriel instead, carrying a syringe and flasks of clear fluids. Behind Gabriel came Danielle, hair pulled back in a ponytail, wearing a tank top and shorts that stirred the embers of desire, deep inside. Thinking hard, trying to sort out what had happened, he frowned at her. She'd been on the jet and then she'd undressed him and helped him into bed. Now she carried a steaming cup of coffee and he wanted some.

Gabriel scowled at him. "Amigo, it's good to see you're awake, but you look like hell. What have you been doing, trying to crawl out of bed?" His friend tut-tutted like a querulous mother hen. "I've got more meds for you. I think you're trying to get pneumonia again. What did you do, sleep out in the rain? Are you hungry?"

Danielle clutched the cup of coffee and stared at him, eyes wide. Voice raspy and weak, he replied. "Gabriel, I need to get to the bathroom. Hey, Danielle, can I have a sip of coffee?"

Danielle's face broke into a huge grin as she stepped to the bed and sat down next to him. Her hands shook and he thought she might spill. "The coffee is fresh and it's Starbucks Italian Roast. I made it just for you."

When she leaned toward him, he forgot about the coffee. Staring down the front of the tank top, he wished he had the strength to lift his hands. The cup touched his torn lips and he grimaced, sipping through the pain. How long had it been since he'd had Starbucks? With a pang of sadness, he remembered. The day he'd told Danielle good-bye, she'd sat and held the coffee for him because of the casts on his arms. He hoped to God he never had to tell her good-bye again. But most of all, he wanted to be alone with her, and then he wanted to make love to her, over and over, for a long, long time.

CHAPTER NINETEEN

Two Weeks Later –Second Week In August
Chad leaned back, put his hands behind his head and sent Gabriel, Michael and Ralph a satisfied smile. The motley group slouching comfortably on chaise loungers had orchestrated and successfully executed what FOX News called the *Epitome of Treason*. He'd laughed out loud when CNN's anchor dubbed their tour de force the *Escape of the Century*. In his opinion, the fact that their rescue of Rowan had dominated cable news for over a week called for a celebration.

The FBI and CIA made dire predictions of recapture and prosecution, but the powers that be in both agencies were befuddled and enraged. The disappearance, without a trace, of the country's most wanted homegrown terrorist *and* his family *and* associates, for the second time, had given the media endless fodder. The reputations of both agencies were in tatters. That the CIA's G650 remained missing, tucked away inside Jerry and Bryan's hangar at Atlanta's Hartsfield-Jackson International Airport made their coup all the more sweet.

The four of them had agreed to meet on the beach for drinks and an update on the tasks they'd assigned each other, germane to the welfare of the small group of people at the estate. Exile in paradise was how he described it to Bettina. Taking a long swallow of a potent Jack and Coke, he gazed out across the rolling waves. The sun beat down, but the breeze off the Pacific cooled nicely. All things considered, he thought there were worse places to be exiled.

The only thing that saddened him was the conspicuous absence of the man who'd brought them all together in the first place. So far, Rowan had shown no interest in anything or anyone, except Danielle. But he planned to drag Rowan to the beach as soon as this meeting was over. Whatever it took, his reclusive friend was going to sit and drink with him.

Glancing at the other three men, he smiled. Downing a Red Stripe and belching into his fist, Ralph already looked like a local in his battered fishing hat, faded t-shirt, dungarees that had seen better days and ancient tennis shoes that used to be white with, surprise, no socks. As far as he could tell, the older man hadn't shaved since arriving at the estate.

Gabriel had a ball cap pulled low over his face and wore mirrored sunglasses. Sans shirt and wearing swimming trunks, he looked brown and fit. After gulping a couple shots of tequila, he slid down in the chair and hadn't moved. Michael's wavy black hair scraped the collar of the Hawaiian shirt he wore unbuttoned above cutoffs. The man he'd come to trust and depend on sipped a Budweiser and eyed him placidly. There was no doubt in his mind that Michael had nerves and balls of solid steel.

In his FBI t-shirt, khaki shorts and tennis shoes with socks, Chad felt overdressed and geeky. It figured. Somehow, he never got it quite right. Rowan had always called him quirky, or goofy, not that he minded. Fully invested in the slower pace of island living and the welcomed respite from frantic activity, he yawned and supposed he should get started. "Gentlemen, I'm pleased to inform you that neither the FBI nor CIA has a clue where we are. Their search parameters don't even include the Hawaiian Islands. They've focused so far on the D. C. metropolitan area, Sioux Falls, Chicago and a fifty mile radius of Santa Barbara. The tenor of communication between Ainsley, Capello, and Shemal is bleak at best. The three of them remain committed to the search, of course."

He paused. "Shemal is my major concern. He has global contacts, so I watch his communications closely, especially with the Muslim Brotherhood. The Islamic world is seriously pissed off because, unlike our Intelligence agencies, they know the truth about what Rowan was up to. They want him just as badly if not worse than our own government."

Shaking his head in disbelief, he continued. "Capello is like a rabid dog. His pride took a severe beating in his dealing with Rowan and he can't seem to get past it. Ainsley remains an incompetent idiot." He shrugged. "Nothing new there. At any rate, I monitor the communications of all three, multiple times daily."

Gazing expectantly at the other three men, he waited for one of them to speak. Michael twisted in the white chaise lounge and stretched. "Thanks, Chad. Your work is much appreciated. Now let me see. To date, I've set up electronic surveillance of the entire estate property, including a state-of-the-art alarm system installed in the house, which was no mean feat. The sucker is monstrous, but you all know that."

Smiling lazily, obviously enjoying himself, Michael carried on. "I've appropriated satellite phones for everyone except Derek, of course. We've all got ATM cards for multiple accounts that you set up, Chad. The accompanying identity documents have been handled and I've secured a stash of small arms that I hope we never have to use. And by the way, Rowan's two Glocks, the 36 and the full-auto 18 he likes so much are included in that stash. Of course, he'll never see the 22 again." Michael stopped and grinned. "But hell, at least the CIA has something to remember him by."

Returning Michael's grin and making a mental note to share the security arrangements with Rowan, Chad focused his attention on his former boss. "I'd be curious to know what you think about Derek's state of mind, Ralph. How's the mentoring set-up working out?"

Ralph cleared his throat. "Derek's a good man, but he's having a hard time. He and Marion hit it off, and she's a wonderful confidant. Derek has a lot of hostility toward Rowan, for obvious reasons. Marion says he still feels very protective toward Danielle. The best thing would be for Derek to find another career in different location."

The older man chuckled. "Believe it or not, Jerry and Bryan need a mechanic. I've set Derek up to talk to them about moving to Atlanta and working on their fleet of aircraft. They're willing to enroll him in classes and get him up to speed. The issue is one of identity, and whether he can keep his mouth shut."

Ralph tilted his head back and scratched his neck. "I'm not convinced yet that he can handle this transition, but he told Marion he'd never do anything to endanger Dani, as he calls Danielle."

Chad watched as Gabriel came to life, snorting over Ralph's last comment. "Holy Mother of God, that gringo had better stay far away from Danielle. You know, someone needs to make it clear to this loco chicken bastard that he doesn't have a choice about keeping his mouth shut. Hey Chad, does Derek have internet access?"

Slanting a quick smile at Michael, who sat snickering into his beer, he answered Gabriel. "I've allowed Derek to use a computer, but I route everything he receives or sends to my computer first. So far, he hasn't done anything he shouldn't, but that reminds me. A woman at the airport in Sioux Falls has been a major pain in the ass. I've been monitoring her emails to Shemal since last spring. I finally had a chance to catch up, and *she* is the reason Ralph and I are wanted. She also contacted the FBI about Danielle. So in essence, she's responsible for Rowan's incarceration at Quantico."

Taking a deep breath, angered at the havoc created by the sleazy bitch and what it had cost all of them, but especially Rowan, he continued. "Her name is Marta. She emails Shemal regularly and sends Derek emails asking him all kinds of questions. She's quite brazen about her activities."

Gabriel scowled. "Give me time to think about it and I'll come up with a solution for la puta. And I still think you should let *me* talk to Derek. But anyway, Rowan's progressing well physically. We nipped a bout with pneumonia in the bud, which is a good thing because he seems susceptible to that. His cracked ribs are healing, but still painful." The stocky Hispanic massaged the back of his neck and smirked. "I'd be willing to wager that he hasn't had sex with Danielle quite yet."

Gabriel paused and a frown replaced the smirk. "But amigos, I'm most concerned about his mental health. Danielle came to me a couple days ago, telling me how every night he has nightmares and then can't sleep. She loves him so much, you know? But she's worried sick over him. Bottom line, in my opinion Rowan needs professional help. He exhibited symptoms of post traumatic stress after those CIA bastards worked him over last spring. The days he spent in the brig can't have helped. Michael's mom, Georgia, knows a psychiatrist who works with veterans. The guy's got a talent for tough cases. I'd like to have Georgia contact him about Rowan."

Ralph spoke up. "When I picked Rowan up at that Chamberlain rest stop and had to cuff him, he damn near fell apart. And then, when the SWAT boys got too close at the airport, he lost it. Scared the shit out of me, I can tell you that. If we can get this psychiatrist out here, that'd be great. My only concern is adding another person to the list of people who know where we are."

Looking at the three men, Chad didn't know what to say. Michael leaned forward and swung his bare feet to the sand. "Let me tell you all something. Rowan will snap out of this. Granted, it may take him some time. But when he does, our biggest problem will be containment. Because Rowan is going to be interested in one thing and one thing only, and that's retribution for what's been done to him and everyone he cares about. When that happens, we'll play hell keeping him here."

Michael stood up and crushed the beer can. "I'll give my mother a call. And I'll make it clear to her that the only way we can bring her psychiatrist friend out here is if he understands that he'll be making a permanent commitment to relocate without knowing any details. My mother can feel him out regarding Rowan. It's iffy whether he'll be interested, but we can't do it any other way. It's too damned dangerous, for all of us."

Gabriel slid out of the chaise and stood up. "Agreed, amigo. Keep us informed. I'm going for a swim before I check on Rowan."

After watching the two men amble off, Chad gave Ralph a grim smile. "You know boss, oh hell, *Ralph,* I'm all for helping Rowan with retribution, especially when I think about that bitch Marta, from the airport."

Ralph gave him a sour look. "Let's get Rowan thinking straight first. But then, I'm with you. I'd gladly help find the two jerks that left him hanging in that warehouse office. He's fairly screwed up, thanks to those two. I'm tellin' ya, you should have seen the look in his eyes that day at the airport."

His colleague paused and whistled softly. "If he hadn't been restrained, there's no doubt in my mind that he'd have taken me on, and then made for the closest SWAT guy. And now, I can't imagine delving into his mind. It's my guess that if, and it's a big if, that psychiatrist decides to come out here, he'll be biting off more than he ever dreamed about when he tackles Rowan."

Chad nodded. "What's happened to Rowan is a crime, and I'm willing to do whatever it takes to make things right. Maybe someday we'll have that opportunity. Right now, I'm going to find him and make him sit out here for a while. I'm going to give him his own private update on what we talked about, and I've got some good news for him."

Rowan stepped out of the shower and paused. He heard Danielle talking to someone. She sounded upset. Wrapping a towel around his waist, he walked to the bathroom door and cracked it open. The influx of cool air into the steamy warmth raised goose bumps on his arms. Water dripped down his neck and into the outcropping of hair on his chest. Who was she talking to? When he heard the other voice, instant anger fired in his mind. Fuming, he hurried through the connecting hallway from the bathroom into the bedroom, pulled on shorts and not bothering with a shirt, flung the door open and strode into the living room.

Danielle sat on the sectional sofa with her arms crossed. Derek stood in front of her and swung around to glower at him, resentment etched on his face. "This is all because of you. You swept her off her feet and brainwashed her, ruined her career, and her life. You ruined my life too. I wish you'd never stepped foot in South Dakota."

Shaking with deepening anger, he came face to face with the frustrated man and caught the glimmer of fear in his eyes. Grabbing Derek's arm, he spun him around and slammed him against the wall, ignoring the pain in his ribs and shoulders. Damn, he hadn't lost his touch.

But now the other man squirmed and grunted. "Screw you, Milani. I hate your guts. Too bad you're not still in jail somewhere."

Smoldering rage overtook the anger, and he twisted Derek's arm up, until the moron grunted again. Clamping his other hand on Derek's neck, he applied pressure and listened to him gag. "If Michael hadn't rescued your sorry ass, you'd be in the hands of the CIA right now. Believe me, it's not as much fun as being here."

Leaning close, he whispered in the other man's ear. "You can be glad I don't have my knife dumb fuck, because I'd love to slit your throat." He tightened his grip and watched Derek's eyes bulge in terror. "But I might break your neck instead."

Someone knocked on the door, then opened it, and he heard cursing, in Spanish. A firm hand gripped his shoulder. "Let him go, Rowan, so I don't have to treat him for a broken arm, or worse. Come on, let the stupid gringo live another day."

Gabriel's hand squeezed his shoulder in unmistakable warning. The last thing his ribs needed was for his burly colleague to insert himself into the quarrel. Taking a ragged breath, he dropped Derek's arm, let go of his neck and stepped back. Gabriel nodded at him, eyes wide. "Thanks, Rowan. You had me worried for a minute."

No longer belligerent, Derek leaned against the wall and stared at him in consternation, massaging the angry red marks on his neck. The man's wrenched arm hung limp at his side and his voice was hoarse. "All I wanted to do was talk to Dani, make her see reason. The last thing she needs is to be in this mess. But you, you're *crazy.*"

Danielle spoke from the sofa. "Derek, we've had this conversation before. Why can't you understand? I want to be with Rowan. Get over it and move on with your life."

Rowan saw the despair on Derek's face when the man turned toward Danielle. "If only I could. But thanks to him, I can't, because I don't have a life anymore."

Bitter irony made him laugh out loud. "Welcome to my world, Derek. And let me tell you something, whatever you need to make a new life, I'll make sure you have. But you stay the hell away from Danielle. She chose. I didn't brainwash her. Now get out of here and don't come back."

Gabriel spoke. "Come on Derek, I'll go with you and take a look at your arm and your skinny neck. You're the one who's loco, coming over here. You're damn lucky to be alive, gringo." Waving one hand wildly, Gabriel clamped the other on Derek's upper arm. "Now move it, let's go." With a scowl at him and a grin for Danielle, his friend ushered a cowed Derek from the room and shut the door.

Danielle remained seated, arms still crossed as he sat down beside her. When she looked at him, he smiled and touched her hair. "You OK?"

Smiling back at him, she grabbed his hand. "I'm fine, just mad. Derek never used to be like this. The ugly things he said; none of this is your fault."

Leaning back, he stared at his hand in hers, reveling in the warmth, the simple touch. He didn't think he'd ever move past pure gratitude for her presence in his life. On that level he could empathize with Derek. It must be hell for the guy to be in love with Danielle for years, only to have her make an inexplicable choice like him. "He can't help it, but he's lucky Gabriel showed up when he did."

Danielle sidled closer. "Derek was scared to death. I can't believe what Gabriel said. Would you really have done anything to him?"

Thinking about the knife he sometimes preferred to his pistol, and the alarm he'd seen in Gabriel's eyes, he decided he'd said too much. "Nothing a few aspirin wouldn't fix."

Another knock on the door ended the conversation, and he sighed in relief. Danielle squeezed his hand, jumped up, and opened the door. "Hi Chad, come in. Is Bettina with you?"

Twisting around on the sofa, wincing at his still sore ribs, he saw his tall friend and smiled. "Hey, what's up?"

Chad looked first at Danielle. "Bettina is hoping you'll come over. She wants to cook out on the beach tonight. Actually, we're hoping both of you will join all of us. It should be fun. Marion and Janice picked out some great seafood at the local market."

Chad frowned at him and then looked at Danielle again. Knowing the look on his face had stopped his friend, Rowan glanced at Danielle. A delighted grin lit her features. Goddamn it anyway. His wily colleague knew he wouldn't say no if it meant hurting her. Tone carefully neutral, he replied. "Thanks Chad, that sounds nice."

Chad shifted his gaze and gave him a complacent smile. "You know it'll be fun. And now, if you two have the time, Bettina wants to see you, Danielle. And Rowan, I've got a bottle of Jack Daniel's waiting for us on the beach. I gotta talk to you, brother."

Since when had his goofy friend gotten so slick? At least if he had to spend an evening with his parents, the whiskey would help.

An hour later, relaxing on a chaise lounge, immersed in a comforting haze of single barrel Jack Daniel's whiskey mingled with Coke and ice, Rowan stared at the aquamarine waves and thought maybe he could fall asleep after the nightmares now. Every night he woke up drenched in sweat and terrified, certain he was still in the cell at Quantico. And every night, he got up afterwards and prowled the house, peering anxiously out the windows into the darkness, wondering when a cadre of FBI or CIA agents would burst through the doors and haul him back. Listening to Chad's recitation of what he and Michael had done gave him a much needed assurance of security.

Chad coughed, ending his contemplation. Lifting his eyes from the mesmerizing waves, he saw his colleague grinning at him. "Hey Rowan, I saved the best news for last."

Raising a brow, he gazed at his friend. "What are you talking about?"

Looking inordinately pleased, Chad reached down to the sand for his drink. "Let me explain. See, it pissed me off when I found your financial papers and realized that the CIA had confiscated the funds from your two offshore accounts."

Precious equanimity shattered, he shivered when the condensation from his glass dripped on his bare stomach. "I haven't forgotten."

Chad smiled at him and took a long swallow of Jack and Coke. "Ahhh, that's good. I traced those funds and got your money back. All of it. My father invested it for you, conservatively of course, in various ways, in the name of James

Hawthorne. And Rowan, well I guess you know. It's a lot of money."

"How? You did?" Dipping his head and wiping his eyes, he looked at Chad and then looked away, squinting at the blue-green horizon. Mortified that his lips were quivering, he hoped his friend wouldn't notice.

Chad saved him from having to speak. "Look, it was fun. And it made me feel like I was doing something to help you. It sucked when Michael and Gabriel took you. We didn't know if we'd ever see you again. Both Ralph and I felt so helpless."

Swallowing hard, he met Chad's eyes. "I don't know what to say. They took everything from me, and I never dreamed I'd ever get it back. Thank you."

Chad leaned over and clanked his glass. "You don't have to say anything. Just relax and let's drink for a while. I've missed you, brother."

Angelo Blevins, psychiatrist, Vietnam Vet, and former POW stared at the email and read it again. Georgia Cristo and he had been friends for nearly twenty years, and he'd always thought of her as one of the sanest people he knew. Slowly reaching for his cup of coffee, eyes never leaving the computer screen, he lifted it to his lips, wondering if he needed to adjust that assessment. Several months earlier they'd chatted online, and she'd asked questions about Post Traumatic Stress Disorder, his specialty.

While in the Vietnam War, he'd spent over a year as a POW, courtesy of the Viet Cong. Once back home, his life unraveled while he suffered from post traumatic stress. Eventually he'd recovered and found his own brand of revenge against his torturers by becoming a psychiatrist. Working with down-and-out vets had always been his first love. In fact, he'd retired from private practice to work exclusively with the people no one else wanted. That was part of the reason he'd ended up at the Union Gospel Mission in Sioux Falls.

Unfolding his lean frame from an ancient office chair, he stood up. He needed more coffee to figure out how to deal with the strange email. Pouring another cup of Starbucks, the one indulgence he allowed himself, he breathed deeply, enjoying the aroma. Nothing beat a good cup of coffee. Taking an appreciative swallow, he leaned against the counter in the combination kitchen-living room of his tiny apartment. To say he was intrigued by Georgia's email would be an understatement.

Reflecting for a moment, he realized that nothing tied him to Sioux Falls. At sixty-two he had no family other than an amiable ex-wife and a daughter in her thirties who seemed mostly embarrassed by his lifestyle. He'd wrestled with occasional discontent, a feeling that there must be more out there for him somewhere, if he could only find it. Could this be his chance to contribute, maybe make his mark?

Sliding back into his chair, he perused the email a third time, wondering what in the world Georgia meant.

Would you consider an opportunity to help someone in desperate need, but not in a position to seek therapy? It would mean moving, going off-grid, so to speak, but you'd be working on a project I know you'd love. Come visit at the ranch for a weekend and I'll explain.

Good Lord. Going *off-grid?* Despite his practical nature, she'd hooked him. With a chuckle he leaned back in the creaky chair and hit reply. It looked like he'd be heading into the wilds of northwest South Dakota. Thank God it was still summer.

Feeling disconsolate, Michael flopped into the recliner he'd lugged next to the window in the living area he shared with Gabriel. Feet crossed, hands in his lap, he stared out at the expanse of lawn that ended at the beach and thought about Rowan. If a more strong-willed man existed on the planet, he'd be surprised. He was grateful for his friend's intrepid personality, because if Rowan had given in to Sal Capello, they'd all be sitting in a brig somewhere.

Rubbing his face wearily, he tried to exorcise the disturbing images that replayed in his mind. Thinking that someone needed to know what had happened to Rowan, he'd asked Chad to hack the video records from Quantico's brig cameras. They'd sat together and watched, sickened at the debasement their friend had endured.

Rowan would be the first to insist that he hadn't been tortured, but *damn*. Both he and Chad had ended up drunk, taking shots directly from a bottle of Jack Daniel's to get through the unsettling images. In the end, he knew Rowan would have died before giving up their names or admitting to treason. And he hoped his volatile friend never found out what they'd done and *seen*, because the humiliation would be devastating. He shook his head. There was no telling what Rowan might do.

His lips twisted in a grimace as he thought about the next task he and Chad had agreed upon. After what Rowan had been through, spending a quiet evening with family and friends should be child's play. But Rowan hadn't seen his parents in years because of something that had happened between him and his mother. And now it was his job to talk to Khalil and Janice, to ask them to hold back when they saw their son and not overwhelm him with emotion he couldn't handle.

How would they react? Meeting them, he'd found Khalil to be kind and intelligent, and Janice reminded him of Rowan. He could see the same passion in her eyes. No wonder the two of them had clashed. Dreading the conversation, he decided to get it over with. Hopefully they would understand and cooperate. Gazing out the window for a moment longer, he resolutely put aside his troubled thoughts about Rowan's suffering and stood up.

While he trudged reluctantly through the maze of hallways connecting the wings of the rambling house, he thought about flying back to South Dakota. No doubt Gabriel was antsy to head for San Diego, where his wife, young daughter, and son lived. And he couldn't wait to see Asal, his *honey*, as he called her, because that was the Farsi translation of her name.

Five years earlier, one of their clandestine operations had turned deadly, and Asal Tehrani, an Iranian operative who worked with them on rare occasions, had been compromised. There had been no time to plan, she either left with them, or died. He'd been in love with her for a while, so when they returned to the United States, he'd asked her to be his wife and she had laughingly said, *C'mon Mikey, I'm not a believer in arranged marriages.*

But he didn't care about that. She lived in Pierre, South Dakota's capital, in a house he'd purchased for the two of them, and had never batted an eye at the new identity he'd created for her, complete with birth certificate and social security number. Thinking about her made him smile. Independent as hell, Asal did her own thing, as she proudly told him, although she seemed to enjoy the weekends they spent together. So did he. No one outside their small circle knew about her, not even his parents.

Asal spent her time monitoring and infiltrating numerous Islamic websites, posing as a jihadist. Thanks to her, they'd garnered a treasure trove of valuable information. Because of her finesse, he'd known about Muusa Shemal and his connections to the Muslim Brotherhood before Chad had found out, although he hadn't let on. Asal had discovered Sa-id Harandi's unwilling betrayal of Rowan, too. Someday, when he was sure Rowan could handle it, he'd tell him about the demise of his unfortunate friend. Looking up, surprised to see he'd mindlessly walked right to the door of the Milanis' suite of rooms, he took a deep breath, held it, and knocked.

CHAPTER TWENTY

Standing on the stage with the Imam of his most beloved Houston mosque, Muusa Shemal gazed with pleasure at his gathered holy warriors. Handpicked by him, these men would search diligently until they located Rowan Milani. Since the Brotherhood had finally, by Allah's immeasurable grace, given him permission to pursue the ghost agent in his own way, he had chosen men of Iranian descent to find their brother. He smiled. There could be no sweeter requital than for the man to be vanquished by his own kind.

This time there would be no piddling with American Intelligence agents. Stunned and enraged by the inability of the FBI and CIA to keep Rowan Milani in custody, he'd retreated to Houston for succor. Thinking of the precious resources wasted, he ground his teeth. The Americans were, how had the pundit on one network described them? *Keystone Cops?* They were imbeciles.

This time, when his warriors captured Rowan Milani, they would deliver the jinn directly to Egypt. And, Allah be praised, no one, neither the greedy ones in the Brotherhood who wanted to barter his prize to the highest bidder, nor the cunning man's friends, would remove Rowan Milani from his grasp.

The Imam touched his arm. "Teacher, your warriors await their instructions." Private reverie ended, he smoothed his black-and-silver pinstriped suit and adjusted the red silk tie. Dabbing at the beads of sweat on his forehead with a matching red silk kerchief, he silently thanked Allah for the air conditioning in the cleverly hidden room, built inside a Houston warehouse. Without it, the heat and humidity would have been unbearable. Taking careful steps from the stage to the floor he strode into the midst of his jihadists. The men parted like a subservient river until he stood in the center of the secret sanctuary.

The group of thirty-odd men talked quietly among themselves, casting surreptitious glances his way. Raising his arms and turning in a slow circle, he began. The years of searching, the thwarted plans, and the intolerable loss of his prize lent passion and power to his words. "My brothers, you have been chosen by Allah for a quest. You will devote all your capacities, your mental, spiritual, and physical resources, to finding Rowan Milani, the *Shayton* who has defied the will of Allah, sending our martyrs to paradise at a time of his choosing, ruining countless stratagems for jihad."

Sweat soaked his shirt and trickled down his face. He mopped it off with the red kerchief. "You will scour the internet for information, hack the banking and computer records of every known associate of Rowan Milani, and travel to airports around the globe in search of the aircraft that carried the kafir to freedom. Allah will guide each of you in this holy endeavor."

Breathing hard, he waved the silk kerchief like a red flag of victory. "Clues and a trail will emerge. You, his rightful brothers from Iran, will expose and unearth him. Then you will vanquish the jinn to Egypt to fulfill Allah's destiny for one such as him."

The men exploded as one in a fiery roar of assent, shouts of *Allahu Akbar* punctuating the bedlam. These holy warriors would complete his vision. Arms flung over his head, he shook his fists. "By the gracious mercy and power of Allah, you will succeed."

Rowan sat on the edge of the bed and massaged his forehead, wondering why he'd let Chad talk him into spending an evening with his parents. What could he say to them? Thinking about them brought back too many painful memories, and goddamn it, he didn't need that. If he never saw his parents again, it would be all right with him. Why couldn't he be left alone to deal with his screwed up mind and body.

Danielle poked her head in the bedroom. Eyes sparkling, she smiled at him. "Are you getting ready? Want some help picking out a shirt?" Her smile changed to a worried frown. "What's the matter?"

When she sat down beside him, all thought of his parents vanished. Dressed in a sleeveless halter top sundress that matched her eyes, her skin glowed from the month she'd spent on the island. Sliding his hand down her arm, he wished they could just lie back on the bed. But no, Sal Capello had fixed that for a while yet. Taking a deep breath, wincing at the sharp twinges and frustrated because of the still healing ribs, he fought an uprising of bitter rage at the man who'd inflicted so much pain.

Danielle laid a hand on his cheek, drawing him out of the angry thoughts. "Your mom and dad are excited about seeing you. Your mom was so kind to me when I first arrived. She sat and talked to me, and we even said a prayer for you to be strong, and that you'd be rescued quickly."

Her words refocused the rage, turned it white hot. Janice had no right to shove her religion down Danielle's throat. He stared at her and saw the uncertainty in her eyes. "That was nice. You want to pick out a shirt for me? I'll wear anything but white."

Danielle gave him a quick kiss and stood up, tantalizing in the dress. "Thanks for doing this. I can see it's hard for you. If you ever want to talk about it, I'm willing to listen."

If it were up to him that would never happen. "It's OK, I'm fine. Let's go, before Chad comes looking for us."

She nodded and turned to the closet. "All right, here's my favorite color on you." Her smile was innocent when she swung around with a royal blue Hawaiian print shirt, but he knew better. Amazed at how well she could read him, he stood up and took the shirt from her. He was still buttoning it when she put her arms around him and snuggled close.

Closing his eyes, he lowered his head to her soft lips, giving in to the fierce desire. Letting his hands roam, feeling the firm warmth of her body beneath the cool silkiness of the dress, he heard the catch in her breath. But when he fumbled with eager fingers to untie the halter top, she pulled away.

Desire checked, the rage simmered back and he clenched his jaws, forcing his hands to his sides. "Danielle, why do you do that? You make me crazy and then you quit."

He couldn't miss the bright spots of color on her cheeks. "It's hard for me too, Rowan, and I always end up feeling bad because of your ribs. I'm sorry."

When he saw the frustration in her eyes, he felt like a jerk. He shook his head, knew he needed to get a grip. "No, I'm sorry." Grabbing her hand, he tried to smile. "Let's go and get this party over with."

Janice stood next to Khalil and scanned the large, flagstone patio with its strategically placed lights and artfully scattered beach furniture. Ralph and Marion sat chatting with Derek and Gabriel while Chad and Bettina tended the grill. Michael stood next to Chad, but Danielle and Rowan were nowhere in sight. Breathless with anticipation, she thought about the visit from Michael that afternoon. Rowan's friend had been so kind, so concerned. She and Khalil would do anything for their only son. She just wanted to beg Rowan's forgiveness and tell him how wrong she'd been.

Oh dear Lord, there he was. She took a step forward, only to feel Khalil's hand on her arm. "Not yet Janice, give Rowan some time and space, like Michael told us. Let him relax with everyone first. We've waited years. Surely we can hold off for a few more minutes."

Hearing the firmness in Khalil's tone and seeing the determination in his eyes, her shoulders drooped and she acquiesced. Trying not to stare, she watched Rowan and Danielle surreptitiously. Rowan had shaved the beard and his hair was shorter. But his face seemed hard, and he looked so thin. Smiling at how his demeanor softened when he looked at Danielle, she thought he must love her very much. Her smile faded. So far, he hadn't so much as glanced their way. The look on her husband's face stopped her again. "OK, fine. I can wait."

Surveying his friends and family relaxing together against the backdrop of the molten sunset, Rowan knew he was fortunate. He also knew that there couldn't be a better bunch of people to be stuck with on an island paradise. Why then, did he feel so irritable? Maybe it was Derek, giving him dark glances while he hid next to Gabriel. Or the shy smiles from Bettina. It was a credit to Chad that his impulsive, passionate sister hadn't run squealing into his arms.

Spotting his parents, he frowned. So, they couldn't wait to see him. Well, the sooner he talked to them, the sooner he could be done with them. Jaw set, he looked at Danielle. "Will you help me talk to my mom and dad?" Still feeling bad about his earlier anger, he grabbed her hand and drew it to his lips.

Danielle's brilliant smile lifted his heart, and with her hand firmly in his, he headed across the patio. His mother watched him and so did his father. They stood still as statues, staring at him, and then Janice stepped forward with Khalil lagging behind her. Face to face, he gazed from one to the other. They looked older and excitement lit their faces. But he felt empty and had nothing to say.

Janice took a step closer, reaching out. Seeing his father grimace, he didn't move when Danielle pulled her hand from his, and his mother's quivering arms went around him and tightened in a hug. He winced and she pulled back, hands clutching his arms, looking up at him, biting her lip. He could see her tears, ready to overflow. "Oh Rowan, it's so nice to see you. It's been too long and I want you to know, I'm so sorry, for everything. I was so wrong, all those years ago."

Staring at his mother, the old resentment rekindled by her faltering words, he raised a brow. She was sorry? What the hell was he supposed to say? That he forgave her? Khalil stepped forward and took a hold of her arm. His father looked apologetic. "Hello Rowan, we're so glad to be here. I'm sorry for your mother's outburst. It's just that we're both excited to see you."

Michael appeared at his side with a tall, fizzing glass in one hand and a can of Budweiser in the other. "Hey Rowan, it's nice to see you out and about. I brought you a Jack and Coke. Have a drink." Blue eyes sharp and assessing, his colleague glanced from Janice to Khalil, and back to him. "Janice, how are you this evening? It sounds like you and Marion have prepared a feast for us. Whatever it is smells great. Danielle, you look fabulous."

Grateful for Michael's timely intervention, needing to quench his burgeoning animosity before berating his mother and ruining the evening, he grabbed the drink and tipped his head back. Taking a deep swallow, he realized too late that the mixture must be Jack Daniel's with a splash of Coke. While he inhaled pungent fumes, the whiskey burned its way down his throat. His nose ran, his eyes watered, and he started coughing. Michael slapped him on the back. "Whoa there, take it easy brother. Janice, you wouldn't happen to have a Kleenex, would you? Looks like Rowan could use one."

His coughing fit distracted his mother, and Khalil stepped forward with a handkerchief. For as long as he could remember, his father had kept a pressed white handkerchief in his pants pocket. Shoving the drink at Danielle, who stood next to him snickering, he grabbed the handkerchief and muttered a strangled, "Thanks, Dad." After wiping his eyes and nose, he took the glass back from Danielle, shot Michael a dirty look, and frowned at his parents.

Khalil spoke first. "We are very happy to be here. This is a beautiful place to live. Your mother's going to revamp the landscaping. Can't you imagine the flowers she'll grow out here?"

Janice chimed in, giving him a forced smile. "Oh yes, we're so happy to be here. It's been such a pleasure to meet Danielle, too. You have," his mother's gaze wandered to his wrists, and her eyes widened, "oh dear."

Taking another, smaller swallow of mostly whiskey, he sniffed and wiped his nose again. This was not going well. Looking around for his cohort, he saw that Michael had backed off a few steps and stood sipping the Budweiser, watching the interplay between him and his parents with a slight smirk.

Danielle spoke up. "It's been great to meet you both. I'm so happy we're all here together. The house and the entire estate are amazing. Don't you agree? I'm hoping maybe Rowan will teach me how to surf. He's told me how much he loved the water, growing up."

Grateful for her ability to put everyone at ease, he ignored the pain in his ribs and put his arm around her. "Dad, Mom, I'm glad you like it here. I know it was a sudden change. Ah, it's too bad my problems disrupted your lives." His comments sounded stilted and he panicked. Agreeing to see them had been a colossal mistake. He wanted no part of his mother's remorse or his father's kindness.

Khalil waved a hand and smiled at him. "Nonsense, we're ecstatic to be here. Since I retired a year ago, we had nothing holding us in California. But now, I think your mother needs to help Marion, so we can all sit down to the meal they've worked so hard to prepare."

Janice smiled again, but he thought she looked strained and unhappy. "We are thrilled to be here, and I can't wait to start working on the flower beds. I hope you enjoy the dinner. We prepared some dishes you always liked. Perhaps we can chat later, but your father's right, I need to help Marion."

Relieved to see them go, a headache starting behind his eyes, he watched his father guide his mother toward the others. Michael stepped back to his side, a satisfied look on his face. "That went well, don't you think? You know I've always got your back. Oh, Danielle, I keep forgetting to tell you. My mom loves your mutt. Damn thing follows her all over the place." Saluting them with his beer, Michael turned and sauntered off.

Danielle giggled and he frowned down at her. "Did Michael plan that?"

Giving him a quick shrug, she slid from beneath his arm and grabbed his hand. "Beats me, but it's nice to know Shasta's in good hands. Michael told me his mom picked her up, but my attention has been focused on you." Her smile was sweet. "Let's say hi to Chad and Bettina and get something to eat. I'm starving, how about you?"

CHAPTER TWENTY-ONE

Two Weeks Later – Fourth Week In August
Rowan stared at Chad and Michael in disbelief. "You decided *what?*" When his two friends had asked to meet him in the study, he'd been interested. But now, leaning back against the leather sofa, observing their smug faces, he felt sideswiped and it stung.

Chad sat across from him in a chocolate-brown leather chair that matched the sofa, feet up on the coffee table between them. His friend looked solicitous. "Rowan, calm down, please, and listen to reason. We know you're suffering and need help. That's all this is about."

Glaring first at Chad and then at Michael leaning casually against the wall, he thought nastily that this was about the two of them getting carried away with being in charge and taking care of him. "You could have asked me before you hauled someone clear the hell out here. And from South Dakota?" Thoroughly frustrated, he shook his head, trying to stave off encroaching anger.

Michael shoved off the wall and stalked around the room, running a hand along the floor to ceiling mahogany shelves, filled with what must be hundreds of hard cover books. In the central, communal area of the house and one of the few rooms with no windows, at first Rowan had thought the study seemed cozy, but now it felt closed in and stuffy. A musty scent hung in the air, tingled in his nose and he sniffed, feeling the first inkling of a sneeze.

Michael stopped and stared at him, hands on hips. "It's a done deal, Rowan. The guy's here and he's spent a lot of time studying the information we gave him. He's a psychiatrist with years of experience treating Post Traumatic Stress Disorder. You will meet with him this afternoon, so suck it up and don't be a stubborn jerk."

Chad sighed and smiled kindly. "His name is Angelo Blevins and he seems like a cool guy. To be honest, we figured it would be better if you didn't have time to dwell on him coming out here. If we screwed up on that, I'm sorry. But I'm with Mike on this. Now's not the time for your stubbornness."

Gazing moodily from one to the other, he knew they were right that he needed help. Raising his hands in defeat, he gave each of them a hard stare. "OK, whatever you want, I'll do it. I'll meet with the guy every day for the rest of my life, if that's what you want." He lowered his hands and smacked them on his knees. "But you know what? I was interrogated at Quantico. I didn't have a lobotomy. Would it kill either of you to ask me about what I need?"

Chad and Michael exchanged glances. He saw Michael grimace and give a quick, negative shake of his head before Chad spoke. "Yeah, we know how you were interrogated and that's part of the reason we went ahead and made these arrangements."

Shock crackled through him at his colleague's revelation and he sat up straight. "What did you say? What exactly do you mean, *we know how you were interrogated?"*

His two friends exchanged glances one more time, stoking his anger and frustration to the breaking point. When Chad spoke again, he could see the sadness in his friend's eyes. "Mike and I thought we should know what happened, in order to help you. So I hacked the video records from the brig."

Humiliation burned hot in his face. Breathing hard, fists clenched, he stared at Chad. Shifting his gaze, he saw that Michael had tensed up and stood watching him through narrowed eyes. He struggled to contain his anger. "You had *no* right, *neither* of you. How could you do that?" Briefly covering his face with his hands, he hunched over on the sofa as the anger dissipated into intense hurt.

When he looked up, Michael relaxed his stance and gave him a pleading look, which he thought seemed out of character for his hard-nosed friend. "Rowan, we didn't do it for fun or for some damned voyeuristic reason. We needed to know what techniques the CIA agent employed, so we could help you. Do you realize that you were subjected in *five days* to what CIA interrogators normally progress to in a *month?* We appreciate what you did for us. If you'd given in to that asshole, we'd all be incarcerated now."

Chad nodded and looked grim. "Watching that video is one of the hardest things I've ever done. No one else will ever know what we saw. And when you're ready to take out Sal Capello, I'm with you. We'll make the world a better place, without him."

His humiliation deepened as it dawned on him that Michael and Chad felt sorry for him. And because of their *pity* they'd acted without any consideration for what he might want or need. Goddamn it, they were supposed to be his friends. Looking from one to the other, feeling utterly betrayed and mortified that they'd seen what Sal Capello had subjected him to, he shrugged. "I need some time to think about this. Is that all right with the two of you? Maybe you'd like to consult with your, oh excuse me, *my* psychiatrist and see if it's all right if I *think.*"

Michael raised an insolent brow and headed toward the door. Chad stood up and looked at him. "Rowan, I'm sorry. I wish I could make you understand. Maybe we can catch up later and have a Jack and Coke on the beach."

His plans for the afternoon were none of their business. He raised a hand and dropped it back in his lap. "Yeah sure, whatever you want." Chad looked unhappy, but didn't say anything else, just followed Michael and closed the door, leaving him alone. Taking a deep breath and letting it out slowly, he leaned back again, stretched his bare feet out in front of him and closed his eyes.

Last winter in Denver, sitting on the hard bench in the bowels of the airport, he'd felt like a pawn on a chess board, being maneuvered where he didn't want to go. He snorted. That had become the story of his life. And now he'd been manipulated again, by the men he trusted most. Angrily rubbing his eyes with the heels of his hands, he thought about Michael and Chad. Along with Gabriel and Ralph, they had risked everything for him. Where would he be without his misguided, despotic friends?

The sound of the door snapped his eyes open. Expecting to see Chad or Michael, he frowned at the man who stepped inside and stopped, then stared at him with a confused look on his face. This must be the shrink. Still irritated, he straightened up and leaned forward. "Can I help you with something?"

The man came further into the room, giving him a momentary shiver of fear. What if this was an operative who'd managed to breach their security? But the man stopped in front of him, smiled, and held out his hand. "Angelo Blevins here and you must be Mr. Milani. It's a great pleasure to meet you, although I apologize for disturbing you. I didn't think anyone would be in here."

What could he say to the guy? God only knew what Michael and Chad might have told him. Realizing the psychiatrist still stood in front of him with his hand out, he scowled. Screw him if he thought he was going to stand up and shake his hand. Meeting the curious eyes, he sighed. "Doctor Blevins, my colleagues just informed me that they made arrangements with you to be here. That was not my choice."

The doctor slumped into the chair on the other side of the coffee table. Clasping his hands between his knees, the older man gazed at him quizzically. "Your friends didn't consult you about working with me?"

Smirking at the psychiatrist, he wondered if he was being played. The man looked clever. "That is correct, Doc. Can I call you Doc? Please call me Rowan. Only Georgia Cristo calls me

Mr. Milani, because of an ill-conceived desire to preserve my dignity, which is obviously a lost cause." He clamped his mouth shut. What the hell was wrong with him? He'd revealed way more of himself than he'd intended. And all the shrink had done was sit there and stare at him.

A smile lit Angelo's slender face. "Ah, Georgia, she's quite the lady and a good friend. Please feel free to call me Doc or Angelo, whichever you're most comfortable with." Tucking shoulder length graying hair behind his ears, Angelo frowned at him over narrow, wire-rimmed glasses. "I must confess, it troubles me that you were not involved in the discussion of your need for psychotherapy. Pardon me for stating the obvious, but you are, after all, the intended recipient of my care. It seems only logical that you would have played an integral part in the decision."

Disgruntled and completely disarmed by the canny psychiatrist, he didn't know what to say. Jamming his fingers along the stubble on his jaw, he gazed into the man's perceptive blue eyes and thought, *what the hell*. He was never going to win anyway. "Doc, you're here now. We might as well get started. Want some coffee?"

Angelo's kind face beamed. "Coffee sounds fantastic. I don't suppose anyone out here likes Starbucks?"

Chuckling at the doctor's hopeful look, he stood up. "You're in luck. Starbucks is the only coffee I drink. A pot of Italian Roast is brewing right now. Follow me."

Angelo walked with him to the communal kitchen down the hall where he filled the to-go mug Chad had snagged from his hotel room in Sioux Falls and poured another steaming cup. The psychiatrist gave him a grateful smile and sipped. "Ah, now this is good coffee. Thanks."

Back in the study, he sank into the sofa and put his feet up on the coffee table, staring at the lanky man sprawled in the chair facing him. The good doctor looked relaxed and happy and reminded him of an aging hippy, but he wasn't fooled. The guy was sharp. "All right, Doc. What's next? Thanks to my colleagues, you probably already know more about me than I do. And I'm sure Georgia had plenty to tell you."

Frowning and shaking his head, Angelo held the coffee cup in both hands and looked at him. "Your friends told me you'd been through a rough interrogation period. They provided me with background information and a timeline of events. Georgia said you'd exhibited symptoms of post traumatic stress, which is my specialty, and one of the reasons I'm here."

That sparked his interest. "Yeah Doc, why exactly are you here? Living in Sioux Falls, you had to see and hear something about this mess. Hell, you could be assisting America's most wanted homegrown terrorist." He drew a quick breath. It hurt to say it out loud. What was it about the shrink that made him spill his guts without even realizing it?

The psychiatrist sipped coffee and regarded him with the penetrating eyes. "Last March I remember seeing you on a stretcher, being taken from a warehouse, if I remember correctly, and of course I watched the coverage of your supposed rendition. When you surrendered last month, I watched that as well. And now, your disappearance from Quantico has captivated the media and the entire country.

When Georgia approached me, she made it quite clear before identifying you, that I would be in a position to assist someone who needed my specialized services but was not able to ask. Rowan, I know you're innocent. Helping you regain emotional health would be my pleasure. In fact, I would consider it an honor."

The last thing he wanted to talk about was his emotional health. Thinking about what the tricky shrink might get him to divulge left him uneasy. Just drinking coffee with the guy was exhausting, and he didn't like the feelings the doctor had stirred up in a half-hour of chatting. But more than anything, today he wanted to be with Danielle. "Well Doc, I've got another appointment. How about tomorrow, same time, right here? That fit into your schedule?" He couldn't help snickering. This was his personal, private psychiatrist, after all. "Oh yeah, there's one last thing. How much did my colleagues offer to pay you to come out here and tell me what to do?"

Angelo stared at Rowan's back as his new patient strode away with a slight limp, seemingly without a care. It was a façade, of course, but he marveled at the man's demeanor. Barefoot, wearing a rumpled, unbuttoned shirt over cutoffs and clutching a Starbucks mug, Rowan had shown him how to navigate the labyrinthine house. Then the brooding man strolled with him to the brick walkway and pointed the way to the beach. After that, Rowan had sneered at him and said, *see ya later, Doc.* He didn't think he'd ever seen eyes so cold and mocking. And yet, he sensed good humor and kindness in the troubled man, all but lost beneath layers of what he knew must be truly abysmal pain.

Whew. Georgia hadn't been kidding when she'd said this would be a challenge. Rowan Milani got all his juices flowing. The man was hurting and his well-meaning friends had wounded him even more by acting without his consent. Shaking his head over their thoughtlessness, he decided to get more Starbucks and jot down his initial thoughts. Chuckling over their shared enjoyment of what constituted a great cup of coffee, he realized he'd found a starting point in developing trust with the wary man.

Goodness, then he needed to figure out how to send some money to his daughter, the Union Gospel Mission in Sioux Falls and maybe even his ex-wife. The amount Rowan told him would be deposited in an account for him every month was nothing short of staggering and significantly more than he'd been promised. There had to be a way for him to share it without giving away the identity of his patient or his whereabouts. He'd have to consult with Chad or Michael about that.

Feeling more energized than he had in years, he took a moment to enjoy the warm breeze fluttering the palm branches, the sugar-white ribbon of sand and the turquoise water. His life had definitely turned an interesting corner. Smiling to himself, he shrugged. Looking back had never been his style. The future stretched ahead, full of interesting possibilities for him and his new patient. He couldn't wait to get started.

Sitting cross-legged on the blanket he'd arranged on the sand, Rowan tossed back a hefty shot of Jack Daniel's. After meeting with his colleagues and talking with the sharp-witted psychiatrist, he needed the whiskey. Relishing the burn down the back of his throat, he splashed more into the glass and wondered what was keeping Danielle. He'd already poured her favorite wine.

Stretching and twisting his back, he considered the state of his body. Soreness lingered in his shoulders, along with a stiffness he figured would probably be with him for the rest of his life. Some of the scars from last spring had started to fade. But most important, no more aching twinges plagued every breath.

Deciding his ribs had healed enough, he'd asked Danielle to meet him at a hidden section of beach. Tucked into a curve in the shoreline and partially shaded by a cluster of palms, it provided the privacy he craved. It wasn't the Four Seasons, but it beat the house, where someone always seemed to be knocking on their door. And he wasn't in the mood for interruptions. Not today. Danielle walked around the bend and waved. "Hi. Sorry I'm late. Bettina gave me the third degree, so I finally told her to tell everyone to leave us alone for the afternoon."

Downing another gulp of Jack Daniel's, he watched her walk toward him in the deep sand. The enticing bounce of bare breasts under her t-shirt and the natural sway of her hips beneath short shorts had his palms sweating and his pulse pounding in his throat. Blinking in the dappled sunlight, he gazed up at her. "Hi Danielle. Have some wine."

Sliding down next to him, she took the glass and watched him through a long, slow swallow. "Mm, thanks, this is the best wine. Hey, I ran into Michael and he told me about the psychiatrist." She sipped more wine and then frowned, laying her hand on his arm. "I'm sorry they did that without consulting you."

The feather light touch of her body against his chased the jumbled thoughts away. He twined his fingers in her hair, enjoying how the sunlight sparkled through it. "The shrink is OK. And he likes Starbucks."

Danielle laughed out loud and tipped her head back to finish the wine. Staring at her smooth neck, he followed suit and drained the whiskey, tossing the glass to the sand beyond the blanket. When she slanted a brow and laid back in the shade, he looked down, mesmerized by how her breasts filled the t-shirt. She ran her tongue provocatively around her lips and his mouth fell open.

Giggling, she pushed herself back up beside him and slid her hand inside his shirt, trailing her fingers from his chest to his belly, pumping his heart rate higher and giving him instant goose bumps. "Rowan, take your shirt off, would you? Want me to help you? Do your ribs still hurt?" She paused, swirling her fingers in the fine hair around his belly button, giggling again when he grabbed her cool, dry hand with his hot, sweaty one. Her voice became wistful. "Do you realize it's been almost six months since we flew to Chicago for the weekend?"

Nodding as he pulled the shirt off, he smiled at her. "Yeah, I know how long it's been. But hey, my ribs don't hurt anymore."

Eyes wide, she put her hands on either side of his face. "I can't believe it. What are we waiting for?" Wrapping her arms around him, she pulled him down with her to the blanket. Her fingers left a trail of fire on his skin, moving playfully down and helping him out of the cutoffs, then tingling up his sides, dancing across his shoulders, and raking deep into his hair.

Arousal rolled through him in burning waves and he kissed her hard, heard her soft moan when his tongue touched hers. Eager for more, he slid his hand beneath her shorts and she lifted her hips to help him pull them down. When he slipped his hand under her t-shirt and felt her tremble, saw her chest heaving, he could barely whisper. "We gotta get rid of this, Danielle. It's in my way."

He waited while she pulled the t-shirt over her head and then lost himself in her body. God, she was so soft all over. When he explored with his hands and lips, tasting and teasing with his tongue, she arched her back and gasped, sending his heart rate skyrocketing.

She was everything he could ever want. Then the steel door slammed shut, echoing in his mind, sending him back. Alone in the frigid cell, nose burning at the stench of sweat and urine, he remembered what he'd wanted so desperately to tell her while he suffered, cuffed and chained, staring at the concrete floor.

He lifted his head and shuddered. Danielle opened her eyes. "What's the matter?" Her hands, warm on his chilled skin kept him anchored in the present.

Breathing hard, he looked down at her. "In the brig at Quantico I," he paused, touching her face with shaky fingers. "I thought I'd never see you again and I wished, I wanted so badly to tell you how much I missed you and how much I loved you."

Danielle stared at him intently, and her hand gripped his arm. When she spoke, the ferocity in her voice made him shiver. "It's all over. Just make love to me. *Right here.* Right now."

Unexpected tears welled in his eyes, and he blinked them away. "Danielle, you know that's all I ever want to do."

The smile she gave him was tender. "I love you so much, Rowan. And I can't wait any longer." Her hands were warm and gentle on his body. "Please, let's do this."

EPILOGUE

September 11th

Rowan walked toward the pool house for his morning workout, a beach towel slung over his shoulder. Situated east of the house, surrounded by palm trees and a tangle of overgrown grass and shrubs, the secluded facility was one of his favorite places. Stepping off the brick walkway onto the sandy path leading to the door, he reflected on the routine, the deceptive semblance of normalcy his life had fallen into. Making love to Danielle, if he was lucky, constituted the beginning of his day. While she showered, he grabbed coffee and headed out to swim.

The Olympic-sized pool allowed him to vent his growing resentment over the destruction of his career and reputation, the scars on his body, the limp he couldn't conquer, and the screwed up mess in his mind. He swam hard, pushed himself viciously until his chest heaved and ached. Then he worked out, forcing his shoulders, wrists and hands through the exercises Michael's father had taught him. After that, he hit the weight machines until his muscles burned. Another swim helped him unwind, and he finished by soaking in the hot tub.

The exercise always made him hungry, and he munched through a couple peanut butter and jelly sandwiches and took his coffee with him to meet Angelo. The shrink had grown on him, although more often than not, he needed solitude and the bottle of Jack Daniel's when their sessions ended. Sometimes he wanted to choke the perspicacious psychiatrist, but Angelo seemed to know when his rage threatened to overflow and backed off accordingly. The bitch of it was that the guy got him thinking about things way more than he wanted to.

His afternoons consisted of drinking alone on the beach if Angelo's insights proved to be too much. If not, he went fishing with Ralph. Now that they weren't boss and subordinate, the tension between them had evaporated, and their friendship had grown even stronger. Ralph's wife Marion made monster cookies for him and served them warm out of the oven with big glasses of milk, to fatten him up, she said, and he liked that. She was easy to talk to, and he could relax because she never prodded him with embarrassing questions about how he was doing. Nope, Marion just accepted him without judgment, like she always had, and he liked that, too.

During the evenings, he and Danielle curled up by themselves or met up with Chad and Bettina. They watched movies, read books, and caught the news. Sometimes he and Danielle just talked, about all kinds of stuff. Well, she talked and he listened. He loved to tweak her and then wait while she reacted. Her passionate responses gave him an excuse to get his hands on her before she could do something to him. And more than anything else, he wanted his hands on her, all the time.

This morning he'd planned to commemorate the attacks of September 11, 2001 and pay his respects to Michelle by watching the memorial services at Ground Zero in New York, where he'd been every year until this one. Scanning the channels and settling on FOX News, he found that he'd forgotten about the time difference, and the memorial services were over. Instead, a serious reporter anchored a special on America's most wanted homegrown terrorist. *Him,* for God's sake, complete with pictures of his parents and the house in Carpinteria, California where he'd grown up. They'd found his high school senior picture, another from college, his FBI ID shot and finally, the photo taken at Quantico's brig. He almost didn't recognize the long-haired, bearded man who looked into the camera like a cornered animal. But he was well acquainted with the terror mingling with rage in that man's eyes.

They had video too, of him on a stretcher and from the day Ralph escorted him across the tarmac in chains. Watching his halting steps toward the Bureau's jet, he shivered. He could still feel the weighted, padlocked chain around his waist and the cold metal on his wrists and ankles holding him captive. The anchor talked knowledgeably about how he'd become radicalized, about his traitorous escape and the terrible blight he'd caused across the country and hell, around the whole fucking world.

After that the anchor reported on the FBI and CIA's joint efforts to find him, and their newest angle, a fifteen million dollar reward for information leading to his apprehension. That made the sweat bead on his forehead. Any number of greedy entrepreneurs would be inspired to search for him. As his aiders and abettors, Ralph and Chad had rated only five million dollars each, and that made him laugh out loud. His colleagues would feel slighted.

While the reporter pontificated about the importance of bringing him to justice, of making him an example, the simmering rage boiled over. *Goddamn it.* They couldn't do this to him. *But they had.* Dealing with the specter of recapture and the constant reminders of pain and degradation had too often left him bereft, floating in miserable limbo, but not anymore. Not after listening to the lies and distortions that left his reputation in tatters and would surely encourage loathing in the very people and the country he'd risked his life to protect.

Flinging open the door to the pool house and stepping into the welcoming humid warmth, he decided that as soon as his workout was finished, he'd find Michael. If anyone could figure out a way to eliminate the men who'd cost him so much, it'd be his hard-ass friend. For the first time since the CIA thugs had abducted him six months earlier, he wondered what had become of his pistols. The two guns were another part of him that he'd lost.

Frustrated and angry at the gross injustice and all the lies, he dove into the pool and started swimming. With each stroke, he envisioned them. Seth Hancock, Lucien Talbot, Sal Capello, Rodney Ainsley and the master, the orchestrator of the destruction of his entire life, Muusa Shemal. He would find a way, somehow, to exact revenge for what they had done. Nothing would make him happier than placing a forty-five caliber slug between the eyes of each man, courtesy of his Glock 36.

An hour-and-a-half later, he slid into the hot tub, letting his body sink beneath the water. The frothing jets eased the soreness in his shoulders and helped him relax. Now maybe he could think about what he needed to do. Pushing himself upward, he heard a shriek. Shoving his hair back, he shook water out of his eyes and scowled.

His mother stood next to the hot tub, hands over her heart. "Oh dear Lord, Rowan, you scared the living daylights out of me."

Bottles of cleaning fluids rolled crazily across the tiled floor, and a plastic bucket lay on its side next to a pile of rags. Water dripped down his face while he stared at her. "Mom, what are you doing in here?"

Looking flustered, Janice squatted down and turned the bucket upright, glancing at him while she reached for one of the bottles. "Your father and I come over here once a week. You know how your father likes to tinker. While I clean, he fixes. Over the years, quite a few things around the estate have fallen into disrepair, and he stays busy." His mother glanced toward the door.

Sure enough, his father came striding into the pool area wearing a tool belt over stained, tan cargo pants and a clean white t-shirt. Khalil looked happy. "Good morning, Rowan. It's nice to see you enjoying yourself."

Wishing he'd come earlier to avoid them and wondering how he could make them go away, he faked a smile. "Hi Dad, looks like you've got a project going."

Khalil paused, looked at Janice and winked, then turned to give him a brief grin. "Yes, I've got several projects in the works. See you later."

Suspicious, he watched his father walk away, whistling off-key, like he always had. Janice stuffed the rags and bottles into the plastic bucket and stood up, wiping her hands on her jeans. "Could we, I mean, would you; Rowan, I need to talk to you."

Sighing, he let his head droop and washed a hand over his face before looking at his mother and considering his options. Janice stared beseechingly, hands clasped together. It was much easier to simply stay away from his parents. That strategy had been successful until this morning. But he couldn't deliberately hurt his mother.

Blowing jihadists to kingdom come with his Glock 18 didn't bother him. But God help him, he couldn't bring himself to tell Janice to get lost. Not when she stood in front of him with tears glistening in her eyes, looking sad and hopeful at the same time. No, he'd been had. "Sure, OK Mom. Just let me get out of here."

Climbing carefully out of the hot tub, he draped the towel around his shoulders and slid into a lounger. Water dripping everywhere, he put his feet up and stretched out, letting his wrinkled hands lay in his lap. Janice perched on an adjacent deck chair and leaned forward. "Thank you so much. This means everything to me. For a long time I've wanted to talk to you in person. It's no good on the phone or in an email, to say what I need to, especially on this day."

Annoyed with her meandering and the reference to 9/11, he frowned at her. "Let me help you out, Mom. You're sorry, right? You want to apologize for things you said a long time ago. Well, all right. I accept your apology. And you know what? You can forget about it. Because the last thing I want is to relive any of that."

Janice blinked at him. Her mouth formed an O and she raised her hands as if to stop him. "No, it's not that easy. You don't understand."

He interrupted her. "Look, I do understand. You want forgiveness, absolution, or whatever your religion calls it. You want me to say I forgive you? Accepting your apology is the same thing, isn't it? But if it makes you feel better, I forgive you. Now, can we agree not to discuss this again?" Waiting impatiently for her to reply, he realized his whole body had tensed up. He took a deep breath, twisting his shoulders and forcing his clenched fists to relax. Why couldn't she move on and leave him alone?

His mother huddled on the chair and wiped at the tears that had trickled down her face. "Thank you, for your forgiveness. I know I don't deserve it. For years I've agonized over how terribly I hurt you and I'm so sorry. I was foolish and full of such harsh judgments, but I've learned about grace." Janice paused, and then gave him a timid smile. "Oh, Rowan, God loves you. He cares for you and wants to help you. And your father and I want so badly to get to know you again. Being here, having that opportunity, is an answer to our prayers."

Barely able to keep his temper in check, he quit listening and shook his head. Nothing had changed. Janice still couldn't resist any excuse to shove her religion down his throat. He swung his feet to the floor and stood up, glaring down at her with his arms crossed. "Enough, OK? We're stuck here together for the foreseeable future. If you want to get to know me, then we have to move on. And one other thing. Don't hound me about how wonderful God is, all right? Is that too much to ask?"

Janice stood up to face him and he noticed that her hands were shaking. "Whatever you want is fine with both your father and me. All that matters to us is a relationship with you and Danielle. She's a lovely woman, and we're so happy you've found someone like her."

Janice quit talking and looked at him, biting her lower lip. Surprised at her willingness to concede, he searched her face for mendacity, but saw only determination. Her eyes were nearly as dark as his and reflected the same impassioned persona, which made him uncomfortable. Weary of the exchange, wanting only to escape, he sighed. "OK, great. You're right about Danielle and thank you. I'm grateful for her every day. But I have to go now. Some other time maybe we can talk more."

When he turned to leave she grabbed his arm. Irritated, he pivoted back toward her. Janice gave him a faltering smile. "Thank you again, for everything. We are grateful to be here. Your father worried about being deported to Iran because of all the lies. He couldn't survive something like that, and neither could I. You're a wonderful son and so good to us." She squeezed his arm and let go. "I just wanted you to know that."

Rendered speechless, he could only nod and turn away. Unreasoning anger swept through him as he wiped stinging tears from his eyes. Her words had touched him, and he didn't like that, at all.

Sitting in companionable silence with Michael on the patio overlooking the Pacific, Rowan was glad that no one else was around. Sunlight glinted on the waves and the rhythmic rush of the water calmed his mind. Glancing at his friend, he took another bite of his peanut butter and jelly sandwich, thinking about what he wanted to say. Swallowing and sipping his coffee, he laid the sandwich down and wiped his mouth with the back of his hand. "I can't ever repay you for getting me out of Quantico. If you hadn't, I'd be in Tora right now." An involuntary shudder caught him off-guard, and he took a steadying breath.

Michael frowned and shifted in his chair, fiddled with his cup of coffee and shrugged. "All in a day's work, my brother, you know that. You don't owe me anything."

He stared into the always assessing cobalt eyes. "Well, I'll be on the owing end to both you and Gabriel and your parents for a long time as far as I'm concerned." He sighed. His colleague would surely gloat over his next admission. "You know, the shrink was a good idea."

Michael chuckled, lips twisting in a wry smile. "I know and you're welcome. Be sure you mention that to Chad sometime. The poor guy has a conscience, unlike you and me. He still feels bad about doing that without consulting you."

Relieved more than he'd like to admit by the subdued response, he nodded. "I'll talk to Chad. But Mike, I've got a question. Do you still have my guns?"

His friend's face broke into a huge smile. "Damn it, that's the last thing I expected you to ask me about. Hell yes, your 36 and18 are here. Didn't Chad tell you about the cache of small arms I collected? Your pistols are part of that and speaking of the 18, I'd like to take that sweet baby back to South Dakota. Anyway, you gave me the 18 after the Mexico operation and Chad nabbed the 36 before the FBI or CIA found it. The suppressors for both pistols are in the gun cases, with the weapons. You can practice all you want out here and not alarm the locals."

Pure pleasure coursed through him at the thought of his personal weapons being in his hands again. It felt good to think that he could put even one part of his life back together. He'd been helpless for so long. But now, he couldn't wait to feel the solid, balanced weight of the forty-five caliber 36 in his hands, breathe in the acrid scent of gunpowder when the tendrils of smoke rose from the barrel, and run his finger along the smooth steel slide. "Thanks Mike. I can't tell you how much I appreciate that. I hope I can handle them. After, well, I've been working out. But my fingers tingle sometimes and I can't tell if my hands and wrists are getting stronger."

Michael looked at him and then looked away, staring at the water while he spoke. "You'll handle those weapons just fine."

His friend dragged his gaze away from the hypnotic waves back toward him, the normally mocking face serious. "Rowan, I need to tell you something. Asal discovered who betrayed you to Muusa Shemal."

Nonplussed, he could only stare. How many more revelations could he handle? "OK, lay it on me."

Michael glanced at the ocean again and sipped his coffee before speaking in a low voice. "I'm sorry, it was Sa-id Harandi. According to Asal's internet sources, Shemal tortured him for at least a week, until Sa-id identified you and then the bastard slit his throat. *Washington Post* archives have the story of his disappearance and later the discovery of his body, if you're interested."

Grief for his gentle, courageous friend brought stinging wetness to his eyes for the second time that morning, but he blinked it away, embracing deepening anger instead. His emotions were on a rampage, and it was starting to piss him off. Sadness overcame the anger as he remembered New Year's Eve, the last time he'd been with his friend. He rubbed his eyes and gave Michael a bitter smile. "Thanks for telling me. You know, somehow, the monsters who've perpetrated this debacle on me and everyone else out here have got to be held accountable."

Michael folded his hands in front of him on the table. "What do you have in mind?"

Watching Michael's face, thinking about the wheels turning behind the fierce eyes, he leaned back, braced his hands on the table and let the pent-up frustration and rage fuel his words. "What I want is retribution, for everything that's been done. I want to eliminate the principal players."

He snorted. "And for God's sake, when I turned on the TV this morning, you want to guess what I saw? Someone put together a cozy story about America's most wanted homegrown terrorist. *Me.* Goddamn it, that's not right. I want my country to know I'm innocent."

The vehemence drained away and his shoulders slumped. "This crap will never be over. I know that. I'll be wanted by the CIA, the FBI, the Muslim Brotherhood and hell, all the radicals, for the rest of my life, but I can't sit and do nothing."

Michael shot him a speculative look. "Let me think on this for a while. It's going to take some detailed planning. Rowan, I have to ask, are you willing to leave here? Because you understand, what you want to do will be difficult from a remote location."

Nodding at his colleague, he slurped the rest of the coffee, angered at how the cup rattled when he sat it back on the table with a shaky hand. Eyeing the half-eaten sandwich, he wondered if he'd ever recover or be himself again. Just the thought of captivity sent panic rippling through his gut.

Lost for a moment in memories of utter helplessness, hard fists and cold steel cuffs, he shuddered. Blinking to clear the images, he took a deep breath and met Michael's concerned gaze. "Eventually, if it's necessary, I'll start the ball rolling with Chad and Ralph. But first, I need to spend some personal, quality time with my 36 and 18." He managed a smile. "I've missed those damn pistols."

Michael looked relieved. "And I've missed you, Rowan. It's great to have you back."

Twisting uncomfortably on the leather sofa, Rowan wondered if meeting with his shrink on this particular day was a mistake. The study felt claustrophobic. After watching the disturbing images of himself on TV and then talking to his mother and Michael, he already wanted and needed to hit the beach with the bottle of whiskey.

Angelo sat across from him in his usual spot and looked at him, hands folded in his lap. "Rowan, if you feel up to it, I'd like to talk to you about September 11, 2001. From what you've told me, that day played a pivotal role in your life, precipitating your involvement in black ops and the private jihad that's netted so many dead Islamists."

He stared at the psychiatrist and tapped his fingers on his knees. Blowing out a gusty sigh, he wished the conversation wouldn't go down this road, then figured, as he always did when faced with the psychiatrist's gentle probing, *what the hell.* "Well, you see Doc, after September 11, 2001, revenge was all I cared about. When I heard that the President was discreetly looking for an American who could speak Arabic and Farsi, had a Middle Eastern background, someone who could handle a gun and a knife and wanted to serve his country, I knew I was that man. I've never looked back, never regretted even one life that I've taken."

Angelo looked thoughtful. "Do you realize that you've never told me why you chose that path? Did something happen to you personally on that day or were you, like so many other Americans, inspired to serve because of the horrific act of terror on our own soil?"

Jaws clenched, he stared at the psychiatrist. It had been ten years and he'd never talked to anyone about losing Michelle on that day. Ralph had held him in his arms when he collapsed while watching the tower implode, knowing in that moment that he'd lost everything. But other than his fellow workers at Ground Zero in the days afterward, he'd never brought it up to anyone else, and over the years, he'd shoved the terrible pain deep inside.

Now he felt his chest tightening and tried to take a deep breath. How did Angelo do this to him? "That morning, my fiancée Michelle was having breakfast at Windows on the World. She was pregnant. I've never told anyone else. We'd only known for a month. But sometimes I still think about it. A baby, for God's sake, and you know, a family."

Angelo leaned forward and he could see the compassion in the older man's face. "I'm so sorry for your loss, Rowan. If you feel up to it, tell me more. Sometimes walking back through the memories facilitates healing, if you're guided by someone skilled in the art. I'd be happy to walk through those memories with you."

A shuddering sob escaped from his lips. He looked at the doctor, panic-stricken. He drew a sharp breath as the sense of an overwhelming presence shimmered around him. He remembered that presence. The voice, filled with kindness, whispered through his mind. *Don't be afraid, Rowan. Let me help you.* What the hell was happening to him?

Angelo stared at him, a puzzled look on the kind face. "Are you all right, Rowan? I'm sorry if I spoke out of turn. My passion is for healing, but if you're not ready, I understand."

For the third time in a few hours, tears filled his eyes. Hot and stinging, they ran down his cheeks while a hard lump in his throat made speaking impossible. He opened his mouth and closed it as a tidal wave of emotion rushed over him.

Sobs he couldn't stop shook his shoulders. It was as though someone had opened the floodgates in his heart. Hunched over on the sofa, thankful for the heavy shelves of books that absorbed the sound, he gave up and wept, covering his face with his hands. He must be losing his mind.

Eyes tightly closed, he didn't move away when Angelo sat down beside him and put a comforting arm around him. Inexplicably drawn, he leaned into the other man's shoulder until the tears subsided. Exhausted, but feeling more at peace than he had in years, he took an unsteady breath and opened swollen, aching eyes. Angelo sat watching him, a patient look on his face. Shock rolled over him and he turned sharply to where Angelo should be, sitting next to him.

The psychiatrist looked embarrassed. "Rowan, please accept my apology. I've never been so insensitive before."

Still disconcerted, he blinked at the doctor. Now he needed the solitude of the beach, where he could think and try to make sense of what had happened. Thinking how good a cool wash cloth would feel on his burning face, he took a deep breath. "It's all right, Doc, don't worry about it. You know, maybe we should take a break. It's ah, I've never done this before." He needed to leave, before another wave of emotion blindsided him. Standing abruptly, he nodded at Angelo. "If I need you, I'll find you. Otherwise, I'll catch you in a couple days, or whenever."

Angelo stood up, brow furrowed. "Are you sure you're all right? I don't want to leave you hurting. Do you need to talk or would you like some company?"

Company was the last thing he wanted. "Nope, I'm fine, Doc. No worries. I'll see you later." Before Angelo could say anything else, he slipped out the door and shut it quietly.

Heaving a ragged sigh, Rowan gazed for a moment at the closed door and then headed outside, down the brick walkway toward the beach. Head bowed, hands stuffed in the front pockets of his cutoffs, he walked. The sand burned the bottoms of his feet until he hit the water, enjoying the coolness as the waves crawled up over his ankles. The breeze refreshed him and he stopped. Lifting his head to the noon-time sun, he closed his eyes, taking deep breaths of the salt air.

Opening his eyes, he sighed again and kept walking. After mindless minutes, he found himself on the hidden section of beach where he and Danielle still liked to meet. They kept a couple beach towels in an old wicker basket and he grabbed one, spread it on the sand and plopped down. Drawing his knees up, he wrapped his arms around them and buried his head. Oh God, not again. Clenching his jaws, he tried to brace himself, but it did no good.

Another wave of raw emotion rolled over him. After all the years, he grieved for Michelle and the child whose eyes he'd never gaze into, the likeness he'd never have the pleasure of contemplating. The overpowering presence settled around him and the voice spoke again. *I held them in my arms, Rowan. They were never alone.* It was too much. His body shook as he wept. He'd never allowed himself to cry, and now he couldn't stop.

After a while his sobs subsided, and he raised his head, resting his chin on his knees. His head ached, his eyes burned, and he'd never felt so empty. Before he could absorb that, another wave of sadness covered him, and he grieved over the wreckage of his life, the career and the reputation he'd been so proud of, the staggering humiliation, the wounds to his psyche and the scars on his body.

Each degrading act he'd endured played in his mind as he sat, hands over his face, tears running freely, while the shimmering presence settled around him yet again. The voice whispered with such tenderness he could barely breathe. *Each time they hurt you, I was there beside you.* At last the images stopped, and he lay flat on his back, wrung out, with an arm across his eyes. His enervated mind couldn't process anything else. He fell into deep, exhausted sleep.

Someone whispered his name. "Rowan, are you awake?" Gentle fingers traced the line of his jaw and then his collar bone, slid across his chest and down to his belly, making him shiver. "Rowan, it's time to wake up."

Mouth open, he laid on the towel feeling like he'd been run over by a truck. His lips were caked with fine, salty sand. It layered his neck and chest beneath the shirt he never buttoned and gritted under the waistband of his cutoffs. The arm over his eyes felt like a lead weight. He coughed and grimaced as he sat up. "What time is it?"

Danielle sat cross-legged next to him on another beach towel, smiling while he stretched and yawned. Then her face turned serious and she grabbed his hand. "It's six-thirty already. Angelo called me earlier and said you were upset after your meeting. I thought you'd probably be here. Are you all right?"

Blinking at her through burning eyes, he didn't know what to say. He felt like hell. "I'm fine, just tired and cold. When we get back, I'm going to take a shower and hit the sack." He gave her a crooked smile and squeezed her hand before letting go and struggling to his feet. Reaching down, he grasped her hand and pulled her up. "Wanna go to bed with me?"

She slid her arms around him and murmured into his shoulder. "You look like it's been a rough day. I'm so sorry. I wish you'd talk to me, so I could help you." Her voice sounded so wistful and sad, he felt guilty. Her hands roamed up into his hair and pulled his head down. She kissed him softly and he knew his lips must feel like sandpaper, but she didn't seem to mind. And God, she felt so good and so warm pressed against him.

If only he had the energy, he'd make use of those beach towels. But the weariness he felt was more than bone deep. It had invaded his soul. Danielle pulled away and he could see the concern in her eyes. He put his arms around her, letting his hands wander down to her hips. "Don't worry, I'm OK. You're right though, it's been a long day; draining." Hesitating, knowing he'd probably regret it, he continued. "We can talk for a while, but I'm not sure how long I'll last."

She looked up at him in the fading light. "This is never going to be over, is it? They're never going to let up about you or believe that you're innocent, are they? Oh my God, I hate the people that did this to you."

Crushing her close, he whispered into her hair, watching as the waves closed over the sun, leaving a faint golden sheen atop the inky darkness of the water. "Someday, somehow, I have to make them believe."

An hour later, Rowan sat curled up on the corner of the sectional sofa in his favorite spot, temporarily revived by a steaming hot shower. He'd pulled on a pair of ragged jeans and in a moment of bitter irony, an old FBI sweat shirt, another item Chad had snagged for him out of his hotel room in Sioux Falls. Sipping whiskey, he glanced sideways at Danielle, sitting next to him with a glass of wine, her legs entwined with his. Heaving a sigh, he wrapped an arm around her. It was time to make good on his promise to talk. "Something strange happened today, while I was with Angelo."

Surprise mingled with curiosity in Danielle's face, and she took a swallow of wine before tilting her head toward him. "Really? What happened?"

Obviously she hadn't thought he'd talk. Damn it, what if another blast of emotion he couldn't manage came over him? It was too late now, though, because he could see from the look on her face that blowing off the whole thing would only whet her appetite. And he didn't have the energy to resist. "It's hard to explain. See, a couple times, when I was, I thought, you know."

Thinking about the brutality always made him queasy. Danielle cupped her hand on his cheek. "Is this something that happened at Quantico?"

He nodded. "And once before. But at the end, in Quantico, I knew it was all over. Next stop Tora Prison, and I'd be lost forever. Then, I don't know how else to describe it, a *presence* surrounded me. It talked to me, told me to ask for help. So, I did."

Eyes like saucers, Danielle sipped her wine and snuggled closer. Her voice was quiet, almost reverent. "Wow. What an incredible experience." She paused and placed her hand on his cheek again. "You've been through so much. I'm glad you decided to talk to me. What happened next?"

Giving her a weak smile, he shrugged. "Well, here we are. Today, Angelo asked me about September 11, 2001 and wanted to know if something personal had happened to me that day. I told him about Michelle." He let his voice trail off. No way could he tell Danielle the whole story, he was too exhausted. Rubbing his eyes, he sighed. "But anyway, all of a sudden, that presence surrounded me again."

Danielle twirled her wine glass and gazed calmly into his eyes. "You can tell me anything, Rowan. I'll listen anytime." Tears sprang into her eyes. "You didn't have to surrender, but you did, for me." She sniffed and smiled, blinking the tears away. "I love you so much."

Amazed as always by how much she cared for him, he finished the Jack Daniel's, thankful for the whiskey's warmth spreading through his body. But then the shattering emotions he couldn't escape gripped him again. The lump in his throat hardened and tears stung his eyes. He tried to swallow, irritated by the hoarseness in his voice. "You know I love you too. I'd do anything for you, Danielle."

Fearful that he'd break down, he looked at her helplessly, his voice a whisper. "All I want to do is forget." He stopped again and took a deep breath. "But that presence offered kindness, to *me*. I still don't understand why, and I'm sure I never will."

Touching her fingers to his lips, Danielle gazed at him, the compassion in her face nearly undoing his shaky composure. "You don't have to say anymore. I get it."

Surprised, he wiped the tears leaking from the corners of his eyes and twisted around so he could face her. "You do?"

Pulling her legs up so she could wrap her arms around her knees, she gave him a sweet smile and nodded. "What I mean is this: I get what you're trying to tell me. After being treated like a traitor and being beaten, along with whatever else that CIA agent did to you, to experience kindness must have been incredible."

Taking a shuddering breath, he nodded. "Yep, you're right. Even now, I feel like I don't deserve what's somehow being offered. And I'm not entirely sure what that is." A huge yawn interrupted him and he wiped his running nose with the back of his hand.

Danielle looked like she was just getting warmed up and watching her made him even more weary. "Rowan, how can you say you don't deserve kindness, wherever it's coming from? I wonder. After talking to your mom a few times, it seems like, I don't know, maybe this presence is God wanting to help you."

Too tired to get angry at the mention of his mother and her religion, he could only stare, wishing he'd refilled his glass of Jack Daniel's. "Nothing my mother says to me about God makes any sense. I don't even know if I believe in God. And anyway, if that's who was talking to me, which I doubt, he wouldn't want to help me, of all people."

Danielle wrinkled her nose. "What makes you say that? Why wouldn't God want to help you?"

Thankful that the hellish wave of emotion had retreated, at least for the moment, he looked at her and wondered how he'd gotten himself in so deep. They'd never talked about his past and all the martyrs he'd sent to paradise. Wishing with all his heart that he'd never agreed to have a conversation, he sighed again. "Because I've killed way too many people, more than I can count. But you didn't know that, did you?"

Danielle opened her mouth to speak, but he shook his head. "Let me finish. They were terrorists, and I eliminated them on behalf of the country that calls me a traitor now, but still, I don't think God would make a distinction." The bitter longing that welled up inside him was almost as bad as the raw emotions he couldn't control and surprised him just as much. Why did he care whether a God he wasn't sure existed wanted to help him or not?

Danielle chuckled and tapped him on the chest with an index finger. "I know, but I think you're wrong. You make things way too complicated."

He scowled and grabbed her finger. "Wait a minute. How could you know about the terrorists I've killed? Did Michael or Gabriel tell you? And what do you mean, *I* make things too complicated?"

Danielle's eyes held a defiant glint when she looked at him. "Gabriel and I have talked a couple times. And when you were in the hospital, I wanted to know what was going on. I was hungry to learn everything I could about you. Bettina told me about when you were kids growing up, but also that you'd changed a lot."

She paused and he watched as embarrassment tinged her cheeks. "So anyway, Chad left your laptop with me one time when he and Ralph went down to the cafeteria to eat. The flash drive was with it and I read everything. Didn't you get the gift I left for you? I put a note with it, telling you I was grateful for all you'd done."

Dumbfounded at her admission, he let go of her finger and dug in the front pocket of his jeans, pulling out the coin she'd given him. Ralph had passed it back to him one afternoon while they were fishing. Happy to have it again, he'd stuffed it in his pocket and kept it with him. Now he laid it in his palm. "I got your note, but I didn't realize you were talking about the black ops. Getting the note and this coin meant everything to me. I'm sorry I didn't mention it before now."

Danielle had tears in her eyes again. "I'll never forget that awful day. Saying good-bye to you was the hardest thing I've ever done, and I don't want to say those words to you, ever again."

He stuffed the coin back in his pocket and reached out to wipe away the one tear that had slid down her cheek. "Me either."

When she smiled, he sagged in relief. So damn tired he could barely think, he just wanted to end their conversation and go to bed. But then she nailed him. "Rowan, look, you make things complicated because your thoughts about God are all tangled up in the crap your mom told you years ago. Even she admits it was garbage, so maybe you should let it go. Then you can start to get acquainted with that presence or being, and I think it's entirely possible that it's God. Maybe that's how you'll find healing for all the horrible, evil things that have been done to you."

Wanting to run far away from the draining emotions and even the thought of making God's acquaintance, he drew her into his arms and held her tight. His only hope was to tweak her, get her mind on another track, and maybe even make her mad. "Like I said, nothing my mother says to me about God makes any sense.

But you are incredible. You make way too much sense. I knew there had to be more than one reason I fell in love with you. Your mind outdoes your fabulous body sometimes and damn, now *that's* saying something."

Snickering while she squirmed, he was glad she couldn't get a hold of him or see the smirk on his face. This was going to work magnificently and he might even get some sleep. "Rowan Milani, that is the most chauvinistic thing you have ever said to me. You know, sometimes you are a first-class jerk, and if you weren't so damn good looking, you'd be sorry."

Keeping her trapped in his arms while she huffed, he yawned again and let his chin rest on the top of her head. "Nah, I'm not a chauvinist, I'm just a guy. And hell, people have been telling me I'm a jerk for years. But as long as I've got you, I'll never be sorry. Now c'mon, let's go to bed. I've got big plans for that great mind of yours, first thing in the morning."

THE END

Mary Yungeberg

Consummate Betrayal

Mary Yungeberg

Picture by Julia Wollman

Mary has been an avid writer all her life. After numerous freelance articles published in a variety of magazines, along with several careers, she chucked her "real world" job to pursue her dream of writing thrillers. CONSUMMATE BETRAYAL is the first in the Rowan Milani Chronicles. UNHOLY RETRIBUTION is the sequel and A DIFFERENT MAN is the third installment in the series. All three books are available in print and digital formats.

Mary is passionate about inspiring women to live with purpose and pursue their dreams. She is a strong believer in empowering women to defend themselves. She loves the sport of shooting and capably handles her two Glock pistols. When she's not at the shooting range or working on the next installment of the Rowan Milani Chronicles, you may find her burning up the pavement in her black Mustang convertible.

She lives in eastern South Dakota with her husband and Lucy, an intemperate Rat Terrier who runs their household.

For more information about the Rowan Milani Chronicles, visit Mary's website: MaryYungeberg.com.

Consummate Betrayal

Made in the
USA
Lexington, KY